MW01657006

Emerald Bruises

Emerald Bruises

Book Two
The Jewelry Box Series

by

New York Times Bestseller
Pepper Winters

Emerald Bruises
Copyright © 2024 Pepper Winters
Published by Pepper Winters

All rights reserved. No part of this book may be reproduced or transmitted in any form, including electronic or mechanical, without written permission from the publisher, except in the case of brief quotations embodied in critical articles or reviews.

This is a work of fiction. Names, characters, businesses, places, events, and incidents are either the products of the author's imagination or used in a fictitious manner. Any resemblance to actual persons, living or dead, or actual events is purely coincidental.

This book is licensed for your personal enjoyment only. This book may not be re-sold or given away to other people. If you would like to share this book with another person, please purchase an additional copy for each person you share it with. If you are reading this book and did not purchase it, or it was not purchased for your use only, then you should return it to the seller and purchase your own copy. Libraries are exempt and permitted to share their in-house copies with their members and have full thanks for stocking this book. Thank you for respecting the author's work.

Published: Pepper Winters 2024: **pepperwinters@gmail.com**
Ebook Design: Cleo Studios
Paperback Design: Cleo Studios
Alternative Cover Image: Julia Cherrett Valareign (etsy)
Internal Images: Julia Cherrett Valareign (etsy)
Editing by: Editing-4-Indies (Jenny Sims)
Proofreading by: Christina Routhier
Indian Sensitivity Reader & Hindi Translation: Shabnam Arora
French Translation: Aurélie Gordio
Audio Narration: Luke William Bromley & Lucy Jessica

OTHER WORK BY PEPPER WINTERS

Pepper currently has close to forty books released in nine languages. She's hit best-seller lists (USA Today, New York Times, and Wall Street Journal) almost forty times. She dabbles in multiple genres, ranging from Dark Romance, Coming of Age, Fantasy, and Romantic Suspense.

For books, FAQs, and buylinks please visit:

https://pepperwinters.com

Subscribe to New Release Newsletter by following QR code

EROTIC ROMANCE 'SPECTACLE OF SECRETS' STANDALONES

One Dirty Night
(Ella and Nicholas)

FORBIDDEN ROMANCE

The Luna Duet
Lunamare (Book One of The Luna Duet)
Cor Amare (Book Two of The Luna Duet)

FANTASY ROMANCE

Destini Chronicles
When a Moth Loved a Bee

DARK ROMANCE

Goddess Isles Series
Once a Myth
Twice a Wish
Third a Kiss
Fourth a Lie
Fifth a Fury

Monsters in the Dark Trilogy
Tears of Tess

Quintessentially Q
Twisted Together
Je Suis a Toi

Indebted Series
Debt Inheritance
First Debt
Second Debt
Third Debt
Fourth Debt
Final Debt
Indebted Epilogue

Dollar Series
Pennies
Dollars
Hundreds
Thousands
Millions

Fable of Happiness Trilogy
Book One
Book Two
Book Three

SEXY ROMANCE

The Master of Trickery Duet
The Body Painter
The Living Canvas

Truth & Lies Duet
Crown of Lies
Throne of Truth

COMING OF AGE LOVE STORY

The Ribbon Duet
The Boy & His Ribbon
The Girl & Her Ren

Standalone Spinoff
The Son & His Hope

STANDALONES

Destroyed – Grey Romance
Unseen Messages – Survival Romance
One Dirty Night – Erotic Romance

MOTORCYCLE CLUB ROMANCE

Pure Corruption Duet
Ruin & Rule
Sin & Suffer

ROMANTIC COMEDY written as TESS HUNTER

Can't Touch This

CHILDREN'S / INSPIRATIONAL BOOK

Pippin and Mo

UPCOMING RELEASES

***For 2024/2025 titles please visit** www.pepperwinters.com*

RELEASE DAY ALERTS, SNEAK PEEKS, & NEWSLETTER

To be the first to know about upcoming releases, please join Pepper's Newsletter (she promises never to spam or annoy you.)

Pepper's Newsletter

SOCIAL MEDIA & WEBSITE

Facebook: Peppers Books
Instagram: @pepperwinters
Facebook Group: Peppers Playgound
Website: www.pepperwinters.com
Tiktok: @pepperwintersbooks

Dedication

To all those lovers of morally grey heroes.
The shades of darkness, the sometimes wrong, and their constant struggling.
To stay good. To stay decent. To do the right thing…
Only to shiver in ecstasy when they go bad.

Letter from the Author

The Jewelry Box Series is a work of fiction, but it is a dark read. Almost every trigger that can exist, exists within this tale. Blood play, breath play, non-con, dub-con, degradation, pain, despair, betrayal, hope, and faith.

Please take the warning seriously. This book is explicit, erotic, despicable, and downright monstrous in some places. There is love, yes, but first you have to go through a hell of a lot of depravity to find it.

Please read responsibly.

Pepper x

Prologue

Henri

LONELINESS AND NAUSEA.

Two things I'd been afflicted with since I was old enough to know I was different.

Different from the boys in the playground—boys who had mothers who hugged and loved them.

Different from the men in the bars—men who could laugh and flirt without feeling sick to their goddamn stomachs for what they truly wanted.

Loneliness and nausea.

My barometer of right and wrong.

Loneliness pushed me into the dark.

But nausea kept me in the light.

I hadn't realised how much I relied on those two afflictions.

How much I needed to live in constant motherfucking pain.

Until the moment both emotions switched off.

The moment Ily kicked me in the nose and fought me with all her terror and heartache, my moral compass well and truly shattered.

I'd been wrong when I thought I'd been born with a broken one.

My compass had just been different from everyone else's.

I'd carried it my entire life—relying on it to keep me normal.

Loneliness was my North.

Nausea my South.

East and West, my right and wrong.

But now…I was lost.

Plummeting into perpetual darkness where I'd always belonged.

No, not just darkness…

Freedom.

Freedom from sickness.

Freedom from loneliness.

Free to be entirely…

me.

Chapter One

Ily

I'D NEVER WISHED FOR DEATH before.

Even on my darkest days when I wondered why I'd been abandoned on the steps of a hospital, I'd always been grateful to be alive.

I might have been born unwanted, but I'd been cherished from the moment Krish spotted me. I'd become a sister and a daughter. I'd been kissed and hugged, doted on and adored. If anything, I was grateful to my birth mother for giving me up because I'd found exactly where I was supposed to be.

So no…at no point in my blessed, happy life had I ever heard the whispers of giving up.

Until now.

"*Fade away*," hissed a drugged delusion.

"*Die so you don't have to feel the pain*," whispered a roaring tiger head mounted on the wall.

The dead zoo crushed me from all angles, puncturing me with antlers, horns, and tusks. Even if Peter hadn't forced psilocybin down my throat, I would've struggled in this room.

Struggled not to hear the phantom screams of death.

Struggled not to be affected by the stagnant energy of slaughtered things.

But with the drugs?

I didn't stand a chance.

Henri's voice trickled down and down into my soul.

"I told you what would happen, little nightmare. I told you what exists inside me. I told you." Over and over again, his raspy, drunken voice repeated. *"I told you what would happen. I told you…"*

A vortex.

A spinning, sucking hellhole binding me to the X-shaped cross where he'd imprisoned me.

I shuddered as his tongue slid over my cheek one last time, catching stray tears before he pushed away.

He sighed as if he hadn't taken a proper breath his entire life. He flexed his shoulders as he finally slipped into who he truly was. The illusion of him with bat wings and vampire fangs returned, painting a morbid fantasy of his shredded, skin-webbed wings fluttering behind him, kicking up dust motes, and sending feathers of dead birds shivering.

I blinked and tried to see past insanity. Tried to cling to sanity.

But it was no use.

I only saw a fallen angel.

A devil born from a man.

With a huff, Henri unwound his fingers from my throat. They fell away, trailing down my chest before he put distance between us, coating me in ice after he'd burned me with brimstone.

I couldn't breathe as he stumbled back, alcohol stealing his steadiness. With a groan, he raked both hands through his hair and looked at the domed ceiling. With his head tipped back and blood streaking his upper lip from my kick, he looked as if he implored the heavens to give him a second chance. To let him fly into the clouds and save him from the despicably dark things crawling through his spirit.

But no deity answered.

No spearing ray of light appeared.

The fog swirling by his legs only grew thicker, congealing like blood as his chin tipped down again, and he sucked in another huge breath.

His hands balled. His tattered wings retracted and folded down his back, the bone-clawed tips kissing the bloodstained carpet below.

And then…his eyes locked on mine.

"I told you what would happen, little nightmare. I told you what exists inside me…"

Every atom inside me froze, all while my hallucinations grew stronger.

The unexplainable attraction I held toward Henri chose that moment to tear out my stupid, useless heart. His grey gaze was the hook, puncturing the pathetic organ. His cold smirk the line, tugging on my ribcage. And his blackened voice the final yank, ripping me from existence, delivering me flopping and gasping at his feet.

"*I'm finally free.*" His voice echoed in my buzzing mind. "*Free.*"

I trembled as he smiled. Not the fake, perfected smile of a cop playing the role of a sadist but a monster who was truly, finally *free.*

He's free, and I'm…

dead.

"*Let yourself die. This is just the beginning…you don't want to endure the end,*" a hummingbird whispered.

"*Death is better than what he's about to do,*" a crocodile, forever trapped in water-like epoxy, croaked.

"I'm glad you decided to finally stop fighting who you truly are, Henri." Victor's vile tone cut through my delusions. "Just in time, I might add. Then again, I'm still unsure if I should let you live or die…"

"You'd kill me the moment I've come alive?" Henri muttered. "Bit unfair."

Victor didn't reply for a while, his face carefully cold. Finally, he said scarily softly, "I'll postpone my judgement until after…how about that?"

"Fine." Henri nodded, his face etched with shadow.

For a moment, I saw things as they truly were.

Henri just as a man—his black t-shirt rising and falling with heavy breaths, his black slacks so severe compared to his bare feet.

Peter just as a slave—kneeling on blood-dripped carpet, the cuts across his torso like red scripture scrawled into his skin.

And Victor as a king—sitting with his legs primly crossed on a rattan peacock chair. His lambskin slippers tapped out an impatient beat while his black dressing gown parted, showing navy silk pyjamas beneath. His hands folded over the gun he'd held to my head, resting like a deadly pet on his lap.

With a tight smile, Victor ordered, "Now you've strapped her down, choose a weapon."

"A weapon?" Henri's voice dabbled with drunkenness, lazy and hostile.

Victor pointed at the table full of rusty, unhygienic torture devices. Even the barbaric thousand-year-old instruments displayed in the Tower of London were better looked after. Two of the knives had dried blood on them, and the thumbscrew looked as if it had a torn piece of flesh.

Oh God…

My delusions pounced again.

New wings sprouted from Henri's back, and the blood-speckled white carpet beneath my bound and buckled feet poured like a river, swirling around Peter's knees across the room.

Peter gave me a despairing smile.

His dark honey skin began to glow as if he'd been anointed by the divine.

Strands of light feathered from him, dancing past Henri and soaking into my chest.

I sucked in a breath.

I felt Peter's regret at drugging me.

Tasted his fear.

Heard his sorrow.

With lamenting birdsong erupting around the room, I forgave him.

Forgave him for drugging me.

For making this impossible for me.

For destroying me.

With a soft growl, Henri swayed toward the table holding such nasty things. In my narcotized eyes, the weapons morphed into sentient beings, vampiric daggers just begging for a bite and hissing clamps just waiting to suffocate.

Running his fingers over the array, Henri selected a particular blade. Holding it up to the glittering chandelier, he ran his thumb over the dull rustiness. His nose wrinkled as he slammed it back down again. "They're not sharp enough to cut cleanly."

Victor smirked. "That's the point. Makes you work a little harder for those sweet drops of ruby."

Nodding as if he followed Victor's twisted logic, Henri slowly stepped away from the table. "But what if I don't want to work harder? What if I want her blood to pour easily, freely, and all over my goddamn hands?"

Victor shrugged. "Then I'd say you're shit out of luck, as I don't have anything that sharp."

"I do." With a smirk, Henri shoved his hand into his right trouser pocket.

No…

Sanity came roaring back.

Don't show him.

Don't reveal what you smuggled in—

"I want to use this, if it's all the same to you." With a flourish, Henri held up the fatal little switchblade I'd woken up to him inspecting in his room. A blade he'd hidden the moment I'd noticed and then smothered me with his half-naked body to keep me quiet.

I gasped as memories of what he'd done after that ricocheted through me.

I relived it, not just recalled.

A movie of us played out before me. A doomed, depressing hologram as Henri rocked against me, rubbing my clit with his cock, offering me chocolate in the form of an orgasm. An orgasm that'd torn through me. An orgasm that was the last piece of goodness I'd ever feel.

Victor stiffened in his chair, his fingers tightening around the gun. "You brought a fucking *knife* into my home, Ward?" Raising the weapon, he aimed the muzzle at Henri. "Care to tell me what that was for?"

Henri didn't look at me.

No shred of the man who'd begged me to play along with him existed.

He was merely an animal that'd prowled out of its cage—a beast slowly growing accustomed to its new freedom. "If you must know, Vic, I brought it as protection."

"Protection? From what?"

"From you."

Victor scowled. "Why would you need protection from me? We're the same…you and I. Or at least…that's what you've attempted to convince me of. Whether I believe it or not remains to be seen."

Henri shrugged and flicked open the switchblade. He hissed under his breath as he ran his thumb along the sharp, pointy end. "To be honest, I'm having a hard time remembering much right now. My mind is quiet for the first time in decades. My thoughts are so fucking calm, it's eerie." He slur-chuckled and tapped his temple with an unbalanced sway. "Must be the booze."

"Possibly. Or…it's because you're finally done with bullshit. I saw the change in you when she kicked you. I see it still." Victor studied Henri before standing and gliding like a creature of the night toward a narrow chest of drawers. "I'm still open to killing you if you don't fully step into who you truly are, but…I'm willing to see how far you'll take this. If I didn't know any better, I'd say you were finally waking up—just like you said—and that's why you're no longer afraid."

Opening a drawer, he rummaged around before removing something. Oiling his way back to Henri, he said, "Hold out your hand."

Henri spread his fingers and offered his palm, his arm unsteady. "I'm not afraid of you, you know."

"Oh, I know." Victor smiled like a doting father as he dropped the item into Henri's grip. "You were afraid of yourself."

Henri shuddered and fisted the item. "Fuck yes, I'm afraid of myself. I've been afraid all my life."

"And now?" Victor crossed his arms. "How do you feel?"

For a moment, Henri didn't answer. He studied whatever Victor had given him before his imaginary, drug-given wings flared with a dry rustle of skin and bone.

And when he spoke, I felt it in the core of me.

"For the first time in my life, I'm not nauseous."

"Nauseous?" Victor raised an eyebrow. "You're going to have to explain that one because I don't follow."

With a heavy sigh, Henri blinked as if he finally saw the truth.

A truth that he could be honest about things he'd hidden from all his life.

A different sort of confession to the ones he'd given me.

A *real* confession.

Wiping his mouth and schooling his tongue not to give in to drunken slurs, Henri muttered, "All my life, I've felt sick if I ever contemplated taking what I needed. I gagged on the poison inside me. I begged to throw up this curse before it killed me. But now…" His chin tipped up. His eyes locked on mine. "That sickness is gone. I feel so fucking strong. Like I'm invincible. Untouchable..."

My mind blended fact and fiction as Henri prowled toward me and pressed the knife against my cheek. "I'm really, truly free."

I sucked in a breath.

He forgot about Victor.

He spared no thought for Peter.

It was just him and me.

Bad and good.

Alive and dead.

"Do you know what I wanted to do when I first saw you at the bar, Ily?" He dragged the sharp, sharp knife down my chin, along my throat, and over my flimsy white negligée. "I wanted to hurt you. I wanted to bend you over right there and fuck you hard enough to make you scream."

I couldn't catch a proper breath as he swirled the dagger around my nipple.

Gone was our pantomime.

Our script in cinders all over the floor.

"I told myself those thoughts were wrong. I pretended that the moment I noticed you, something didn't crack inside me." He laughed under his breath. "I lied."

His eyes never released mine as he placed the item Victor had given him on the table beside us. His gaze no longer shimmered with righteous silver but turned a flat sterling of corruption.

Rocking back on his heels, he tested the hooks holding my golden collar and cuffs before nudging my ankles with his bare toes, ensuring the buckles he'd bound me with held.

Only once he was satisfied I was well and truly at his mercy did he drop the final pretence and give in. With steady hands, he grabbed the neckline of my negligée, then sliced it with his knife. Fisting the shredded lace, he yanked.

Hard.

The rip of it tearing in half matched the ripping in my heart.

Fresh tears stung.

Zebras brayed.

Wolves barked.

Every inch of me trembled as Henri shoved aside the scraps of my ruined lingerie, baring my nakedness to a thousand dead eyes, one slave, and a monstrous ringleader.

But none of them mattered as Henri dropped his stare to my breasts and devoured me by sight alone.

"Fuck, you're stunning." He palmed me, fisting delicate flesh ever so cruelly. "Ripe and young, pure and brave."

Tears welled hotter, wetter.

I didn't let them fall.

Not for him.

Not for death whispering in my ears or terror fisting my crazy-winged heart.

"You'll sob for me before the night is through," Henri breathed as he pressed the tip of his knife against my neck. "You'll bleed for me every night. And *fuck*, that turns me on."

"*Die now…before it's too late*," a swan crooned.

"*Choose to drift away where he can't hurt you*," a sparrow chirped.

"Use the pipette dropper I gave you, *mon ami*," Victor said as he settled back into his peacock chair for the show. "Count each droplet you draw from her. One hundred and two, don't forget. That's about five millilitres, give or take."

Five mil?

Practically nothing.

Barely anything.

Yet…*it's everything.*

My blood.

My lifeforce.

Mine.

Not his.

My mind suddenly swarmed with gushing crimson.

Litres and litres, buckets and buckets.

My throat sliced and gaping.

My skin turning white as red spilled all over the floor.

Ignoring Victor, Henri shifted closer. His thigh wedged between my spread and naked legs. The softness of his slacks against my pussy added another element of insanity. Softness equalled kindness. Softness equalled our pact, our deal, our vow.

But everything was broken now.

"Please..." I whispered.

My first word in so long.

My first plea of many.

"Don't. Don't do this, Henri."

He shuddered and closed his eyes.

And I hoped...just like I'd hoped in the library when he told me he was a cop.

I hoped he'd choose me.

Choose us.

Only this time, when he opened them again, there was no promise to save me, no oath to protect Peter, no admission that he was good.

This time...only a monster stared back.

"You don't have permission to call me that. I'm your lord and Master. Address me as such." With a flick of his wrist, he cut me.

I cried out as his knife punctured and pierced.

He groaned as hot blood seeped free.

A different kind of haze corrupted his shadow-stained eyes. Not alcohol. Not nausea.

Peace.

The longer he stared at the rich blood rolling its way down my throat, the more savage his stare became.

Sharp with fatal diamonds.

Twinkling with lust and glimmering with sick need.

It was true, then.

Eyes truly were the windows to people's souls, and I couldn't look away as Henri—the man who'd caused feelings and unwanted desire—vanished beneath Henri, the ruthless Master.

And I couldn't help it.

The drugs in my system drowned me again.

I lost myself as Henri bent forward, grabbed the glass-blown pipette, and pressed the tip to the blood he'd drawn. With fierce attention, he sucked it up, trapping red in the dropper.

The room erupted with a cacophony of noise.

Bird song, cheetah snarls, elephant trumpets.

"Die."

"Stop breathing before he steals your breath."

"Stop bleeding before he steals your life."

"Die!"

My ears rang.

My heart thundered.

Blackness coated my vision as Henri placed his knife down and held out his hand. With drunk-defying precision, he opened his palm and squeezed the blood-engorged pipette.

Almost in slow motion, ruby droplets rained.

"One," he murmured.

"Two." He shuddered.

"Three." He licked his lips.

"Four." He pressed his red-spotted hand to his throat.

Not looking away from me, he smeared my blood along the same area of his body where he'd drawn it from mine. "Four droplets. Ninety-eight to go." He shivered as my blood baptised him just like he'd christened me in his cum on the maypole.

A different sort of ritual.

A perverse little ceremony where he truly became the devil.

Manifestations of my insanity revealed onyx gates of hell swinging wide behind him. Gargoyles flew out of the fog swirling thicker and higher around his legs. Scorpions and salamanders, hell beasts and death hounds…they all stalked and prowled toward me.

I struggled in my binds as one smoke-curled hound sniffed right between my bare legs.

Tears I'd forbidden from falling threatened to rain faster than my blood.

I choked on salt.

I gagged on sorrow.

Victor chuckled as I spiralled down, down, down.

Far worse than before.

More deluded than before.

Instinct overrode everything.

The urge to fight and war and *run.*

I fought my binds. I yanked my arms and kicked my legs. The clink of my collar on the hook behind me rang out like a church bell.

Peter balled his hands and never looked away, his eyes blazing messages to calm, to accept, to drift.

But it was too late.

I'd fought it for as long as I could.

I'd clung to flashes of sanity.

I'd done my best to salvage the script Henri and I had written.

But as Henri dropped his red-smeared hand and fisted his erection, falling on me for more, it was over.

His gut-wrenching groan tore me open.

He shimmered in a mirage of delusion as bat wings flared wide and fangs elongated to pierce his bottom lip.

Everything vanished.

The room.

The animals.

Peter.

Victor.

Hell.

All that remained was *him* as he held up his knife and searched for a new place on my body to slice…

Chapter Two

Henri

I'D NEVER FELT THIS WAY before.

Never been so…empty.

Empty of attempts to be better.

Empty of hope that I was good.

Even the night I'd tried to butcher myself and willingly summoned death, I hadn't reached this level of emptiness. This aching, quaking *freedom*.

The sharp scent of Ily's blood shot up my nose. The droplets I'd smeared on my neck infused with my body heat, permeating around me like some deviously bad aftershave.

My cock throbbed to draw more, desperate and *painfully* insistent.

I'd been inside this girl twice. I'd come four fucking times today and shot back a shit ton of alcohol, yet…her blood was the worst kind of aphrodisiac.

Far more potent than just sexual conquest.

Far more carnal than just a quick fuck.

This new throb ached in every vein and vessel, soaking into my teeth and deep into the empty chambers of my long-dead heart.

I'd always felt less removed from the animal kingdom than my fellow humans. Always felt a scratching in my bones and skin as if I could change shape and grow fur. I'd often imagined my teeth growing into sharp canines and my nails into savage claws.

But that was when the nausea always found me—slapping such stupid ideas away, smothering me in humanness, sending me bolting for a bush or toilet to vomit in.

But now?

I felt…*healthy*.

Energised.

Reborn.

No sickness. No churning gut. No reprimanding inner voice telling me to be better.

I'd *tried* to be better.

I'd tried so fucking hard.

But *this* was better.

Giving in.

Going home.

Becoming who I truly was.

It was motherfucking liberating.

Blinking slightly hazy eyes, I focused on the sparkling jewel bound to a cross before me. Whatever I'd felt for this slave? The overwhelming crush I'd harboured? The nonsense belief I could save her…all faded into a different sort of conquest.

I cringed at my embarrassing past and all my struggles.

I turned my back on the man I could never be.

My past self fucked me off.

His patheticness.

His weakness.

His desperation to be normal.

Fuck that.

Why be normal when I could be *this*?

This powerful. This free. This *whole*.

Never again.

Never fucking again would I kill myself trying to be something I wasn't.

And it's all thanks to her.

Letting my cock go, I traced the dagger along her pretty cheekbone. Such flawless skin. Such an angelic colour as if she were borne from sunlight and butterscotch. "Ah, Ily…" My hand was steadfast and stable as I scribed an H over her cheek—not cutting, merely autographing her with invisible ownership. "You freed me, little nightmare. Your silly little kick unlocked every part of me."

She stretched on her tiptoes, tipping her head back as if she could escape my knife. "This isn't you. It's not." She squeezed her eyes closed and shook her head, her collar jingling on its hook. "You don't have wings. You aren't some son of darkness. I'm hallucinating, and this will all be over soon—"

"It's already over." I dragged the dagger along her jawline. "The moment you kicked me, it was all over."

"Don't." She strained from my blade, lengthening her neck, revealing the small cut I'd already made and inviting a thousand more. "Please. Stop. Please, *please* stop."

Dropping my head, I pressed my mouth to the wound I'd caused. I tongued the cut, my stomach snarling for sustenance. To taste her. *Truly* taste her in a way I'd never tasted anyone.

I'd never gone that far, despite my dreams and longings.

Never drawn another's blood and feasted, despite my tastebuds turning every other food to ash.

But only a faint metallic flavour teased me, the wound already sealing and refusing to give me its gift.

Fine.

I still had ninety-eight more droplets to draw.

Pulling away, I studied her fear, her tension, her twitching, jerking terror.

As much as her beauty beguiled me, I saw the truth now.

She was just a girl. A toy. A belonging.

My belonging.

To do with as I please.

Painting her plump pink lips with the sharp tip of my blade, I shivered as she gasped in panic. Her body twisted in the binds, the clink of the buckles around her ankles music to my fucking ears.

"You should really thank me, you know," I murmured, utterly entranced with the way brutal metal threatened to puncture her fragile skin. "This knife is sharp and clean. Far, far better than those disgusting ones Victor offered."

A string of words escaped her in a language I wasn't familiar with. Peter gasped behind me, obviously understanding her.

Breathing hard, she repeated them, over and over. A mantra.

Her pretty voice filled the room, weaving around dead animals, invoking a spell that only freed me further.

I smirked and waited for her to open her eyes.

Her voice slowly drifted off; I grinned the moment her golden gaze met mine. "No amount of prayers or chants can save you, little nightmare."

Her lips twisted, fighting tears.

My entire body stiffened, transfixed on the glossy-wet glitter in her eyes.

With one hand, I adjusted my hard-on, just daring her to cry in my presence.

With monumental effort, she sniffed back every sorrow and trembled in her imprisonment. Bound and subservient, her forced submission seeped into my mind, adding yet another layer of freedom.

Sighing with utter relief and newfound power, I hunted for a new spot to cut.

Ily moaned in utter despair as I drew my knife across her neck, over her shoulder and down, down her arm. She flinched as I kept going, stopping on the paper-thin skin of the inside of her wrist. The golden cuff keeping her arms spread had already bruised her. Slight redness from her struggles marred the perfection of her flesh. "You know…I never intended to use this blade like this, but it's fitting. It's new. A virgin to blood…just like me."

Gritting my teeth, I added pressure to the blade right over the web of veins keeping her alive.

Ily's self-control broke.

She thrashed and fought. Jerked and jangled. The cross didn't budge. The buckles didn't unbind. Her collar and cuffs held, trapping her in helpless fury.

Nowhere to run and no way to hide.

I let her tire herself out.

Never lifted the knife point from her wrist.

Only once she panted and her head hung with defeat did I raise an eyebrow and push down. "That was pointless."

She cried out as my switchblade punctured her.

"Pointless but oh-so-fucking satisfying." I couldn't tear my eyes away. Just a tiny nick but in the perfect spot. "Your heart is pumping; your blood is flowing. See how quickly it pours for me now?"

Blood oozed far faster than the slice on her neck, rolling with shiny, lustrous crimson. It threatened to plop off her arm before I snatched up the pipette and sucked it into the glass tube.

She moaned again as I collected her lifeforce. The wound didn't give up much. After all, I'd merely scratched her.

I had no intention of rushing this.

No intention of giving up this heady, arousing superpower.

Raising the pipette, I held it to the chandelier.

Light shone through her trapped blood, turning pink and almost translucent. I swear I saw sparks of life within, tiny flecks of her soul that she'd never get back.

Stabbing the knife into my waistband, I held out my already blood-smeared palm and squeezed the black rubber tip of the dropper.

One by one, red droplets fell.

"Five." The first scarlet splash landed like a tiny starburst. "Six." It joined its bloody twin. "Seven." I shuddered as my voice darkened. "Eight." Euphoria opened its pearly gates and let me in. "Nine." The alcohol in my system no longer had any hold on me, burning away beneath the flames of sadistic truth. "Ten." The final drop settled on top of all the rest—a tiny puddle of copper-tainted wine.

My mouth watered.

I raised my hand to my lips.

The urge to take communion filled me. Not the spirit-forgiving kind where sins were erased by the body and blood of Christ but the spirit-freeing kind where sins stepped fully into the light of night.

My tongue snaked out.

Ily looked away as if she couldn't watch.

And the tiniest tug in my heart stilled my scarlet drink.

Not yet.

I paused.

I'd ignored every devilish voice my entire life. I'd shut them up and shoved them into the dark.

Willingly listening now was a novelty.

Not yet.

After.

You taste her, and it's all over.

You'll snap.

I had a solid point.

Slapping my palm over my wrist, my nostrils flared as her blood stung me. The same wrist where I'd drawn it from Ily—claiming it as mine.

Her eyes widened as she watched me paint her essence against my overheated skin. Sweat rolled down my back. Heat scorched my veins. And the sensation of her energy seeping and tangling with mine made my heart pound a drum of fucking ecstasy.

Giving in to the urgency percolating in my belly, I stepped toward her other outstretched arm.

She flinched as I wrapped my fingers around her wrist, shoving the cuff a little higher to access the spiderweb of red and blue beneath.

"This isn't real. Not real." Her head hung low as I fisted my knife from my waistband and pressed it against her skin. "It's just a bee sting. A thorn. Nothing more than *ahhh*—"

I pierced her.

Barely there.

A tiny incision.

Blood immediately beaded.

Swapping the blade for the pipette, I repeated the ritual: sucking down hot, metallic vitality.

My hand—that always used to shake as I did my best to trap myself within—was wondrously steady as I squeezed out all the droplets I'd claimed.

"Eleven." I struggled to breathe as her russet blood seduced me. "Twelve, thirteen, fourteen, fifteen." I pinched the dropper, releasing a final one. "Sixteen." Five droplets all congealing into one silken ball of ruby.

My teeth ached to suck down her flavour.

My heart bucked against my ribs.

But I kept enough control to smear Ily's blood over my matching wrist, joining us in three ways. Three points of energies and souls.

In some dark recess of my mind, I truly felt a binding taking place. A black sort of tethering, braiding her heartbeat to mine. Her blood to mine. Her fear and futile future to *mine.*

An idea unfurled.

Too fast to stop.

Too delicious to refuse.

Swapping the pipette for the knife again, I ran the glinting tip right down her sternum.

Ily struggled and gasped, her eyes wild as she saw things that weren't real in a room that most certainly was.

I'd never been so clear-headed. So potently aware of every desire and desperation.

Pity she didn't feel the same.

Pity she allowed her catatonic terror to turn her inside out.

It would be so much more fun if she was truly with me and not skittering between reality and wherever else her mind had taken her.

"Not real," she whimpered as I shifted my blade slightly to the right, hovering over where her flurrying heart hid beneath flesh, muscle, and bone.

"Not real. He's not real. This isn't real. He's not a vampire. Not a demon. Just a man. Just a—"

"You're wrong." I chuckled as I pricked the swell of her upper breast, sighing heavily as red, red blood appeared.

She cried out and fought, her collar making that delicious mocking jingle against the hook holding her in place.

"I'm real. You're real. *This* is real." It was second nature now to gather up her blood in the cleverly designed glass tube. Sucking it up, I siphoned red from her body to paint mine.

This wound bled a little more.

I'd lacerated a little longer.

Marked her a little deeper.

The pipette was full by the time the cut forbid me anymore.

Her gaze tipped up, her eyes blazing gold and almost holy. I froze as I tripped into her celestial stare, once again seeing an angel I'd ensnared from the heavens and dragged down to wicked hell.

Unlike before, whenever I'd see a stunning woman and fought disgraceful urges to hurt her, I no longer hated myself. I no longer punished myself. No gush of sickness. No urge to purge myself from sin.

This was how things were always meant to be.

Victor was right.

Life existed in balance.

Predators and prey.

Monsters and meek.

I couldn't change who I was; I'd only killed myself by trying.

The world needed men like me because goodness couldn't exist without evil. Light couldn't shine without darkness. And Ily would never have existed if she hadn't been born for me to ruin.

No, not just ruin.

Shred apart.

Feast upon.

Consume.

Placing the pipette and knife on the table holding all manner of torture devices, I grabbed the back of my t-shirt and wrenched it over my head.

Ily shivered as I stood before her bare-chested. Her eyes skittered over me. Her lips thinned as she shook her head and saw things I couldn't see.

"Just a man. He isn't made of smoke or shadow. He's not scaled like a dragon or—"

Grabbing her chin, I forced her eyes to lock on mine. "What do you see when you look at me?"

Fresh tears glimmered in her stare. The glossy wetness punched me in the stomach, and my cock almost crawled out of my trousers.

Biting her bottom lip, she tried to pull her jaw out of my control, but I merely tightened my grip. My fingers hurt her. I knew they did. Her body tightened with pain. Her eyes flared with discomfort. But she didn't speak. Didn't obey. She merely slipped into the language I couldn't understand, making sinister things slither through me.

"Fine. Keep your secrets." Letting her go, I grabbed the pipette and held out my palm.

My body was oversensitive.

My pulse haywire.

My instincts off the fucking charts.

Numbers were nothing to me now.

Words nothing more than barbaric human communication.

I was above such things.

Yet I had to count…

"Seventeen." Victor's cool, collected voice interrupted my black-dripping thoughts. "You're at seventeen." He smirked as I shot him a look. "Don't worry, I struggle to keep count too when I'm in the midst of this game. It's addictive, isn't it? Illuminating and invigorating." Leaning forward, he licked his lips as he studied Ily and her four shallow wounds. "By the time you're done, she'll be marked and blooded, and you…"

"Will be the man who signed and drank her."

He canted his head with dark respect. "Precisely." Waving his hand, he grinned. "Continue. I'm rather enjoying the show. In fact." Snapping his fingers, his gaze shot to Peter still kneeling on the rug. "I'm in need of a skilled mouth, my sweetling."

Peter couldn't hide his gulp of disgust.

His skin already held the remnants of a Master cutting him.

His face gaunt.

Eyes broken.

He couldn't look away from Ily even as he crawled on hands and knees to Victor and waited patiently while Victor shimmied on the chair and yanked down his navy pyjama bottoms. A small part of myself that used to know what jealousy felt like, what covetousness and resentfulness burned like, watched the well-trained slave as he reared up on his knees and fisted Victor's thick erection.

To think I cared that he was aware of Ily.

So what?

He's nothing.

Victor gave him a doting look, running his hands through Peter's dark brown hair. "I'm so glad you're back to behaving, Peter darling. Please don't disappoint me like that again. It hurt."

"I won't, Sir V."

Victor shuddered as Peter gave him a hand job, his gaze still pinned on my trophy strapped to the cross.

Ily breathed shallow and quick; her entire attention locked on Peter.

There was that connection again.

Some sort of bond that had no fucking right to exist.

My chest swelled with possession.

Ily studied him with despair and pity.

But Peter watched her with respect and hope.

Hope?

Fuck.

I saw through all his training.

I arrowed straight to the truth he couldn't hide.

He wasn't just aware of her; he *wanted* her.

This obedient, broken little slave had enough audacity to want what was *mine.*

"If you ever touch her, I'll make you wish you were dead," I hissed, jerking his gaze to mine. "I see what you feel. I see you wanting."

Victor stilled and grabbed Peter's chin. "Is this true? You? Out of all my jewels? You would be stupid enough to lust after what isn't yours?"

Peter dropped his eyes. "She's new, Sir V. I'm merely concerned her mind will break if you play with her too long."

"That's not your concern now, is it?"

"No, Sir V."

"Your only concern is how to please me." Victor's voice turned to acid. "So…please me."

"Yes, Sir V." With a final snatched look at Ily, Peter leaned forward and deep-throated his Master's cock.

Ily let out a savage little scream.

Another stream of foreign language spilled out of her.

She thrashed and fought.

Her belly flexed with panic. Her legs flailed uselessly.

I crossed my arms while she lost herself.

I sank even deeper into the heart of darkness that made everything so viciously free. Her goodness was what made her sad for Peter. Her kindness would be her downfall. I wanted to take every shred of that empathy and sympathy and burn it to fucking dust.

Raising the pipette again, I squeezed out her clotting blood.

"Seventeen." I grunted as the plop stained my palm.

"Eighteen." I groaned as Ily stopped fighting and hung dejected and drained in her chains.

"Nineteen. Twenty. Twenty-one. Twenty-two." I kept counting, losing myself deeper and deeper with every drop. "Twenty-three, twenty-four, twenty-five." By the time drop number thirty puddled in my hand, I could barely stand up straight.

I ached.

Fucking *ached* to snap every restraint and be done with this fucking game.

I wanted to drink from the source. Lap from her vein. Count as each bead soaked directly onto my tongue.

Ignoring the sucking noises behind me, I smeared my palm over my heart in the exact spot where I'd drawn the blood from Ily.

Her eyes met mine.

She shook her head with a wet-sad stare.

And I lost myself.

Time ceased to exist as I cut her again, this time above her belly button, slicing through perfect tender skin. Ten droplets from there. Ten to mark my own stomach.

My eyes drifted to her bare pussy.

To the trimmed line of curly black hair.

To the part of her that I'd claimed twice, yet hadn't truly mastered.

She'd given me her body because she believed I was better than what I was.

It was time I took her against her will because I would never be anything more than a beast.

With steadfast hands, I unbuttoned and unzipped.

Shoving down my trousers, I wrenched off my boxers and stood before my jewel as bare as her.

She didn't react.

Her eyes filmed over with horrors.

Her skin pallid and cold.

I didn't like it.

I *hated* it.

She'd given me no reaction when I'd been an idiotic wannabe hero—a monster doing his best to be a saint. She'd frustrated me as I'd used her, and she fucking irritated me now that I obeyed no such pact.

I wanted her tears.

Her struggles.

I wanted her to *break*.

Yet she merely blinked with dead eyes and did her best to ignore me.

Let's see how she ignores this.

Dropping to my knees between her spread and buckled legs, I looked up at her as if I truly did dwell in hell. She stiffened as I pressed the knife against her ankle, nicking her with a nasty flick.

Tears trembled on her lower lashes, but she didn't try to kick me again. Didn't mutter words I didn't know or see things I couldn't envision. She merely sighed and closed her eyes as if she sought inner peace.

Allowing her to avoid me for just a little longer, I siphoned up her blood, surprised at how many drops filled the pipette.

I must have cut deeper than I thought as fifteen pretty beads of blood filled my palm.

I smeared them on my matching ankle before reaching for her other one.

She didn't even suck in a breath as I sliced her again just above the leather binding her.

Not as much in this harvest.

Merely eight little droplets to stain my skin, painting me in primitive ink.

What's that? Sixty-three so far?

My mind didn't want to keep count anymore.

It wanted more than just one hundred and two measly drops.

It wanted *all* of them.

As I worked my way up her legs, cutting and drawing, counting and smearing, my humanity kept falling away. Stripping me from clothes, shoes, and belongings. Erasing money and hardship and ego. I reverted to my ancestors who painted their conquests on cave walls. Celebrating their hunts as they killed their prey and used the blood of their meals to tell stories of their mightiness.

The insides of her knees bled nicely. Giving me thirty combined from both.

Ninety-three.

Panting heavily, swallowing hard against the vicious urges to taste, I reared taller on my knees and clamped my hands on her hips. The slim switchblade kissed her where I held it, the dropper in my other hand.

Her eyes flared wide.

Her breath caught.

My thumbs moved of their own accord, caressing her like I'd done in the past when all we'd had was secrets and whispers.

I did my best to stop, but they kept stroking her delicate, almost translucent skin.

She shifted in her binds.

Her pulse pounded against my fingertips.

Her skittering heartrate revealed the truth.

"Does it hurt, little nightmare? Or will I find you're secretly wet again?"

Ily looked away, colour scalding her cheeks.

Victor cursed. "Sheath your teeth, you little cunt."

Peter didn't reply but a gagging noise sounded as if Victor shoved his jewel's face deeper onto his cock.

My own cock reached breaking point.

I no longer felt drunk on booze but entirely high on Ily's ungiven surrender.

Nine drops remaining.

A mere nine little ruby tears to finish this morbid game.

And I knew exactly where I'd bleed her.

Glancing down at my nakedness, I traced my knife along the red, ugly scar above my femoral artery. Or at least, I'd thought that was where it lurked. I'd tried to find it. Tried to slice it. Tried to bleed out all over the goddamn floor.

I'd failed and left myself with a nasty reminder that I couldn't even kill myself successfully.

For months, that'd gnawed away at me. Shamed me. Destroyed me.

A constant reminder that even though I wanted so fucking badly to be good, that was never an option for me.

But now…I'd reached the bottom of my downfall. Black clouds above me. Midnight fog around me. And I'd never breathed such sweet air, never stretched in such welcoming oblivion.

That scar was now a promise.

A vow that I'd found where I belonged.

I was home.

Looking up, I caught Ily studying my puckered scar.

In a moment of lucidity and ill-advised empathy, she whispered, "What happened?"

I grinned at the softness of her voice, the imploring hope that I'd return to her and be the jackass who thought he'd been falling for her.

I couldn't wait to teach her that that jackass was now dead.

"I survived." I ran my thumbs on either side of her pussy, tracing the hypersensitive, ever-so-fragile skin. "And for the first time since that day, I'm glad I did because now…I get to play with you."

She shuddered.

Her collar clinked against the hook.

Her entire body broke out in goosebumps.

"Please, Henri."

"Not my name anymore, little nightmare. I told you that."

"Please—"

"Hush." Pressing a kiss against her left upper thigh where her flawless skin mocked my scarred one, I poised the tip of my knife. "This one might hurt."

Not giving her time to tense or slip into whatever subspace she found sanctuary in, I cut.

Not too deep—I wasn't feeling murderous. Just deep enough to grant her a matching defection, completing our ceremony of blood and belonging.

Scarlet instantly gushed.

Hotter than before.

Redder than before.

I went to press the pipette against her dribbling crimson, but…

I reached my limit.

Stabbing my knife into the carpet by my knee and tossing the dropper over my shoulder, I threw Victor a savage grin. "I'm done playing your game, Vic. I'm going to play my own now."

Ily jerked as I fell on her.

She cried out as my mouth locked over the bleeding wound.

Life ended.

Death paused.

The world screeched to a stop.

Every sense, every fucking synapse zeroed in on her sweet, sharp decadence.

My heart smoked as that first taste, that first delicious *dangerous* taste seared onto my tongue.

Fuck.

Me.

Never.

I'd never tasted anything so raw and earthy and…so bitterly carnal.

My cock speared upright with throbbing starvation.

My hands tightened around her hips, dragging her into me.

My tongue licked at her wound, forcing her to give me more, give me everything.

Ily's cry seeped into my ears.

My mouth stung.

My body vibrated.

Lust ripped violently through me.

Yanking my lips away from her thigh, my eyes locked on her pussy.

So close.

Right there.

The stupid rules I'd made of not tasting what wasn't mine incinerated.

My laughable boundaries shattered as I shifted on worshipping knees and claimed her.

My lips locked over her clit in one smooth domination.

"No," she screamed. "Don't."

I licked her. Hard.

"No, *uhhhh—*" Her refusals ended with a moan that set my hair on end. The same sort of moan I'd heard in her sleep. A wanting moan. A desperate moan.

I didn't hesitate.

My tongue slipped deeper, past her clit, hunting for that wet, dark heat.

Unlike our pantomimes and the moment when she'd writhed on my hand at dinner, she wasn't wet.

This game hadn't scrambled her right and wrong or made her lust.

But I didn't care.

I'd taken her lifeforce.

She existed within me now.

We were one.

And I wanted all of her.

I wanted her weeping and writhing.

Shattering and begging.

I want in.

With both hands clamped on her hips, I ate her, *devoured* her.

I plunged my tongue inside and suffered a second fucking reckoning.

Her blood was sharp and stannic. Full of iron and minerals.

Her pussy was silky and sweet. Full of pleasure and promise.

The two flavours blended and turned me into an animal.

I didn't hold back.

I fucked her with my tongue without any worries of being too hard or too vicious. I gave her brutal. I gave her cruel.

Her entire body twisted and thrashed in her binds. The insides of her thighs quivered to get away from me. The buckles held her spread. My nose nuzzled her clit as I inhaled deeply, soaking my lungs with her perfect scent.

She struggled to speak.

Her whimpers turned me the fuck on.

And when her body gave in to my attack and surrendered?

Yeah, it was all fucking over.

My hands moved without permission, my left soaring up her body to fist her breast and my right dipping between her legs to penetrate two fingers inside her.

She burst into flames.

Her skin heated to a thousand degrees.

Her head tipped back as I finger-fucked and tongued her. Licking her clit all while my fingers plunged deep.

This was for me.

Everything I claimed, *I* wanted.

Yet I couldn't deny the thrill of making her come apart.

Of taking away her control and turning her entire body against her.

The first ripple of her pussy around my fingers made me grunt with approval. The gush of wetness made my entry slick and smooth.

I kept going.

Kept pushing, breaking, claiming.

It didn't take long.

Unfortunately for her, I was a fast learner.

She'd taught me what she liked when I dry-humped her to completion in my room.

I might not know her last name, but I knew she liked it hard.

So…I gave her hard.

Motherfucking ruthless.

And she came.

Wake after quaking wake.

Pulse after shuddering pulse.

Her body milked my fingers.

I couldn't help myself.

Withdrawing my hand, I plunged my tongue back inside her, needing to feel the quivering sensation in my mouth—to taste her release, drink down her unwanted orgasm, and prove to her that she might hate me but her body fucking *loved* me.

My chin and five o'clock shadow were drenched as her fierce climax faded almost as quickly as it'd pounced.

Her cuffs jingled as she trembled. Her chest flushed. Skin sweaty.

She'd fallen down the other side of a craggy, blissful mountain.

I wanted to fall too.

Fumbling with the buckle around her ankle, I unthreaded the loop and let her go.

Just one.

A single leg.

The one I'd cut to match mine.

With blurry eyes and horror on her beautiful face, Ily cringed away from me as I swooped to standing and grabbed her knee. Hoisting her leg as far up my thigh as possible, I spread her at my mercy.

Our eyes locked.

Our panting matched.

I expected her to tell me no.

To scream or beg as I fisted my erection and guided it to where it needed to go.

But she didn't.

Her mouth merely fell wide as I breached her.

I didn't look away as I sank deep, *deep* inside her.

Her head tipped forward almost crashing against the base of my throat as I shifted her higher and forced her body to accept all of me. Her wetness helped me glide. Her residual pleasure-pulses threatened to make me come.

And when I slotted all the way in, we both groaned.

I rocked my hips, feeding her my throbbing length.

Her eyes snapped closed as her body clenched around me.

Right there was our first moment.

This was sex.

Not those other pathetic moments where I'd been too shit terrified to enjoy being inside her. Terrified at losing control.

Those had been pretend. Make-believe. Survival.

This…

This was *real.*

This was mine.

She was mine.

I thrust.

All.

…and thrust.

Fucking.

…and thrust.

Mine.

Victor's grunt echoed behind me as he reached his own climax, no doubt spilling down Peter's throat. I didn't look over my shoulder. No one else existed apart from this jewel that'd bled for me, this gorgeous temptress I'd conquered and enslaved.

I withdrew and drove back in, shuddering as her body welcomed with such tight condemnation. All the barriers and chains I'd wrapped myself in detonated. Ily might have unlocked my cage with her ill-advised kick, but sinking inside her was the final strike to the bomb that'd been waiting to explode ever since I was born.

My insides shattered.

My heart imploded.

Shrapnel fell around my feet, confetti made of morals and scruples and ridiculous, useless integrity.

I'd been born alone; I would die alone.

There was no need to try to be a man deserving of a wife and life.

All that fucking pressure.

All that bullshit at being better…it all collapsed inward.

My pace increased as I rode the woman who'd freed me.

My body sank into hers. Over and over. Driving in and out, relentless with primal pounding. The faster I fucked her, the more my mind became a smoking wasteland. A battleground where I'd slaughtered my past and stood victorious on the pile of my defeated bones.

I no longer needed such fragile, frivolous things.

I didn't need them because…I was no longer human.

My lips pulled back as I sank on my heels and thrust up. Ily bounced in my hold as I jack-knifed into her again and again.

My eyes fell on the cuts I'd given her. No longer bleeding, her skin glowing angry and red. Each laceration looked like red liquorice—lashes of addictive bitter sugar just for me.

Falling on her neck, I tongued the small wound and groaned as her entire body shuddered against mine.

She didn't speak. Didn't react.

But I felt her.

Inside me.

Around me.

Her soul and her body, stealing all of me just like I'd stolen all of her.

"Fucking hell," I groaned as every muscle clenched, climbing up that delirious mountain where bliss could turn a man mad.

My mouth hovered over Ily's. Our lips parted, breaths mingling.

All it would take was a tip of my chin and I'd claim yet another piece.

A kiss.

A wet, deep, *vicious* kiss.

But…something stopped me.

Our eyes locked, scattering the urge and giving me a far more urgent one.

I begged to see her cry.

I wanted to drink down her sadness just like I'd drunk down her essence.

I *needed* her to cry.

To complete my transformation and ensure I never forgot just how untouchable I was. How utterly invincible I was now that I was me. The *true* me. The monster I could never quite tame.

Even as I thrust into her hard and fast, and her eyes glowed with unwanted pleasure, she withheld her grief. For the first time since we'd met, she had control over her sorrow, and it fucked me off that she denied me.

The longer I stared at her, the quicker our bodies collided.

Her teeth clamped into her bottom lip, and my forehead crashed on hers as I threw every shred of my hell-damned soul into this.

This moment of absolute awakening.

I'd never been so profoundly, so *painfully* aroused.

So aware of everything.

Every slide and slip. Every ripple and flutter. Every grunt and gasp.

No thoughts. No ethics. Nothing to ruin the absolute perfection of this moment.

So many layers of freedom.

So many levels of release.

Ah fuck.

That word triggered another release.

One that'd haunted me since the moment I'd first punctured Ily's virgin skin.

Blinding, brutalizing pleasure shot down my spine and curdled between my legs. Tighter, stronger, it festered in my belly, snarling to obliterate.

I held off for as long as I could.

I rode Ily for as long as possible.

I never wanted to leave this nirvana.

But as Ily struggled and her voice once again slipped into a language I couldn't understand, I was no longer the Master but at my monster's mercy.

My shoulders rolled. My breath caught. My entire body quaked with sweet, savage agony. I roared as my balls tightened, cock thickened, and jets of crippling, consuming rhapsody shot out of me.

Ily cried out as I spilled inside her.

Her eyes closed as I jerked and shivered in the throes of the best fucking orgasm of my life.

I couldn't breathe as I kept twitching, totally consumed with how liberating it was to come with blood on my tongue and truth in my twisted heart.

All other climaxes paled.

None of them ever granted me such transcendent peace.

As the last pulse of my pleasure subsided and I focused slowly on the room full of a thousand dead creatures, I froze, just for a second.

A familiar second.

One where my tongue turned sour, just waiting for nausea to pounce.

I tensed against the noxious sickness that always made me pay.

But…nothing.

Blissful, wonderful *nothing.*

For the first time in my godforsaken life, my stomach growled for a different reason. Not to throw up the awful things I'd done but to fucking celebrate.

Hunger shakes caught me unaware.

My body chose that exact moment to make me stumble beneath starvation.

With a grunt, I withdrew from Ily and tripped away from the cross.

Keeping her eyes on the floor, she drew her free leg to her other, contorting her body to an uncomfortable angle as she crossed her ankles and snapped her thighs together.

Despite her best efforts to hide, she couldn't stop the creamy white trail of my semen leaking out of her.

My cock twitched in pride.

My chest swelled with ownership.

I'd walked into this room a pathetic shadow of my true self, and now…with Ily's blood staining my body and my cum staining hers, I felt complete.

Grabbing my trousers from where I'd kicked them off, I slipped them up and fastened the zipper. With a satisfied sigh, I turned to face Victor.

He stood beside the backgammon table that'd been righted from me crashing into it. Fresh platters of food waited, summoning me to devour. He saluted me with an onion tartlet. "Well done."

I tipped my chin and stalked toward him.

I couldn't ignore the urge to eat anymore.

Snagging a salt-encrusted cracker with what looked like duck pâte and some microgreens, I shoved it into my mouth. The booze in my system was a distant memory.

"How does it feel?" Victor asked quietly, throwing a look at Peter who kneeled by Victor's feet. "Are you finally free?"

Bracing myself, I sank my teeth into another delicious morsel and chewed.

I waited.

I swallowed.

I searched inside for that debilitating nausea, daring it to creep over me and make me vomit all over Victor's lambskin slippers.

Still nothing.

My shoulders rolled with such fucking gratefulness, I almost stumbled.

Did this mean I'd never have to puke up my rotten guts anymore?

That all I had to do to find a cure was stride over that mythical line I'd always avoided?

Perhaps my constant state of sickness had been yet another symptom of my denial?

It seemed so.

It felt so.

And slowly, the biggest smile of my life spread my lips.

Grabbing a handful of perfectly seasoned peanuts, I shoved them all in my mouth and laughed. Victor's question bounced around in my wondrously empty mind, and my body turned jittery with relief.

Bursting at the seams with emotions I didn't know how to fucking process, I strode to Victor and slung my arm around his slender shoulders. Peter shot me a look before his gaze sneaked back to where Ily hung silent and miserable in her binds.

"You know what, Vic?" I kissed the cocksucker on the cheek. "I feel fan-fucking-*tastic*." Glancing at the spread of snacks, I shrugged. "In fact, I've worked up quite the appetite."

"Oh?" Victor chuckled and stepped out of my half embrace. His eyes narrowed, full of unreadable things. "You've indulged in enough pussy tonight I'm sure, so what are you hungering for now?"

"A juicy bloody steak."

Peter winced.

Ily gagged.

And Victor merely smiled like the reptile he was, still watching me a tad too closely. "As you wish. Peter, take Ily to see Dr Belford and then put her to bed. I expect to see you both bright-eyed and bushy-tailed in the morning."

"Yes, Sir V." Peter staggered to his feet, flinching beneath bruises slowly blooming on his throat. Bruises Victor had given him or another

Master before Ily and I found him in the corridor?

Either way, my heart didn't skitter like it used to.

The hero inside me didn't rise to save the day.

That motherfucker was dead.

Good riddance.

"Come along then, *mon ami.*" Victor strode to the door and cracked it open. He shook his head just once at the guards—guards who'd been briefed to kill me if I'd failed. Immediately, all four bowed and siphoned out into the night.

Looking me up and down as if he still didn't trust me, Victor said, "I'll wake the chef and celebrate with you. After all…it's not every day I have a hand in freeing someone who was so determined not to be freed."

I smirked and strode past him.

I walked on fucking sunshine and rainbows. "Guess I owe you a thank-you."

"Guess so." Victor laughed softly as he slipped beside me.

The door slowly swung closed, blocking off the dead zoo, my past life, and the girl who'd been the crux of my transformation.

I didn't look back.

Chapter Three

Ily

I MANAGED NOT TO CRY.

I didn't cry as Henri cut me.

Didn't cry as he fucked me.

Didn't cry as Peter gently unbuckled and unshackled me, shoved off the tatters of my torn negligee, or when he slipped his kind arm around me and guided me, ever so tenderly, to Dr Belford's private rooms. The same rooms he'd been slipping out of when we'd found him an hour or so ago.

God…has it only been an hour?

Eager dawn did its best to lighten the midnight sky, quickly glimpsed in the arrow slits along the corridor as we moved like ghouls in the dark.

It couldn't have been a single hour.

I felt ancient.

A time-worn antique that no longer knew how to walk or talk or breathe.

Peter didn't say a word as he knocked softly on the door and waited for an equally soft voice to grant us entry.

I didn't cry as he guided me inside just as Dr Belford clicked on a lamp and shrugged into a pink fleece dressing gown. Didn't cry as she took one look at my naked, cum-smeared, blood-letted state and patted the operating table shoved against the wall of her private sitting room.

Everything about her space scrambled my head.

She was as much a prisoner here as us. Once a slave and now the tending physician to a hundred more, she'd invoked Victor's generosity enough to warrant clothes that weren't see-through and rooms with locks on the doors. Yet even in her quaint lounge with its grey couch and normal-looking glass coffee table, the large metallic cupboard with neatly typed labels on its many, many drawers screamed surgery.

Trembles found me as Peter helped settle me on the white-sheet-covered table. He didn't speak as he went to Dr Belford's couch and snagged the thick yellow-and-cream knitted blanket that looked homemade.

Dr Belford went to argue but then nodded. "You can't take it down to your quarters, but you can use it while you're here. Not my rules, you understand. If it were up to me, you could take every damn thing he's given me and share it around."

"I know." Peter gritted his teeth and bundled me up. He wrapped me so tight, drawing the corners beneath my chin, he almost choked me.

Sighing heavily, he kissed my forehead and spoke to Dr Belford. "He used a clean blade. Shallow cuts. She didn't bleed much."

"How much is much?" Dr Belford asked.

"I think Victor ordered about five mil or so."

"Good. At least she doesn't need a transfusion."

I shuddered.

The fact that she had the ability to do such a procedure painted horror stories in my head.

I huddled deeper into my borrowed blanket.

Opening a few drawers of her medicine cabinet, Dr Belford selected whatever she needed, then came to join us by the wall. Placing a small metal bowl, iodine, some antiseptic cream, and beige bandages and band-aids beside me, she looked at me carefully. "I need to tend to you, okay? I'm just going to slip the blanket down and the moment I've cleaned your wounds, you can have it back."

I knew she spoke.

I saw her lips move.

I heard her words fall.

Yet…there was a strange kind of separation. A fog that wasn't quite a fog. A silence that never quite faded.

I shivered as she glanced pointedly at Peter until he stepped away. Once he no longer clutched me in the blanket, she gently pushed it off my quaking shoulders and inspected the cuts Henri had given me.

Cold air licked me.

Pungent antiseptic stung me.

I didn't look.

I just stared at nothing.

At a single speck of dust on the flagstones.

A speck that danced and morphed into tiny replicas of my past.

A teddy bear I'd given to Krish from my own collection.

A Barbie doll I'd dressed up in a matching saree when we went to our neighbour's son's wedding.

A quartz crystal tower that I used to meditate with that Father gave me on my tenth birthday.

The drugs still twisted my reality.

My thoughts still gluggy and nonsensical.

But they weren't as chaotic as before.

Not as technicolour or fantastical.

While Henri cut me, I'd been swept away by them. Pinwheels and fireworks exploded over my vision as the pain in my body became colour in my fractured mind.

I'd sunk into those refractions.

I'd studied the shapes my mind conjured depending on what part he sliced.

When he cut over my heart, I recognised the flower of life pattern from my pendant Krish had given me. The pendant Victor had stolen.

I'd heard that symbol was revered.

Part of the sacred geometry of energy and accession—portals into other realms.

I'd tried so hard to step into a portal and be gone.

To sink into a meditation and be free of him.

But each time he cut me, I couldn't escape my mortal body or the burning, slicing agony.

And so, I'd been trapped.

Mindless by a drug that faded but refused to let me go. Imprisoned by cuffs and buckles, completely at Henri's mercy as he mounted me.

That was where the numbing fog first found me.

Where all feelings and hopes I'd nursed for Henri Ward died a quick and silent death.

Not because he'd transformed into a heartless beast but because the psilocybin chose that moment to do what Peter said it did.

It ignited my blood.

It heated my clit.

It triggered my hurting, horrified body into despicable desire the moment Henri licked me.

I'd hated all of them.

Despised them.

As Henri performed such a sensual act and somehow made it an act of sabotage, I cursed *everybody*.

I hated Peter for drugging me and leaving me at the mercy of a substance that tore apart my mind before tearing apart my body. I hated Victor for hurting so many and the guards for keeping everyone in-line.

But I hated Henri most of all.

I hated him with the fire of a thousand suns I was named after.

I wanted him dead even as I came on his tongue.

My orgasm was detested and defective with none of the tingling magic of enjoyment.

Psilocybin might have given me sexual sensitivity, but it'd failed at quickening my heart.

It taught me a valuable lesson.

Yes, it could prepare my body for sex.

Yes, it could make me find a biological release.

And yes, it could protect my mind from the pain of unwanted coupling.

But when it came to granting me peace in this hellscape, it failed spectacularly.

I felt empty.

Cavernously, gale-howlingly *empty*.

The numbness spread as Dr Belford tended to me.

Exhausted anaesthesia crept over me, bringing listlessness and coldness as she cleaned the cut on my upper thigh and gently placed a plaster over it.

I was detached and paralysed.

But I didn't cry.

Didn't cry as the blanket was once again tucked under my chin and held in place by Peter. I didn't cry as Dr Belford packed away her things and asked if I wanted any drugs to dull the pain.

"No drugs," Peter said. "*Ever.* Put that on her file or whatever notes you keep on us. No drugs, got it?" He shuddered and shook his head. "I-I gave her psilocybin. She reacted poorly. She's still suffering and it's all my fucking fault."

"Your fault?" Dr Belford laughed tragically. "None of this is your fault, Pete."

He looked away. "I shouldn't have forced her to take one. I thought…I thought I was protecting her. That she'd slip away like the rest of us. Have a little trip into fantasy land and come back to earth when it was all over."

"Didn't she?" Dr Belford frowned, then shone a pen torch into my eyes.

I didn't even flinch.

Didn't cry.

Didn't cry.

"Her pupils are heavily dilated."

"Will she be okay?" Peter asked, his voice cracking with guilt.

"She'll be fine. She just needs to sleep it off."

"Yeah, for the two hours left of the night."

Dr Belford stepped away. "I guess you better get to sleep quickly then. You both need some rest."

Peter nodded and went to unwrap me from my cocoon.

"Wait." Dr Belford placed a hand on his bare arm, studying the cuts she'd already tended on his skin. "You're shaking, Pete. Did something else happen?"

He scoffed under his breath. "Nothing that will kill me. Unfortunately."

"Did Victor make you serve again?" Her lips twisted in disgust. "Knowing what Master K did to you?"

"He doesn't know. He never wants to know. He sees I'm still standing, and he's satisfied." He hung his head. "And don't worry. He only made me blow him. That I can handle. Nothing a little finger down my throat when I get back to our quarters won't fix. At least he didn't fuck me. That…that would've been agonising."

With a wince, Dr Belford whispered, "Use that numbing cream I gave you. Rub it in. I know you have a thing against suppositories but I'm telling you—"

"I have enough people sticking things up my ass without me joining in." Peter chuckled blackly.

"Regardless, insert one for the next few days, and whatever tearing you're suffering from will heal far quicker."

"Yeah, yeah." He waved her concern away. "I'll survive. I always do."

Not believing him, Dr Belford glanced at me. "Did her Master have intercourse with her?"

"Yep." Peter shuddered. "Hard."

Cupping my chin, Dr Belford filled my faltering vision. "Did you split? I'm aware Peter doesn't want to give you any more drugs, but I have others as well as psychostimulants. Paracetamol, ibuprofen, codeine. I even have liquid morphine…when the occasion calls for it."

I didn't answer her.

The effort was too much to swallow and blink and speak.

"I've got some stashed downstairs. If she wants some later, I'll give them to her," Peter said quietly.

"Okay." Stepping back, she grimaced. "In that case, off with you both. Sleep is the best healer, so go get some."

"Hear that, Ily?" Peter grinned far too wide for my benefit. "*Chalne ka samay ho gaya.*" (Time to go.)

The Hindi words sank into my cotton wool head, reminding me that I'd implored in it, chanted in it, begged in it.

It'd been as useless as English because I was still here, still trapped, still lost and alone and so, *so* afraid.

But I didn't cry.

Didn't cry.

I shivered as Peter stole my blanket and folded it neatly back into place on Dr Belford's couch. Taking my icy hands, he guided me off the table, then tucked me like a terrified naked duckling under his wing and guided me through the citadel.

The journey went unnoticed.

The chilliness of the morning utterly unable to match the frostiness of my soul.

We met no one.

Heard no one.

Just two bleeding ghosts in the night.

The entire time we walked, Peter stayed silent. He didn't try to pry me from my fugue, and I didn't try to offer him comfort.

Our silence did that for us.

It cloaked us and made us invisible.

By the time we'd climbed down all the stairs and entered a familiar corridor, I didn't want to be around others.

I just wanted to be around him.

I burrowed into his chest.

He hugged me tight as he pushed open the entrance to the slave quarters.

The huge carved door swung wide.

Warmth from sleeping bodies welcomed us. The soft snores of those in sweet oblivion made me viciously jealous.

I drifted toward the huge room holding a sea of white-shrouded beds. I could vaguely make out the one that Peter had said was mine. Smooth and empty, beckoning me to tumble atop it and forget.

Forget.

I needed that.

Badly.

So I went.

"Wait." Grabbing my wrist above my cuff, Peter tugged me to a stop.

I stopped.

I blinked.

But I didn't cry.

Didn't cry even though a million tears pressed like daggers behind my eyes.

Didn't cry even though every word, every breath, every gasp and heartbeat throbbed and ached and *burned* with sorrow and grief and misery.

I blinked again as he cupped my cheek and guided me to the left. "Come with me."

I followed.

Padding barefoot and bare, caped in goosebumps and scribed by Henri's wounds, I had no free will left.

Tugging me past the kitchen with its huge fridge full of fruits and vegetables, past the monstrous-sized bathroom with iridescent tiles shimmering from the floor to ceiling, he didn't stop as we skirted the wardrobe large enough for a Broadway show, morbidly depressing with only negligées and lingerie on neat tidy hangers.

Finally, he pushed open the door at the end of the jewel's private corridor.

A room I'd never entered.

"In here." Slapping the switch by the door, I flinched as rows upon rows of illumination flickered on, dancing over a treasure box of gold, gems, and jewelry.

The drugs in my system painted a hulking dragon in the corner. Smoke curling from its scaly-purple snout, its horn-tipped tail slinking around the many, many drawers and baskets full of priceless loot.

I wanted to ask what this room was. To know why it looked like a vault full of forbidden fortune.

I tried to blink away the illusion of a lavender-skinned possessive dragon as another plume of smoke snaked from its nose.

But…I had no energy.

No strength.

But at least I didn't cry.

Didn't cry.

"Pete?" Kirk appeared on the threshold, rubbing sleep from his eyes and flicking us a worried glance. His white pair of boxers didn't hide his impressive bulge. "You guys were a while. Everything okay?"

Peter let me go.

I drifted forward like dandelion fluff on the wind.

His voice licked at my heels. "I'm worried about her."

"Why?" I felt Kirk's stare on me. "She looks in one piece, minus a few cuts."

"Her body maybe, but I'm petrified that I broke her mind."

"How would *you* break her mind?" Kirk choked. "Wait. Y-You didn't touch her, did you, man? Fuck…you're not…you don't have *feelings* for her, do you? I mean, I saw the way you looked at her in the showers. I know you think it's your responsibility to look after us all, but you never looked at any of the others like—"

"Quiet." Peter interrupted. "It's not like that."

"You sure about that?" A scuffle sounded. "She speaks Hindi…same as you. That similarity seems to have caused an instantaneous bond—"

"I said *quiet*," Peter hissed.

"Not until I make you see sense." I looked over my shoulder as Kirk grabbed Peter by the elbow and growled, "You saw what they did to Macy and Sayd. The moment Vile Victor found out they were in love, he tortured the fuck out of them."

Wrenching his arm from Kirk's urgent fingers, Peter threw me a scowl. "I'm not falling for her. I just…feel responsible—just like you said. It's my fault she's like this."

I didn't care they spoke about me as if I wasn't there. As if my mind truly had broken and nothing was left of me.

The numbness reached my ears, turning the volume down on everything around me, including Kirk's and Peter's fierce whispers.

Ignoring them, I padded closer to the baskets of glittering jewels. The dragon puffed a warning tower of smoke in my direction as I sidestepped her prickly tail and reached out to touch a moonstone ring.

A tingle of power shot into my fingertips.

I didn't know if it was real or drug-induced.

I searched my fractured mind for memorised facts on this particular rock.

Moonstone.

Found mainly in Sri Lanka and Southern India. Supposed to be calming, connected to the moon and feminine energy with the power to manifest dreams into reality.

All my dreams are broken…

My heart wrenched.

My soul cracked.

But I didn't cry.

Yanking my hand back, I ran my fingertips over a million other baubles and keepsakes. Garnet and emerald. Pearl and sapphire. Necklaces, bracelets, rings, cuffs, hair clips, and earrings.

More than a jewelry shop.

More than I'd ever seen.

My skin prickled as Peter appeared on my right and Kirk on my left. Kirk stayed quiet, but Peter took my hand and looped his fingers tight with mine.

Kirk sucked in a breath.

"Do you see what used to belong to you?" Peter whispered, maybe to avoid the cameras or maybe just because the witching hour demanded respectful quietness.

I blinked and met his ardent stare.

Did he mean…

No.

He couldn't.

I looked back at the rows upon rows of gemstones. Inlaid in silver, gold, and copper.

Thousands of them.

Thousands of mementos and treasured things that once used to belong to…

I gagged and stumbled back.

My ribs shattered.

My insides tore.

But I didn't cry.

Didn't cry.

Peter moved with me, tucking hair behind my ear. "They used to belong to jewels like us. Others who have come and gone. They served, they disappeared, and yet their precious things from a previous life live on, tormenting us, haunting us, reminding us every goddamn day that there might only be thirty of us now, but there have been hundreds before."

Kirk wiped his mouth. "Fuck, man. I thought you were trying to cheer her up."

"I need her to find what's hers. I need her to have a reaction. The sooner she snaps out of this, the sooner I can—"

"What's going on?" Rebecca and Nancy appeared, draped in comforters from their bed, shuffling like dopey zombies in the dark. "We'll get told off if we're caught wandering around."

"Then go back to sleep," Peter snapped. "We're coming. I just…first, I need to see if Ily can find something from home. I-I think it will help."

"Help how?" Rebecca asked, scooping up a handful of necklaces.

They pooled through her fingers with strings of gold.

"I gave her psilocybin—"

"Oh, you shouldn't have." Rebecca dropped the necklaces. "I overheard her telling Sonya that she had a bad reaction to weed once. She's probably one of the unlucky few who don't react well to substances."

"Yeah, thanks for that, Bex." Peter rolled his eyes. "Unfortunately, I didn't have that information and figured it out the hard way."

Nancy came toward me and stared into my eyes. A daisy crown appeared on her head, quaint, fragile little flowers weaving through her fiery strands. Didn't matter they were an illusion, they seemed real and far too delicate for this place.

"She definitely looks out of it." Nancy snapped her fingers in my face.

I didn't flinch.

Didn't have the energy.

"She hasn't said a word since Ruby Tears." Peter sighed.

"Uh-oh." Both girls looked at one another. "I know how much that gutted me the first time." They shared matching grimaces. "You just need to give her time, Pete. You can't rush her. She'll deal with it in her own way."

"She needs to do something," Peter muttered. "Her silence is freaking me out."

"What do you want her to do?" Kirk snapped. "Scream?"

"If it will help…then yeah."

"Nothing will help." The blue-eyed, black-haired slave who'd been Victor's choice at the orgy-dinner appeared. Behind her trailed in four others. Two boys, two girls. All of them in various states of nakedness and sleep.

One of the boys said, "Come on, let's go to bed. The sooner she falls unconscious, the sooner her mind will come to terms with what happened."

Peter marched into his band of surviving jewels. A discussion sprang up. Some heated words broached higher than a whisper.

I ignored all of them.

I bowed my head at the silent dragon still puffing in the corner and let the sparkling gems seduce me.

A large pendant of snowflake obsidian caught my attention.

Snowflake obsidian.

Formed by volcanic eruptions in Italy, Scotland, and other wonderful far-off places. A stone believed to help heal trauma, shock, and dissolve both physical and spiritual pains.

I clutched it tight and kept walking.

So many.

Too many.

A crypt full of memories from those who'd worn, revered, and appreciated these gemstones.

A tomb of dead jewels who would never be found.

I dropped the snowflake obsidian.

My palm burned.

It belonged to someone else.

Someone who'd been tortured, brutalised, and murdered.

My eyes stung.

My breath caught.

My insides twisted into a million knots.

But I didn't cry.

Didn't cry.

I moved to the next basket and ran my cold-frosted fingers over hundreds of beaded bracelets. Just like mine. Too much like mine.

I would never be able to tell which were the ones Victor had taken off me, and I didn't want to. They hadn't worked. They hadn't protected or saved me.

The weight in my chest grew and grew.

The pressure in my head swelled and swelled.

The dragon hissed, and my heart fissured.

Just a crack.

But it caused a gaping abyss in my chest.

But I didn't cry.

I stayed dry-eyed and silent.

I didn't think about what Henri had done.

I didn't think about what he would do next.

I just kept praying to the mountains of jewels and—

I froze.

My heart stopped.

Resting in the last basket on the top row.

Glinting green and placed just so, rested my aventurine pendant from Krish.

For a second, I had no reaction.

The pressure inside me, the tears I refused to shed…they didn't get worse or better.

But then the crack in my heart gorged agonisingly wide.

An earthquake shook me.

A soul-shake.

A heart-break.

The crack became a chasm.

And my spirit fell out.

Screaming.

I gagged on despair and fear and loss. Horror waterfalled and flooded me until my faltering heartbeat roared in my ears.

I reached for my pendant.

The flower of life stone slipped elegantly off the pile of gems.

Slipping, slipping, as if it'd been waiting for me to claim it, and my inner breaking destroyed it.

With a sharp wail, I lurched through the illusion of the dragon and ran headfirst into crippling, clotting agony.

With quaking hands, I snatched up the stone.

I ran my thumb over the emblem that I knew better than my own face.

I saw Krish's smile as he gave it to me.

Felt his unconditional love as he secured it around my throat.

Heard his wise, quiet voice telling me I was special. So special.

And I broke.

I didn't cry.

Didn't cry.

I *sobbed.*

Falling to my knees, I pressed the last piece of home to my chest and splintered.

A wounded noise fell out of me.

Breathless and tragic.

A gasp, a rock, a gag, a grunt.

And then, I was nothing but tears.

Gushing wet, ugly, *violent* tears.

I wasn't aware of hands tugging me away from the shelves.

I wasn't conscious of an embrace given by the one slave who'd done his best to save me.

I lost myself to grief.

I cried and cried and *cried.*

I wailed.

I screamed.

I purged every cut and siphoned every droplet.

I couldn't suppress Henri's relief at being free.

Couldn't forget the change in him or the loss at his downfall.

All my hate.

All my worry.

All my fear and pain and terror poured out of my eyes and all over the floor.

I cried and cried.

I cried into dawn.

I cried into hell.

I kept crying until…I couldn't cry at all.

Chapter Four

Henri

I BASKED IN THE SUNRISE.

With an unlit cigar in one hand—courtesy of Victor after our perfectly rare-cooked steak—and a glass of rich merlot in the other, I bathed in the brilliant colours of nature.

Spools of gold crept over the horizon, followed by the intoxicating flush of a well-delivered bruise: purples and blues, followed by shades of reds and streaks of pain.

I sipped the wine, comparing the tart richness of grapes to the earthy rapture of Ily's blood and…I waited.

I didn't light the cigar.

I didn't shift from where I sat in the grass. The manicured green perfection cushioned me like the thickest, softest carpet.

After my five a.m. dinner with Victor, he'd retired to bed, and I'd strolled outside for some fresh air. Every mouthful of our shared celebration had been divine. Every swallow stayed exactly where it was supposed to.

The meat soaked up the rest of the alcohol, slowly bringing me down from the savage high of monster-hood, hovering me somewhere in the middle of human and beast.

I'd waited for shame. For disgrace and self-reproach, but so far…nothing.

I didn't wonder what'd become of Ily.

Didn't think of my brother or how he'd kill me.

My mind was empty, blissfully empty.

And I hoped it would *stay* empty.

But…just in case it didn't, I wanted to be on my own.

I needed to find out how much of this transformation was true.

A terrified part of my psyche kept waiting for me to revert.

To snap back into the weak, sniffling bastard who'd suffocated me my entire life.

For the hero to beat back my villain and shove me into another worthless cage.

I'd gone most of my life suffering sickness that could spring from nowhere.

And…after tonight, I couldn't quite trust that I was cured.

I hoped so.

I tentatively believed so.

But…I had to wait.

And so, I kept sipping vintage wine and watched the sun come up.

By the time golden rays peaked over the guard towers and the men on watch turned off the spotlights aimed at the drawbridge and moat beyond, I closed my eyes and flopped heavily onto my back.

I opened my arms for retribution.

I swallowed hard to entice the sourness of penance.

But still…nothing.

No nausea.

Not even a stomach squeeze.

Slowly, a soft smile tipped my lips.

I closed my eyes to the incandescent sunrise.

I sank inside myself, into all the corridors and forbidden chambers that I'd been too shit-terrified to venture into.

I made myself take inventory.

Forced myself to recall my childhood and puberty full of loneliness and suffering. I remembered the urges that'd crippled me and relived what I'd done to Ily.

And…as I sank into the very soul of my monster, another lock fell away.

The final lock.

The last chain.

Motherfucking tears came to my eyes as I exhaled with bone-shuddering gratitude.

No regret.

No remorse.

My worthless spirit didn't try to drag me back into unachievable light but was perfectly content to stay in these comforting, worshipping shadows.

I was changed.

I was *freed.*

I didn't turn into a rampaging lunatic intent on raping, pillaging, and murdering.

I didn't sprout fangs or a tail or go loping after a full moon.

I was still just a man.

A man who was finally honest.

Sitting upright, I tipped the rest of my wine onto the grass, tucked my unsmoked cigar into my trouser pocket, then shot to my feet as if I weighed nothing at all. No longer burdened. No longer drowning beneath anchoring lies.

I strode calmly and confidently toward the fortress where I'd been forced to step into me.

My thoughts were still my own.

My heart still beat, my senses still worked, I still breathed and existed.

All my life, I'd been so afraid of personal acceptance that I'd built up a fantasy that the day I became who I truly was was the day I died for good.

But I didn't die tonight.

I'd metamorphosised.

I'd shrugged off the ill-fitting chrysalis.

And now, I flew.

Chapter Five

Ily

CLOUDS IN MY HEAD, MY mouth, my ears, my heart.

I groaned and tried to crawl my way out of the fuzzy, foggy entrapment, only…something heavy pinned me down.

Sleep dissolved instantly, slamming me into a vicious headache. My hand raised to try to rub away the discomfort, only that was trapped too. Blinking away threads of nausea and confusion, I raised my head and froze.

I lay in the jewelry room.

Naked as the day I was born.

Dressed in a few scant band-aids, I slowly shifted against heavy, crushing body parts and sat up.

The people surrounding me mumbled with annoyance. Some rolled over and slung arms and legs over their closest companions. Others huddled deeper into their dreams as if unwilling to come back to reality.

A circle of them.

A hoard of them.

Just like all the jewels dumped into baskets and draped over each other, Victor's jewels did the same thing.

And I sat in the middle of what looked like a massacre.

Bare limbs punctuated by scant white blankets drawn from single beds. A blend of skin colours, hair colours, bruises, cuts, and pain. I hadn't met all the slaves serving in this fetish-filled stronghold, but seeing them all in one room made me freeze.

At first, I thought it was another illusion. It had to be the drugs. Because if it wasn't...

I choked.

The strangeness of an arm missing a hand or a hand lacking a finger or two. The sickening realisation that one girl was missing an ear, and another had a puckered scar running from her temple to her chin.

The longer I stared, the more maiming and torture appeared. Red scars and silver scars, raised ones and neat ones, almost every jewel had some imperfection, granted by a Master who ought to be *dead.*

Swallowing down a gush of venomous empathy, I rubbed my face and stopped looking.

It's the drugs.

You're still under the influence.

That's why you're in the middle of mostly nude strangers.

I braced myself and tried to see past the history of abuse and focus on why they were all curled around me, tighter and tighter, forming a spiral of body parts with me in the centre.

What happened?

Are they okay?

My breath came shallow, my throat stinging from all the salt I'd cried last night.

Last night?

More like only an hour or so ago.

Sunshine poured through the high barred windows and the door to the cavernous bathroom glowed with burning sunlight.

Too bright.

Far, far too bright for my sorrow-stinging eyes.

My bladder pressed uncomfortably, and my hip ached from sleeping on the stone floor.

But I wasn't cold.

If anything, a sheen of sweat covered my chest thanks to the body heat of so many.

I-Is this real?

And if it is…how had they survived such torture and unhappiness?

I'd only spent one evening being molested, and I'd shattered.

It made me feel stupidly weak compared to the Chinese girl missing two fingers and the black woman with only one ear.

A dark-haired head closest to me suddenly rose.

I stilled as Peter opened blurry, bruised eyes and pushed himself upright with a groan. Kirk's arm fell off his bare waist, and Rebecca mumbled in her sleep, cuddling closer to Citra, who rested her head on Nancy's thigh. Dane, with his mohawk, snuggled into Corine, and she burrowed closer to a boy I didn't know.

I was literally in the middle of warm skin and brave hearts.

"Hey," Peter croaked.

I swallowed, coughed, and swallowed again. "I-I'm not imagining this?"

Gently extracting one of his legs from beneath a sleeping girl I hadn't spoken to, he eased his knees up and hugged them. "Your crying woke them. They came to see if you were okay."

I flinched.

I couldn't fully remember.

Didn't *want* to remember.

The crack inside me had been enough.

The release of all those hot, painful daggers behind my eyes and the churning, heart wrenching grief inside me.

I'd held back the tears for as long as I could.

But when I broke? Well…

I shrugged. "I'm sorry for the scene I caused."

Shaking his head, he gave me a soft smile and cupped my shoulder. "I'm not. It was a relief to have you let it out. To have you purge what happened."

I flinched as images erupted.

Henri.

His knife.

His cuts.

His tongue…

I recoiled from Peter's hand, cupping my breasts and shifting my legs to hide the very part of me Henri had taken without consent.

How could I forget even for a moment?

How had my mind pushed it away long enough for Peter to remind me?

The awful thing was, I didn't need reminding.

Last night was a part of me.

It'd changed me on a cellular level.

And I had no idea who I was now that it was over.

I shuddered as more images returned.

The breaking, the bleeding…

The shallow cuts on my body would heal, but my heart never would.

Devastated didn't come close to how I felt. Betrayed? Of course. Confused? Definitely.

But guilt curdled most of all.

He'd asked me not to fight him, and I'd fought.

He'd begged me to remember our promise, and I'd forgotten.

I couldn't forgive what he'd done, but I couldn't lay the blame entirely at his feet either.

Peter dropped his hand and stiffened. "You're thinking about him."

I looked up and met his soulful brown eyes. "W-We had a deal…and…I broke it."

"*We?*"

I slouched, aware I'd almost slipped. Henri's secrets. Henri's covert mission. I might hate what he did and vaguely remembered hating him with a thousand suns last night, but…if there was the slimmest chance he could pull himself back from this, then…I couldn't spill his truth.

This was bigger than me.

This was for them.

"Doesn't matter." I rubbed my face. "None of it matters. It's done."

"That's it, huh? You were in pieces last night. You almost turned catatonic in my arms as you cried. It took all of us hugging you to stop your shivering long enough to get you to sleep, and now you're just *forgiving* him? I mean, I've seen some sick shit in this place and dealt with a hundred broken people, but that? Wow."

"Of course I'm not forgiving him." I scowled. "It's just…complicated."

"Complicated?" He bared his teeth. "It's the simplest thing in the world, Ily. He hurt you. I drugged you against your will. Be mad at me. Be mad at him. Be mad at the whole goddamn world, but don't you *dare* shut down on me again. You shut down, and it's all over in here. I won't let you check out. I won't let you fade away. And I definitely won't let you take responsibility for what he did."

I glanced at the maimed jewels again. A question suddenly popped into my head. "When you brought Victor into the library—when Henri was about to take me the first time—why…why did you tattle on us? I always wondered if you were playing a sort of game or…" I narrowed my eyes on a pretty jewel missing an entire hand. "Or was it because you feared he'd cut me into pieces? That Henri would do to me what others have done to you?" My heart flopped out of my chest. "H-How much have you seen, Peter? How much death have you witnessed? *Aap kaise jeevit reh sakte ho? Unmein se Koi bhi kaise jeevit reh sakta hai?*" (How can you keep surviving? How can any of them?)

He shrugged. "That's a lot of questions, and I have no answers." His eyes told me everything he didn't. "We keep surviving because we don't have a choice, and you…you almost gave up on me last night."

"No." I shook my head. "I just…the drugs made me fight him. H-He told me not to." I reached for his hand. "I agree I lost myself for a moment, but you don't understand. There was so much riding on me keeping my wits. That day in the library, he made me promise not to fight. He—"

"That fucking asshole." Shooting to his feet, he didn't care he woke ten others or a ruckus of grumbles echoed as jewels slowly sat up. "He made you promise not to fight?" He bent and glowered. "And you agreed? Fuck, if that isn't one of the most twisted—"

"It's not. It would make sense if you knew why—"

"I don't need to know. I know him. I know others like him. I know he enjoys the hunt, the tease, the toying. He told you not to fight because he fed off your trust and obedience. He made you believe he'd never do to you what others have done to us. But wake the fuck up, Ily! He cut you, raped you—"

"I don't need you to remind me, Paavak."

"Peter," he snarled.

I stood too, still cupping my breasts, then giving up. It wasn't as if everyone hadn't already seen me or that a dozen other naked jewels scattered by my feet. No one ogled me. No one cared.

Lowering my voice, I whispered in Hindi, "*Main ab theek hoon. mujhe lagata hai, Davaaon ka Asar khatam ho gaya hai. aaj sab kuchh behatar hoga...aap dekhenge.*" (I'm okay now. The drugs are gone, I think. Everything will be better today…you'll see.)

Blackness stole over his face. "Everything will be better? How can you say that? Are you deluded?"

I reared back. "No, I'm—"

"Trying to see good in a shitty situation?"

"Yes, I—"

"Don't." Bending down, he snatched something from the floor. His linen pants brushed against my legs as he grabbed my hand and shoved my aventurine pendant into my palm. "I need you to stay strong. I'm aware I'm contradicting myself when it comes to you—I tell you to run. To stay. To trust. To give in. I have so much advice, and none of it can truly save you. Perhaps I should let you have your fantasies that he's different and won't hurt you. But after last night…how can you even want to believe that?" He hung his head. "I just…I just need to know you'll be okay. Tell me you see him now. Tell me you're prepared for how bad he'll get and that you're strong enough to bear it, and…I'll back off, alright?"

"Pete feels responsible for you," Kirk whispered from the floor. "He feels responsible for all of us."

I tensed.

My fingers curled automatically around my warm, carved pendant. "You're not responsible for me, Peter. You can't take our wellbeing on your shoulders as well as your own suffering."

"Don't waste your breath." Rebecca laughed sadly as she hauled herself upright and wrapped her comforter around her bareness. "We've told him that. We tell him every night. Doesn't stop him, though."

Glancing at all the jewels slowly climbing to their feet from our strange sleep spiral, Peter muttered, "We all agreed when Yasmin died that we'd look out for one another."

I flinched. "Did a Master kill her?"

"No." Peter sighed with a slouch. "She did that herself."

"She committed suicide?" My eyebrows rose.

"Might as well have." Citra sniffed sadly.

Peter shot her a look, then locked his stare on mine. "She didn't tell us how badly she was hurt after a Master beat her. She shut down and went quiet. No one noticed her fading away. She even served her Master again, all while her body kept dying. By the time she woke us the next night and said she didn't feel well, it was too late. She died of internal bleeding."

I placed my hand on his arm. "I'm so sorry."

"Don't be sorry. Just don't do what she did. Don't shut down—"

"I give you my word, I won't do that." I hated the panic glazing his eyes. The out-of-control helplessness. The tragic inability to make a difference. My voice shook with conviction. "I promise."

He nodded without looking at me.

I dropped my eyes, hating that I'd made another vow.

I didn't seem very good at keeping them.

Opening my fingers, I studied my pendant.

The weighted agony of grief swelled all over again.

Homesickness and horror. Panic and pain.

I wanted so, so badly to leave.

To run out of this claustrophobic, sadistic place and never look back.

But…a heavy sense of calm forced back the avalanche of terror.

I'd spent my entire life caring for Krish. I hadn't been his parent in the terms of physical things. Our mother and father did a fantastic job of keeping him fed, clothed, and content. But I was the parent of his soul. I was the only one lucky enough to connect with him on the level where he was most comfortable. Sometimes that was a silent level. Sometimes almost mystical. When others couldn't get through to him, I could, and…that was a gift, never an obligation.

I closed my eyes and sank into a split-second meditation.

I tumbled so deep, so true, I knew without a shadow of a doubt that I was meant to be here.

Not to endure.

But to *survive.*

To help all these forgotten slaves survive.

To help Peter survive.

Sucking in a deep breath, I did my best to gather up the remnants of the girl left over from last night. I refused to let my broken heart jump to conclusions. Henri had been drunk. I'd been drugged. We both did things we shouldn't.

Today is a new beginning.

Today is the day help will come…you'll see.

Fisting my pendant, I went to thread it around my neck.

Peter curled his fingers around my wrist. "You can't. No jewelry apart from our collar and cuffs." Flicking a look toward the bedroom, he forced a smile. "Seeing as you'll be the only one not storing drugs in your pillow, keep it there. Touch it. Sleep with it. Don't use it to remember a life you can never go back to but to stay alive in this one, no matter the cost."

Exhaling heavily, I studied him.

What changed for him to encourage me to stay breathing when last night, before the orgy-dinner, he'd said I'd be better off running into electrocution to avoid whatever a Diamond Kiss was?

No answers appeared in his guarded stare.

He was right that his advice was contradicting and confusing.

But for now, I just nodded. I refused to remember him blowing Victor in that animal carcass-filled room. I refused to accept that I'd have to watch him pleasure other Masters before I managed to get him free. If he needed me to promise that I'd stay fighting, then I'd keep fighting. For him. For all of them. "I'll put it under my pillow."

"*Achchha.*" (Good.) He never looked away. The moment stretched far too long before he ducked his head and pressed a fleeting kiss right on my mouth.

I froze.

Kirk sucked in a breath.

Rebecca went to say something, but two tall shadows appeared in the door frame. "What the fuck are you all doing in here?"

Slaves scattered.

Some bolted past the two guards. Others backed away into the corners of the room.

Peter gulped and slowly turned to face them. He kept his head bowed and body as meek as he could make it. "Nothing. Forgive us."

The taller, broader of the guards with a shiny bald head spat, "Get up to breakfast. You're late. All of you."

Peter shot a look at the clock where my delusion-dragon had sulked last night.

8:19 a.m.

"*Fuck.*" Peter went deathly still before he shot into action. Spinning to me, he snatched my pendant from my hand and threw it back on the baskets of gemstones. Raking his eyes over the crowded room, he hissed, "Run."

The guards stepped aside as jewels charged down the corridor and vanished.

"Come on." Grabbing my wrist, Peter dragged me into a gallop.

Past the bathroom.

Through our quarters.

Right through the citadel and into the glaringly bright, horribly new morning.

Chapter Six

Henri

MY TEETH TORE INTO A wonderfully warm baguette with lashings of ice-cold butter.

I'd never tasted anything so delicious.

I couldn't remember ever having such a voracious appetite.

I'd only slept a couple of hours before my stomach woke me for another meal, and I'd stepped into the most sublime morning, walking around in hyperawareness.

My deliberate cold shower felt like pristine snow against my skin.

My toothbrush like minty bubbles in my mouth.

Even my clothes felt better than usual, and they weren't even mine.

The grey t-shirt and jeans I'd chosen from the wardrobe were far more like my usual style back home before I had to pretend to be a rich son of a bitch who lived in tailored suits and rubbed shoulders with sadists.

But…I didn't have to pretend anymore.

I *was* a rich son of a bitch, and…for the first time in my sorry excuse of a life, I was brave enough to call myself a sadist.

Sadist.

I chuckled as I ripped off another hunk of bread.

Sadist…

What exactly did that word mean?

I'd never really bothered to look it up.

All I knew was it meant someone who got off on inflicting pain or humiliation on others. Well…if that was the true definition, I'd been doing that my entire life. To *myself.* But at least the masochistic part of me was dead and buried and this morning was just. So. Fucking. *Glorious.*

Reaching for the sweating butter, I added another curl just as thirty jewels, in boxers, negligees, and nakedness, tumbled out of Victor's castle and tripped into the garden. In a flurry of feet, they darted to the front of the deck and kneeled, one by one, into a tidy horizontal line with bowed heads and praying hands.

Victor strolled out from the banquet room that spilled with its many open doors onto the deck, his right hand holding a plate topped high with sugary treats. Behind him, the huge dining room with carved architraves and exquisite works of erotic art, held a buffet fit for a court of a hundred kings, offering delicacies from roasted pheasant to saffron-infused scrambled eggs.

His team of waitstaff inconspicuously kept everything flowing, even with quite a few men selecting their favourite dishes. The barista who hand-delivered my latte—the perfect accompaniment to my fresh-out-of-the-oven baguette—must've roasted the beans in fucking heaven because I'd never tasted such a fine brew.

Everything tastes better when you're free.

I smirked.

Fuck yes, it did.

And the best part?

I wouldn't be seeing any of it later.

My pathetic sickness was over.

Resting his plate of mini pastries on my table, Victor slipped his hands into his silver slacks and strolled to the edge of the deck. Rocking on his heels, he surveyed his jewels as if they truly were sheep who'd been drawn into a tight flock.

Halfway down the line, my gaze snagged on Ily.

My heart quickened.

Desire pricked my veins.

Her skin glowed in the golden sunshine, highlighting a few ugly band-aids hiding the cuts I'd given her. She kept her chin low and eyes hooded. Her blue-black hair shimmered with sapphires but looked unkempt.

Shifting forward in my chair, I narrowed my eyes.

In fact, blood still smudged her in places. A perfect crimson fingerprint on her left breast where I'd squeezed as I'd driven my tongue inside her.

She hasn't showered.

If someone shone a blacklight on her, they'd see streaks of my cum between her legs.

I'm still inside her.

My cock rose.

I pressed it down.

Last night had been the best orgasm of my life; I wanted another.

Now.

I wanted to fuck her in the light of day. In front of others, I didn't care. I wanted to test my power and hammer a nail into the coffin of the heartsick idiot I used to be.

"Is there something you wish to tell me, my sweetlings?" Victor smiled kindly, interrupting my fantasy of snapping my fingers and summoning Ily to blow me under the table.

The tiniest part of me still feared that regret would swarm the moment I saw Ily again.

Could I truly, fundamentally change in a single night?

But…seeing her now?

That answer was yes.

Yes, I was changed.

Yes, I was free.

But most of all…I was still *me.*

Still me and open to all feelings—no longer wanting to ignore any of them. That heady rush of possession and aggressive wave of jealousy only made my need for her erupt into a fever I never wanted to cure.

You're never going back…are you?

The inner voice sounded like a wing-torn angel who'd judged and tormented me my entire life.

I chuckled under my breath and shook my head.

No, I was never going back.

Not for anyone or anything.

Not for a brother I didn't know or a girl I'd only just met.

I liked my little nightmare.

I *still* liked my little nightmare.

But why would I ever want to free her when the outside world didn't understand me, my blood kin wanted to kill me, and the girl I part owned could run away from me?

Fuck that.

I'm home.

She's home.

And we're never leaving.

Victor huffed when no one responded to his heavily veiled, dangerously soft question. His loafers skimmed the deck as he paced up and down, up and down. Clucking his tongue, he said, "Let's start off easy, shall we?"

A few heads came up before ducking quickly.

"Can someone please explain why my security footage showed all my precious jewels were missing from their beds this morning?"

Shoulders hunched; hands balled.

"Or perhaps you can explain why you all ended up in a skin

sandwich on the vault room's floor?"

Ily flinched and raised her head. With bravery glittering in her strange golden stare, she opened her mouth to—

"I had a nightmare," Peter blurted. "I, eh…woke them by accident, and they followed me into the gem room." He hung his head. "They were only trying to console me, Sir V. I'm sorry—"

"Ah, Peter." Victor ran a hand over his mouth. "Will you ever stop trying to take the blame?"

Peter hunched lower.

Ily inched closer, pressing her naked thigh to his linen-covered one.

A flare of annoyance cut through me. I put down my baguette before I throttled it.

A stagnant pause before Victor quit his pacing and faced his row of bruised and obedient jewels.

For the first time, I noticed some of them were missing a few pieces.

A finger, an ear…

My heart stung for a moment, then went quiet.

Butchering people wasn't on my list of proclivities, but I had no morality left to judge those who did.

"You know lying never works because I see all things." He tossed a smirk over his shoulder, looking directly at me.

My instincts prickled.

What the fuck was that?

Looking back at his slaves, Victor added, "The skin sandwich I can tolerate. Everyone needs some comfort once in a while, and I'm not such a harsh Master to deny you a platonic hug every now and again. However…" His voice grew icicles. "I saw a kiss that shouldn't have happened, and my guests were inconvenienced by all of you being late." He tapped his Rolex. "Twenty-three minutes late to be exact." He sighed dramatically. "Whatever shall I do with you?"

Marching to my side, Victor placed a hand on my shoulder. "Henri, you decide. After all, the kiss involved the jewel you paid so handsomely for."

"Excuse me?" My voice darkened. "Ily *kissed* someone?"

Her chin tipped up, defiant or just despairing…I couldn't tell.

Our eyes met for the first time since I'd sunk inside her last night.

I waited all over again for some shred of the idiotic tosser I'd been. For crushes and obsessions to pounce.

But my head remained clear.

She belonged to me. Her every breath, touch, kiss, and fuck was *mine.*

So who the hell dared to steal one?

Standing slowly, I narrowed my eyes on Peter.

"*You.*" I stalked toward the edge of the deck. "I told you last night what would happen if you ever touched her."

Other guests settled deeper into their chairs, sipping coffees and biting into berry muffins. Silence fell in the gardens. Even the birdsong and happy crickets quietened.

Peter kept his eyes on the grass.

The same grass where I'd finally sunk into the epiphany that I was free.

Flexing my hands, punishments collided in my head.

A whipping might be apt.

Castration was probably going too far.

Slipping my hand into my pocket, I fingered the black device that brought such swift discipline. Pulling it out, I let all the jewels see what rested in my palm. As expected, a few whimpers rang out, followed by an entire line-up stiffening into stone.

Ily dared to press closer to Peter, fucking me right off.

Spinning on the spot, I raised the electrocution remote. "Is this what you had in mind for discipline, Vic?"

Victor chuckled and sat in the very same chair I'd vacated.

Very delicately, he pushed aside my half-eaten breakfast and folded his hands in his lap. The way he moved reminded me of a cat about to kill something. The way he watched me said I was his prey.

Which didn't make a shred of fucking sense.

I frowned as Victor watched two black-suited guards roll out a narrow table with a large flatscreen on it. Once it was in prime position on the deck, he nodded his thanks as a retreating guard placed a remote control beside my abandoned coffee cup.

Picking it up, Victor stroked it like it was a pet anaconda. "I'll answer your little question in a moment, *Ward*, but first…indulge me in some of mine."

I didn't like the way he stressed my last name.

I didn't like that he smiled at me the same way he smiled at his godforsaken jewels.

The old me would've broken into icy sweat by now.

The new and improved me just stood there.

Bold and careless.

Crossing my arms, I tipped my chin. "Got something on your mind,

Victor?"

"I do actually. Allow me to show you." Angling the remote at the TV, he clicked it on and revealed a scene that felt like foggy déjà vu.

Drifting a little closer to the screen so the sun glare didn't obscure details, I frowned at the still image of my arms wrapped tight around Ily, my mouth pressed to the corner of her eye, her naked body draped over my lap on the busy acorn-motif carpet of the library.

That felt like decades ago.

My heart skipped then settled. "You're interrogating me on transgressions I've already explained?"

Victor pursed his lips. "Just indulge me for a few minutes, *mon ami.* I'm aware you said your fetishes include tears and whispers."

A few guests snickered around the deck.

The jewels behind me stayed eerily silent.

"Amongst my top five, yes. But you already asked what I was doing when you came to find us. And I told you."

Funny, the thought of whispering to Ily now leaned toward telling her exactly what I wanted, rather than doing my useless best to save her. I no longer wanted to whisper for her to play along but to truly confess that her blood made me throb and her tears made me ravenous to break her.

"Tell me again if you don't mind." Victor tapped my empty coffee cup with the remote. He grinned, but it didn't reach his eyes. "Go on. Don't be shy. After all, there's no secrets between us."

There he went with the cryptic crap again.

Yesterday, I would probably have had a panic attack and overcompensated with some heavy-handed confession of wanting Ily in pieces.

Today, I merely shrugged and released a part of my untameable darkness. "Fine. I drank her sadness."

"Why?"

"Why? I don't know. Why do we like the things we like? I've always been drawn to tears. Probably another throw-back to my fucked-up childhood."

"Oh? How interesting." Victor took a bite of his mini blueberry danish. "Please…do continue."

Ignoring the guests and their judging eyes, I said, "My mother would never touch me…unless she was crying. The nights when she sobbed for no apparent reason were the nights she actually looked to me for comfort. She never went as far as to hug me, but she did tolerate *me* to hug *her*. I guess you could say my adolescent mind figured I needed tears to feel affection, and the adult part of me morphed that into something sexual."

"An understandable conclusion." Victor nodded. "I always enjoy hearing guests psychoanalyse themselves." Clicking the remote, he skipped to a short silent video of Ily trapped in my hold, wedged against the bookcases, our eyes locked as I whispered something with far, far too much emotion.

Shit, had I truly entrapped her that tightly? Whispered that fiercely? Passion dripped from my every word and motion. The way I looked at her blazed with possession even then. And the way she looked at me…

I paused and assessed the quick knot in my gut.

She looked at me as if terrified but also willing to trust. The way her mouth twisted and eyes widened. The way her bare skin glowed as I cupped her throat and hissed into her ear.

I hadn't been able to see her gaze then.

But I saw it now.

Saw the flash of heat. The heaviness of her lashes as I nuzzled against her neck and said whatever stupid thing I said.

"And this?" Victor paused the video.

At least it had no sound.

No way to know all the broken promises I'd made or the jumped to conclusions she believed.

"Merely a silly little game." I didn't shake or sweat. I had nothing to hide now. Sure, I was a fraud yesterday, but this morning, I was one hundred percent one of them—an unredeemable, irreprehensible bastard—and I no longer suffered shame because of it.

"I told her that I wanted to—"

"Let Ily tell it." Victor held up a hand, pointing the remote at my jewel frozen on the grass. "Sweetling…?"

Ily swallowed hard and refused to look at me. Slowly, she raised her chin. "H-He said he wanted to make me his in every possible way. To tear me apart. T-To bleed me and drink down every drop."

My eyebrows rose.

Her memory was impressive.

The fact I'd tasted her blood made me shiver.

Her willingness to lie for me had almost brought me to my knees in the library. But here, in the bright light of a wonderful new day, I just pitied her.

All those lies I said under the guise of truth. All that honesty I spoke under the cloak of fibs. If I had my way, I wanted every despicable thing

I'd confessed to come true. The tart pinch of her despair already coated my tongue, making me goddamn starving.

"Thank you, my pet. That was almost verbatim." Victor nodded with a sharp edge. "Almost as if you were reading from a rehearsed script."

Ily's gaze snapped to Victor's.

Mine narrowed.

Was that a lucky guess, or was he fishing?

Sighing happily, as if he enjoyed toying with us, he pressed the remote again.

The next scene made me flush with embarrassment.

A few guests chuckled. One even commiserated. "Don't worry, Ward. I threw up the first day I gave in, too."

"Pussy," another whispered.

Victor merely waited for me to explain.

I scowled at the image of me on my hands and knees, dripping wet with the shower raining and my fingers clutching at the tiles. My back arched to hurl. My face tortured with nauseous misery. I didn't need the video to show that my cock still glistened from being inside Ily the first time.

Tied to the maypole.

Taken so damn hard because the moment I sank inside her, I couldn't stop.

Ily sucked in a breath on the lawn.

My skin itched.

I didn't want her seeing that.

But then again, she'd already seen me at my weakest. Acted along with me at my dumbest. She'd not only obeyed me, but I had a sneaking suspicion she felt sorry for me.

My fingers dug into my biceps as I crossed my arms tighter. I went to lie. To blame something I ate or jet lag or exhaustion, but…I didn't *want* to lie anymore. Not because five guards inconspicuously joined us on the deck, fanning out with their hands hovering over concealed weapons but because I'd changed last night and didn't want to undo that change.

I liked my freedom far too fucking much to turn my back on it.

"So, Henri?" Victor canted his head. "Do you have an explanation for this one?" He scowled. "Were you throwing up from fucking your jewel or for giving me two million euros for the privilege?"

A man snickered. "Nothing worse than forking over cash you don't have, huh?"

"Knew he was an idiot." Someone chuckled.

"Neither." I smiled. Genuinely. Full of goddamn relief that that little malady was a thing of the past.

"Pray tell," Victor murmured.

"My guts have always been sensitive. I told you that last night. I guess you could say my body took it upon itself to keep me from straying."

"Straying?"

"Into the dark."

"So this is you purging the darkness of rape?"

I shot a look at Ily, needing her to see my face when I confessed, "It wasn't rape. She consented."

Another ripple of laughter was followed by a hissed gasp from Ily.

Peter didn't look up, but his entire body tensed.

Glancing back at Victor, I flung open my rotten pages and became an open fucking book. "When I whispered to her…I might have said some things that made her play along with me."

"Such as?" Victor narrowed his eyes.

I dabbled with stepping over the line of who Ily thought I was, but Victor didn't need to know. That part of the pantomime was over. Ily would've figured out I wasn't a cop after what I did last night.

I'd never been one. Would never become one.

That knowledge would hurt her almost as much as my switchblade.

That reminds me…I left it in Victor's dead zoo.

I wanted it back as a keepsake for the night I awakened.

"I told her if she behaved, I wouldn't let anyone else have her. I asked her to trust me. That everything I did to her was for the greater good."

Peter let out a tortured sort of noise.

Ily remained deathly silent.

Greater good.

In the library, those two words had churned my stomach something terrible. Here, not even a ripple.

"Interesting. So *that's* why she went from a barbed-tongue witch to an obedient little toy so quickly?" He watched me as if he knew more than what he let on.

Keeping my guard up, I nodded. "Clever, huh?"

He studied me closely. "Some might say you collared her mind…which seems far more effective than just collaring her body."

I bowed my chin. "I'll take that as a compliment."

"You do that." He didn't smile, though, merely clicked his damn remote again. "I suppose you'll have an equally understandable explanation for this too?"

The screen erased my retching episode and replaced it with a photo of me leaning against the bathroom door, knees up, elbows wedged on them, hands buried in my hair.

I looked like a miserable fool.

I'd fallen asleep.

Ily had eaten all my room service.

I'd dry-humped her into an orgasm before thinking I was ever skilled or lucky enough to turn off the signal scrambler.

That'd been the end of our alliance.

I waited for a streak of remorse.

But only a faint tinge of nostalgia came.

I'd liked her pliant beneath me.

I regretted not fucking her when I had the chance.

"So?" Victor rolled his hand. "Go ahead and explain."

I shrugged, not appreciating him exposing what a heartsick imbecile I'd been. "I wanted things I still wasn't prepared to accept. I was exhausted by the struggle. I needed space, and she was in my bed. The bathroom offered the only privacy."

"I see."

I didn't like that response.

Placing the remote ever so carefully on the table, Victor steepled his fingers. "There are only three more teeny tiny things to show you. So far, you've been honest. I suggest you keep being honest because I'm telling you now, I'll sniff out any lies."

"Lies?" I bared my teeth. "I've told you the truth—"

"And I just told you I'm aware of that. That's what pains me so." He glanced at the guards. They all drifted forward, closing ranks and trapping me in a wide circle.

"What the fuck are you doing, Victor?" I didn't move.

Where could I go?

But I did lower my arms and ball my hands. "You planning on shooting me because it took me a day to accept who I am?"

"I'm deliberating shooting you because I can't get a read on you. I know you're telling me the truth about what you want. I saw for my own eyes how much you enjoyed playing Ruby Tears. You're not faking your needs, Ward. Nor are you gagging on the actual act. But you *are* keeping things from me. Things you think you've hidden because you think you're clever and can win at this game. A game that I've been playing *since you were fucking born.*"

The savagery of his last sentence stunned even him.

He flashed me a regal smile, then ran a hand through his greying hair. "Forgive me. My temper sometimes gets the better of me."

I stilled.

Why would his temper be up?

What the fuck happened between our enjoyable dawn dinner and now?

Licking his lips, he continued in a calmer, colder tone. "I know you've seen the cameras everywhere. I don't try to hide their existence. I also don't hide that everything that goes on in my home is recorded—not for bribery or control over my guests but to protect my precious gems." Waving at the line-up of jewels on the grass, his voice lowered with patriarchal concern. "Before I put cameras everywhere, a few of my guests were…*overzealous* with their affections. My jewels suffered needlessly, and I lost a few thanks to reckless unrestraint. Now, everyone knows they're on camera, and if I see anyone maiming, butchering, or killing a jewel, they answer to me. Sometimes in the form of a fine and sometimes in the form of permanent removal from my home."

Permanent?

Did that mean death?

"There's only one place I allow my guests privacy, and that's on the shitter. The tiniest blackspot in my omniscience." He smiled graciously. "After all, no one needs to see that."

"How generous of you," I snapped, my own temper finally waking up. "Get to the goddamn point."

"My point, *mon ami*, is this..." Pressing a single finger on the play button, the TV screen exploded with another video of Ily and me. Almost as if he'd plucked the scene from my previous thoughts, I stared at my half-naked body wedged over hers in my bed. Her legs wide enough for me to press in that perfect spot, her white negligée bunched around her waist, and eyes wide as I kept her wrists pinned above her head.

Raising the volume on the TV, Victor shot me a scowl.

And there, barely audible thanks to our careful whispering, was my voice, hoarse with need and fraying with self-control. "We both…have to use you again. Possibly in…room…play up for…cameras. I won't treat you kindly…when…show. So…if you…then use me. Right here.... No regrets..."

My mind rushed with things to say.

But Victor merely held up his hand and skipped to another video. "Hold that thought, Henri. I'm sure you'll have plenty to tell me after the next two. How about you watch first and then see if you can dig your way out of this fucking hole you've dug yourself into, hmm?"

With a finger stab on the button, he started the next one.

Ily argued with me by the door as I'd prepared to slink into the night to try to turn the scrambler off. She'd offered to come. Made reasonable points about why she should. And I'd hesitated because the thought of putting her in even more danger than I already had crippled me.

I scoffed at my past self.

I might hate this inquisition, but I hated last night's version of me even more.

Watching that version on TV, seeing how wound up I was, how twitchy—almost like a crack addict around a fresh line of cocaine—was hard to stomach.

I was beyond fucking grateful I was no longer that weak or helpless.

Crackling sound rasped from the flatscreen, fanning out amongst the guests, jewels, and morning birdsong, patchy and bad quality, only snagging a few of our whispers.

My mouth moved; broken words spilled out. "I won't need…won't be seen."

Ily asked something inaudible.

My lips curled back. "Yes…guards…lazy….Anyone thinks…I was roaming…the dark…ride will be here…be over."

The sound quality filled with static as Ily argued, and I hissed back.

Finally, the most condemning part came in Ily's soft, sweet voice. "I'd rather you…hurt me….This is bigger…. It's…them—all those...slaves—and…I can't…down. *You* can't let them down."

That last line was spoken far too clearly, far too passionately.

The jewels all shifted behind me, not daring to speak, but their fidgety body language blasted their confusion.

Crossing my arms, I merely arched an eyebrow and waited.

One more video.

What could possibly be any worse?

Victor pressed pause and narrowed his eyes. "I'll let you in on a little secret, *Ward*." He stressed my name again, his temper clinging sharply to every letter. "I was going to kill you last night. That paperwork I was doing so late? That was this. I was up late because of *you*." He pointed the remote toward me. "It took all my fucking willpower not to shoot you in that corridor. But…I decided to see how deep you'd entrench yourself, and…somewhere along the way, you made me doubt. *Again.* The moment I think I know who you are, you become someone else, and I'm getting really fucking sick of you playing me for a fool."

I shrugged, keeping my cool in the face of his blazing fury. "You're not a fool."

Ignoring me, he snarled, "You entered my home and went behind my back in every possible way. You denied yourself, all while thinking you're *better* than us. You had the fucking audacity to come into my fucking sanctuary and try to *steal what is fucking mine!*" Scratching his freshly shaven cheek, he sucked in a calming breath. "Sorry, I'm a little frustrated with your lack of respect. Shall we watch the final video?"

I just nodded as the guards crowded me a little tighter.

Victor pressed play.

And I laughed as our little video journey went full circle and returned to the library.

I knew my fate before a single word was spoken.

I had Ily shoved against the bookcases, glowering at her as if I wanted to eat her alive.

Audio crackled.

Static and scuffling.

Ily gasped as my fingers dug into her hips, and my life ended in her perfectly clear, horribly condemning whisper, "—undercover." *Unintelligible whispering.* "…mixed signals." *Unrecognisable murmurings.* "…meant to come? …sent…to…jewels? Y-You're a cop?"

Chairs slammed back against the deck as men all shot to their feet. Some started toward me, fury on monstrous faces.

The guards tightened ranks.

Guns were pulled out of holsters.

The slaves behind me broke out in urgent whispers.

Ily's horrified gasp clutched at the back of my neck, but I only had eyes for Victor.

I never looked away from him as he rewound and replayed the sound bite.

"—undercover." *Unintelligible whispering.* "…mixed signals." *Unrecognisable murmurings.* "…meant to come? …sent…to…jewels? Y-You're a cop?"

Only once Ily's shocked but hopeful voice faded into the morning sunlight did he stop the video and lean back.

He didn't speak.

Didn't have to.

Two guards marched toward me and pressed two guns against my temples.

I went cold inside.

Mercifully, exquisitely cold.

How fucking tragic that today was the first day of my life that I learned to live. That food finally tasted sweet, and my senses finally knew joy.

So short-lived.

Twenty-nine years of struggle and for what?

Such a goddamn waste.

I wished I'd embraced my darkness a decade ago.

At least I would've *lived.*

I waited for it to end.

For the pop of a trigger and then nothing.

But…time dragged on, screeching, *stretching.*

My heart picked up the longer they didn't kill me.

I bristled and wished they'd get it fucking over with.

Least I could rest then.

Rest just like I'd predicted.

Alone. Always alone.

Guests shouted at Victor to give the order.

Ily said something that was lost in the mutterings of other jewels.

My world drew to a pinprick of just Victor.

Waiting…

Waiting…

"Any last words, Henri Ward?" Propping his elbow on the table, he ran his finger over his bottom lip. "Any words for your superior officer? Want to tell me what police force you work for? How long you've been undercover? If there's any more of you disgusting little *rats* trying to gnaw their way into my paradise?"

The guard on my left shifted, pressing the muzzle of his gun harder into my skull.

Victor sighed heavily as if it genuinely pained him to do this. "You know, *Henri*…you're the first to fool me. I have a knack, you see. A gift at seeing predators where others only see men. And you…you *are* a predator. I see it even now. Maybe that's why you were chosen for this assignment. Maybe your captain saw that in you and decided to throw you into our den…or perhaps you're the best fucking actor I've ever seen, and I should present you with an award. Either way, the fact remains…you lied—"

"I didn't lie." I growled. "Not to you anyway." I shrugged. "At least…not about everything."

"Kill the snitch, Vic. Blow his fucking brains out." A guest I hadn't spoken to sidled up to Victor. "I'll do it. Always wanted to know what it felt like to shoot someone point blank."

Victor held up his hand, stilling the guards and their shaking arms from the weight of outstretched guns. "Patience, everyone. He's dead. But…I do have a certain fondness for him, and so…I'll let you speak, *mon ami.* One last time."

One last time.

Those words echoed in my empty mind.

One last time to breathe.

To exist.

What I'd fucking give to have one last sip of Ily's blood and one last taste of being inside her.

The icy stillness inside me solidified into a glacier. Everything began to sparkle as frost and icicles formed.

What would I give?

Honestly? Truly?

I'd give fucking *everything.*

Just like I'd been willing to give everything to a brother I didn't know and a girl I'd only just met. I'd spent my entire life trying to live according to others, but here and now…I had to make the choice to live for *me.*

And the only way to do that…

I chuckled as realisation struck me like a fist.

Fuck.

I had to let Ward die.

Had to turn my back on everyone and everything.

Transform into who I'd always been.

Without any life raft to go back.

Stepping out of the guards' imprisonment, I didn't stop marching until I grabbed a chair opposite Victor and sat down. The guards trailed me, unsure what to do.

"You gonna let him get away with this, Vic? Shoot the cunt," a guest shouted.

"Don't!" Ily screamed.

"Do it." Another guest.

But Victor didn't say a word or order my execution, so I smiled and not only became an open book, I wrenched out every sin and secret and prepared to dump them on the plate in front of him.

"I'm not a cop."

He nodded as if he expected me to say something like that. "Forgive me if I don't believe you."

"The things you heard. The whispers we shared…it was a method of control."

"Again, I don't believe you."

"Okay then…I asked her to play along with me. I told her not to fight back, and I'd get her out of here. I told her I'd been sent to free your slaves by doing whatever was necessary."

"*That* I believe."

"I told her for me to achieve such things, I had to wait for backup to arrive and that meant having to pretend. I confessed that even while I 'pretended' to be abusive…I would enjoy it."

His eyebrows quirked. "And she went along with it?"

"She did." I resisted the urge to turn around and find her. "She gave me her consent. For all of it. Hence…it was never rape."

"Interesting." He toyed with a mini pastry. "If that's true and you don't give a damn about her…then this won't bother you." Snapping his fingers, he barked, "Roland. Grab Ily and bring her here."

"Be my fucking pleasure." Roland shoved the rest of whatever he was eating in his mouth, then wiped crumb-covered hands on his shorts. Leaving the throng of other cop-detesting guests—all of them lined up and salivating at the thought of my murder—he shot me a wicked grin, then shot down the steps to the grass.

His large belly jiggled beneath his maroon polo, and his khaki shorts strained over his ample backside as he snatched Ily around the elbow and hauled her to her feet.

Possession rose ugly inside me.

I wanted to rip his motherfucking hands off for touching what was mine.

But I stayed silent and stoic as he dragged her into motion.

Peter restrained himself from reacting, but I saw the look between them: the quick bolt of terror and powerlessness, support and commiseration.

Ily tripped as Roland cuffed her around the ear. "Walk properly, or I'll make you crawl."

Bracing herself, she figured out her feet and lurched up the deck in his grasp. Her bare, stunning skin looked sacrilegious beside him. The cuts I'd made—all hidden beneath plasters and bloody fingerprints marking her as mine—roared our history, all while another man dragged her around like she was his.

Shooting me a scowl full of hate, Roland stalked right to our table, kicked aside the two unoccupied chairs, and tossed Ily toward us.

Her eyes met mine, wide and worried as Roland grabbed her nape and shoved her face first, right between Victor and me. Her golden cuffs and collar clanked against the table, her wrists knocking crockery and scattering the condiment caddy to the floor.

Every instinct roared to slit Roland's throat with the butter knife, but…whatever new game this was, I had to win.

And I have to keep my wits.

Settling into my chair, I cocked an eyebrow. "Trying to prove that your guests jump at your every command and your jewels have no control, *Master Jeweler*?"

I stressed his title like he'd stressed my name.

He didn't seem to care; merely laughed under his breath. "Oh no, my lying friend. Merely trying to see how far you'll go to prove you're not what you truly are."

"You think by tossing Ily on my plate, I'll what? Confess I'm a cop?"

"I think watching Roland fuck her in front of you will force you to admit the truth. Especially if I promise to stop him if you merely admit that you're a snitch and a rat and a motherfucking dead man."

"Ah." I nodded. "Gotcha."

"So…?" Victor raised an eyebrow. "One last chance, Henri. Will you or will you not admit you're an officer of the law? Are you from an English force? French? Interpol? Who?"

"I told you." I refused to look at Ily, panting with pure fear on the table. "I'm not a cop."

"Roland." Victor flicked his snuff-watching, necrophiliac friend a smile. "Fuck her."

"About damn time." Roland ran sausage fingers down her spine and shoved his hand between her legs.

"Get off me, you sick *bastard*!"

She screamed.

She thrashed.

Her sudden ferocity knocked Roland off balance, sending him reeling. Swooping upright, she looked as if she'd run, but then with the softest snick of a remote, she gasped, went rigid, then flopped back over the table, twitching and moaning in agony.

Victor held his electricity remote directly against her collar, his blue eyes dead of emotion. "Do I have to do everything for you, Olivan?" He rolled his eyes at Roland.

Roland fumbled with his zipper. "No, *bijoutier*."

"I'm surrounded by idiots." Removing his thumb from zapping Ily, Victor waited a few seconds for her to stop convulsing and then nodded. "Get your cock out and fuck her then. Let's see how many thrusts it takes Henri to admit he's—"

"I'm not a damn cop." Rage accented every word. "And if he sticks his dick in her, I'm going to be *extremely* pissed off."

"Why? Because you promised to save her before any other man had a taste?"

"No. Because she's *mine*. We had a deal."

"Deals have a habit of expiring if one party is a conniving snake." Victor looked idly at Roland as he shoved his shorts down and revealed a stubby, fat cock.

Ily gathered her strength and tried to kick backward, aiming for his knee as he wedged a hand on her nape. "Don't touch me, you diseased—"

"Shut up." Roland pressed his naked thighs against her ass. "Or I'll rip out your ungrateful tongue."

He bent his legs.

He fisted himself to—

"I told you." I launched out of my chair and round-housed him right in the face. "I'm not. A. Fucking. Cop!"

One punch.

That was all it took.

He must've had a glass chin because one second, he was standing; the next, he was out cold on the deck.

I flexed my fists.

Hitting him felt far too good.

It took every restraint not to start kicking him and never stop.

I needed a release for the churning, *burning* energy inside me.

Ily soared upright. Her chest rose and fell, her skin flushed. The way she looked at me pinched with betrayal, yet…beneath that betrayal lurked hope.

Hope.

I knew I shouldn't, but I *liked* the way she looked at me. I liked that she still believed I was better than what I was…even now.

Breathing hard, I sat back down and raked both hands through my hair. Focusing on Victor, I said, "Look, I apologise for hitting him but…just *listen* to me. I'm telling you the goddamn truth. Ily jumped to conclusions. I never said I was a cop. It was her little fantasy, not mine.

And I went along with it because it made my task far easier."

Victor raised a hand and pointed at another guest. "Larry. Fuck her."

"I'll do it." A dark-skinned guy grinned. "I can make her scream far louder than Larry can."

"Fine." Victor shrugged. "Someone do it. I'm getting sick of this asshole lying to me."

Ily stepped back, only for a guard to train a gun on her.

Victor pulled out his own gun from the back of his trousers, waggling it at my heart. "If you even think of hitting Ian as he takes what I've so kindly given him, I'll shoot you and be done with it. Sure, I want to hear you admit your lies, but you're vastly over-estimating my patience to waste any more time on your pathetic little—"

"I admitted I was sent. My task was to find out where your estate was and rescue your slaves."

Lowering the weapon, Victor watched Ian cross the deck and take up his position behind Ily. I couldn't watch as he fumbled with his belt and zipper.

"You're a slippery son of a bitch, I'll give you that." Victor scowled. "How can you be tasked to come here and not be law enforcement?"

"I had a different kind of overlord, but…I'm no longer loyal to him." I spread my hands. "You have my word, Vic, whatever I am…I am *not* a cop."

"Who sent you?"

Hesitation filled me. Just a little bit. But enough. "Doesn't matter. All that matters is I let Ily think I was a cop, but I'm not and—"

"It's true." Ily flinched, then sucked in a breath. Ignoring the Master behind her as he finally withdrew his cock and pumped himself a few times, she scrambled for fresh lines, believing this was yet another act, another stage. "It's my fault." She pressed her hands on the table. "It was me who—"

"Quiet." Ian shoved a fist against her shoulder blades, shoving her cheek first on the table again. Her collar clanged like a dinner bell.

Her eyes locked on mine.

Bleeding with trust.

Still.

I drew back.

Still?

Even after what I did to her last night?

She still thought I was…good?

What a silly, *stupid—*

"Do it, Ian," Victor drawled. "He's being stubborn. Rape his little crush and—"

"There's no way for me to convince you that I'm not law enforcement." I curled my hands, ready to punch another bastard in the nose. "I have no badge number to give you or a secret phone number to call. You know yourself that I haven't been able to ring for help because your technology keeps this place so well hidden. You're far too smart to think I'm a threat to you."

I narrowed my eyes on Ian, who pressed his cock against Ily's bare ass.

And fuck, it was hard.

So fucking hard to stay seated and not wrench his dick off with my bare hands.

She closed her eyes.

Her breath turned shallow.

"You know how I feel about compliments." Victor smiled tightly. "Get on with it."

Ian shifted, widening his stance.

The guards lined up on either side of me, cold guns wedged against my temples again.

At least if they shot me, Victor would be covered in brains and bone.

But so would Ily.

And I'd already scarred her for fucking life.

And if you want to keep scarring her, then ***do*** *something.*

I had no more loyalty.

No more heroic need to be good.

There's no need to hesitate.

Tell him…

"Out of curiosity's sake…" I did my best not to snarl as Ian angled himself down. "What would I have to do to stop all of this?" I fiddled with a discarded napkin, unable to keep my fingers still.

Victor huffed. "Nothing. You betrayed me. You came into my home under false pretences and thought you could take me down." His blue eyes darkened. "Is your name even Henri Ward?"

And there it was.

The question I didn't even know I'd been waiting for.

The question that would either save me or ruin me.

Leaning back, ever so fucking grateful my heartrate slowed and my hands stopped shaking, I shook my head. "Nope."

"No?" Victor cocked his head. "What do you mean, no?"

"I mean, Ward is not my last name."

"Yet another falsehood it would seem." Victor sighed as if he truly hated everyone. "Tell me, if it's not too much of a fucking *inconvenience,* Henri, what is your real name, and why should I care?"

I flexed my shoulders.

I cricked my neck.

Ian went to thrust.

"Order him to stop, and I'll tell you everything." I raised an eyebrow. "And I promise, you'll want to hear what I have to say."

Chewing on the inside of his cheek, Victor pondered for a moment before waving his gun at Ian. "Wait."

"But I'm—"

"I said *wait.*" He cocked his chin.

Ian muttered a few choice curses as he backed up and stuffed his erection into his jeans.

Ily didn't move.

Didn't even open her eyes.

I was grateful.

Grateful she wasn't going to be a distraction because I really couldn't afford to be distracted as I said goodbye to every future I'd envisioned and embraced a new one.

"My last name is one you've heard of." I smiled as cold as him. "Apparently, you've known of my brother for quite some time."

Intrigue flared in his eyes. Victor leaned forward a little. "Your brother?"

"I'm not a cop."

"Even if that's true, it won't save you."

"You're right that I was sent here by someone. I've admitted that a few times now. I was ordered to report your location, count your slaves, and summon mercenaries to slaughter you."

Victor's gaze flickered to the guards.

The guests all took a big step back, waiting for the bang.

Ily stiffened on the table.

I shrugged. "I'm not afraid to admit my intentions toward you weren't honourable, and for that, I'm sorry."

Ignoring my apology, Victor's face etched with ruthlessness. "You're really not helping your case."

"I'm not, am I?" I smiled thinly. "I did my best to do what I was tasked with. I tried to ignore the allure of this place and pretend I wasn't seduced by the very real, very uncomfortable realisation that I'm more like you than I wanted to admit. More like you than him, anyway."

"Him?"

"My brother."

"Ah yes…the suspense is killing me."

"I came to end you, Victor Grand, but…I've changed my mind."

"Oh, you have, have you?" His fingers traced the trigger of his gun. "And don't think I didn't notice the use of my surname. Only a very few people know it. So…who told you?"

"My brother."

"Yes, this fucking brother. Who the hell is he?"

"He shares the same curse I do, but…he decided to keep fighting it like a lifelong disease. Me? I've decided to stop chasing a cure. I'm done. You helped free me last night. You and Ily…and now that I'm fully infected, I'm aware there's no other place for me."

"You're definitely infected with something," he muttered. "Insanity would be my first guess."

"Aren't we all a little mad?" I laughed. "But at least we accept it, unlike some."

"Some being…?"

"My brother."

"Fuck you and your dramatic delays, Ward. *Get to the goddamn point!*"

"I like it here, Vic." I smirked. "I like who I am here."

"How nice." He smiled with unveiled sarcasm. "I'll be sure to put that in the review book."

"I like part owning Ily, and I like being *me*."

"Doesn't change—"

"I don't want to die."

Victor snorted. "Pity—"

"I want to live, Vic."

"That won't—"

"I want to stay."

"Your enjoyment of my home is flattering but—"

"I am what you see. You weren't wrong. And I wasn't acting. I'm a sadistic son of a bitch, and I can actually accept that now…thanks to you."

"Lies—"

"*Truth.*" Leaning forward, I draped my arm over Ily's bare back and clamped my fingers over his wrist. Smiling with every blackness inside me, I squeezed him. "I want to stay, not just for this weekend or a single month. I want to stay forever. I want that lifetime membership. And in order for you to trust me…I'll tell you who I truly am."

Victor sucked in a breath, glanced at my hand locked on him, then raised a single eyebrow. "Go on then, I'll bite. Tell me…who are you?"

My soul shivered.

My heart thundered.

And all I said was, "I'm Henri Mercer, brother to Q Mercer, and it's a pleasure to officially meet you."

Chapter Seven

Ily

CHAOS ERUPTED.

Guests started yelling.

A gun fired by accident, the bullet whizzing into obscurity.

Jewels scurried away, hiding behind bushes and hedges.

And Victor shot to his feet so fast, he almost went ass over heels. His gun went flying, skittering under a table.

Spying a chance to run, I bolted off the deck and into Peter's outstretched arms. Without a word, he dragged me behind one of the many happy-babbling fountains, this one with a heron peering down at us with a fish in its mouth.

Skidding to my knees, I turned back and watched the anarchy unfold.

In a vicious flash, the guards yanked Henri from his chair, kicked the back of his legs, and slammed him to his knees.

Their fingers squeezed around triggers.

I stiffened for a second bang.

Victor threw up a hand. "*Wait*!"

Everyone froze.

Slaves and Masters combined.

A prickly, powder keg of energy consumed the entire garden as waitstaff darted back inside.

Victor stalked to stand over Henri. Holding out his fingers, he waited for one of the guards to pass him a gun.

With an evil sniff, he pressed the muzzle squarely on Henri's forehead. "You're a *what*?" His hiss reminded me of a thousand cobras, a hundred rattlesnakes. His tongue seemed forked, his face completely inhuman. "Say that name again, I fucking *dare* you."

Henri didn't shiver or try to get away. His voice was steady and sure. "I'm a Mercer. I'm the bastard son of Quincy Mercer the First. He kept a stable of slaves in France. He raped my mother for over a decade."

Victor bared his teeth. "I'm aware the late Quincy Mercer shared my interests but the current one—"

"My brother. He goes by Q."

"*Yes*, I'm aware," Victor hissed again. "That motherfucking cocksucker."

"Don't think cock is his flavour of choice, but I tend to agree with you." Henri shrugged. "I've only met him once, but he didn't care at all about trading my life for what he wanted."

"He's the one who sent you?"

"He is." Henri's back rippled with righteous strength. "I've been honest, Victor. Every confession about what I want and every urge I feel has been the godawful truth. I was born to a monster and I've been one ever since. My brother figured he could use that against me, but…pity for him, I've found where I belong."

My heart pounded.

I didn't understand.

W-What's going on?

So…he's not really a cop?

Keep up, Ilyana!

Peter wrapped his arm around my shoulders as Victor loomed over Henri. He swayed on the balls of his feet, grinding the gun into Henri's forehead. "There's no record of you in any of the files I have on that bastard. No link. No alert. I've been thwarting his attempts to find me for years, and there hasn't been a fucking *whisper* of a brother."

"That's what made me perfect for the job." Henri dared rise higher on his knees, pushing against the gun. "You say you see me. You do. I didn't lie about any of it. In fact…" He swatted at the gun, then looked over his shoulder, his eyes skating over scattered jewels until stopping on me in Peter's hold.

He scowled but said softly, "The only one I truly lied to was Ily. I lied when she thought I was a cop. I lied when she thought I would let her go. I lied when she thought I was good."

Terror crawled up my throat.

I shook my head, hating that truth blazed in his grey stare.

No longer troubled. No longer shadowed.

All his whispers about enjoying what he'd have to do to me. All his urging not to fight him because it would trigger something he couldn't control.

Oh God…

"Don't look at her," Victor barked.

Henri ripped his gaze back to him. He splayed his hands like a martyr. "If the truth can't prevent you from killing me, then so be it. At least you know I'm not a cop." He closed his eyes, seeming perfectly at peace with Victor's power over his existence.

If he shot him—

God, I'd lose it.

I'll be all alone.

Have you not been listening?!

You've been all alone since the moment he noticed you!

I shook my head, scrambling to stay faithful even after I'd fucked everything up last night.

No…this…this has to be another attempt to stay undercover.

He's still good. Still trying to save us.

I'd clung to that the entire time I'd been spread over the table.

I'd made a prayer out of hope as not one but two men prepared to rape me.

I couldn't just let that go.

Couldn't just stop…hoping.

It was messy and complicated, but…*he's still going to get us out.*

After all, he would know the names of others in this sordid underworld.

He would know how to use them to his advantage.

What he did to me last night was just a gigantic mistake…by both of us.

Isn't it?

But Victor…hesitated.

The way he studied Henri tore apart my hope, one stupid strand at a time.

Chewing on his bottom lip, he threw up his arm for silence as his guests all bickered and gave him orders to murder. "Shut up, all of you."

Removing the gun, he raised his hand for Henri to stagger to his feet. "You have five minutes."

Henri stood to his tall height, bowing his chin respectfully. "What do you want to know?"

"All of it." Pointing at the chair Henri had been sitting in, Victor took his and lowered himself ever so slowly. "Go on, then."

Sitting down, Henri placed his hands on the table. "Guess I'll give you the highlights. I had no idea of my origins until a few months ago. I actually tried to kill myself one night when I lost control thanks to too much alcohol."

Wait…he tried to kill himself?

My heart twisted agonisingly.

"I was sick of fighting the darkness inside me and when I found out about my brother's existence, I went to him for help." Henri chuckled blackly. "His idea of help was throwing me to you and seeing if I'd survive."

"And he thought you could win against me?" Victor tapped his finger on his pastry plate. "Did he give you any training? Preparation?"

"Nope." Henri shrugged. "He gave me a list of names—guests he knew visited you regularly—and told me to pick one to befriend." His eyes sought out the bastard Roland, who'd finally woken up from Henri knocking him unconscious.

Slowly, Roland picked himself up from the deck and rubbed his jaw.

My skin crawled from the memory of him naked behind me.

The imprint of his grotesque—

I shuddered.

I wished Henri had killed him, not just stunned him.

"Six months it took for me to get Roland's trust," Henri continued. "I played the part, all while knowing I wasn't playing, not really. Don't get me wrong, I despised the videos Roland made me watch. He's one sick fuck—like I told you at dinner, I like them warm and alive—but he did arrange a meeting with you."

Roland threw Henri the finger, still nursing his jaw.

"Did you tell your brother about that meeting?" Victor asked softly.

"I did." Henri nodded. "He was aware."

"And how did he intend to come after you if you were successful in hoodwinking me?"

For the first time, Henri's shoulders tensed, but then he rolled that tension away. "He gave me a pair of cufflinks. They contain a GPS tracker."

I gasped.

So that's why he leapt down my throat when I knocked them off his bedside.

They're our only way out.

Victor's face darkened. "You brought them into my estate? When I gave you such welcome hospitality?"

"They're useless…as you already know. However, if it will make you feel any better, you can have them."

Victor rolled his eyes. "How generous."

Henri smirked. "Know what else is generous?"

He scowled, taking Henri's bait. "What?"

"The fact that I paid you two million euros."

Victor stilled. "Your money is the same as everyone else's."

“But that’s the thing…it wasn’t *my* money.” He cocked his head as if he had a great secret, his short dark hair catching the sun. “I’m practically penniless. Remember how I said I like reading? Well…I like writing too. I’ve been trying to write a book for years, all while I kept my bills paid with bar work and the occasional stint at labouring.” Reaching across the table, bold and frankly stupidly reckless, Henri snatched the baguette off the plate in front of Victor and sank his teeth into it. “You won’t begrudge me a final meal, will you, Vic?”

Victor’s brows furrowed, not really paying attention. He seemed hung up on a prior sentence but couldn’t untangle it. “Did you sell the rights to this book? Is that where you got the money?”

Henri swallowed and shook his head. “That would still make it my money…wouldn’t it?”

A guest suddenly marched forward. “This is bullshit, Vic. Kill him for the traitor he is. He’s ruining my appetite.”

“I agree with Kyle,” another said. “He’s a fraud.”

Roland marched into the fray, his face bruised. “I’m so sorry, Master Jeweler, I had no idea he was such scum, such a fucking con-artist. Allow me to kill him for you. Let me right my mistake.”

Henri threw him a scowl, but Victor still didn’t say anything.

He kept his dark blue eyes locked on Henri, his silver shirt and slacks almost blinding in the glare.

And Henri just stared back.

Unafraid.

Or…very good at hiding it.

Peter’s arm tightened around my shoulders as if he expected another gunshot to go off any second. He tugged Citra into our huddle too, pulling her from where she’d been hiding close by. He tried to push our heads down so we wouldn’t see Henri’s skull shatter apart.

“Don’t.” I shoved him off.

“Ily—”

Crawling away a little, I shivered as a few Masters on the deck noticed me.

I froze and kneeled, cupping my bare breasts.

What did I think I could do?

Rehearse another script? Begin another pantomime?

Henri was the leading star, and there were no lines left for me.

It’s all a lie anyway.

No…

I-I couldn’t believe that.

If I did, I’d snap.

I needed to have faith in *something.*

It just sucked that I had no idea what was real or fake anymore.

It felt as if hours ticked past, but finally, Victor's lips twitched.

Slowly, terrifyingly slowly, the twitch morphed into a smile, and the smile cracked into a laugh. And once he started laughing, he got louder and louder until he reached across the table and dug his fingers into Henri's shoulder.

He shook him and waggled a finger in his face, his laugh almost obscene.

Guests froze.

Guards shot each other a confused look.

Slaves retreated deeper into the gardens.

And Henri merely raised the half-eaten baguette in a toast. "Exactly."

Exactly what?

"Oh, this is too *parfait.*" Victor threw his head back and laughed his damn ass off. Only once he wiped tears from his eyes did he stand and announce to all of us: "It seems that the very man who has been trying to ruin me for years has been very generous indeed."

"I don't get it." Roland sulked. "What the hell is so funny?"

Turning on him, Victor snickered. "Q fucking Mercer paid *me*—a trafficker he's been trying to stop for years—two million euros for a slave."

"What?" Roland wrinkled his nose. "But Henri paid—"

"Idiot." Swatting Roland around the head, Victor turned back to Henri. "Answer my next question with every drop of honesty because it could very well be your last."

Henri squared his shoulders and nodded. "Ask."

"How much did your brother give you to oil your way into my confidence?"

With only the slightest hesitation, Henri answered, "Thirty million."

Peter grunted as if someone struck him.

My heart stopped.

How strange that it was *this* moment where the house of cards Henri had stacked before me finally tumbled. I'd believed he was a poor government worker…*lies.* I'd believed he was a darkly tangled cop who still erred on the side of good…*lies.* I'd believed it was my fault he snapped last night because I couldn't stop the drugs from making me fight…*lies.*

Card by card.

Lie by lie.

The softest puff of wind and they all scattered, leaving me completely alone and unprotected.

Goosebumps pricked and I huddled on the grass.

Tears stung my eyes, but I refused to let them fall.

All my grief.

All my guilt.

They dried into shrivelled husks and stabbed like poisonous thorns deep inside my stupid, *stupid* heart.

Waiting until his guests quietened again, Victor stepped into Henri and asked, "How much is your life worth to you, Henri *Mercer*? What would you be willing to pay to survive?"

Bowing his head, Henri's voice shook with true passion. "To survive? Not a single penny. But to thrive? I'd give you everything."

Victor couldn't stop the flare of respect in his eyes. "I hear your truth, just like I see who you are. Yet…" He cocked his head, studying the man he'd been moments away from killing. "You're aware of what I'll do to you if you're lying, correct?"

Henri nodded coldly. "I'm aware."

"If I find out this is another ruse, I'll collar you and cuff you and make you serve in the dungeons until you scream for mercy. Only once you're buggered, butchered, and barely recognisable will I put you out of your misery. Does that change any of your answers?"

I shuddered.

Henri didn't.

"Not a single one." Henri kept his chin high. "I'm related to the man who's been trying to take you down for years, and I'm telling you, with my hand on my blackened heart, that I forsake every connection I have with him."

Taking his time, Victor finally sniffed. "Would you be willing to prove it?"

Henri frowned. "Not sure how I can, but sure. If it'll keep me alive and ruling as a Master and not a slave, I'll do whatever it takes."

"Good." Nodding as if a new contract had been signed, Victor stuck out his hand. "You and I have another date in my office. If you can prove you are who you say you are, then you can thank me for my benevolence by gifting me every euro Q Mercer gave to you." His teeth flashed. "You do that, and…I'll give you a home for life."

Henri shifted with infinitesimal emotion, but then his spine braced, and he slipped his palm into Victor's. "Deal."

Yanking Henri into him, Victor hissed, "This doesn't mean you're off the hook. It just means you don't die today."

"I understand."

"You're on probation, *Mercer*." Victor blinked. "Strange…I never thought Ward suited you. And now that you mention it…you do look a lot like him."

"His wife seemed to think so. She welcomed me with open arms. Pity he didn't."

Victor snickered. "You know he'll stop at nothing to kill you now, right? Seems as though you're trapped between two enemies."

"But maybe one day we can be friends." Henri chuckled. "Now that this nasty business is behind us."

"I guess time will tell." Victor pointed a finger in Henri's face. "But no more pussyfooting around. You want me to trust you? Then trust your-fucking-self. No more thinking you can be both monster and saint."

"Way ahead of you. Last night was my awakening."

"Good boy." Victor's lips curled into a savage smile. "You won't have any objection to taking your sweet, far-too-trusting jewel into the snuffbox, then?"

"Not at all." Slowly, Henri turned on the spot. "I'm looking forward to it. Whatever it is."

His eyes sought me out, searching for me in the guests and jewels, flaring as he found me alone, marooned on the grass.

Unlike before when he'd looked at me, no flash of togetherness forked between us. No secretive alliance bound us. No forbidden emotions webbed the longer we played our dangerous game.

He looked at me as if he finally accepted I belonged to him and was impatient to begin a very different story.

Stalking down the deck steps toward me, he cupped my elbows and helped me stand.

My skin recoiled.

My stomach revolted.

It took every effort not to spit in his face and *run*.

Running his thumbs softly over my skin, he dropped his stare to the red smudges still dirtying me from last night. "Watching those men touch you made me fucking rage, but seeing my fingerprints marking you in blood makes me so goddamn hard. You're mine now. You're truly, officially—"

"Get *off* me." I squirmed to get away. "You're a damn liar. You *lied* to me. You lied to me every time you opened your lying mouth!"

His fingers tightened into ice picks. "And now, I'm telling you the truth."

"I hate you." I struggled and jerked. "You'll pay for—"

"I've been paying my entire life, little nightmare. It's time someone else paid for a change."

"And you've decided that *I'm* the one who has to pay?"

"I didn't decide." He shrugged. "Fate decided the moment we noticed each other at the bar."

"Screw you." I balled my hands, renewing my efforts to get free. "Do you honestly think you'll get away with this?"

"I seem to be so far, yes."

My heart cracked all over again.

Eyes prickled my skin from everyone watching. Jewels, Masters…every single person judging me for being so stupidly naïve.

There was no such thing as goodness in him…only evil.

I went limp in his hold. "Was any of it real?"

His fingers gentled on my elbows. "Most of it was. Especially the part where I told you not to fight me." His eyes softened with sick gratitude. "Last night was the best night of my life, by the way. I want to thank you—"

"Fuck. You." Temper turned my limpness back into struggles.

"Keep fighting me, Ily." He smiled. "You saw what happens when you do, and I'm fairly certain I'm getting addicted to you. So…keep fighting. I beg you."

I immediately turned to stone.

He huffed. A sadistic twinkle appeared in his grey gaze. "Spoilsport."

"Go to hell."

"Nothing's changed between us, you know," he murmured. "I still want you. I still find you the most delicious creature I've ever seen. The only thing that's different is I'm no longer hiding how I feel—"

"Pity that you now disgust me."

"Ah, don't say that." He smirked. "Your body likes me…I know that for a fact."

Not caring that everyone watched us. Not caring how dumb I'd come across, or how pathetic I'd turned out to be, my voice cracked as I clung to hope one last time. "You let me believe you were a cop."

"You were the one to jump to idiotic conclusions. To believe I could ever be good enough."

"You lied to me. About *everything*."

"I told you. Not everything." He sighed. "If you must know, I tried. I really did. I hoped I'd have enough strength to ignore temptation and do what my brother asked of me. Unfortunately, you're far too fucking tempting, and I'm so much happier now I've given in."

"You're the reason I'm here, you bastard." I struggled again, fruitlessly. "You said you would get me home."

"Ah, little nightmare." He pressed the softest kiss on the tip of my nose. "You are home. We both are."

Victor's footsteps echoed as he came down the deck steps and joined us on the lawn. "No more whispering, Mercer. Everything you say to her is for all our ears."

"No problem." He smiled in a way I'd never seen. No strain. No stress. Only peace.

I forced myself to look into his eyes, searching for any shred of the Henri I knew before. The man who'd convinced me so entirely. The trickster who played me so spectacularly.

If I hadn't cried my soul out last night, I would've shattered into tears.

Now…only numbness.

And betrayal.

And fear.

His gaze glittered back, silver and clear, his face unmasked and relaxed. Dragging me into him, he shifted his hands to my face.

A million needles stabbed me from his touch. I tried to push him away, but he just tightened his fingers until my cheekbones threatened to snap. "I want you." Running his roughened thumbs over my cheeks, he reminded me of all the moments he'd stroked my hips with such tenderness.

He'd caressed me beneath Victor's nose.

Touched me gently all while apologising for hurting me.

I'd believed in those pets. I'd gathered courage from his kindness.

I didn't care he'd straddled the border of light and dark.

I'd *trusted* him.

But now…that light extinguished.

"I need you to know that despite my urges and all the depraved things I'm going to do to you, I'm not a psychopath. I'm not compensating for something. I'm of sane body and mind."

"Hey," a guest grumbled from a nearby table. "You saying the rest of us are lunatics?"

Henri didn't answer him, his breath hot over my lips. "I know that you're different and accept you'll always have a strange hold over me. I'm fully fucking aware of how hard I get around you and even with so many other jewels at my disposal, I only want you. Whether that obsession will last remains to be seen, but for now, I'm indulging in whatever little crush Victor thinks I have and letting myself off the leash entirely." He kissed my cheek with exquisite worship. "Know what that means?"

I clenched my teeth and didn't reply.

Goosebumps scattered as he pressed a line of the softest kisses across the bridge of my nose to my other cheek. He moaned as he inhaled me. "It means that you belong to me. You will bow for me. Open for me. Moan and bleed for me. I will not spare you. I will take everything you have, and it will be my greatest fucking pleasure to rule you. Don't go looking for the sniffling fool who brought you here. Henri Ward is dead, which means I should probably introduce myself. My *true* self. The Master you now belong to."

Wrapping his fist in my hair, he pushed me slowly but firmly to my knees.

Our audience watched it all.

I winced as his fingers tightened in my strands.

And I wished the earth would break apart and whisk me away as he said, "My name is Henri fucking Mercer, and you, little nightmare, are mine. Body, mind, and soul."

Chapter Eight

Henri

MY MIND SWAM WITH POWER.

My cock swelled.

The temptation to order her onto all fours grew by the moment.

What's stopping me?

I'd unshackled myself from normal society. I now lived in a Garden of Eden where beasts ate forbidden fruit and dined on feminine flesh.

Swallowing hard, my hand strayed to my jeans button—

"Fuck, you're an eager one now you've slipped the noose. Temporarily, I might add." Victor's voice cut through the lustful buzzing in my blood. "Keep your cock where it is. We still have a matter of identity confirmation and payment before she's yours again, Mercer."

I whirled around, Ily's thick, black hair still in my fist.

The animal inside me prowled too close to the surface.

I'd already hit Roland for touching what was mine.

I prepared to hit Victor for denying me my rights.

Victor cocked his head, daring me to do something very ill-advised.

I blinked a few times to rid the shadows curling over my stare. When I could talk like a man again, I snapped, "In that case, I wish to make a bargain."

"A bargain?" Victor snickered. "I just let you live, you ungrateful bastard. I think—"

"I'll give you everything Q gave me. I won't begrudge a single euro...all I'm asking for is full ownership of Ily and your agreement no one else will touch her."

Ily went stiff by my feet.

A few jewels gasped. Guests all voiced their very loud, very annoying opinions.

Slipping his hands into his slacks, Victor cocked his head. "I'm aware my cameras could have better audio. That you almost got away with your little act if it wasn't for the moments when your conscience almost broke you. Yesterday, your desire to own her came from the idea you could keep her safe…so why should I believe this request is any different?"

Pulling Ily to her feet, I tightened my fingers in her hair. "She was my first. The first to set me free." My voice turned hoarse with possession. "And honestly? The thought of anyone else tasting what is mine, using what is mine, *hurting* what is mine? Well…" I shrugged. "Let's just say it makes me fucking murderous."

For a long time, Victor just studied me. Then he completely changed the subject. "Before we go up to my office, there's the simple matter of discipline."

Whose discipline?

Mine?

Guests who'd broken off and sat muttering over their forgotten breakfasts perked with interest. "Finally gonna punish them for being late, Vic?"

"Indeed." Victor nodded. "Well, Henri is."

I narrowed my eyes. "Punish who?"

"My jewels of course."

It felt like another test. To see if I'd baulk.

Never again.

I sniffed. "How do you want me to do it?"

"Use your imagination." He grinned. "But I expect you to punish them all. In one fell swoop."

I frowned. "Does the remote allow you to shock more than one jewel at a time?"

"Yes. If they're touching." Victor smiled slyly. "In fact, they enjoyed touching so much this morning, I say we return the favour."

My heart skipped, then went quiet.

My mind shot back to what Victor had accused. That Peter had kissed Ily. He'd put his mouth on hers. On what was *mine*. Fury boiled quick and black.

Letting Ily go, I pointed to where Peter kneeled by the fountain.

She wanted to touch him so badly?

So be it.

Backing up a little, I snapped my fingers. "Every jewel, get back in line. *Now.*"

A scurry of feet on pristine grass. A quick shuddering of hedges as they crawled from behind sculpted animals.

One by one, they all resumed their meek kneeling pose, close but not too close, heads bowed and waiting.

"Go join them, little nightmare." I arched my chin at the trembling slaves. "Sit beside Peter."

Her upper lip curled as if she wanted to throw some violent words my way before she obeyed and went to him. An Indonesian girl had to scoot sideways to give her space, pressing them all a little tighter.

Victor didn't interfere, nor did he instruct.

He might not have shot me, but I was on thin ice. The hairline cracks were there. The occasional groan as stability threatened to give beneath my feet.

Grabbing the remote from my pocket, I held it up. "How long is usual for this type of infraction?"

Victor pursed his lips. "Let's do ten seconds."

"That's it?"

"That's plenty." He scowled a little. "They still have a full day of service before them. Don't rob their ability to behave just because you're feeling…how did you put it? Murderous?"

"Only murderous if someone touches what's mine."

"Ah, so that's why you're so eager." He grinned as his eyes skated to Peter. "You really shouldn't have kissed her, my pet." His loafers hissed through the grass as he stepped a little closer. "And if I find you doing it again, I'll cut out your ungrateful tongue." He laughed quietly. "I know, I know…I've threatened to do that before, but you always convince me to let you keep it because you use it so well. But there will come a time when even a good blowjob won't save you."

Peter bowed his head. "Yes, Sir V."

Taking the lead, Victor splayed his arms, encompassing the line-up of thirty jewels. "You all looked so cosy this morning, cuddled happily against each other. Why are you so far apart now?"

The jewels all flicked each other a worried glance before ducking their chins and inching closer, thighs to thighs, hips to hips. When no space existed, Victor sighed as if they'd disappointed him. "Hold hands, my sweetlings. There you go."

In a blur of obedient motion, each slave clasped the hand of their neighbour, creating a damn daisy chain of half-naked, fully-bare humans. Bruises glowed on some, cuts on others, Ily seemed to shimmer the brightest as she tipped up her nose and clasped the hand of the girl on her left and Peter's on her right.

Her eyes dared me to punish her.

My thumb hovered over the remote.

The jewels waited.

Silent and dull, broken into submission from so many mornings like this. So many days of unavoidable pain and constant agony.

My heart stirred.

Of course, it did.

I was a monster, not heartless.

To have their freedom stripped away. Their dignity bought. Their bodies rented to the highest bidder must be hell on fucking earth.

But…like Victor said: without predators, prey ran amok. I'd merely stepped over that dividing line and became the one who preyed instead of got preyed on.

I stepped forward. "For what it's worth, I'm sorry. I take no pleasure in punishing you in this way, but it's necessary and it'll be over soon."

Ily caught my stare.

Her face filled with loathing.

I aimed at Peter and pressed the button.

He jerked instantly.

His hands clamped down on those he held, feeding the current all the way along the line.

I'd expected it to feather out like a wave. Oh no. It bolted through every bone and nervous system connected to Peter's in a single, savage moment.

I didn't count the passing seconds.

The ability to use numbers and words escaped me as I locked my gaze on Ily and watched her entire body ripple with electricity.

The eeriest thing was the silence.

Guests muttered and chuckled behind me, but not a single slave screamed.

I didn't think they could with a million forks of lightning firing through their system.

"Enough, Mercer. Enough."

Victor's curt command brought me back, and I released the button.

The eerie silence became gasps for breath and guttural groans for mercy. One by one, the jewels let go of one another, shuffled to make space, then hugged themselves as residual jerks worked through their frames.

"Corine, I'm well overdue my morning massage," a guest behind me barked. "Hurry now."

With a weary sigh and tears in her eyes, the girl who'd been fucked by Peter last night clambered to her feet and went tripping up the deck. She dropped to her knees beside a toned gentleman with dark brown hair.

He saw me watching and narrowed his eyes.

Checking to see if Victor looked at him, he flipped me the bird, then clicked a leash to Corine's collar and led her crawling behind him into the castle.

My gaze drifted over the other guests.

All of them either drew fingers over their throats to symbolise my death or outright ignored me.

Guess I hadn't won any friends the moment they heard the word cop.

"Peter, sweetling." Victor drifted forward. Waiting until Peter raised his head, he ducked and captured his jaw. His fingers turned white he gripped Peter so hard, but Peter didn't react. Didn't pull away. Didn't flinch.

Ily did.

Her hands balled in her bare lap, forming weapons that she could very easily throw at Victor only to lose and be punished all over again.

Stalking to join them, I snapped my fingers—getting rather good at this whole owning a pet thing. "Ily. Heel."

"*Heel?*" Her upper lip curled. "Seriously?"

"Now." I scowled.

"Fuck you, Henri *Mercer*. Fuck you for every day you made me think you were different."

Ducking to my haunches, I ignored Peter's sharp inhale as I pressed my mouth to her ear, resorting to our previous game of whispers. Only this time, I didn't beg her to obey me or stop fighting. This time, I merely said, "I *am* different. Just like you are. Want to know what I think? I think we were meant to notice each other. This was meant to happen. You were always meant to be mine."

Shoving me away and crawling backward, she bristled with hate. "I'll never forgive you for this. *Never*."

I shrugged. "You have my permission to hate me, little nightmare. I can't control your feelings. However, you *will* acknowledge me as your Master, and you will come if I desire it."

"I would rather have sex with Roland."

I rocked back on my feet, cupping my chest. "Ouch. That was low."

"That's how despicable I find you."

"But that's not what your body will say when I've got you spread on my cock again."

Standing as graceful and as elegant as a swan, Ily stepped into me.

I swooped upright as she stabbed her finger into my grey t-shirt-covered chest. "One day, I will find what scares you the most. One day, I will find your greatest weakness, and when that day comes…I'll fucking *ruin* you with it."

I shivered.

Couldn't help it.

She was just so goddamn beautiful when she was mad.

Dropping my hand, I rearranged my swelling erection and shot a smirk at Victor. "Do I have time to play before we go to your office, or do I need to restrain myself?"

Letting Peter go, he swayed upright. "You're alive by my grace only. Proof and cash…those are the only things that will give you that life back."

"Fine." I removed my hand. "Let's get it over with then."

Victor chuckled. "For someone treading the plank, you're mighty cocky."

"Only 'cause I know I'll be getting back on the boat." I winked. "To play on your analogy, of course."

"We'll see." Giving Peter a soft smile, he said, "I know you had a rough night with Master K, my pet. I saw the footage of what he did to you. I don't like that you broke one of my rules and hate that you forced me to punish my entire jewelry box of precious gems, but…I think you need an afternoon off to contemplate your actions…and to heal."

Peter blinked as if he'd never heard such an offer. "Eh, are you sure?"

"Are you questioning my command?"

"No, Sir V. Never." Climbing to his feet, Peter kept his eyes downcast. "W-What should I do?"

"Whatever you like." Victor shrugged. "You're free from service until tonight. Go sleep. Go sunbathe. Go for a fucking swim for all I care. All I ask is you relive the mess you caused and strive to do better." Patting his cheek, Victor sighed dramatically. "Actually, you know what? The air in here is a little too serious for my taste. I think we all deserve a little fun."

Ily sucked in a breath, sensing the underlying monstrosity of his tone.

"I think a treasure hunt is in order, don't you?"

Peter couldn't hide his cringe. "Y-Yes, Sir V."

"I'm putting you in charge of arranging it. You know the typical rewards. Gather up as many prizes as you see fit and scatter them around the estate. You know what I expect." Grabbing Peter's collar, his gentille persona vanished. "And don't think you can just include prizes that benefit you and yours. Include prizes for my guests too, please. Otherwise, we'll have to have another discussion."

Peter shuddered. "Yes, Sir V."

Letting him go, Victor wiped his hand on his trousers. "By the way, were you in any way responsible for Ily's strange condition last night?"

The question was phrased so gently but a quiver of daggers rested inside.

Peter glanced at Ily. He opened his mouth—

"I let fear override my common sense," Ily snapped. "He didn't do a damn thing."

Victor grinned. "You know, loyalty toward a friend over loyalty toward a Master often leads to the worst pain of all."

Her nostrils flared.

Looking back at Peter, Victor said suavely, "You know I'm aware of your illicit apothecary, correct?" He chuckled as Peter stiffened into concrete. "Relax. I'm not going to punish you for it or even take away the pills you hide in your pillowcases. I tolerate Dr Belford's substance smuggling because when one of you self-medicates, my guests always comment what a good fuck you were."

Rearranging his cock, Victor shrugged. "I even partook in one myself when Rachel came to me a few nights ago. It was…fun."

"I…" Peter scrambled for something to say, lost for words. "I, eh…" Flicking Ily a look, he finally found courage and blurted, "I drugged Ily without her permission. That's why she reacted so strangely."

Wait, what?

I studied her closely.

So that was why she fought?

Why we both snapped?

I snickered at the serendipity.

Victor got me drunk, and Peter got Ily high.

It seemed those two ingredients granted me the perfect panacea to be free.

Have to try it again sometime.

"I thought you did." Victor nodded sagely, then turned to Ily. "What did he give you, sweetling? And why did you react so badly? Only for my records of course. I have a vested interest in your mental and physical health." He sighed as if it truly dismayed him. "Tina kept things from me once, and it turned out she had a rare type of aggressive cancer. If only she'd told me sooner, I might have been able to treat her."

"Perhaps she took the sickness as her ticket to freedom?" Ily hissed.

"There are far worse things than dying."

Peter shot her a warning look.

"Yes, there are." Victor nodded. "So I suggest you keep that in mind when I'm being so cordial and forgiving. I know you're still new, and that fire of yours will most likely reemerge now that you've seen the truth of Henri's lies, but I suggest you think long and hard about being argumentative."

"You know what? Fuck you too. Fuck *both of you.*" Ily sniffed, throwing me a fiery glower.

My hand twitched, but Victor just snickered. "One day, my pet. One day. Perhaps even together."

She gulped.

My temper prickled. If Victor thought he'd share an Ily sandwich with me, he would find I had a few terms and conditions if he wanted Q's fortune.

"So?" Victor looked back and forth between the two jewels. "What was the drug that made Ily react?"

Peter balled his hands, well used to answering when asked. "It was psi—"

"Why?" Ily interrupted. "So you can use it as a weapon against me? Drug me each time I'm misbehaving?"

"That's up to Henri to decide." Victor shrugged. "Or whatever Master is currently ruling you in the future. I merely want to know so I'm aware of what can kill and maim. Do you think I intend to kill my jewels through allergies? That the notes I have on Rachel and Colin with their peanut and sesame intolerances are a dastardly plot to murder them?"

"I wouldn't put anything past you." Ily crossed her arms, not caring she stood naked or that my bloody fingerprints still branded her.

"I'll take that as a compliment, and perhaps you should take it as a warning." Victor grinned far too white and wide. "For now, though, I'm impatient to see if Henri can finally be trusted, so…I'll find out another day."

Patting Peter's bare shoulder, he added, "I expect a fantastic treasure hunt tonight. And don't forget. Good things come to those who accept their place and respect their Masters."

"Yes, Sir V."

"Good boy." Victor's hand dropped away. "I'll tell my friends you're out of bounds for now. You even have my permission to tell me if anyone disobeys that order."

Peter's cheeks pinked beneath his natural dusky tan. "Thank you, Sir V."

"Run along now." Dismissing him with a wave of his wrist, Victor pinned his eyes on Ily. "You see, my pet? See how generous I can be when a jewel has earned my affection?"

Peter gave her a tight grimace before he left and vanished into the castle.

Only once he'd gone, did she reply with fangs, "I see you using kindness as another form of control."

"I don't know if I prefer this real version of you or the one who was acting because she believed her new Master was a cop." Victor chuckled. "You were so much quieter and amenable yesterday."

"Yesterday, I believed in a lie."

"Yes, I suppose you did. Pity that."

Withdrawing a leather leash from his pocket, he tossed it to me. "Bring her with us. If you are who you say you are, then I suppose you better keep her close. You have a long task ahead of you, Henri. You skipped straight to the obedient slave thanks to whispers and lies. But today, she won't obey. Today, she'll fight, and I can't wait to see how you'll break her."

Ily's mouth parted in unwilling awe as she stepped over the threshold of Victor's office.

The leash tugged her collar, snaking its way into my palm as I guided her to the button-leather couch Victor had lounged on while I'd transferred two million euros.

I'd paid that money to be the one to fuck her on the maypole.

Now I was about to pay for the right to stay and fuck her for the rest of my life.

Funny that yesterday I'd had such qualms about even touching her, yet now I had overflowing urgency to touch her *everywhere.*

"Sit her down, Henri, and come here." Victor pulled out the chair in the centre of his very long work area. He didn't bother powering up the four computer screens down one end or even flip up the laptop at the other. He merely leaned under the desk, typed in a code with soft beeping noises, and a fortified drawer popped out.

Is that where he keeps the scrambler?

Curiosity flared. Not because I still attempted to live up to Q's ridiculous mission but because cloaking this place with a dead zone of technology was rather genius. The thought that I'd never be online again was a small price to pay for peace.

Letting go of Ily's leash, I pointed at the couch. "Sit down. Don't move. Don't speak."

"I'm cold," she muttered as she perched on the icy leather. Her nipples had pebbled into dark pink ice-cubes the longer we'd walked through the stone castle. Sunshine spilled into Victor's plush office from the doors leading to his patio with snarling gargoyles and weeping angels, but the inner temperature of the fortress bordered on arctic.

"If you do as you're told and aren't a nuisance, I'll get you something to wear when we're done."

She looked as if she'd spit some sort of slur but then she lowered her eyes and nodded.

My heart kicked at the obedience.

My cock thickened for—

"Henri. Now," Victor ordered, fishing out a cell phone from the hidden drawer.

Giving Ily one last lingering look, I padded over thick gold carpet toward him. I no longer fought terror at being found out but slipped deeper into my new skin. "What do you want me to do?"

Ignoring me for a second, he fiddled with the phone. Scrolling through his contacts, he chose a name I didn't see, then stood up. Grabbing my hand, he shoved it into my palm. "By the way, your suicidal mission last night of breaking into my office and turning off the scrambler? It would never have worked. Want to know why?"

My hand closed around the phone. The line kicked in, faintly ringing whoever Victor had selected. "Why?"

"Because the scrambler isn't here. It's not in my castle. It's not even on my island. It's up there." He pointed at the gold-embossed ceiling.

"Up where?" I scowled. "You just said it wasn't on your island, so it can't be on the roof."

Victor sighed and squeezed my shoulder. "You're quick, Mercer. And that's why I like you."

I paused, thinking about it. But the ringing stopped, and a faint voice echoed from my palm.

I froze.

"You better get that." Victor chuckled. "Oh, and the scrambler is on a satellite. Programmed to follow my home through space and earth's spinning. Only a code will turn it off, and only I know the code. It's not written down anywhere. It's not accessible by any of my computers. This is the only phone that taps into it and allows calls outside, and even that is restricted by another code. My internet goes through the satellite and is encrypted before connecting to the world wide web. So you see, *mon ami*…don't beat yourself up that you failed. You failed the moment you agreed to do your brother's dirty bidding. Don't feel bad that you're far too smart and far too honest to be his bitch."

Patting my cheek with affection rather than condescension, he moved to sprawl in a grey leather recliner in a puddle of sunlight. "Get that. Before they hang up."

My heart kicked just a little as I raised the phone to my ear. "Hello?"

"*Bonjour*?" a feminine voice responded in flawless French. "*Je pensais que personne n'était là. Puis-je vous aider*?" (I thought no one was there. Can I help you?)

I slipped into my first language, my heart still thumping from Victor's speech. "*Qui… qui est-ce*?" (Who…who is this?)

"*Qui êtes-vous?*" (Who are you?)

Her crisp, almost prim voice jogged my memory.

Fuck.

Suzette.

Q's housekeeper.

I'd only met her once, but she'd struck me as a feisty woman who would fight to the death for those she loved.

I flicked a look at Victor.

Jesus, just how far did his reach go?

He had my brother's home number in his phone. Probably had his address and all his allergies too.

Victor saluted me with two fingers before cupping his chin and resting his elbow on the armchair.

Sitting heavily, I pinched the bridge of my nose and prepared to have a conversation that would ensure I could never step foot outside Victor's fortress again.

"Put it on speaker," Victor whisper-muttered. "I want to hear if Quincy truly knows you." He grinned as he glanced at Ily as if she was in on this morning's entertainment. "I'll be able to tell by his voice, you see. Are you ready, sweetling? Ready to know if the man who's been fucking you truly is a monster of the Mercer line?"

Ignoring him, I put the call on speaker and replied to Suzette, "*Passez le téléphone à Q …s'il vous plaît. Je dois parler à mon frère.*" (Put Q on the phone…please. I need to speak to my brother.)

"*Henri*?" Her voice rose into glass-shattering octaves. "*Est-ce vraiment toi*?" (Is that truly you?)

She said my name like my mother used to.

Onn Ree instead of Hen Ree.

"It is. I don't have long, and I need to speak to Q. Is he there?"

"He just got home!" She slipped into English, copying me with a happy giggle. "He and Tess took Lino to the neighbouring farm to pick out a goat. He wanted one ever since Tess read him a book about the hen, the duck, and the billy goat."

I swallowed hard as phantom tugs of the old me banged on the cage within my heart. Seemed when the monster sprang out to play, the human part was locked firmly away. If I didn't know any better, I'd say the pains in my chest were another level of betrayal.

I struggled to speak around the sudden rocks in my throat. "Y-You're saying…I'm an *uncle*?"

Suzette paused. "Oh…" She didn't say anything for a while, then rushed, "Q didn't say anything when you came for dinner because he's extremely protective of their son. Don't…don't take it personally."

How else was I supposed to take it?

Fucking hell.

If I wasn't sure I was making the right decision, I was now.

Fuck him and his perfect fucking family.

Fuck him and his adoring beautiful wife.

Fuck him and his doting darling son.

I didn't need them.

I had something he could only dream of—freedom to be my true self without any restraints or regrets.

"*Henri*?" Q's voice shot down the line as if he'd yanked the phone from Suzette's hand.

He pronounced my name like it should be spoken, making me despise *all of them*. Seemed anyone who ever called me Onn Ree didn't fucking care about me, and I was done.

Anger built.

Unbelievable, *unbearable* anger.

"Is everything okay?" Q asked. "Are you safe? The tracker isn't working, and I feared—"

"You feared what? That I'd gotten myself killed?" I snarled, spitting out streams of fury. Fury I hadn't even known I harboured. Fury that'd been stealthy and oh-so-fucking serene, just waiting for this moment to froth.

He sucked in a breath.

For a moment, neither of us spoke.

Then he chose diplomacy and calm. "Where are you? I'll send a team to get you. What happened with the meeting you said you set up with the Master Jeweler? Did you meet with him?"

I shot Victor a look.

He smirked right back.

"Oh, I met him. Victor Grand is exactly how you described him."

"You went to his island?"

"Yep."

"And he let you return? Just like that?" His voice darkened. "What did you have to do to convince him to trust you?"

"What slave did I have to fuck do you mean?"

The line seemed to tremble. "Did you touch one of them, *brother*?"

I locked my gaze with Ily across the room. Her golden eyes shimmered with tears, but the salty liquid remained firmly trapped by her thick black lashes.

A flash of all the moments between us.

The visceral reaction I'd had when I first saw her.

The disgust at offering her money for her soul.

The desire as I bid for her at Victor's twisted auction.

The absolute despair as Victor poured alcohol down my throat.

And finally, the excruciating freedom as she kicked me in the nose.

Like a scrapbook—a Rolodex of unforgettable evolutions.

Settling back in the chair, I tore up that scrapbook and blew the confetti right in my brother's face. "I met a girl. A sweet, innocent, *wonderful* girl. With one look, I knew she was different, and if I'd been better, been normal, who knows? Maybe she would've become my wife one day. But because I'm my father's cursed son, I stole her instead of wooed her. I offered her a million euros of your money to sell me her soul, and…she took the deal. I gave her to Victor, and he opened up his island."

Q's matching fury crackled down the line. "Ignoring everything you've just said so I don't have an aneurysm, if you only offered her a million, why did I notice a transaction for two?"

I flinched, remembering his strict condition of monitoring my account. He'd be able to see what I spent, but he couldn't stop me from spending.

He'll have a nasty shock this afternoon when the balance is set to zero.

"Because I gave it to Victor."

"You *what*?"

Victor snorted and slapped his thigh, having a great ole time.

"You gave *my* fucking money to a motherfucking *trafficker*? *Es-tu fou putain*!?" (Are you fucking insane?!) Q roared, his voice echoing in every corner of the office.

"For the first time in my life, I'm clearheaded, actually." I buffed my nails on my jeans. "And if you're close to having an aneurysm from that part of the tale, allow me to tell you the rest." Keeping my eyes off Ily and Victor, I murmured, "I fucked her. I claimed her. I bound her to a cross and drew her blood. And you know what? It was the best night of my life. All that fucking loneliness…all that struggle…it's gone. I've found where I belong, and it's right here. With a slave all of my own. A jewel to keep for as long as it pleases me."

"You're still there?" Q asked, deceptively soft. "With Grand. Right now?"

"He is indeed." Victor stood from his chair and sauntered over. "Hello, my old nemesis. I suppose congratulations is in order for your son. I didn't know you'd multiplied. I can't tell you what a pleasure it is to—"

"Fuck you," Q spat. "You think you're safe? That I'll never find you? Think again. I *will* find you, Grand. And when I do—"

"You'll have to kill your own kin to get to me." Victor laughed. "Think you can do that?"

"He's fucking dead already," Q hissed. "I should've done it the night he tripped over my doorstep. No matter, I have a rosebush patiently waiting to feed on his rotten heart."

I didn't flinch.

Didn't care.

As far as I was concerned, this conversation had done all it needed to.

Q had made it abundantly clear we were family, and now I never wanted to speak to the bastard ever again.

"Any last words, Vic?" I raised my eyes.

Victor leaned over the desk, deliberating.

Neither of us saw Ily bolt from her spot on the couch and fly across the room.

"Help! *Please help*! My name is Ilyana Sharma. My father is a cardiologist at the Royal Brompton Hospital in London. Please tell Krish I'm—"

Victor backhanded her.

She switched from flying toward the phone to flying backward.

She landed flat on her back, gasping for air, winded and wide-eyed.

The golden carpet cradled her as she squirmed and choked, her hands clawing at the thick strands.

I shot to my feet and dashed to her side, completely forgetting Q until he seethed, "I'm coming for you, Ilyana. I vow I'll find you, and I'll fucking kill my brother for what he's done to you."

The line went dead.

I tossed the phone away.

With slightly trembling hands, I gathered Ily into my arms and stood with a grunt.

She still struggled for breath; I spoke over her bird-like gasps. "I'll transfer the rest of his money to you in the morning. I don't want a single penny of what's his. But…a million of that is hers. I promised it to her the night we met, and I intend to pay my debts, especially seeing as I'll be claiming every shred of her soul."

Victor slowly picked up the phone from the floor and tapped it against his thigh. "You're honourable. I like that in a friend. Consider your request granted."

"Good."

"That…" He raised an eyebrow. "That was an interesting conversation."

"Are you satisfied?" I cocked my head, hoisting Ily a little higher in my arms. "Satisfied I have nowhere else to go and nowhere else I'd rather be?"

For the longest moment, he studied me, studied Ily in my arms, then the strangest, softest affection appeared in his navy stare. "You know, Henri…I'm also well acquainted with loneliness. It's a curse, you see. A curse for those who recognise the world for what it truly is."

I scowled. "How do others see the world?"

"They see it as their God-given right to find a mate, have a litter of children, shackle themselves with a house, a mortgage, a pet, and a lifelong tax bill. For those who don't want that or don't fit into that pre-programmed mould, we're forever on the outskirts…alone."

Ily gagged and then sucked in her first proper breath.

I rocked her without thinking, tenderness as fierce as my lust. "So that's why you made your own world? On this island?"

"Exactly." Coming toward us, Victor pressed a doting kiss on Ily's cheek before cupping mine. "I like you, Henri. Despite our rocky beginning, I do believe you're finally seeing the light. And for the first time in decades, I see myself in another. All my other guests? They're a temporary fix to the loneliness that can still haunt…even in this paradise. You remind me of myself when I was your age. You remind me that I don't have children to leave my utopia to. You remind me that there is more to life than fun and fucking."

Stepping back, he shrugged almost self-consciously. "I'm glad I didn't have to kill you."

I half-smiled, Ily growing heavy in my arms. "Yeah, me too."

"You're still not home free." He waggled a finger in my face. "It will take years for me to fully trust you, but…you just chose me over your own flesh and blood. And I can't help but be swayed by that. And so…" He padded back to his desk and locked the phone away. "Keep being who you truly are, Henri Mercer. Share all your parts, not just the dark and disturbing. Allow yourself to be vulnerable. Allow yourself to be happy. And perhaps…one day, that lifetime membership you've fought so hard to earn might turn into something far, far more."

I stilled. "What does that mean?"

He sighed and simply said, "I'm in need of an heir, aren't I? Eventually."

Ily coughed on a breath; I stumbled back. The punch of acceptance from a man who'd been seconds away from shooting me made me feel as if I'd been the one winded.

Not sure how to reply, the weight of the past few sleepless nights, the exhaustion of decades of pretend, the pain of losing everything and gaining a very different future chose that moment to choke me. "D-Do you trust me enough to allow me to spend the rest of the day with my jewel? Alone…in my room?"

He flipped open his laptop and nodded distractedly. "You have full reign of my home, *mon ami*. You know there's no escape…by scrambler or by brother. You're locked here by your choice." He looked up and smiled. "I will no longer demand anything of you, and you are free to do as you please. The matter of the funds can be taken care of another day."

I nodded my thanks.

And without another word, I carried Ily down the stairs, entered my room, kicked my door closed, and laid her exquisitely gently on the bed.

Chapter Nine

Ily

WE SLEPT FOR THREE DAYS.

Exhaustion came for both of us and shoved us down, down into its cloying, clinging grip. I tried to fight it off. Tried to summon enough strength to slink out of bed and return to the jewel quarters, but the moment Henri placed me like spun glass on his mattress, handed me another black t-shirt from his wardrobe, and held back the covers for me to clamber beneath, I couldn't keep my eyes open.

He didn't march to the bathroom to hide.

Didn't touch me or hurt me.

He merely unbuttoned his jeans, undressed to his boxers, then crawled into bed beside me.

He plummeted into sleep quicker than I did.

I had a few seconds where I could've slit his throat with…something. Maybe a shard of glass from breaking the vanity mirror or even the sharp little pins from his cufflinks abandoned on the bedside table.

But then everything went black.

And I slept.

We slept through lunch and dinner.

We stumbled blurry-eyed and silent to the bathroom to relieve ourselves and drink some water.

We tried to stay awake, but the emotional and physical burnout wasn't done.

I slept beside my enemy and didn't give a damn.

By the end of the second night, we roused ourselves just enough to order room service. We ate in caustic silence, devouring the most heavenly mushroom and pumpkin risotto. The fresh cheesy bread filled my stomach with carbs, and before I knew it, we were fast asleep again, completely unconscious, side by side, until another dawn shone, and the sun slowly cured our debilitating fatigue.

I treated myself to Henri's shower.

His back had been turned to me as I woke and noticed the clock next to the unicorn-murdering goblin hinted noon wasn't so far away.

I'd never slept so long or so deeply.

I didn't know if it was the fact I hadn't slept for a few days previously or my terror and heartache had wrung me dry, but as I stood beneath steamy, burning droplets, I felt more myself than I had since I went to the train station with Samuel and headed through the tunnel to Paris.

A lifetime ago.

A world past.

Tipping my face into the heavy stream, I sighed.

Did that Q guy hear me clearly enough? Had he found my father and told him what'd happened? Was he on his way to find me and the other slaves?

Three days was a long time.

Three days could be the difference between sexual servitude and freedom.

My skin prickled with awareness.

I jumped as I looked to my left and spotted Henri watching me. His grey eyes sharp and savage, no longer hazy with sleep.

Instinct made me raise my arms and cup my breasts, turning my hips so he couldn't see. But then remembrance made me flinch, and I let my hands fall.

He'd seen everything. Touched everything.

The fact that I'd fallen for his falsehoods—lies that left me with a horrible aftertaste—didn't change the fact that he'd kept me from the grasp of others and I'd been given a blessed honeymoon in this place.

Unlike wedded couples who went at it like deviants and consummated their marriage with love and joy, this wedding had been cemented without a single touch. Three nights of nothing but sleep. In our dreams, I'd become his. In our nightmares, he'd bought me.

I hate him.

Ignore him.

Running my fingers under my awful collar, I choked down

claustrophobia as I rinsed away any dirt beneath. Repeating the process with my cuffs, I managed to ignore him during my entire wash.

Only once I'd sluiced off the soap and had nothing else to do but get out did I gather my courage and face him.

I froze.

Ever so slowly, he stripped off his underwear, kicked them into the corner, and entered the shower. The large, black-tiled space with its massive rain head and bench seat had seemed cavernous with just me inside.

Now, it felt like the tiniest prison.

My skin prickled as he reached around me and gathered a handful of soap from the dispenser.

A whiff of honeysuckle and jojoba fragranced the steamy hot air as he ran his hands under his arms, over the scant hair on his sculptured chest, and down, down to his hardening cock.

Look away, Ily.

Look away now.

I tried.

I really did.

But my eyes glued themselves to his fist. My breath turned thin as he worked himself. My heart floundered like a dying thing as any sign of flaccidity turned into velvet-wrapped steel.

Nudging me out of the way, he stepped under the stream, hissed at the hot temperature, then turned it down until icicles dripped from the showerhead.

I gasped and dashed to the glass door.

Only, his hand lashed out, snapping around my cuffed wrist.

I flinched as his fingers tightened, pressing against my pounding pulse.

Yet he didn't say a word.

Not a single one.

He held me and rinsed in snow, then flipped the water back to hot and yanked me under it.

I spluttered as he pressed me against the chilly tiles and dropped his hand between my legs.

I shot onto my tiptoes as a single finger found me, slipped through my shower-wet folds, then penetrated.

Good God—

The invasion.

The *intrusion.*

I gritted my teeth as he stroked me.

I didn't fight back as he hooked his finger and found that disloyal, deluded spot.

My tummy clenched as he continued to touch with all the arrogance of a man who knew I had nowhere else to go.

The stagnant silence and heavy weight of cursed synergy between us only made my heart thunder harder.

Bending his neck, he pressed his mouth to the vein in my throat.

I didn't know if he meant to kiss me or bite me, but all my senses shot to where his lips caressed, scrambling as his one finger became two, and he *still* didn't speak.

He rocked his hand between my legs all while his cock hung heavy and hungry between his.

Billowing steam thickened, obscuring his face as he pulled away from my neck and ensnared me with his silver stare.

Every urge and self-preservation ordered me to look down. To bow or kneel or do any number of things to get him off me and far, far away.

But a guttural groan fell from him as his fingers feathered inside me, and my body finally answered.

Against my will.

Against the very fabric of right and wrong.

I grew wet from his skilled touch.

I had no power over the tingles and tugging.

My cheeks blazed as he worked me deeper, harder, his hand pumping in that perfect rhythm, his thumb finding my clit and forcing me deeper, deeper into a vortex that promised sublime shattering.

I grabbed his wrist and tried to stop him.

His tendons flexed beneath my hold, but he never ceased.

His fingers withdrawing and thrusting, in and out of me.

Our gazes locked as he forced me higher on my tiptoes, knowing I couldn't run. Couldn't scream. Couldn't stop this.

He might've been speaking the truth that our previous couplings hadn't been rape, but now I knew who he truly was.

And this…this wasn't wanted.

I opened my mouth to tell him no. To see if that word held any power.

But his hand clamped over my lips, and he shook his head.

The first communication in three days.

With the stealth of a terrifying beast, he pressed his cheek to mine and breathed, "On your hands and knees, little nightmare."

My eyes flared as he removed his fingers and reached out of the shower for one of the many towels on the rack. I scowled as he brought it beneath the spray and hot droplets instantly drowned it, making the plush white cotton go soggy.

Slapping it onto the floor, he pointed at it.

He didn't speak again.

Didn't have to.

We both knew who the Master was, and I cursed him all over again as he clamped a hand on my shoulder and pushed me down.

And down.

And *down.*

He didn't stop pushing me until I kneeled on the towel.

The moment I kneeled, he twisted me away, then pressed on my nape, urging me forward.

I deliberated fighting.

I imagined so many scenarios of kicking his legs out from under him and killing him with a heavy fall. I pictured grabbing the showerhead and ramming it down his throat. I entertained myself with visions of strangling him with the towel or bludgeoning him to death with the soap dispenser.

But all of that took strength and speed.

And he already had me on my knees.

And, out there, lurked a hundred more like him.

And every single one of them would gladly trade places to hurt me.

What was worse?

Being fucked by a man who'd already been inside me or fucked by someone new?

What would break me less?

Being taken by a man who'd never lied or the one who made me hope?

With a despairing sigh, I stopped straining against his hand and tipped forward.

I gripped the slippery tile. My knees grateful for the towel's cushioning.

Heavy water pummelled between my shoulder blades, slightly too hot, prickles of heated pain.

My dripping hair hung around my face, and I refused to look behind me.

Refused to see how hard he was.

How desperate he was to fuck me.

Grabbing another towel, the wet slap of it sent a flush of

goosebumps and terror.

The shudder of him falling to his knees behind me made me beg to be anywhere else.

His fingers found me again, testing my readiness, granting me at least some consideration to prepare me.

That's for him, you idiot.

Fucking something wet and hot was one thing.

Fucking something dry and frigid was entirely another.

I choked on a sudden sob.

Frigid.

Sam had used that word.

I'd thought his accusation was the worst thing to ever happen to me.

Now, I'd give anything to go back to that nightclub and thank my stupid ex. Thank him for name-calling and setting me free. Thank him for showing me that it wasn't the end of the world to be told your sexual prowess was worse than a blow-up doll because I would've given anything, literally *anything*, to never have sex again.

Henri's fingers withdrew and landed slippery on my hip.

He caressed me like he had in the past.

Before, I'd stupidly associated those little swirls with our own version of Morse code.

A silent little message just for me.

His fingers said…*stay calm.*

I've got you.

We'll survive…together.

But now?

What a mockery.

What a goddamn lie.

My head dropped as deeper sorrow twisted my heart.

But I didn't cry.

I would *never* cry again.

Not for him.

Not for them.

And definitely not for me.

I shivered as he ran his thumbs over my hipbones one last time, then reared up and pressed his thighs to the back of mine.

My ears strained for his voice.

For him to tell me to obey and play along and it will all be over soon.

Poisonous words sat on my tongue to reply.

To tell him to jump off a cliff and die, only…

He stayed quiet.

Just a breathy little groan as he notched his crown inside me and paused.

His fingers gripped my hips, his knees spread mine a little more.

The broadness of his cock sent messages of conquest throughout my entire body. He hadn't even filled me, yet he'd conquered me just by holding me in place, knotting us together like animals, dragging out the moment of suspense. Not giving me peace, not penetrating or pleasuring or putting me out of my tangled, terrible misery.

I waited.

I waited just like I'd waited for help to come.

And when I didn't think I could wait any longer, he pressed a kiss to the beads of my spine and—

Thrust.

All the way in.

Thick and hard, long and dominating.

I cried out.

I gagged on a scream.

He growled as he seated himself ever so deep inside me.

He folded over my back, wrapped his arm around my chest, and palmed my swinging breasts. His hand clutched far, far too tight.

His teeth sank into my shoulder as if to scar me with ownership, and then…he rode me.

He didn't have sex with me.

He *rutted.*

He turned off his humanity and mated me like a monster.

And all I could do was brace.

Brace against his pounding. His punishment. His pulsing, maddening thrusts.

I hated that the small fire he'd kindled grew brighter and brighter flames.

I hated that my hips started matching his, slapping us together with wet sucks from the shower and loud claps from our skin.

I hated that his teeth started to feel good.

The way he pinched my nipples felt good.

The way he drove again and again felt oh so fucking *good.*

And I had a choice.

A single choice in that single sinful moment.

Come and claim this forced sex as mine.

Or let him come and think he ruled me.

As darkness wisped over my sanity and despair cancelled out my dignity, I made that choice.

I changed beneath him.

I felt the sick mutation as I became someone I didn't recognise.

No way out.

No way free.

So…I had to find my own freedom.

Peter was right.

The trick to existing in this place was embracing the very thing used to shackle us.

Sex.

Sex was for them.

Sex was theirs, and we were the vessels to take it.

But what if I made it *mine*?

The moment the thought unfurled, the darkness stopped wisping and pounced. It clouded my head, clotted my heart, and my body decided it'd had enough of being taken and took instead.

A vicious, vanquishing orgasm sliced deep, *deep* inside me.

Pleasured by Henri's rampant fucking, stabbed again and again by his conquering cock, I gave in to heat and fire and magic.

And when that magic burst, I let loose all the agony inside me.

I came.

I came hard.

I came from my G-spot—a mythical place but now fully real.

The power of it awakened and corrupted me.

The clenches felt fiercer, deeper, stronger than any other; I lost myself to pinwheels and light sparks.

I'd never come this way before.

Never felt my body gush or grasp so greedily for harder, faster, more, more, *more*.

In one ripple, I was addicted.

I clamped down on his invasion and demanded he give me everything.

And from behind me came the most animalistic roar.

Henri had no choice but to give in to me.

I ruled him.

Commanded him.

I made *him* break.

He came.

As he spurted rhythmically and ruthlessly inside me, I finally knew

how I would survive.
Not together.
Not with him.
But alone.
By myself.
In this cesspit of sex and sedition.
Until one day, I was free again.

Chapter Ten

Henri

THE SUN TRIED TO BLIND through shut eyelids.

Its heat threatening to burn me, its ever-constant presence both condemning and soothing at the same time. The musical splashing of the waterfall cascading down river rocks and into man-made rockpools serenaded the blissful afternoon.

I'd found heaven.

And for the first time in my life…*I'm happy.*

My fingers tightened around the leather leash I'd held ever since I'd snapped it onto Ily's collar and guided her from my room. The sun lounger I'd claimed smelled faintly of coconut lotion from previous pool goers, and the lazy lap of water on its pebble-lined shore matched the waterfall's song.

I'd chosen this pond-inspired pool after perusing Victor's estate. A similar one existed closer to the castle, but this one…with its natural contorting, real lilypads, and croaking, cheeky frogs hinted it wasn't just a chlorinated pool masquerading as a pond, but a true filtered ecosystem complete with reeds, boulders, and a deep end where little minnows had swum between my toes as I'd dived down into the chilly depths.

That reminds me, it's almost time for another dip.

Sweat glittered on my skin, and my stomach growled faintly for food.

If my appetite stayed this ferocious, I'd have to hit the gym I'd found earlier today as Ily trailed silently behind me.

When we'd left my room, I'd expected Victor to leap out of the shadows and cart me back to his office, but I hadn't spotted him. Other Masters ignored us. Other jewels kept their heads down. I'd taken their uninterest to familiarise myself with everything.

I wanted to know the lay of the land: where the kitchens were, the slave quarters, the recreational spaces, and the many other nooks and crannies such a place like this could hold.

After all, this was my home now.

I could never leave.

For two hours, we'd followed stone corridors and stuck our heads into rooms dripping with obscene decadence. Turned out, Victor's dead zoo on the top floor wasn't the only trophy room, and we'd come across the weaponry—all swords, daggers, pistols, and blades chained to the walls—then followed the animal skins into a gaming room, billiard room, another small library, conservatory, day spa, and endless other solars, parlours, and receiving rooms.

I expected Ily to gasp or comment on some nicknack or drapery, but she remained prickly and poised. She drifted after me like the nightmare I called her, moving like a queen draped in my black t-shirt, haunting me with every word she didn't speak.

Her unspoken emotions crackled like a storm with every step; she showed no signs of being impressed as we dawdled through the indoor Grecian-style swimming pool and cut through the fully equipped gym where other guests worked out—some with jewels tethered to the treadmill, keeping them close in case the urge struck.

She'd stayed deathly silent as we made our way outside, found this idyllic pond-pool with no other guest or jewel partaking, and staked our territory for the afternoon.

I'd expected her to speak once I'd dropped a few towels onto the grass for her to sit on and pointed at her to settle in the shade of a large black umbrella. I tried to come up with something to say as I took the lounger and stripped off my t-shirt and shorts, leaving me in a pair of black boxers.

My throat itched with words, and my ears ached for her voice, but it seemed neither of us had anything to say.

Just like we hadn't had much to say as she'd shattered around my cock, fisting me so damn tight I'd had no choice but to come with her. Her orgasm literally bruised me, and I couldn't figure out if I floated on a semi-high from making her come that hard or because she'd made me explode just as badly.

As we'd panted on the tiled floor, still joined and sticky, I'd had a flush of the old me. The human part of me who wanted to stroke her and kiss her and say thank you. But she'd ruined it by shoving me away, shooting to her feet, then stumbling from the shower.

In one move, she reminded me all over again that just because I could take her whenever I damn well wanted didn't mean she would ever feel the same way I did.

At least she hadn't gone far.

I'd found her sitting on the ugly throne in the corner of my room, t-shirt clad, hair brushed, her eyes on the carpet and hands clenching the armrests.

I supposed that would've been the perfect moment to say something.

To discuss what I expected from her. To somehow understand how three days had passed in a fugue.

How had we slept so long and deep? Had she ever crashed that hard before?

I certainly hadn't.

Even after my mother's funeral or the long trip to visit my brother—both events crammed with sleepless nights—I hadn't fallen face first into oblivion and struggled to crawl my way out.

Whatever had happened or whyever our bodies had chosen that exact moment to shut down didn't really matter.

It'd happened.

We'd been at our most vulnerable, and neither had harmed the other.

That meant some trust must exist.

And now…we were awake.

Rested.

Conscious.

We had the rest of our lives to talk, and I had no intention of letting her ignore me.

Perhaps that's why she hasn't spoken a word to you?

Because everything you've ever said to her was a lie.

I shifted on the lounger.

Not everything.

I'd been honest. Too honest.

I couldn't help that she'd chosen to hear good in all the bad.

That was a her problem, not a me problem.

And besides, I still kept my end of the bargain.

Just because I'd chosen to stay and keep her didn't mean I'd ever let another man fuck her.

She's mine.

Through and through.

I doubted the attraction I had toward her would fade and…that was fine with me.

I didn't see the problem feeling something for her because that was the part I'd been denied my whole life. I'd turned into this twisted fucking thing because I'd been prohibited love in all forms.

Could I help it that I wanted to feel love as much as I wanted domination?

That I needed to be affectionate, all while making her bleed?

Opening my eyes, I squinted behind the dark aviators I'd found in the wardrobe.

Clenching my belly, I sat up and swung my feet into the soft, spongy grass.

Ily didn't react.

Sitting in a circular shadow-puddle made by the umbrella, she sat cross-legged like an enlightened saint. Her forefingers pressed together to form infinite circles, her palms up on her knees, her back as straight as the wand inked into her spine.

One of the towels I'd given her draped between her legs, hiding the fact she wore no underwear, and my borrowed t-shirt bunched enticingly around her hips.

I waved my hand in front of her closed eyes; she didn't so much as twitch.

Was she asleep again? In a trance?

Snapping my fingers by her nose, I said, "Wake up, you've done enough sleeping."

Her golden gaze shot wide.

I swear they shimmered with pure light before she scowled, and they filled with hate. "It's rude to interrupt someone who's meditating."

"Oh, that's what you were doing." I eyed her stiff posture. "Funny enough, one of the girls I used to work with at a local pub said I should try that. Said it would help with whatever sadness she saw in me."

Her eyes narrowed. "I don't see sadness in you anymore. I only see a devil." Dropping her hands from their strange position on her knees, she balled her fingers. "I see horns and bat wings, bone claws, and…" She drifted off before asking, "Do you know how you looked to me the other night? How my delusions painted you?" She shook her head. "Of course, you wouldn't. Why would you? You were so drunk on your own fantasy that you were completely unaware of mine."

"That wasn't my fault. Peter confessed he drugged you against your will."

"He did it to try to protect me."

"Sounds as if he only made it worse."

"Perhaps." She shrugged angrily. "Or it just revealed your true colours, and now I'm aware of *exactly* who I belong to."

The rush of her admitting she belonged to me almost made me tumble off the lounger.

My heart fisted.

My stomach clenched.

It took all my discipline not to yank the leash and order her onto my lap.

"I'm glad you've finally accepted your place." My voice sounded hoarse and thick.

"My *place*?" She laughed icily. "My place is back home. My place is with my brother. My place is with the guy who made me believe in him, believe his lies, believe he was good and kind and courageous."

I stilled. "I'm still that guy."

She laughed. Far too shrill and manic to be considered sane. "Tell me, *Henri*," she spat as if my name contaminated her tongue. "Was any of it real?" She held up her hand before I could speak. "And I don't mean the things you said to me. The remarks that 'I'm different' and you're 'aware' of me. Spare the seduction spiel, okay? I might've bought it back at the club and clung on to that stupid hope, but you proved—very ardently—that you're incapable of feeling anything but lust and selfishness."

Gritting my teeth, I focused on controlling myself.

Ily took my silence as the perfect opportunity to add more fuel to my already burning fires.

"Can you believe I actually thought you were with someone else on the outside? That you were a good little undercover cop, doing his job—which included doing me—but you kept yourself bound and almost bashful because you belonged to another." She huffed. "I actually felt *sorry* for you. Sorry you had to touch me in ways you didn't really want to. Sorry you had to stray so close to the line you said you always struggled with."

My heart skipped a beat, picturing myself with anyone else but her. The picture looked all wrong. Distorted. It was her or no one. I'd chosen her. *Fate* had chosen her. We were a done deal for life as far as I was concerned.

I might be a monster, but I had the unswerving loyalty of a monogamist.

Probably because the privilege of having just one person to call my own was enough after a lifetime of nothing. Sure, I could dabble with Victor's jewels. Who knew, maybe I would get the urge, but why did I need another when I had *her*?

"You're mine, little nightmare." I leaned over her, fisting the leash binding her to me. "And I'm yours. The sooner you stop fighting that, the sooner we can begin our new life together."

"New life?" She wrinkled her nose as sparks flew from her eyes. Yanking at her collar and bashing her golden cuffs together, she snarled, "This is no life. You *stole* my life—"

"Life comes in all shapes and sizes."

"And all sorts of pain and suffering."

I pursed my lips, allowing her that one. "There will be pain, but…I'll protect you at the same time."

She threw up her hands with a frustrated, unhappy groan. "This is what I'm talking about. Do you honestly not see the problem?"

"Problem? What problem?"

She cocked her head as if she truly didn't understand me. "Answer me truthfully—"

"I always do."

"Will you draw my blood again?"

"Definitely." My tongue tingled instantly. "You taste like fucking nirvana."

She shivered. "What else…what else do you plan on doing to me?"

"Honestly?" I shrugged. "Everything." Reaching out, I ran my thumb over her cheek. "I want to whip you until you writhe. I want to mark you until you're mine. I'm fighting the very real urge to order you to blow me right now because watching your gorgeous mouth form such fighting words is making me as hard as those fucking boulders in the pond."

Shoving my hand away, she gulped. "H-How can you talk about abusing me and look at me the way you do?"

I smirked. "And how do I look at you?"

"Like…like…" She huffed; words tumbled in a rush. "Like you're falling in love with me."

"Would it be so bad if I did?"

"No one in their right mind could fall for someone they want to abuse."

"I never claimed I have a normal mind."

"You're sick," she whispered. "Every single bastard in this place is sick."

"Perhaps." I stroked the leash. "But that doesn't stop the fact that I've been single most of my life, so I've missed out on the correct etiquette of a relationship. Just because I've stepped into my true self doesn't make my past any less true. I'm still the guy who's been excruciatingly lonely until the night I found you. The moment I saw you, that loneliness just seemed to…go away. And now that I have you? *Truly* have you. In a place where no one can take you away from me? I can't explain the relief, the joy, the—"

"Stop it!" she shouted. "Just stop all your damn mind games. Stop—"

"Games?" I scowled. "No games. Truth."

She laughed and looked me dead in the eyes. "Perhaps that's your greatest fear, then. Loneliness."

"My greatest fear?"

"I warned you I'd find your ultimate weakness, Henri Ward. I won't stop. I'll never stop until I find the one thing you're most afraid of. Then I'll use that knowledge as a pitchfork and ram it into your devilish heart."

Nursing the flames she caused in my chest, I forced restraint and flicked a look across the far stretch of garden between us and the gothic-inspired castle. I was grateful we were far from the main residence. That the pond we sat at nestled beneath the towering walls of the keep where drawbridges and moats kept us protected.

I liked talking to Ily.

I'd always liked talking to her.

But I couldn't imagine other Masters spoke so freely or allowed their jewels to get so stroppy.

Running my thumb over the leash, I dabbled with the idea of telling her to bend over instead of finishing this conversation.

The longer she spoke, the harder I got.

The more she tried to break me, the hotter I became to break her.

Not raising my eyes, I studied the leather strip.

She wanted my greatest weakness?

Fine.

I had a sneaking suspicion what that was, and if she was half as intelligent as I thought, I was surprised she hadn't figured it out by now. I all but confessed it in everything I told her.

"It's not Ward any longer. And it's not really Mercer. It's just Henri…while we're alone. But when we're in company, I suggest you call me Master H…just to avoid any issues."

"I hate you," she hissed almost too low to hear.

I pretended her curse didn't strike like a stinging arrow in my heart.

Keeping a smile on my lips, I murmured, "And you could just ask, you know. Ask me what my greatest weakness is. I'll tell you."

She laughed again. "As if."

"I would." I looked up, drinking in her magnificence. The sapphire glow of her blue-black hair, the way her skin gleamed just a little bit darker than mine, how a lone freckle stamped a beauty spot right beneath her right eye. If she one day told me she was a fairy and the inked wand on her back was real, I would probably fucking believe her.

She'd certainly cast a bastard of a spell on me.

For the first time, I wondered if I would've been able to resist temptation if I hadn't been tasked to capture her. If I'd been given any other slave that wasn't her.

I'd believed I'd stayed firm in my resolve because I'd *felt* something for her.

I'd tried to do the right thing to save her.

But now…with hindsight screwing me up, I feared the moment I caught the curse of true feelings was the moment I'd fallen.

Given in.

Broken.

Not because I couldn't stomach the thought of hurting her but because I couldn't fucking handle never seeing her again.

I stiffened.

Not only had I bought myself a lifetime stay at the greatest sadistic hotel ever built but I'd ensured she would stay right by my side.

Together.

Just like I wanted.

Raking both hands through my hair, I sat a little taller and looked down at her. For all intents, she wasn't just my slave; she was my wife. Just like I told Q she might've become if I'd been normal. And, like any doting husband, I wanted to share every part of myself with her.

"Go on," I urged. "Ask me."

She studied me for an age before finally slouching as if I stole all her fire. "Fine. What's your greatest weakness, oh great Master II?"

My lips twitched, but I didn't rise to her bait. "I thought it was obvious. It is to everyone else."

Her nose wrinkled.

Dropping to my knees before her, I ran my knuckles over her perfect, slightly sweaty cheek. "No guesses? No theories?"

Ripping her face from my touch, she glowered. "I would've said your brother…but you proved that wasn't the case."

Temper sparked just a little. "That was a stupid little stunt you pulled in Victor's office, by the way. Telling Q your name. Where your father works." I pouted. "He learned your full name before I did."

"Did you stop to think it might be because he deserves it and you don't?"

"It doesn't matter anyway." I sighed. "He told me he's been trying to bring Victor down for years. He's not been able to before, and he won't be able to in the future. The best he can do is tell your parents you're alive and belong to me."

She shivered as if her body couldn't handle the level of her loathing.

She didn't speak.

I tried to smooth the thorns between us.

"Sharma." Leaning close, I sniffed the sweet fragrance of her skin. "Ilyana Sharma. Is that Indian? Was that what you were speaking on the cross? Hindi? Why do you have a wand on your back?"

She cringed away. "You lost any right to ask me questions the day you lied to me."

"You're the one who jumped to conclusions."

"You're the one who let me."

"I'm sorry."

"No, you're not."

I huffed. "You'll want to talk to me one day, you know. To share your family with me. Your childhood and all the moments that made up your life before we met."

"Doubt it."

"We're stuck with each other. *Together*, remember. Forever, actually. I was literally just thinking our relationship is almost like a marriage—"

"A what now?" She coughed, but her cheeks pinked. "You…you think I'm your *wife*?"

"Would that be so bad? I'm aware I'll never get a wife the usual way, and…I rather fancy playing the fantasy that you're mine in that way. Monogamy would be rare in this place, but I'm far more drawn to the thought of never sharing you than I am—"

"Wow, you poor, deluded fool." She shook her head, her eyes narrowed and nasty.

I reared back, instantly on the defensive. "What was that for?"

Tears sparkled in her stare, but they didn't fall. "Do you truly think others won't fuck me? Won't abuse me? What about the day you grow bored of me, huh? Bored of cutting me and bruising me and move on to another pitiful jewel? Do you honestly think we're in some sort of *relationship*? God!" She threw her hands at the sky. "You're crazy. I knew it. You're—" Her wild gaze fell to my upper thigh where my scar hid beneath black boxers. All her fury seemed to snuff out. "I take that back. No one should be called crazy. If Krish were here, he'd tell me how wrong I am to judge you. How I'm in no position to…" Her lips twisted as her eyes flickered with shame. "Y-You tried to kill yourself."

I froze.

The change of subject threw me, but I nodded slowly. "I did."

"Why?"

"Because I hurt someone against my will. Because I couldn't live with the pain of what I am."

She sniffed sadly. "Yet you're okay with hurting me?"

I couldn't hide my wince.

"Know what I think your greatest weakness is, *Master H*?" She shifted to her knees, her fury returning. "I think it's love. I think you've wanted it for so long, you've forgotten what it truly means. Or maybe you never really knew. Either way, I think you believe that this"— she waved between us —"could somehow *become* love…if you stay faithful and guard me from other bad men. You're ignoring the fact that you've destroyed my life, stolen me from my home, and collared me to you. You think by buying my body, you've bought my heart and soul, but the truth is…" She sighed and put her hand on my knee as if, even now, her sweetness and compassion didn't want to hurt me. "The truth is that you will *never* be able to buy those. You will never be able to make me love you. You will never call me your wife because the only thing that we are is…enemies."

I deserved that.

I did.

Yet I wasn't prepared for the dagger stabbing through my ribs and puncturing everything vital inside me.

I grunted as if her words had the power to slaughter all the newness inside me—all the welcoming darkness—and shove me back into a loveless, lonely existence.

I might have feelings for her.

I might want to keep her.

I might hurt her and fuck her and have deep, dark urges.

But under no fucking circumstances would I let her ruin my one chance at happiness.

In the distance, a man strolled toward us. Suave and confident, long-legged and lean.

Victor.

Shit.

Rising from the grass, I sat back on the lounger and judged his stride. I guessed we had a couple of minutes before he arrived. A few more moments to talk freely before he reproached me on my behaviour.

I didn't care that cameras probably eavesdropped and recorded us from the battlements. I wasn't embarrassed for being honest. I didn't care because I was past caring. But I did have something to say. Something Ily needed to hear.

"I appreciate you letting me know how you feel, so…allow me the same courtesy." Pinching the bridge of my nose, I gathered my thoughts before dropping my hand and looking up. "Regardless of how you feel about me, the truth remains that I feel strongly for you. You're right that I don't know what love feels like. I've never been given it. No one seems to want it when I try to offer it. So perhaps I'm doing it all wrong." I looked at my hands. "All I know is, I'm free in this place. Free on an island, locked in a fortress, when out there, in that loveless cold-hearted world, I was afraid, alone, and dying. The night I saw you was the first time in my life that I felt something *in here*." I punched my chest. "I felt it as cleanly and as viciously as if you'd reached into my chest and signed your name on my heart. I don't care if you don't believe me. I don't care if you think my version of love is toxic and wrong. I'm not even saying it *is* love. All I'm saying is…I want you. I want to keep you. And I want you to play along with me."

Silence fell.

Victor came ever closer.

Ily shook her head, digesting what I said. Finally, she choked, "Even now? Even after everything you've done to me, you're still asking me to *play along with you*?" Rage painted her cheeks bright red. "Are you deliberately trying to be cruel, or are you just that fucking clueless?"

"You played along so well with me before. It was us versus them. We were a team…a partnership."

"So you could free us!"

"Yes, well..." I had nothing else to say on that matter. "I can't describe how it felt to be connected to someone after being so alone. To have you. To hear you defend me and have you comfort me. I-I was more drunk on the fact that you were willing to trust me than I was fucking you the first time."

She sucked in a thin breath.

"That's not to say I didn't lose myself the moment I sank inside you. Jesus Christ, the moment I entered you, my body became yours. I know you felt it was different between us. I *know* you did." My voice turned dark. "You came in the shower this morning. You came so damn hard I can still feel you squeezing me. You gave me no choice but to shatter with you. So how do you explain that if you aren't as aware of me as I am of you?"

Her chin tipped haughtily. "Why? Does it bother you that you can't own my pleasure the way you thought you did? That you aren't the master of my body just because you leashed me?"

"No, it bothers me that you're not being honest."

"Like you are?"

"Yes," I snapped. "I will never hide myself from you. I will never keep things from you, and that's why I'm—"

"Tell me, if you're feeling so chatty all of a sudden..." She balled her hands. "If Victor tells you to cut off one of my fingers or my ear or even a hand…will you?"

"What? No, of course not." I scowled. "Why would I rob your body of its parts when it's your body that I want to rule?"

"Other Masters do. Or are you deliberately ignoring the fact that some jewels are missing pieces? Do you honestly not care that you're abusing the very same people you promised to save?"

"I've accepted their place, just like I've accepted mine. And yes, I'm aware. I noticed the other morning. But I'm not like that."

"But you want to hurt me?"

"I do."

"Then don't you see the hypocrisy? You say you're not into butchering me, but you're okay with people who are? There's a word for that, you know…complacency. Complacency is just as bad as the one committing the sin."

"I think I preferred you asleep. Least your tongue was quiet."

"You could just cut it out." She shrugged as if she truly didn't give a damn. "Ensure I'm forever your meek little *silent* slave."

"Tempting." I laughed under my breath.

She gasped. "You're a mess, Henri. You think you're free? You're not. I truly do think you're giving me your truth, but in reality, you have no *idea* what that truth is. You're happy to turn a blind eye to what others do if you get what you want." She shook her head with all the gravity of a judge. "And that doesn't just make you monstrous. It makes you *inhuman*."

I stiffened. "I'm human, little nightmare. And…just because I don't agree with some of what goes on here doesn't mean I have to partake." I shrugged and gave her another truth. "You heard my brother. He'll kill me if I ever leave this place. I've made my bed, and I'm happy to lie in it. Just like I'm happy to lie in it with you."

She rubbed her brows as if I gave her a headache. "Tell me…if Victor offered you another cross to strap me to and another blade to cut me with right now…would you do it?"

"Another question you already know the answer to. Yes," I said with no hesitation. "Yes. A thousand times yes for a thousand bleeding droplets."

"So…knowing that you want that, knowing that you *need* that, how the hell can you sit there and talk about love and marriage and—"

"I can because I feel both. Light and dark. Good and bad. I want to own you. So fucking badly. I want to tell you to crawl to me, bow to me, give me access to everything you are. I have depraved and perverted urges. And yes, I will hurt you, as often as I damn well feel like, but I will ensure no one else lays a finger on you. I will protect you…if you play along with me again. If you—"

"Pretend I'm your wife?"

"No, just…I don't know. Pretend—"

"That I enjoy it? That I'm turned on by you whipping and demeaning me?"

"No, I—"

"Do you expect me to kneel at your feet in worship instead of contempt?"

"*Bon Dieu, ferme-la seconde.*" (Christ, shut up for a second.)

I shot a look at Victor heading in our direction.

So close.

Too close.

Hurry.

Leaning forward, I clamped my hands together. "Having you play along with me when you thought I was a cop and my every touch would get you free was one of the best experiences of my life, but…I was also frustrated. The fact that you submitted? That you restrained your natural instincts to fight? I…I appreciated it but also hated it."

Our eyes met in a collision of sparks.

She curled her upper lip. "You told me not to fight because you'd snap."

"And you fought anyway."

"And you snapped spectacularly."

We glared at each other.

Finally, she asked as quietly as a raindrop, "What are you saying? What the hell do you want from me?"

Victor waved, striding closer and closer.

I waved back before fisting the leash and dragging her into the cage of my spread thighs.

She fell into me.

I caught her.

I held her cheeks and whispered deep in her ear, "Fight me, Ilyana

Sharma. Go to war with me. Make me earn your blood, your screams, your pain. Play monsters with me. Play house with me. Play in fucking hell with me. Cry for me when I have you bound and bleeding, and then accept my worship when it's over. Let me punish you *and* idolize you. I don't just want your fear, I want your lust too. I want your mind, your heart, your soul, and I don't care that I can't buy them. I'll earn them…one delicious bruise at a time."

She struggled to get away.

I held her tight.

Tracing my thumbs over her cheekbones, I stared into her stunning eyes. "Play with me, little nightmare, because my greatest weakness is *you*, and the day you understand that is the day our true games begin."

Chapter Eleven

Ily

HENRI'S WORDS SPUN AROUND AND around in my head.

"My greatest weakness is you, and the day you understand that is the day our true games begin."

The gardens swirled.

The pond shimmered.

Talking to him was like trying to write the rulebook on psychological warfare.

Trying to make him see that despite his perversions, he still had a soul only fell on deaf ears. My attempt at making him see he wasn't like the others flew right over his head.

Can it be true?

Could he honestly be that clueless where feelings were concerned? Was he so denied affection and togetherness that he truly had no idea how to care for someone, how to love?

Good grief, that was terrifying, horrifying…the most alarming thing he could've said.

In trying to understand him, I'd found out the worst.

How could you manipulate someone who saw nothing wrong with hurting a girl they admitted they had feelings for? How the hell could he speak about monogamy in the same breath as wanting to hurt me?

I hated the word crazy after hearing it slung around so often about Krish, but…wow…*I genuinely think he's truly crazy.*

Which meant I was in even more danger than I'd feared because crazy was unpredictable and capricious and—

"Finally!" Victor's obnoxiously smooth French accent sailed from behind me. "I was beginning to think you'd died in your room."

Letting me go, Henri stood politely. Pointing at a spare lounger, he grinned. "Morning. Or rather, afternoon."

"Almost evening from where I'm standing." Victor chuckled, sitting primly on the spare white-and-aqua-striped lounger. His black shorts and charcoal polo made him look like a soul-sucking parasite. His eyes flickered to me, collared, leashed, gagging on rage and fear.

"*Bonjour*, Ilyana. My, my, what a pretty name." His voice tightened just a little. "Tell me, is that Arabic for sun ray and shining light?"

I went deathly, horribly still. "How…how do you know that?"

"I told you, I like to know everything I can about my jewels. I researched you, and even though your surname is Indian, your first name is not. It's a bit of a conundrum and one I'd like to understand."

Flashes of memories—told to me via my adoptive mother's bedtime stories.

The note on my baby blanket.

The scribbled message from my birth mother, read by my highly sensitive brother and incorrectly deciphered, which landed me with a name that dwelled every day in my light-hazel eyes.

I would never give up that priceless moment.

Ever.

An even worse thought came.

He'd researched me.

He'd heard me mention the hospital where my father worked.

Krish—

Good God, Il…what have you done?

I yanked the leash out of Henri's hand and went to swoop to my feet. Only, Henri clamped his large hand on my shoulder, keeping me kneeling.

I struggled, but his fingers bit deep and painful.

Hating him, I hissed at Victor, "You didn't hurt my family, did you? Don't hurt them. Don't—" My voice ended in a choke.

Fuck, how could I be so *stupid* to give out my name, even on the microscopic chance that Henri's brother might find me? I might've condemned them to thugs going around and murdering them.

"Ily, quiet." Henri squeezed my shoulder.

"Don't touch me!" I scratched my nails over his wrist, desperate to fight. "Let me go. God, *please* let me go. I have to go back to him. He'll be so worried. So scared."

"Who will?" His voice darkened.

"Her brother," Victor said without a ruffle. "He's autistic. Very selective with who he speaks to apparently. Hasn't spoken a word since she went to Paris."

"Leave them the hell alone!" I hurled myself toward him.

Henri dragged me back. Hooking his fingers into my collar, he pressed me against his legs. "Calm down."

"Tell him not to hurt them."

"Sweetling, do I look like the type of man who goes around murdering innocent people?"

I coughed.

I literally couldn't breathe correctly.

"Is that a trick question?" I wanted to rub my eyes and wash my ears out. "You're a trafficking psychopath."

"No, no, no, my pet, I'm a trafficking *connoisseur.*" Glancing at the large pond-pool, watching a flittering emerald dragonfly, he said, "Besides, I have no need for your family. As long as you keep behaving like a good little jewel, I promise I won't disrupt your loved ones' lives any more than it already has been by losing you."

Tears.

Hot, *agonising* tears.

I wanted to cry.

To wail.

But I swallowed them back.

I would never, ever, not a single droplet, ever, *ever* cry again.

I'd made the vow in the shower. I reaffirmed it now.

Never.

No matter what they did to me.

No matter how bad it got.

Henri would never drink my sorrow again because one day, *I* would be the one drinking *his* tears. I would find a way to make a grown man weep.

No, not just weep, *sob.*

And then I would walk away and leave him in the same pieces he'd left me.

Pinning my attention on Victor, I couldn't control my sick, shaking rage.

Without a word, I raised my hand and gave him the finger.

He laughed, then clucked his tongue at Henri. "Tell me, how goes the obedience training? Not that well, by the looks of things. Remember the twelve levels of ownership?"

"I haven't forgotten," Henri muttered, his fingers bruising my shoulder. "Something about ownership over her body, mind, pleasure, senses, impulses…"

"Submission, liberation, life, and soul." Victor cupped his hands between spread legs. "It's a long process but very rewarding when you feel every layer break." Cocking his chin at me, he added, "You need to start on her lessons. I expect you to keep her in-line. I won't have her disrupting my other jewels. Already, Peter has behaved much better since she's been missing from the stable for a few days."

My ribcage tightened, a wishbone stabbed into my heart. I wanted to ask about the others. Peter and Citra, Corine and Kirk. Sleep might have nullified everything, but now everything was far too sharp and real.

I want to see them.

"I have every intention of keeping her disciplined, Vic." Henri's grey gaze narrowed. "As long as you grant my request that she's mine and only mine."

Victor scowled. "Still making demands?"

"Still wanting what rightfully belongs to me." He gathered my hair, letting the strands spill through his fingers. "We both know I saw her first. I think that accounts for something. After all, I'm here for life…if you'll have me."

Relaxing with a broad grin, Victor nodded. "I must admit, I've greatly enjoyed having you here so far. From the game of intrigue, the mystery of who you truly were, to the very enjoyable conversation with your brother." He laughed. "I can't tell you how much it tickles me that I have a Mercer in my home. And not just any Mercer but brother to the man who's been a pain in my ass for decades."

"I'm glad I turned out to be so entertaining."

Victor sobered up. "Three days, *mon ami.* I've seen some of my guests crash for a couple of days—tiredness always seems to spring the hardest when we take off our masks—but three? Are you okay?" His eyes turned sly and seeking. "No regrets? No wishing you could leave and run home to your little family?"

Henri shuddered. "He isn't my family." Cupping my shoulder, he stroked his thumb in that mocking Morse code, soft and seducing, sending prickles down my back. "Ily is now my family. You are now my family."

"In that case…this is the time to clear up the last remaining rules so we can begin fresh and enjoy ourselves, *oui*?"

"*Oui.*" Henri nodded. "I appreciate the time you gave us to rest and recuperate, but I'm ready to play."

"Excellent." Rubbing his hands together, Victor sucked in a breath. "My first question is…can your brother access the funds he gave you? Can he claw back what he deposited, or is that cash locked in your account?"

Henri flicked me a look. "It's in my name. I gave him access to view the balance through an email statement but nothing else. Unless he commits forgery, it's mine."

"Perfect. In that case, I'm not in any rush for you to transfer the balance to me. Let's agree that the day of your initiation is the day you pay me, fair?"

"My initiation?"

"You're on probation. I'm open to giving you a lifetime membership and surprisingly amenable to the thought of you being a long-term guest. I'm aware if I sent you away, Q would kill you, so…for now, you have my blessing to stay indefinitely."

Henri tipped his chin in respect. "Thank you—"

"And…" Victor shot me a look. "Seeing as you're rather attached to your jewel, I'll agree to extend your exclusivity for the foreseeable future. I've already talked to the other guests, and despite their misgivings, none of them have given me the funds that you will for the privilege, so…you're a unique case, and I'm open to allowing certain advantages."

Henri sat taller. "That's—"

"Just one teeny tiny thing." Victor held up his finger. "When the day comes that I want a taste. When I give the request to fuck her…you will not put up a fight. Not a single fucking word. Do you hear me?"

His words were like a bucket of icy slush.

My shoulders curled.

True horror soaked into my blood, dirty and damned.

I tried to be grateful that no one else would lay a finger on me.

But knowing I'd one day be Victor's?

I wanted to be sick.

Violently, disgustingly sick.

Gritting his teeth, Henri studied me.

His hands flexed. His nostrils flared. He looked positively unhinged.

But finally…he nodded. "If that's the price to keep her for my own, then…I accept."

"*Merveilleux.*" (Marvelous.) Victor stood and swiped his palms on his shorts. "Now we're both on the same page…is there anything you need? Clothing preferences? Medications? Things that you'll miss from the outside world?"

Henri scratched his five o'clock shadow. "Eh…I think I'm good. Actually? You know what? A laptop would be appreciated."

"A laptop?" Victor's brows furrowed. "You know you can't access the internet, no matter how much you gain my trust. You could be my own flesh and blood son, and I wouldn't allow you a phone or social accounts."

Henri stood and adjusted himself. "Not for that. To be honest, I don't miss going online at all. It's a haven to be away from the moaning and the mess, but what I am missing is writing."

"Ah, yes." Victor smirked. "The book you were penning."

"Seems I'll have spare time now. I won't have to work at menial jobs to pay my bills, and well…" He chuckled. "I can only do so much fucking in one day."

Victor grinned, glancing down at Henri's straining boxers. "Tell me, *mon ami.* Have you fucked your jewel today? I've been slack looking at the cameras."

"Once. In the shower." He raked a hand over his face. "I can't stop thinking about it."

"Oh?"

Henri glanced at me.

I glowered back.

"I swear stealing something she didn't want to give me is the best kind of aphrodisiac. I keep thinking that each time I take her is the best fuck of my life, only for it to pale each and every time." He sighed happily. "And when she switched beneath me this morning? When she rocked back and impaled herself on my cock? When I felt her fucking fist me with an orgasm that choked my own release right out of me? Jesus Christ."

I gagged on self-hatred.

Good grief, Ily.

My idiotic plan of claiming sex as my own method of survival seemed to have already backfired in my damn face.

I'd chosen to use him like he used me.

I'd stolen back my power.

Denied him the chance to rule me.

Switched suffering into pleasure and despair into desire and…

I hadn't stopped to think how Henri would react.

How he'd think I *wanted* him.

How I'd just tangled us together in far worse depravity.

My heart jumped on the self-hatred wagon, reminding me that for all his previous comments about playing along in a farce of marriage and monsters, I'd had similar thoughts. I'd compared our three nights of slumber to a strange, unconsummated honeymoon.

Well, we damn well consummated it this morning, and judging by the way Henri stared at me, it was only a matter of time before he had me on my knees again.

"Sounds as if you have a little nymph on your hands. Lucky you."

Victor winked, moving around the lounger and placing his hands on the back of it. "What's the book about?"

"What are all books about?" Henri shrugged with a strange kind of wince. "Pain."

Victor marinated in that answer before asking softly, "Her pain or yours?"

"More like the pain we'll inflict on each other."

He nodded as if he liked that answer. "Fine. I'll get you a laptop. One with writing software but no Wi-Fi chip. Anything else?"

Henri looked at me, his eyes disturbingly direct as if he could see all my secrets. "Maybe a few clothes for her? A robe that isn't see-through? Some underwear so other guests aren't tempted by what is mine?"

Victor snickered and shook his head. "Even now you confound me."

Henri drew back. "I *confound* you?"

"You look at her as if she's a pretty doll that you'll do anything not to break, but I know the moment you hold a knife in your hands, you'll bleed her."

"So?"

"So…I haven't met many Masters who are so willing to be both soft and harsh."

"Isn't that where the fun lies? The hurting and the healing?"

"It's definitely the way to break them into unsalvageable pieces." He smiled dotingly at me. "If you keep spouting feelings at her, only to whip and fuck her like a beast, she'll be so confused and lost, she'll be yours before the month is through."

Henri paused for a horribly long moment before licking his bottom lip. "In that case, I'll make her so lost that she's only found when she's with me."

"Said like a true fucking author." Victor strangled the back of the lounger before pushing off and shoving his hands into his short pockets. "Dinner is at seven. Another show will be provided, and the treasure hunt I had Peter arrange was postponed until you could participate. You're welcome to join us or…I believe a few of my guests have arranged a friendly competition in the billiard room."

"Competition? What sort of competition?" Henri asked.

"Come and you'll find out." Victor smirked. "It's fun. Bring Ilyana. She can play too." Backing up, he dropped his eyes to Henri's crotch. "A word of advice from a seasoned Master to a new one? If you're hard, make her work. Never give up a good erection, *mon ami.* Besides, she's owed some chastisement for her little outburst. You can't let infractions like that go."

Henri shivered and fisted his hard length. "I appreciate the advice."

"Have fun, you two." Victor blew me a kiss. "Break her in for both of us, Mercer. I want her well and truly tamed by the time I have a ride."

A flush of absolute hatred made my mouth twist into a snarl.

Victor didn't notice.

Walking away, whistling like an asshole, he left Henri and me alone again.

Henri didn't move until Victor strolled out of listening distance. For a second, my heart leapt with hope that he was going to whisper this was all a massive, massive mistake. That there was still a script, still a stage, and a curtain, and a hidden director.

But as he sat down on the lounger and threw me a lazy smile, that hope died.

Once and for all.

In a blaze of burning cinders.

His fingers strayed to his boxers.

He fondled himself through the black material.

And then, with clenched teeth and elegant, monstrous hands, he shifted his hips, removed his underwear, and tossed them onto the grass.

Our eyes met.

My heart thundered.

For all my hatred, my body grew hot and heavy.

It wasn't fair that he looked like a demigod on the outside and was a deviant on the inside. The muscles, the shadows, the piercing silver-shadow eyes.

Biting his bottom lip, he fisted himself and dragged his gaze down my t-shirt-clad body.

"*Enlève-le.*" (Take it off.) Pressing his thumb onto his crown, he cocked his head as if daring me to refuse.

Bare.

Dressed.

Made no difference.

Rising on my knees, I swiped the hem up and over my head, cursing the thick cuffs as they caught on the sleeves.

His eyes immediately landed on my breasts. "Christ, you're gorgeous."

A compliment.

A worship.

It made me feel seedy, dirty, and stained by every touch he'd given and every word he'd used to control me.

He squeezed himself. "*Rampez plus près.*" (Crawl closer.)

"Fuck you."

"I intend to fuck *you*. But only once you've sucked me."

"I'd rather bite."

He moved too fast, inhumanly fast.

One moment, he sat on the lounger with legs indecently spread. The next, he grabbed my hips, tossed me onto my hands and knees, and tipped me forward. "I'm warning you now, little nightmare. If I feel the merest graze of your sharp little teeth, I will hit you so hard you'll end up in the moat outside the walls."

"Do it," I snarled. "Beat me so we can both stop pretending you're any better than the other bastards. Prove to me that every sentence out of your mouth is bullshit."

He stiffened.

I tried to fight his hold. "Do it. Go on. I dare you!"

He just knocked my wrists out from under me and pressed my cheek to the grass.

I hated how effortlessly he manhandled me.

I hated the dynamics of weak and strong, slave and Master.

"I curse you," I hissed. "I curse you with every misfortune imaginable."

He paused as if staring at the wand inked onto my back. "You know…I believe you've already cursed me."

"Free me and the other jewels, and I'll uncurse you…how about that?"

He exhaled heavily. "I'm sorry, but no. I'm done trying to be a hero."

"I hate you," I whispered with rancid-dripping passion.

"Don't be so sure." His fingers dipped between my legs, bold and brutal.

I cried out as he sank two inside me.

"Wet." He groaned. "Want to tell me again that you hate me?"

"I hope you burn in hell." I squirmed as his fingers hooked on that traitorous little spot.

"If I'm burning, you're burning with me." He bent and bit my hip. "Anything else to say?"

"Let me go, you bastard."

"Nope, never letting you go again. Anything else?"

"Yes." I looked back at him, a nasty recipe of despair and helplessness making me far crueller than I'd ever been. "No one loves you because you're utterly unlovable. You deserve to be alone and—"

Instant regret.

Hollowing remorse.

Henri looked as if I'd poured acid into his heart.

I froze, completely shocked at how far I'd fallen.

How terrible I'd become.

God, if Krish could see me…he'd be so disappointed, so sad.

"Henri, I—" I clawed the grass. I gagged on apologies. Hating that I wanted to give him a thousand, all while he owed me so many in return.

"It's fine." He huffed, removing his fingers from inside me. "I deserved that. And you're right." His voice turned stark and emotionless. "Loneliness is my cross to bear because I'm not worthy of anything else. You don't have to curse me with it. I already suffer. Thank you *so* fucking much for reminding me."

Arctic darkness wafted from him as he palmed my ass. "This is my fault. I've been too soft on you. I've let you think you have a say in what I will and will not do. But the truth is, you've just reminded me that I can't be two men at once. I asked you to play along with me. To be mine so I can be yours. But…I see now that only *you* can make that choice. I can't make it for you, no matter how much I beg. And so…here is a little lesson."

Pressing his large palm on my ass, he squeezed me fondly. "You need to decide, little nightmare. A decision that will ensure your life here will be heaven or hell."

I didn't want to ask, but the words spilled anyway. "What decision?"

"The decision to play along with me as my wonderfully obedient wife or…be forced to submit as my badly broken slave."

My heart fluttered. "You wouldn't."

"Wouldn't I?"

The way he said it.

No warmth of before.

No connection.

He'd killed our bond the moment he'd bled me in Victor's massacred menagerie.

"Henri…don't."

"Ten strikes." His hand suddenly left my ass, rising above his head. "Five to kickstart your deliberation and five to punish you for ever thinking you could manipulate me. Once you've screamed and your skin is bright red, you will get on your knees and blow me. If you satisfy me, I'll grant you one request. I'll repay you for your obedience, and you'll learn it isn't so bad to belong to me. If you play with me, I'll play with you. We can have more than what the others have. We can have sex, but we can also have closeness, and if I'm perfectly fucking honest—which I always stupidly am with you—that's the part I want the most. I want to feel connected to you while I hurt you. I want to adore you while I heal you. But if you deny me that closeness, then…maybe you're right. Maybe my suggestion of monogamy is ridiculous, and I should just revoke my exclusivity over you and give you to the others."

Before I could reply.

Before I could tell him that he terrified me and not just because of the harm he caused my body—

He struck.

I yelped as he planted a bruising hand on the small of my back to keep me in place, then spanked me hard.

So hard.

Far harder than he spanked me with the book in the library.

That'd been for show.

This was for him.

Only for him.

"Henri—" I scratched at the grass as he struck me again. "*Ahhh*!" Stinging pain. Five fingers of sting. "Stop it. I get your point. Stop—"

A third swat.

Agony layering upon agony.

A fourth, fifth, sixth in quick succession.

Agony, *agony*, and…an awful kind of thrill.

Seven.

I screamed.

I couldn't help it.

I cried out as fire blazed, feeding through my throbbing flesh.

"Henri!" I clawed and mewled, trying so damn hard to get away. But he kept me wedged on the grass, my back locked in place, my hips exactly where he wanted them.

"Christ, you look incredible with my mark on you."

Eight.

I gasped.

Grunted.

My insides trembled.

Clit ached.

Nine.

"It's like a brand. My own brand. A bright red stamp that you belong to me."

I groaned and moaned, grass sticking to my lips and sweaty skin.
Every cell forsook me, turning hot and heavy.

But I didn't cry.

Didn't even have the urge.

I choked back the fiery flush.

I grasped onto merciless revenge.

And when the final strike landed, and Henri stumbled back to the lounger…

As he spread his legs, and dragged me between them…

As he stroked my cheek like he loved me then positioned me like his whore…

I knew exactly what I would do.

I gathered all the wrongness, all the lewdness and…used it to break him.

He wanted to play Master and slave?

Fine.

Let's play.

Sucking in a deep breath, taming my out-of-control panting, I wrapped my fingers around the thick base of him.

I looked up.

His gaze flared with mistrust.

His hand hovered as if to grab my wrist.

I squeezed—

"*Fuck.*" His voice mimicked a thunderstorm. "Behave, little nightmare. Suck my cock like a good little jewel—without teeth—swallow every drop that I feed you, and then…I'll reward you."

His voice stroked the greed in my blood.

I clenched on nothing and hot, hot need.

My fingers tightened around his shaft.

"Ily…" He shuddered, wary of my willingness. "Be nice."

"Oh, I'll be nice," I whispered. "So very, *very* nice."

His cock twitched in my palm, eager and hard.

He was vulnerable—pretty much as defenceless as a man could get, yet…it was his gaze that ensnared me.

Cold but unguarded.

Distrustful but hopeful.

Angry and brutal and full of sadistic power but beneath all of that…lonely.

Even now.

Lonely.

I wasn't his greatest weakness.

It was that.

The two L words.

Love and loneliness.

Two intangible, important things that had the power to destroy him…if only I knew how to wield them.

"Ily…" he breathed as I dropped my lips to his crown. He smelled of sparkling fresh water from his swim and earthy with lust.

I let that lust fill me with newfound hope.

I tucked away the knowledge of what my name truly meant and what he said to me each time he used it.

He wanted a wife who could patch up that loneliness and make him whole?

Well then…

My mouth enveloped his cock.

He jerked as if I'd electrified him.

His hands came up to gather my hair, fisting it in a ponytail so he could watch.

My scalp tingled.

My ass stung.

One delivered with cruelty, the other with caresses.

He was a paradox.

An enigma.

I swallowed him as deep as I could manage.

I'd never liked giving blowjobs.

Even when Samuel and I were happy, it'd been something I did for him, not for me.

But this?

As Henri jolted and groaned, utterly transfixed as my head bobbed up and down and my hand corkscrewed around his length, I felt the first flutterings of power.

True power.

Raw, feminine power.

I could kill him like this.

Could slice a vein and bleed him out.

Cut off his balls and maim him.

I did none of those things.

I became his because, in return, he became *mine.*

I didn't need him.

Not the way he needed me.

And that was my first weapon.

A weapon so wicked, it made me tremble to use it.

"Fuck," he hissed as I tongued his slit. "*Fuck.*"

A sharp, salty droplet coated my lips; I looked up.

His eyes glowed sterling as he gave me every exposed, despairing piece of himself.

I increased my pace, worshipping him with my mouth.

My core clenched.

My nipples pebbled.

Quakes of sexual hunger pulsed through me, and…I made a different choice.

He'd been good once.

We were all inherently good beneath a lifetime of misery and mayhem.

His aggressiveness came from fear of loss, his possessiveness from fear of loneliness.

Therefore, I would give him the things he treasured.

I would be everything he ever wanted without giving him what he needed.

And then…one day, he would wake and see just how far he'd tumbled.

And when that day arrived, he'd save us.

If only to save himself.

Sucking hard, my jaw ached as I worked and licked him. Sucked and devoured him. His skin was so soft, his hardness twitching on my tongue.

His thighs turned to marble around me.

His hands turned to stone in my hair.

I swallowed him down and hummed in the back of my throat.

"Jesus Christ—" His head tipped back. His eyes snapped closed.

He gave me everything.

I took it all.

Dropping my hand between his legs, I rolled his balls between my fingers.

His reaction was instantaneous.

His growl echoed over the pond, scattering dragonflies. "Hell yes. Just like that. *Fuck*, you're good at sucking my cock."

His praise soothed the pain he'd given me but didn't earn my forgiveness.

How strange that Sam said I was terrible in bed, yet Henri acted as if I was his ultimate fantasy.

I hated that ego made me try harder.

Pride made me fall into ruin as I cut free the threads inside me and threw myself into war.

I wanted him to break.

I wanted to be the one to destroy him.

I sucked harder.

I fisted tighter.

"Goddammit—" His voice cracked. "Your mouth…*shit*—"

I did most things on instinct, stroking him, caressing him, finding his most sensitive spots. I studied him, stripped him, stole everything.

My hand dipped lower, burrowing into the dark heat between his legs.

He twitched and groaned.

I did it again.

A flush of salt on my tongue.

Tightening my fist around his iron length, I sucked and pressed three fingers right on the ridged line tracing from his balls to his rear.

Neither of us was ready for his reaction.

Clamping both hands on my head, he surged into my mouth. "Fucking hell. *Yes.* Christ, yes. Take it. Suck me—"

I rubbed him.

He lost all power of conversation.

His body quaked.

His cock pulsed.

His skin became an inferno.

"*Merde*—" He thrust again and again, and…I let him.

I pressed harder and harder against that ridged little spot.

"Goddamn, you're good at that." He clawed his way back to sanity. "Enough. Wait. Too soon. I don't…" He scrambled for self-control, trying to push me away.

I sank all my weight over him, choking on his hardness.

I jerked him off with my right and pressed up with my left.

He didn't just explode, he detonated.

"*Fuck, FUCK*!"

Ribbons of cum shot into my mouth.

The ridged line beneath my fingers pulsed with every splash.

"Fucking…ah, stop, don't—" On and on, thick and salty, he shuddered through his orgasm. Halfway through his shattering, he stopped fighting and gave in.

His voice became a guttural growl.

His fingers buried deeper in my hair.

Thrusting into my mouth, he fed me every spurting inch. "You want it so bad, you dirty, dirty girl? Then open goddamn wide."

I let him empty into me.

Let him shudder with harsh aftershocks.

I drank every drop.

I suffered through disgraceful yearning.

And only once he sucked in a big gasp did I sit back on my heels and hiss as pain and shame and every other abhorrent emotion swamped me.

Ever so slowly, he opened his eyes.

For a second, it seemed as if he couldn't focus, but then he blinked, and anger painted him. "What the hell was that?"

Hiding my wince, I stood and grabbed my t-shirt.

Slipping back into it, I unclipped the stupid, awful leash dangling unforgotten on my collar and tossed it into his bare lap. The loop landed around his erection like a ring toss. "You told me to satisfy you, so…I did." I licked my lips, cursing the earthy taste of him. "Or did I misjudge your reaction? Are you not satisfied?"

"Am I *satisfied*?" He rubbed his face with one hand then threw the leash onto the ground. "I'm wrung fucking dry."

I curtsied with a mocking smile. "Then you're welcome."

He stood too, towering over me. "What are you doing?"

I canted my head innocently. "I'm only doing what you told me to do."

"I don't remember telling you to destroy me with the best blowjob of my life."

I ignored the nonsensical flash of jealousy at the thought of him having other blowjobs.

By who? Did he like them—

Oh my God, who cares?

Not you.

Definitely not you.

With my ass blazing with his ten-spanked handprint, I raised my chin. "Is that everything, *Master H*?"

"Don't." He swiped his boxers from the grass and slipped them on. Gathering the rest of his clothes and the leash, his eyes darkened. "Don't be a bitch."

"Me?" I pointed at myself. "I think you're confusing me with someone else. I'm your obedient little wife, remember?" I licked my lips, deliberately obscene. "I sucked your cock. I drank your cum. You promised me a favour in return."

He held himself exquisitely still. "What do you want?"

To get away from you.

To get away from the truth.

To get away from myself.

"To see the other jewels."

He sighed heavily. "Can you be trusted around him?"

I knew who he meant.

And I didn't need to use jealousy to make him mine. "I like Peter. Very much."

His eyes narrowed into predator points.

"But I like him how I would like a friend…a brother."

"He kissed you."

"Platonically." I sniffed. "He was offering me comfort, that's all."

"If he does it again, I'll be digging his grave."

"He's protecting me."

"*I'm* protecting you."

"Is that what you call it?" I wrinkled my nose. "Hate to tell you, Henri, but what you just did to me felt anything but safe and protective."

"What *I* did to you?" He scoffed. "You're the one who sucked out my damn soul."

"And you're the one who spanked me!"

His gaze dropped to his palm as if reliving his abuse. Finally, he looked up and snapped, "If he touches you again, I'll—"

"He won't."

He studied me as if he didn't believe me.

Finally, he nodded and stepped away. "Fine. You have two hours. Spend it in the jewel quarters. Do whatever you want. But I expect you at my feet for dinner."

He stalked away before I could bow and simper.

I followed him, studying the tension in his shoulders. The jagged rhythm of his step.

He didn't look like a man who'd just come.

He looked like a man conflicted. Confused. Confounded.

And I hated, positively *hated*, that I knew *exactly* how he felt.

As I walked, the thoughts I'd flatly ignored came bounding into my mind.

I bit my bottom lip as I wedged a hand on my lower belly and cursed him.

Cursed the heat between my legs.

The wetness smearing my inner thighs.

And the terrible, awful knowledge that I hadn't just felt pain when he'd spanked me.

Oh no.

That would've been far too easy.

Far too justified and proper.

If only his hand had just delivered demeaning, dementing pain.

If only his cum on my tongue didn't grant me power as well as punishment.

If only I wasn't going as crazy as him.

If only.

If only.

If only my entire body didn't ache for him to finish what his spanking started.

If only I was numb inside, dead inside, protected from his mind games and confessions.

If only I didn't feel lust.

Horrendous, horrifying *lust.*

I'd chosen to claim my sexuality so Henri couldn't steal it.

I'd vowed to break him before he broke me.

But in return…I'd thrown myself into purgatory.

And ensured, in one fell swoop, that we'd become as fatally sick as each other.

Chapter Twelve

Henri

I GLANCED AT ILY KNEELING obediently by my feet.

Her hair shone like midnight cobalt, and her black diamante bra and G-string made her look far too sultry. Dark red lines marked where I'd cut her, healing and visible now she'd removed the band-aids.

Ten minutes she'd been kneeling, exquisitely beautiful and silent on the warm oak floor. Ten fucking minutes and she'd not once made eye contact with me.

Another crack of stone-shaking thunder crashed through the ballroom. A few jewels hunched where they kneeled by their respective Masters. Even a few men flinched, then chuckled at their reaction.

Rain pummelled against the huge floor-to-ceiling windows like liquid bullets intent on mowing through the dining crowd.

The storm had arrived with dark vengeance as the sun set, rumbling distantly on the horizon as I'd sat in the library and chosen a stack of books to take back to my room. By the time I'd returned to my chamber and showered away any trace of Ily's saliva and remnants of my soul she'd devoured, the entire island quaked.

Lightning forked, and the air crackled with electricity, followed a few seconds later by its angry lover with a crash of cymbals that made my bones ring.

I glowered at Ily again.

She didn't twitch like the others. Her eyes remained locked on the legs of the table, her hands loosely joined in her lap.

What had she done all afternoon?

What had she said to the others?

Had Peter touched her? Talked to her?

My hands balled.

I'd stayed busy after escorting Ily to the slave quarters. I'd deliberately distracted myself with the written word, so I didn't march back and demand her company.

The fact that I actually missed her annoyed me.

The fact that I couldn't control my jealousy fucked me right off.

While she was with me, all those feelings of being alone were blessedly deleted, but the moment she was gone…*merde.*

I raked a hand over my face as a demure staff member delivered a silver-ringed plate full of perfectly roasted chicken, salad, and herb-roasted potatoes.

I looked up and smiled. "Thank you."

She startled as if she'd never been spoken to before. Her pretty hazel eyes reminded me of Ily's, just darker and less golden. With a bow, she scurried away like a terrified mouse.

"I appreciate your attempts at being cordial and polite, Henri, but you don't have to do that." Victor appeared from the candle-shrouded darkness. No lights in the ballroom. Just massive chandeliers and sconces all flickering with wax-dripping candles.

I didn't know if he was going for an ancient kind of atmosphere or if the power had cut out thanks to the storm. Either way, the soft illumination painted everyone in a romantic, almost dreamy light.

A random thought popped into my head. "Do your guests play with your staff too, Vic? Or are they off limits?"

Ily sucked in a breath.

Victor laughed as he settled himself in the chair beside me. "Why? Is your eye wandering already?"

"No." I ran my fingers over Ily's thick hair. "Merely wondering how you keep an estate like this running if everyone working in it is fair game."

Victor nodded and waited for a stunning dark-haired, blue-eyed jewel to kneel beside him. Her collar caught the candlelight, dancing tiny flames over her face while the black teddy she wore poured like darkness over her curvy frame. "I see you're already taking an interest in the bigger picture."

I couldn't read him. "Am I allowed to know, or are the secrets of how you run this place forbidden?"

"Forbidden? No, not at all." He grinned. "It's nice to have someone appreciate the level of coordination that goes into forming a utopia like this. My other guests come for a few days and leave. They don't stop to think about how food is delivered and who changes their sheets and towels."

Patting my knee, he glanced around the half-full ballroom, complete with Masters, jewels, and staff. "I'm happy to tell you whatever you wish to know. After all, like you said, you have nowhere else to go. You should know how your new home operates. But allow me to give you a word of advice. If you feel like dabbling with someone who isn't a jewel, you must ask permission first. My staff—cleaners, cooks, waiters, gardeners—are all selected and stolen like my other gems—but…they have been given a different purpose. They sleep in a different area of Joyero and are subject to different rules."

"So they're exempt from fucking?"

"Unless a Master makes a request for one of them to switch roles, then yes. I need them to keep this place clean and tidy. They can't do that on their backs."

Ily wrinkled her nose but wisely stayed silent.

My eyes drifted to the jewel Victor had taken over the table on the first night.

He caught me looking and cupped her chin. "Isn't she something? One day, when you're no longer indulging in your little crush, you can taste her if you wish. I'm selective of who gets to borrow her, but for you…I'll make an exception." He ran a thumb over her bottom lip.

She didn't react, keeping her eyelashes low, shielding her eyes.

"What's her name?" I asked, appreciating her beauty but feeling no kick, no lust. I glanced back at Ily only to be sucker-punched in the goddamn stomach with both desire and connection.

The loneliness I'd felt this afternoon was quiet now she was near.

And I honestly didn't know how to deal with that.

"Rachel." Victor let his jewel go, snapping his fingers for another waiter to bring him a glass of the wine being circulated around the dining guests. "She's a chemist. Or was." He selected a glass from a tray offered by a demure server, then toasted me. "Now she's my personal favourite, and I find her sharp intelligence extraordinary."

"A chemist sounds interesting."

"She apparently used to work for the government. A top-secret project where an aerosol drug created uncontrollable seizures. It became an invisible weapon, you see. To be used in war."

I scowled. "What's the point in war if you're not actively involved in the fighting? It removes the gore and glory."

"Precisely." He nodded. "Tell me." He glanced at Ily, meek and strangely obedient by my feet. "How was the rest of your afternoon? I'm assuming you made her help you with your little 'problem'?"

My hand strayed to press against my cock. "I did."

"And?"

"And…she blew my brains out."

He laughed. "Excellent. I'm happy to hear you're both settling in so well."

A meal was placed in front of Victor; he didn't thank the girl who delivered it.

Stabbing a crispy potato, he shoved it into his mouth and clapped his hands.

Immediately, a spotlight beamed, soft and gold on the black-draped podium at the head of the ballroom. Unlike the olden days, where a quartet would play or a singer would croon, two jewels stepped into the light and bowed.

A crack of thunder boomed.

"Another show?" I leaned toward Victor. "Do you put porn on every night?"

"Most nights." He chewed and swallowed. "If you have any preferences, let me know. I'll ensure a show is designed for your certain tastes."

My stomach tightened as I dropped my eyes to Ily again.

The memory of sinking inside her when we'd been ordered to perform.

The savageness in which I'd taken her.

I wanted to do it again, only this time…I wouldn't rush it. I'd use the toys on offer. Maybe warm her up with a whip.

My hand stung from swatting her this afternoon.

I'd almost convinced myself that I'd come as hard as I had because of what I'd done to her before she sucked me. But…I had a horrible suspicion that the moment her tongue licked me and her hand dove indecently between my legs, I was fucking putty in her hands.

Where had she learned to blow like that?

And why did I hate that she was so good?

Who taught her?

Rage poured through me.

She gave her ex a birthday blowjob.

Jesus Christ, if she'd given him what she gave me, how did the cunt ever let her go?

My hands curled to kill him.

Knowing he'd touched what was mine.

Been *inside* what was mine.

It made me homicidal.

Not noticing my glower, Ily rose higher on her knees and looked toward the stage. No doubt trying to see if Peter was the lead star again. Her shoulders relaxed a little as she noticed the chosen boy, then tensed as she recognised the Viking-looking slave marching around in a tool belt and low-slung jeans.

She seemed as uninformed as I was, which didn't make sense as she'd spent two hours with the jewels.

Shredding some chicken with my fork, I bent down and offered it to her.

She turned to me with a gasp.

"Did you have a nice afternoon?" I asked softly, pressing the tines against her lips.

She opened just enough for me to place the chicken on her tongue.

My cock went rock fucking hard the moment she bit down.

Chewing, she shook her head. "No."

"No?"

She swallowed. "Everyone was still serving. I spent the afternoon alone." Something flickered in her eyes. Something that summoned an answering flicker inside my chest.

"You could've spent it with me."

"Thank God I didn't," she shot back. That little flicker again. A little smoulder. A shimmer of need.

Just like I was a fast learner of what got her off, I'd started cataloguing her tells.

Gathering another mouthful, this time a perfectly seasoned potato, I fed it to her and whispered, "You're frustrated, little nightmare."

"What?" She reared back, the potato fat in her cheek. "No, I—"

"Liar." Ignoring Victor's glance, I cupped her nape and pulled her into me. My mouth landed on her ear. "You made me come so hard this afternoon, I completely forgot to return the favour. You needed to shatter too. You still do. I smell it on you. I see it in your eyes."

"You're mad." She flinched and tried to pull away. Chewing the potato, she swallowed hard. "Get off me."

I only dragged her closer. "Did you get wet from me spanking you? Is that what's got you so hot and bothered? Why you're sitting there so quiet and still? You don't want to move because every twitch reminds you that you're needy and greedy and dying for me to spread you open and stick my tongue deep, *deep* inside you."

She jolted. A breathy little moan. "No. I mean…*hell no.* I hated you hitting me. I—"

"You were wet. I noticed your arousal before you hid it with your t-shirt."

"No, I—"

"Let's see, shall we?" Tossing my fork onto my plate with a clatter, I dragged her up by her elbows. The suddenness in which I scooped her from the floor and draped her on my knee ensured she didn't fight. But the moment I turned her to face away and spread her legs over my thighs, she stiffened into ice.

Victor smirked and fed a few mouthfuls to Rachel by his feet.

He didn't interfere, and the porno began at the top of the ballroom. The guy prowled toward the girl. She wore the scantiest sundress and clung to a dishtowel as if she were a meek little housewife about to be ravaged by the handyman.

Drawing out Ily's discomfort, I turned to Victor. "Who's playing tonight?"

Victor dragged his gaze down Ily's body, spread and trembling on my lap. "Kirk and Suri. A Norwegian boy I stumbled upon a few years ago trying to score ecstasy in the wrong place, and a Persian girl who was given to me in a trade for an alexandrite gemstone."

Ily's head snapped up. Her tension of being held against her will manifested into haughty disdain. "Alexandrite? How the hell did you get your hands on alexandrite?"

I squeezed her breast through her blingy black bra. "Hush."

"Let her speak." Victor chewed his way through a piece of chicken. "You act surprised, my sweetling, to know I have other hobbies outside of skin and sex."

"Oh, I'm sorry." She pressed a wrist to her forehead. "How perfectly awful of me to judge."

"Ily." I pinched her nipple. "Quiet."

Victor stopped eating and gave her his full attention. "Why do you think I'm so interested in jewels, Ilyana? It's not because I randomly chose a theme, you know. It's because I too—like you as I recall—enjoy traveling the world and digging up precious gems. I own shares in many mines. I dabble in a great many things."

"What things?" she snapped back.

He merely gave her the sickest, cruellest smile. "Let's just say, there are plenty other precious trophies that can be mined and not just from rock."

"What the hell is that supposed to mean?"

"It means, shut the fuck up and prove to me that I'm right," I ordered, cutting their conversation off.

She twisted in my arms to face me, her hips still spread over my thighs. "Let me go."

I grinned, wrapping my arms around her and kissing her cheek. "I'll tell you what..."

She stilled into stone.

"I'm going to touch you. I'm going to slip a single inquisitive finger inside you."

She sucked in a breath.

"If…" I ran my nose along her cheek. "*If* you're dry and truly feel no attraction toward me, I'll put you down, feed you every mouthful of this delicious dinner, then allow you to go to bed unmolested."

Rachel flicked us a look, catching Ily's churning gaze.

Ily quickly glanced away, a blush creeping steadily over her cheeks.

"And if I'm not?" she asked ever so quietly.

"If you're not?" I smiled, my cock aching to take her. "If you're as wet as I think you are. If you're as sensitive and ready to snap as I believe. Well then…I'm tossing that dinner into the storm and having you as my meal instead." I patted the table. "Right here. On your back. Where everyone will watch me eat you out, then fill you up."

She shivered and tried to slip off my knee.

"Ah ah, where do you think you're going?"

She refused to meet my eyes. "Henri…"

"Master H, if you don't mind."

Her teeth clenched. "Master H. I—eh, I'm not feeling well. You wouldn't want me to throw up all over you, would you? Put me down before I—"

"Can't fool me with that one, little nightmare." I chuckled. "I'm well acquainted with nausea, and you, my wet, wanting girl, are the opposite of weak and nauseous."

On the stage, the handyman had the wife in a chokehold as his hand strayed down her body and up her dress. With her splayed to the crowd, everyone saw the moment his fingers penetrated her.

A few Masters snapped their own fingers, ordering their jewels to service them while they ate.

Ily bared her teeth in fury. "You're all sick. This whole place is wrong."

"And you're affected by it. Same as me." I kissed her bare shoulder.

"I'm *disgusted* by it."

"You're wet because of it. You're wet because of me…admit it."

"Never. I would rather die."

"Prove it." I looked up, drowning in her golden rage. "Take my hand, guide it between your legs, and show me."

"*What?*" Her eyebrows furrowed into a disbelieving frown. "Y-You can't be serious."

"Show me. And this all stops." I licked my lips. "If you're dry, you're free. For tonight at least. But…if you're wet. If you clench just once around my finger, then…you're never allowed to lie to me again. You give in like I have. You agree to play along with me, just like I asked."

"Play along with you?" Victor cut in. "I thought you said that was over with?"

Frustration built in my blood, scratching at my teeth, reminding me that a beast stalked within me and the longer I teased it, the worse it would pounce. "Not to play along with me to fool you, Vic." I shrugged, not really wanting to share my idiotic fantasy but knowing he'd see it on the cameras anyway. "I'm here for life. I'm never leaving. Neither is Ily. I merely want her to act as though—"

"I'm his perfect little *wife*," Ily spat. "To beg him to beat me. Plead him to fuck me. Pretend I love him." She shuddered with uncontrolled anger. "Of all the twisted—"

"I think that's sweet." Victor sat back and stroked Rachel's hair. "We all need that special someone. I find men are a curious breed. The ones who have been coming here for years all have their chosen jewel. It's rare for them to stray once they've found the one they prefer. If Henri has already found his chosen one, then you should be grateful, my pet."

"I'll be grateful when you're both dead. When *all of you* are dead."

"Well, none of us are immortal, so that will one day happen." Victor fed a piece of chicken to Rachel with his fingers. "But…that's a long time to wait." His eyes narrowed, glinting with explosive temper that he occasionally lost control over. "Now, your Master gave you an order. Open your fucking legs. Take his hand. And show him what he wants to know."

"I don't need you ordering her about, Vic," I growled. "My jewel. My rules."

"Fine." Wiping his fingers on a napkin, he faced the stage.

Lightning flashed through the ballroom, highlighting the erotic tapestries on the walls and statues of winged folk being fucked by demons. All around us lewd artwork encouraged us to join in.

The housewife let out a sordid moan as the handyman finger-fucked her as if his hand was a hammer drill.

An ear-splintering boom crashed right above us as thunder added itself to the electrically-charged air.

Ily's chest rose and fell as if she bordered a panic attack. I searched her eyes for tears. I longed to see salt pour. But, unlike the breaking in the library on that first day, sorrow didn't glow…hatred did.

My heart wrenched painfully.

My stomach chose that moment to turn sour.

I had everything I could ever want, but somehow, the one thing I didn't know how to ask for was now the one thing I would fucking kill for.

"One day, I'll turn your hatred for me into love," I whispered before I could censor myself. "One day, you'll feel for me as strongly as I'm starting to feel for you, and when you do…we'll both be happy here."

Her eyes met mine.

Her loathing morphed into pity.

With ever so soft fingers, she touched my scruff-shadowed cheek and pressed her nose to mine. Her back twisted, her body contorted on my lap. For the longest moment, she didn't speak but then she breathed, "I'm sorry that your childhood turned you into this creature. This confused, lonely creature who doesn't understand the meaning of love. I'm sorry you've never had someone to call your own. And I'm sorry you're searching for belonging in all the wrong places." Pulling away, she dropped her hand from my cheek and lashed it around my wrist. "But allow me to teach you the most important thing about caring for someone."

I couldn't breathe as she shifted and lowered my hand down her gorgeous body. My nervous system misfired. My blood turned to lava. My cock a battering ram of need.

"The day you actually learn what true love is, Henri Mercer, is the day you will know the darkest pits of despair, not happiness." Turning my hand in her hold, she ran her touch over my knuckles and curled my fingers into a fist, leaving just my middle outstretched.

"You think just because you can make me come that I want you?"

Her skin flushed as she moved aside her G-string.

"You think just because I'm wet that I'm secretly in love with you?"

Her eyes darkened to bronze as she guided me lower, lower.

"You think just because I obey you that I respect you?"

I swallowed hard as she hovered my hand above the scorching fire between her legs.

"You don't have a clue how far people will go for love. You don't have the faintest idea how far I'll go to one day be free of you."

I groaned as the first touch of her scalding, sopping heat stung my fingertip.

Her head flopped backward, crashing on my shoulder.

Guiding my finger deeper inside her, she whispered, "You have no idea what I'm prepared to do to deny you every part of me."

With a gasp, she shoved my finger in as deep as it would go.

We both jerked.

Fuck.

Me.

Victor tossed us a smirk as Ily lay spread-eagled on my lap with my finger impaled inside her.

I couldn't stop myself.

My free arm snaked around her.

My hand cradled her fragile throat.

My teeth found her ear.

And my tongue licked down her neck.

Her hips rocked against my finger as hers fell away, delivering herself to me.

Her wetness dribbled over my knuckles.

Her desire stained my black trousers.

The eroticism of the moment ought to have blown my fucking mind, yet…something was missing. Something violently fundamental. Something I only figured out as her pussy clenched around me, and she moaned wantonly in my ear.

I grunted as that knowledge slammed into my despicably deranged heart.

The monster inside me raged.

She hadn't given herself to me.

She'd *taken* from me.

Used me.

Robbed me.

And even as I inserted a second finger and found out exactly how sodden she was, her voice glittered with an oath I wanted to shatter.

"I'm wet because *I* choose to be, not because you made me. I'm needy because *I* rule my body, not you. I want sex because I've decided you can't take that away from me. I don't care about you, *Master H.* I care about myself. I care about my family back home and my brother who is mourning me. I care enough to refuse you a single shred of power over me." Her hand clamped on my wrist again, forcing me to finger her deeper. "So I suggest you remember that when you make me kneel and suck and moan. Remember that *I* choose this, not you. I want this, *in spite* of you. And I will take everything that you give me and make it mine. Not because you own me but because I will never, ever be yours."

I snapped.

My leash tore.

My monstrosity leapt free.

Swooping to my feet, I grabbed Ily by the waist with one arm and swiped my other through the fine china, food, and wine glasses.

Victor leaned back as things went crashing and splintering to the dance floor.

Guests stopped watching the live porn as I tossed Ily on the table and spread her on her back. "This is for ever thinking you can stop me from owning you, little nightmare."

Unbuckling my belt, I unzipped my trousers and yanked out my cock. "This is for telling me exactly what I can and cannot have."

Nudging her knees apart, I dragged her hips to the edge of the table and smeared my erection through the wetness she vowed would never belong to me. "And this is my answer."

I thrust.

Hard.

Fast.

Brutally deep, deep, *deep*.

She cried out and scratched at the tablecloth.

Digging her teeth into her bottom lip, her back arched as she didn't fight.

Didn't deny.

She welcomed me.

Ground on me.

Did exactly what she promised and stole all my power by wanting it.

Her body sucked me into her wicked, wanton spell, and it was me who fucking broke.

Me who roared and punched fists on either side of her rapturous, lust-filled face and jack-knifed my hips into hers.

Me who raged to snatch her from the sky, all while she flew too high out of my reach.

I lost all focus on where we were.

I forgot a storm raged and others watched.

There were no others.

No elements.

No men.

No stars or storms or suns.

Just us.

Alone.

Just me.

Alone.

Me clawing at a woman all while she didn't even notice me. Didn't care about me. Didn't acknowledge me as I fucking drove into her again and again, begging her to feel me, respond to me, to open her fucking eyes and *see* me.

Sickness clawed up my throat as the sensation of losing something I'd never had poured through my fingers.

I took her harder.

Like a beast in heat.

A male desperate to crawl inside his mate.

And in the midst of my musk, she merely trailed her hand between her legs and touched herself. Rubbed herself in ways she hadn't taught me and tore apart whatever propriety and shyness she'd clung to.

She masturbated…and I was just the dildo she used to come.

And she did come.

Hard.

Her belly flexed as her mouth opened wide.

Her cry as she tumbled over the edge echoed with thunder.

Her pussy fisted me.

Her body fell without mine.

Each ripple, every clench reminded me that she'd found bliss without me.

She hates me.

I stumbled back.

My cock withdrew and I wedged a hand into my belly as I folded in half and struggled to catch a breath.

I turned lightheaded, lost—

Another crackle of lightning tore my head up.

Electrical power showered Ily in icy-white sparks as she sat up on the table and dared steal Victor's merlot. Throwing it back, she smiled and tossed the glass onto all the other shattered dinnerware on the floor.

Another boom of thunder.

Followed by the loudest *clang*.

The metallic twang worked its way through my bones like a pebble tossed in water.

Victor soared to his feet and glowered at a man in the corner. A man with a large padded drumstick standing beside a huge circular gong. "You idiot, it's pouring outside. We'll play tomorrow—"

"We're playing now." The middle-aged white guy stepped toward the ballroom doors and flung them wide. Wind funnelled in. Muggy and wet, whipping up tablecloths with mini tornadoes. "You said we had to wait for Henri to stop napping like some hibernating squirrel. Well…he's just proven he's very much awake." Standing with his back to the storm, he grinned. "So, I ask you, guys. Who's ready for a goddamn treasure hunt?!"

"After that display of fucking?" Charles said from the table next to ours. "Hell yes."

"Those who want to play raise their hands," the white guy shouted over the rain.

Every single Master raised their arm.

Victor shook his head. "You're all imbeciles. You'll get struck by lightning."

"At this point, if I don't fuck something my heart will stop anyway." Roland laughed.

Snatching a female jewel from the floor, he pointed at the open doors. "I suggest you run."

Run?

Ily hopped off the table and rearranged her underwear.

She didn't so much as look at me.

The urge to be sick came again, so fucking tangled with possession and need, I couldn't stand upright.

I thought I was free of this.

Free from struggling with feelings I had no capacity in which to feel.

Slowly, Victor marched into the middle of the ballroom and spun on his patent shoes. "Fine. If you're all so eager to get your dicks fried, let the treasure hunt commence!"

"Fuck yes!" Guests pushed away dinners; the porno screeched to a halt.

Victor smiled at them. "Kirk, Suri…you know what's expected." Turning on the spot to look at every slave, Victor nodded at each of them as they slowly staggered to their feet. "All of you know the rules. But…for the new one who just got devoured next to my dinner, allow me to inform you."

Pulling out a stopwatch from his navy blazer, Victor hovered his finger over the button. "You have one hour. Outside, scattered around the grounds, Peter sweetling has hidden multiple prizes. Some contain gifts such as diamonds, cash, a movie, and a cheeseburger. You're searching for large plastic gemstones with a piece of paper inside. Each chit can be cashed in at your discretion. Trifle, indulgent things that are available for any jewel who is lucky enough to find them. I believe there's even a night or two in the bungalow tucked away in the east corner. A night alone…all to yourself."

Ily threw me a look.

Her fierce hatred of me faded into true inklings of fear.

"And…of course there are prizes for my wonderful guests too. A night in the snuff room with no cameras or controls. A few new toys that I have yet to introduce. A day in the dungeons with my permission to do anything they wish. Oh…and one Diamond Kiss."

Jewels shot each other a horrified look then broke into a run.

Darting out the door, they scurried into the storm.

Everyone but Ily.

I frowned as the guests all whooped and groaned, turning into animals. Some went to chase but Victor held up his hand. "Not yet, gentlemen. That's not very sporting."

Roland bounced on the spot, his hands opening and closing.

No one spoke as Victor watched his stopwatch tick down the seconds.

Finally, he pressed the button and nodded. "Your hour starts now. Happy hunting, my friends."

I'd never seen grown men move so fast.

Shoving each other out of the way, they all bolted into the storm. No jackets, no umbrellas, immediately swallowed by the snarling rain.

Sighing happily, Victor returned to our table and gave Ily a look. His eyes turned reptilian before his attention skated to me. "That little display was fucking shameful, Mercer."

"Excuse me?" My mouth went dry as I finally had the brainpower to tuck away my unsatisfied erection and buckle up.

"That jewel of yours might be sweet, but she's slightly psychotic." He sneered at Ily. "She ruled you, Henri. We all fucking saw it. She was the one in power, and if you don't punish her for such a blatant, disrespectful flouting of her place, then I'll do it. I'll take her down into the dungeons and keep her there until she learns, once and for fucking all, that she is nothing more than what we say she is."

I nodded and went to grab her. "I'll take her to my room and start now."

"No, you will join the others." He smiled like a murderer. "And so will she." Sitting back down, alone now the ballroom and his favourite jewel had vacated, he picked up his knife and fork and cut into a potato.

"Run, Ilyana. You have a two-minute head start, and then Henri will chase you. You'll have to decide if evading him or finding treasure will be more important."

Ily met my eyes.

I had no idea what the fuck would happen out there.

But I had a horrible feeling one of us would end up bleeding.

"Now, sweetling." Slowly, Victor pulled out his trusty gun from his waistband. "If you don't start running in five seconds, I'm going to shoot you and be done with it. You've pissed me off with your little spectacle. And it's made me very, very eager to remind you of your manners. So…" He smiled. "Five."

Ily stiffened and eased her way around the table.

"Four."

His countdown reminded me of a previous one where he got me drunk and held a gun to her head.

"Three."

I'd snapped then.

Ily snapped now.

With a shaky breath, she bolted.

"Two." Victor watched her go.

"One." He fired a round into the storm, the bullet chasing after Ily as the wind swallowed her up and thunder boomed.

Chapter Thirteen

Ily

I RAN BLIND AND DEAF.

Water poured from the sky; thunder did its best to puncture my eardrums.

My ass ached from the bruises Henri decorated me with, and the cuts from a few days ago reached the itchy stage of healing, twinging as I galloped barefoot over soft, springy grass.

The lacy crystal-studded bra offered no support, and the G-string was as wet as the world around me, thanks to the orgasm still echoing in my blood.

I came.

He didn't—

God, don't think about it.

I balled my hands and ran harder, desperate to flee from what I'd done.

But I couldn't outrun the truth, no matter how fast my feet flew.

The truth that every moment I spent with Henri, the deeper into infernal damnation I fell.

I'd hoped taking back what these men tried to claim would be self-empowering, enlightening.

And it was…

In an awful, horrible kind of way.

It showed me truths about myself I never wanted to face.

Truths of darkness and wrongness and sin.

Everything was black inside me.

Tangled inside me.

I cringed as I kept running.

All my life, I thought I was normal. Normal when it came to sex and love.

I enjoyed a kiss and a cuddle.

Sex in a bed and the occasional experience in the back seat of a car.

I rarely self-pleasured, and if I did…my fantasies stuck to nice men, nice touches, nice—

I'm nice.

I am.

But if I liked nice things and swore I was a nice girl, then how the hell could I be so sensitive, so wet, so violently thirsty for *more.*

Stop it.

You're confused.

You're hurting and lost and desperate.

Yes.

Desperate.

I was desperate.

So, *so* desperate.

To leave.

To run.

To go home.

Yet somehow that desperation had twisted into something sick. A sickness that turned me…how did Victor put it? Sweet but psychotic?

God, am I the crazy one?

Would I destroy myself before I stood a chance at destroying him?

God, *him.*

Damn him.

Smite him.

I hated that my soul shivered whenever Henri spoke.

I despised that my body turned molten the moment he touched me.

Soft or hard. Gentle or abusive.

It didn't damn well matter.

And it *mattered.*

It mattered so, so much because how could I betray myself in that way?

How could I twitch with the undying rage to kill every Master in here? How could I say such nasty things, even if they were true? How could I *do* such nasty things…especially with a man I hated.

I-I put his finger inside me.

My stomach flipped, remembering the way he'd swiped his dinner to the floor and made me his main meal instead. The show of possession. The rage of someone equally unhinged.

I'd practically started coming the moment he'd entered me.

Stop it, Il.

Just…no more.

You're fighting with anything and everything you have. That's all. Your body is a weapon. Your heart is a knife. Use them. Use them until they're dead.

My toes dug deeper.

I hurtled forward.

Swiping rain from my eyes, I did my best to see where I was going.

Uplights twinkled on manicured animal hedges. Fountains babbled and fairy lights swayed in the wild wind.

Despite the churning clouds above, the horizon glowed a faint pearl as if the moon did its best to slip beneath the wet violence, beckoning me to climb the stronghold walls, swim through the moat, and hurl myself off the cliff.

Masculine laughter came from my left, followed by a feminine scream.

My feet immediately switched directions, running away from them despite my heart breaking for the poor jewel who'd just been caught.

Lightning forked above me like a morbid, murderous firework.

I hunched, waiting.

BOOM.

The answering thunder threatened to stop my breaking heart as I darted over the sweeping lawns and toward a part of the estate housing fruit trees and a giant maze.

No way in hell would I go in the maze.

I wasn't stupid enough to get lost and molested, but I did race into the grove of leaves, searching for a place to hide.

An hour.

The game would only last an hour.

If I could hide for that long, then I could ask Henri—as nicely as I could with my newly venom-coated tongue—if I could spend the night with the jewels.

Spending the afternoon alone hadn't been my plan.

I'd hoped at least Peter would've been in the showers or dorm. I needed to talk to someone. To ask if this was normal. To purge myself with confession so these awful, sickening secrets didn't eat me alive.

Instead, I'd spent the precious couple of hours I had in the vault, doing my best to distract myself with necklaces and gemstones because each time I brushed my body, all I could think about was him.

Him.

God, not this again.

Get out, get out, get out!

I needed him.

Needed him to be the cop I believed.

Needed him to be good.

Needed him to save both of us because if he didn't…I had a horrible feeling there'd be nothing left to save.

A few men ran past in the shadows.

I ducked behind a tree laden with apples.

So I'm in the orchard.

Perhaps there were sheds nearby I could hide in. Storage rooms for fruit and other fragile things.

A short celebration from someone who found a prize quickly smothered into pain as a Master found them.

The grunts of sex sounded to my left, followed by the rhythmic growls of someone who didn't believe in restraint.

Monsters.

All around me.

Everywhere.

I ran again.

My toes found painful twigs and crunchy leaves, slowing my speed.

I aimed for the soft grass. I could cover more distance that way. I could perhaps run to the battlement and find an archer's nook.

Darting onto the storm-drowning lawn, I put my head down and raced.

I almost ran over it.

A large plastic gemstone looked as if it'd been dropped by the raging thunder. It sat dull and cloudy as fat raindrops rolled down its fake yellow facets.

It beckoned me forward.

Memories of playing a similar treasure hunt with Krish when we were younger filled my head.

Back then, our parents had hidden large plastic Easter eggs in the garden, holding small toys and chocolates. There hadn't been repercussions for finding them or rape waiting in the foliage.

My chest ached for innocence.

My body reminded me I'd fallen so far from grace.

I bent down to grab the gem…

…just as a man hurtled from the darkness.

He bowled into me, snatched my wrist, ducked and grabbed the large plastic stone, then hauled me into speed.

"Peter?" I gasped, licking at droplets cascading down my face. The wind pinched my bare skin, making my nipples as hard as the diamonds on my bra.

"Run." He put his head down and dragged me. I ran as fast as I could beside him, but he was faster, hauling me to speeds I'd never reached before.

"W-Where are we going?" I panted over the wind.

"I have to find the gemstone with the Diamond Kiss in it. I deliberately didn't put it out. I put it back in the cupboard where all his sick prizes wait, but…he noticed." Sucking in a tattered breath, he ran faster. "I don't know where he hid it, but I have to find it before a Master does."

"Why?"

A crack of lightning lit up his body. Brown hair sopping wet, white tight boxers turning transparent between his legs. His back held a crisscross of swollen ligatures.

I tripped. "Oh my God, your back."

He winced. "Ignore it. Keep running."

"But—"

"But nothing. I have to find that gemstone!"

I couldn't take my eyes off his fresh lacerations as he ran as fast as he could, dragging me like I weighed nothing.

Someone had whipped him.

Recently.

A horrible Master had chained him up, punished him with a whip, and then—

I stopped my thoughts before I could picture him being abused any further.

My teeth ground together; the fury that'd manifested in my heart grew sharper claws.

This place had changed me.

It'd rewired my pieces, and I *hated* that I couldn't afford to care or cry or be nice anymore. The storm couldn't wash away the filth in my blood, but it did drown the old me.

It choked me and suffocated me and my rage chose that moment to spill over.

"*Enough*!" I yanked on his hand.

Our rain-slippery skin broke apart.

He shot forward; I reeled back.

I rubbed at my knuckles where his nails caught me. "I've had enough, Peter. We need to get out of this place. Now. Tonight. *Immediately*."

Breathing hard, he locked his knees and stopped his trajectory. With shaking hands, he opened the large gemstone he'd scooped from the grass and angled the piece of paper toward an uplight aimed at a hedgerow of a squirrel.

Instantly, my mind shot back to Henri, thanks to one of the Masters calling him a hibernating squirrel.

God!

Grabbing my dripping hair, I tried to yank him out of my head.

Enough.

Enough.

Enough!

Screaming under my breath, I stomped toward Peter and balled my hands. "We have to do something. I can't stay here. You can't stay here. *No one can stay here.*" I shoved him in the chest. "I heard jewels being hurt out there. Someone is having sex in the orchard. Someone screamed. They're monsters, Peter, and they're turning me into one. We can't stay here! A-Are you listening to me? We need to fight. There are thirty of us, and I only saw fifteen or so of them at dinner. We can…" I shrugged as the hopelessness of everything sat like a rusty anchor in my chest. "We have to try."

Ignoring my outburst, Peter skimmed the prize. Baring his teeth, he shoved the damp paper into his equally damp boxers and tossed the cracked-open fake gem to the ground. "*Fuck.*"

"Are you deliberately ignoring me?"

"I have bigger things on my mind right now."

"Bigger than escape?"

"Yes, actually." His fury matched mine, both of us raging and taking it out on each other instead of those who deserved it. "If I don't find that gem then someone is going to die. And right now, all I've fucking found is a goddamn cheeseburger chit!"

"Wait, what?"

He huffed with a morose slouch. "Someone will die, Ily. Someone is going to die if I don't find that Diamond Kiss." Shooting forward, he snagged my hand. "Come on. He might have hidden it in the maze."

Pulling against him, I stopped him from breaking into a run. "We'll find it. I promise. I'll help you look, I swear. But…this might be our only chance to talk." I pointed at the cascading sky. "The storm is muting us. If there's cameras out here, they can't hear us." I squeezed his hand. "We have to make a plan, Peter. You know that, right? We have to get out of here…before it's too late."

His eyes bugged. "Wh-What are you saying?"

"I'm saying you heard what Henri told me. I stupidly thought he was a cop. I went along with him because I thought he would save us."

His entire body tensed. "Oh yes, I heard alright. We all did. We heard that bastard admit that he used words to bind you into obedience. It all makes sense now why you didn't just tolerate what he did to you but seemed morbidly *grateful.* You acted as if he was your friend, and that? Fuck, until the moment you kicked him in Victor's trophy room, I actually feared you were touched in the head."

"I know how it must've looked."

"No, I don't think you do." He sighed sadly. "You let a part of yourself fall for him. Fall for a lie, and now that part is at his mercy because you can't take it back. He owns a piece of you. And that's why you're so desperate to run. It's not because you're finally seeing that there's no such thing as rescue but because you know in yourself that you're already his and your freedom ended the moment he used kindness to kill you."

I stumbled backward. "You look as if you blame me for that."

"No. I pity you." He swiped at rain rolling down his neck. Lightning shone, jagged and silver, followed by its clashing, booming mate.

With another heavy exhale, he stepped into me and wrapped me tight in his cold, wet arms. "What he did to you—the lie that he'd save you? That has to be one of the most fiendishly cruel things I've ever come across."

A watery laugh spilled from me, soaking into his damp shoulder. "If you can say that after enduring this hellhole for so long…? God, I-I find that totally terrifying."

"Me too." He squeezed me tighter. "But there's a difference between physical warfare and psychological. Most Masters that come here focus only on flesh, but him? He seems particularly skilled at messing with your mind."

Ain't that the damn truth.

I sagged in his embrace. "He definitely gets under my skin."

"Please, *please* don't let him get any deeper."

Rain fell on the top of our heads.

Echoes of what Henri told me when we first arrived repeated in the droplets splashing around us: *"Every thread is breaking. Every decency is fading. And I have to say…death might be worth the price of letting go."*

Death.

He'd turned his back on all the good pieces of himself. He'd chosen death and the sick, sadistic journey toward it.

So…why shouldn't I join him?

Why should I keep my morals when those very morals got me into this mess?

Anger trickled through me as I tugged away from Peter's arms.

I gave him a sad little shrug. "Seems I stupidly fell for your fantasy of someone coming to save us. I *believed* in him."

He winced. "And that's what eats me up. When I saw the video of you guys in the library, I believed it myself for a second. I believed he was a cop and here for us. Fuck, I wasn't prepared for how it made me feel. Such *hope*, Ily. Such agonising, demoralising hope. It tore through me before I could stop it. And you? You hoped for far longer than me, so I can only imagine what it's done to you. I'm sorry. So, so sorry he manipulated you."

My cheeks grew hot. "If anyone deserves an apology, it's you. Have you not seen your back? Good grief, Peter, it's—"

"Sore but survivable." He forced a smile. "Like I just said…body abuse is one thing, but mental abuse? Dangling hope in front of you? Making you consent to what he did to you?" He shook his head. "I told you he's one of the worst, and you didn't believe me. But you believe me now. I know you do. And I get why you think tonight would be a good night to form an army and go to war. But—"

"Tonight *is* a good night."

"Tonight, I have to save one life, not kill us all."

"If we stand up together. We could win."

He huffed and grabbed my hand. "We'll talk and search. We've already wasted too much time. Come on."

Breaking into a jog with him, I did my best to share my probably lethal, terribly suicidal plan. "Henri might've lied, but I didn't. I made a promise to get you guys out. I'm not giving up just because he has."

He shot me a look as we splashed through rain and grass. "What the hell are you saying?"

"I'm going to try. I have to. This is not how this ends. For any of us."

He slammed to a stop again. "You can't be serious. Have you not been paying attention? There's no way off this stinking island. None." Waving at the high battlements in the distance, he shrugged. "How do you plan on getting past those, huh? How are you planning on stopping the guards from shooting you?" Grabbing his collar, he yanked it. "How are you planning on stepping one foot past the electrical fence and not dying for the privilege?"

Goosebumps skated over me. "I-I don't know—"

"You try and kill them, and they won't just kill you back, *jaanu*. They'll make you beg for it."

I froze as the Hindi term of endearment fell from him.

Homesickness suffocated every muscle, every synapse, thought, and feeling.

My feet staggered as if he'd physically slapped me with memories of safety and love, only to dump me back into a storm on rapist island.

He caught me with a wince. "Sorry. I-I slipped."

"It's fine."

"None of this is fine, Ily." He stepped into me and cupped my cheek.

I shivered as his eyes softened in ways they really shouldn't.

Grabbing his wrist, I whispered, "You shouldn't have kissed me…back in the vault."

He froze.

Arguments crossed his face before he shrugged stiffly. "It was just another slip. That's all."

I didn't know what to believe but I nodded and moved away. "We have to get out of here. Please tell me you're ready to fight. Five years is enough. You deserve—"

"I deserve?" He laughed icily. "What I *deserve* is the right to kiss whoever I damn well please—if she wants me back. What I deserve is not to have a dick up my ass every fucking day!"

Pinching the bridge of his nose, he exhaled hard. "Look, I hate being the voice of reason all the bloody time, and I love your warrior spirit, and *of course* I want out. I want out every fucking second of every fucking minute but…it's impossible. There *is* no way out. Not unless you're willing to go to the next incarnation and say farewell to this one."

I drew back. "There *has* to be a way. Henri took me around the citadel today. I saw the armoury. So many weapons, Paavak. We could figure out a way to steal them and start killing the Masters in their sleep."

He chuckled with a terrible sigh. "You're turning out to be quite the murderess." He turned solemn. "What about the karma you'll have to repay?"

"I'll deal with that in the next cycle. I'm sure I'm allowed to take a life if it saves countless others."

"And you figure you can just waltz around with a machete and slice off the heads of those who own us, huh?"

"Well, not quite like that—"

"You think you can fire an old musket—probably with no gunpowder or ammo—before a guard can shoot you with his Glock?"

"No, but—"

"Come on. Let's keep searching."

I fell back into a jog with him, my thoughts colliding. Every scenario I imagined included innocence triumphing over evil. The powers of good on our side, carving a path of righteousness.

But in reality…Peter was right.

Every move we made was recorded.

Every item we touched was catalogued.

If we stood a chance of uprising, we had to be smart.

"Tell the others," I spoke around my quickening breaths. "This isn't over. We'll come up with a plan. I'm going to get home to Krish, one way or another. I have to. And I'm not going to stop until you're back with your family and—"

"Well, well, well…what have we found here, boys?" Three Masters appeared from the storm's shadows.

"Ah fuck." Peter immediately skidded to a halt and stepped in front of me. Bowing his head, he tried to be subservient but his fists curled. "Evening, Master R, Master D, Master L."

The three men chuckled. "Always so polite, little Peter."

Peter stiffened and backed into me, subtly pushing me away.

One of the Masters noticed. "Aww, lookie-here. Peter's feeling protective of the new girl." He elbowed the man closest to him. "Fancies her for himself, I reckon." Looking us up and down, he snickered. "Figured you'd get your dick wet in the storm, huh? No one would see you fuck a fellow slave, is that it?"

Peter didn't reply.

My eyes narrowed.

I recognised one of them from the debacle at breakfast when Henri announced his last name was Mercer. I still didn't understand why that was such a big deal, but I sensed the big problem currently stalking toward us.

Larry.

A weedy youngish guy with a paunch for his belly and noodles for arms. Probably made millions off some software app, turning a lifetime of being bullied into becoming one himself.

"Roger, I don't know about you, but I think I've found all the treasure I'm interested in," Larry said.

"Yep." Roger, with a receding hairline and a body toned from the gym, chuckled. "I think you might be right, mate."

"Run along, Peter. We'll give you a free pass, despite your selfish attitude." The third guy smiled thin and sly. "Go away. We're interested in her tonight, not you."

Peter backed up again, keeping me behind him.

His entire demeanour slipped from fearful to flirty. "You know…I always have fun with you, Master D. How about we go inside and—"

"I see what you're doing." Master D smirked. "And it won't work."

Peter braced himself, his voice turning cold. "Alright then. How about this? No one has found the Diamond Kiss yet. Run along and keep searching and—"

"If I wanted to kill someone, I could just kill you right now." Larry chuckled. "Hey, Daxton? Fancy participating in a bit of murder tonight, or would you rather stick your cock in the forbidden jewel?"

"Or we could do both?" Daxton grinned at the other two. "Fuck her and kill him? That might be fun."

"Vic would be mighty pissed." Roger wiped his forehead free from rain. "He told us that she's off limits, and we all know Peter has been groomed to be his manservant. How about we fuck both and kill both? That way he can only be pissed once?"

"Your reasoning is sound." Daxton laughed. "I could get down with that."

A flash of lightning.

A sonic boom of thunder.

"Hang on…he could revoke our memberships," Larry muttered. "Do we really want to run that risk?"

"Meh." Roger shrugged. "I hear he's leaving tomorrow on another hunt. He won't miss these two when he brings back shiny new jewels to play with."

"Fine." Larry pushed his sodden shirt cuffs up his arms. "I'm keen." His beady eyes flicked between Peter and me. "Ready to play a new game? This one's called Suck and Scream."

For a second, no one moved.

The rain kept pelting; the moon kept trying to sneak beneath black turbulent clouds.

Outwardly, I didn't twitch.

But inwardly?

I broke.

I screamed at the howling wind.

I punched the sky.

I shredded the stars.

I hated this…this *helplessness*. This *uselessness*. This tragic inability to say **NO**.

Every atom inside urged to fly far, far away.

I wanted to transform into the fledgling monster inside me and tear these bastards into bloody, messy viscera.

I didn't want to play by their rules anymore.

I didn't want to abide by *any* rules.

I wanted revenge.

War.

Carnage.

But I was just a girl.

Helpless and useless.

Dripping in a storm.

"Get on your knees, Peter," Larry ordered, pointing at the grass. "We'll let you watch. How about that? We'll even let you jerk off before you die." He snickered. "Hang on. Daxton? Didn't you say he gave great blowjobs?"

"Yeah, man. Sucks the cum right out of you."

"Excellent. New plan. You stick your dick in him, and I'll take first dibs on her."

"Whoa. Who put you in charge?" Roger scowled. "We take a vote."

"But I spotted them first." Larry pouted like a petulant four-year-old.

"Don't care." Roger stepped forward. "That Henri cunt has been keeping her out of our reach. I want to see what's so magical about her pussy to keep him going back for more. I'm first."

"Both of you can have a rub and tug. I'm gonna have first ride." Daxton stepped forward, his hands already unbuckling his belt. Everyone's clothes clung to skin and limb. Water sluiced down faces and the garden lights jerked and jumped as rain continued to pour over their lenses.

My heart pumped so fast it smoked.

I actually smelled it.

The burning, charring scent of soot and sorry organ.

Fear I'd never felt before burned me alive.

Peter trembled; all his bravery seemed to desert him. "I, eh…" He swallowed hard as five years of abuse strangled his throat. "He…I mean, Master H won't appreciate you touching what's his. He—"

"Can take a running leap off the cliff for all I care," Daxton muttered. "I didn't like that Henri fellow the moment he arrived, and I dislike him even more now. Know what I think? I think he's still a cop. I think Victor is wearing rose-fucking-glasses where he's concerned and I'm performing my duty as a fellow Joyero member in getting rid of him."

Larry nodded. "So we're gonna do it then?"

My head snapped up.

Do what?

"Yeah, yeah. We'll kill him. Just have to bide our time for a bit. You know Victor doesn't like us brawling."

"I've got one of the guards on a bribe retainer. He'll give me his gun when we choose to shoot the bastard," Larry said.

"Perfect." Roger nodded.

"Are we gonna stand around all night and fucking chinwag?" Daxton barked. "You." He shoved a finger in Peter's face. "Kneel. Now."

Peter's knees visibly wobbled.

A horrible lifetime of obedience swayed his legs to bend.

But…he glanced over his shoulder at me.

Our eyes met.

And something happened.

The uselessness, the helplessness—every tragic lesson taught by fists and kicks—all faded from Peter's harrowed stare.

All his abuse.

All his pain and rape and degradation.

It curdled into one mass of addictive, noble fury and he nodded just once. "You know what, *jaanu*? Fuck it. *Main aapke saath reh Kar yuddh Karnes ke like tayyar khadi hoon.*" (I'm ready to go to war with you.)

His words hadn't even sunk in before he threw himself forward and tackled Daxton.

The Master tumbled like a rotten building, crashing against the grass as puddles went flying and another fork of lightning flashed.

"*Run, Ily*!" he screamed as the other Masters swarmed him.

A flurry of feet as they all kicked him.

A single scratch of time where Peter chose to protect me all while knowing it was pointless.

And I made an equally pointless decision.

I roared and threw myself at Larry. The smallest one. The only one I might have a chance to overpower. "Get *off him*!"

He grunted in shock as I punched like a wild thing. My knuckles bloomed with pain. Something cracked in my hand. My arms turned into dead weights as I threw hit after hit as strong and as savage as I could.

"Jesus." He ducked his head. "Someone get her the hell off me!"

Arms snaked around my waist.

Unfightable strength pulled me back.

I stood breathing hard as Roger clamped his hands around my

throat, his fingers strangling above my collar. "Do that again and I'll kill you *then* fuck you."

In a dripping black part of my mind, I actually preferred that option.

At least I wouldn't be alive to feel him pierce my body.

Peter grunted again as Daxton scrambled to his feet and kicked him right in the kidney. "Motherfucker! How dare you jump me, you little whore."

Larry smoothed his thin mousy blond hair and marched toward Peter. Kicking him for good measure, he bent down and snapped a leash to his collar. Wrapping the leather a few times around his hand, he braced himself as if Peter would take off like a rabid dog. "For that you can watch all three of us fuck her. How does that sound?"

Roger chuckled as Peter spat a glob of blood on the grass. It shone like oil in the darkness.

"Know what I think, boys?" He laughed again, his fingers tightening around my throat. "I think he's got feelings for this one."

"Oh?" Larry tugged Peter's collar, jerking him back. "Is that true, little whore? Fancy that you're in love with the new girl?"

"Stop it," I spat, squirming in Roger's suffocating choke. "Leave him alone."

"Oh, this is too perfect." Larry danced on the spot. "Tell you what. Confess you love each other and once we've had our fun, we'll let you have *your* fun."

Peter looked away, glowering at a rabbit-shaped hedgerow.

"Nothing to say?" Daxton asked, toeing Peter in the thigh. "Go on. All you have to say is 'I'm a whore and I'm in love with another whore.'" He ducked down and grabbed Peter by the ear. "Admit you have feelings for her, and we'll let you fuck her."

Peter's dark eyes narrowed. "Let her go. Her Master will only make your lives miserable. Play with me. Fuck me. You know I'll make it far better than a newbie who doesn't know how you like it. I'll even let you—"

"Shut up." Grabbing the leash from Larry, Daxton dragged Peter by his collar over to me. Grass and mud stained his legs as he struggled to crawl, choking as his collar cut into his windpipe.

Dumping Peter at my feet, Daxton grinned. "How about you, pretty new girl? Do you have feelings for the boy who's sucked far more dicks than you?"

My back prickled with sobs.

Panic etched the corners of my mind.

Self-preservation urged me to check out.

Turn blank and mute and go.

I couldn't look away from Peter kneeling before me.

His eyes so worried.

His heart so weary.

Just like all the others.

Corine and Citra, Kirk and Dane.

So many broken faces.

But the one face that stuck in my mind on repeat was *his*.

The man responsible for all of this.

The man who was my eternal enemy.

Henri fucking Ward.

I hated that my heart clung to his image.

An image before his lies crashed like a house of corrupted cards.

He might've fooled me into thinking he had feelings for me. I might've fooled myself into thinking I had them for him. But there, in a storm with demons surrounding me, I truly accepted that I was alone.

I'm alone and…about to die.

Unless…

Sex was sex.

My body was just a body.

They can't touch me…not truly.

No matter what happens to my mortal form.

I'm the watcher within.

And…I don't have to watch.

Raising my head, I prepared to step into battle, just like Peter.

This would probably destroy me.

I would never be the girl I once was.

I would hate every moment.

Die every second.

But…I'd do it because I was brave enough.

Brave enough to fall in love with thirty jewels and be willing to trade my body, my life, my very soul so they could be free.

Reaching down, I caressed Peter's wet cheek just as another sheet of lightning turned midnight to daylight. The answering thunder throbbed in my teeth as I gave him a quick, quavering smile. "I'm okay. I'm choosing this. You don't have to fight for me."

The three Masters chuckled and crossed their arms. No doubt waiting for me to spout my undying affection and pledge us as soulmates.

Peter wasn't my soulmate, but he was my friend and purpose.

I'd been brought here to save him.

And so…I'll save him.

As many times as I can.

"Ily…" He clamped his hand over mine. "Don't."

"It's okay. I'm fine. Everything is fine." Tugging my fingers back, I wriggled my feet deeper into wet earth.

I visualised a cord of grounding light.

A cord that would keep me safe until all of this was over.

Rain seemed to pour faster, heavier, baptising me further into a hell.

Starlight descended on my shoulders, glowing from behind black-blotting clouds.

I might never get free.

I might never see Krish again.

But I would damn well fight for as long as my body allowed me to.

My father's voice echoed in my head; a moment of sage wisdom.

"All things pass, my daughter. Good and bad. Happy and sad. This too shall pass. And you are brave enough to be patient."

Backing away from Peter still gasping on the ground, I reached for my bra strap.

All three Masters pinned their greedy gazes on me.

My stomach turned into a slicing barbwire, butchering me from the inside out.

But my voice didn't shake as I said, "Let Peter go. If you agree not to kill either of us, I won't tell anyone what happens here tonight. My Master will never have to know. Victor doesn't have to know. Just…let Peter go, and I won't fight."

"Ily, please don't." Peter shifted in the muddy grass, his hand reaching for me. "I didn't ask you to trade yourself—"

"Won't fight, huh?" Daxton chuckled even as his eyes flared with lust. "But what if we *want* you to fight?"

"Then…I'll fight." I shrugged. "It's simple. I'll do whatever you want if you just let Peter go."

Peter shook his head. "Ily, please—"

"Done." Daxton, who seemed the ringleader, clapped his hands. "Larry, find a tree and tie Peter to it. We'll let him go after we've had our fun." His smile was pure filth. "Can't have her reneging on her offer by releasing him too soon."

Crowding me, he cupped my cheek and dropped his gaze to my bra. "We're all gonna fill you up, pretty girl, and only once you're dripping will we let you both go."

My heart buried itself as deep as it could into courage. "You promise you won't kill us?"

"Cross my heart and hope to die."

Oh, you'll die.

One day.

By my hand if there's any justice.

I nodded and clamped down on my rapidly rising terror.

God, Il.

Now what have you done?

You stupid, stupid girl.

Propositioning was one thing…but going through with it?

My eyes flickered to the two men behind Daxton.

Three men.

Three.

My vision went hazy.

Sobs suffocated in my throat.

I clung to tattered strength as I met Daxton's dark eyes again and nodded. "Fine."

"Take off your underwear. I want to see you."

"Ily, run!" Peter shouted. He earned a kick to his gut from Larry.

He cried out, groaning in agony.

"Come on, whore." With a curse, Larry dragged Peter through the squelchy grass back to the orchard bordering the lawn. His silhouette, as he tied Peter's leash to an apple tree, then lashed it around his throat so he couldn't unclip it, seemed utterly demonic.

With an arrogant laugh, Larry returned, leaving Peter almost choking, surrounded by blood-red apples.

The storm blurred my friend.

I couldn't see his eyes.

It's for the best.

I didn't want to see him while I submitted to this.

My teeth clacked together as Daxton stepped back and unbuckled his trousers. "I gave you an order, jewel. Strip."

"Seeing as Dax has decided he's going first, I call next," Roger barked, already unzipping and kicking off his drenched jeans.

"Fucking assholes," Larry spat. "I always get sloppy seconds."

"Sloppy thirds, actually." Roger laughed.

"If you don't strip, I'm going to hit you and not stop until you do," Daxton breathed, almost inaudible in the storm.

With trembling hands, I obeyed.

Unfastening my bra, I tossed it to the ground, then stepped out of my G-string.

I didn't mourn them.

They'd offered no protection anyway.

My body is just a body.

I'm the watcher within it.

My bones started to rattle with terror.

Don't watch…

I flinched as Daxton put his hand on my shoulder and pushed.

He kept pushing until my knees gave out, and I crashed to the grass.

Don't watch.

Shucking off his black trousers, he tossed them into the rain. His erection stabbed white and long in the night.

Don't watch.

Placing his bare, dirty foot right between my breasts, he kicked me hard enough to scoot me off my knees and onto my back.

I landed with a wince and swallowed a scream as he grabbed my ankles and spread my legs.

I stared at the sky.

At the curtain of twinkling, twirling droplets falling straight from heaven.

Each one was a perfect universe.

Each one full of life to nurture the soil, the earth, the planet.

My heart hurled itself against my ribs as Daxton lowered himself onto me.

Don't watch.

As my body was grabbed by bruising fingers and his weight crushed me into mud, the rain seemed to slow. Prismatic droplets hovered, shooting silver with lightning, then exploding into crystal snowflakes with thunder.

My eyes closed, eyelids pummelled by rain and anchored by lashes weighing as much as the world.

A sweeping, comforting undertow dragged me down and down and down.

I disconnected with my body.

I went empty.

I followed that grounding cord of light as it ushered me away to safety.

I let go.

I fell.

I didn't watch…

Chapter Fourteen

Henri

VISION WAS A FUNNY THING.

I'd once read—on a marathon binge about the make-up of the world and why we fucking existed—that the world was holographic. I read that within every raindrop, blooddrop, breath, and cell, we carried the entire code of the cosmos.

I hadn't understood what the author had been jabbering on about. How the quantum realm was just energy waves until we actually looked and then it became whatever we decided it should be.

But…as I ran through rain and lightning, I began to understand.

The storm fragmented reality—twisting normal things and making them otherworldly.

The thunder rearranged the frequency of the very ground I ran over, making the earth fizzle and fry beneath my feet. The dense liquid in the air saturated my lungs with newness and power, making it hard to breathe.

All of that tried to distract me.

But something drove me.

A gnawing in my chest.

A jagged kind of needling.

Urgency I'd never felt before hurtled me through the rain in search of something…someone…her.

The girl who'd run.

The girl who'd awoken me.

The girl I had to find.

The undone weight between my legs kept me far too ferocious. The memory of her using me to chase her pleasure only ensured I chased her to relieve mine.

She owed me.

I wanted her to put me out of my misery.

To accept her place.

To respect me instead of ridicule me.

I *needed* her.

I needed her to need me.

I need…more.

I ran harder.

Searching.

Needing.

A plastic gemstone glittered at the base of a goddess statue, her marble hair cascading to the ground and her arms wrapped around a bowl of forbidden fruit.

I didn't care what was inside.

The only treasure I wanted was Ily.

But I snatched it up anyway and kept running.

Where are you, little nightmare?

Hunting her was not good for my sanity.

With every step, I reverted deeper and deeper into a prehistoric animal.

I couldn't stop images of what I'd do when I found her.

How I'd fall on her, fill her, bite her—

Christ.

"Ily!" I charged through bleeding water and flinched beneath the might of nature. "Where the fuck are you?"

I wasn't the only animal out here.

There were others.

Too many others.

She's not safe.

Up ahead, my eyes locked onto a scene.

A scene I couldn't make sense of.

A crowd of blackness.

Two creatures of darkness.

And there, on the grass, a third fell onto whatever prey it'd caught.

A part of me cringed in sympathy.

Whoever had been caught would suffer.

But…I had no time.

No morals to stop them.

I have to find her.

I went to veer to my left.

To leave the predators to their kill.

But…

Something.

Unexplainable wisdom.

The harshest throttle of knowing.

My hand clutched the stupid gem, and my legs slowed.

A man's shout rippled through the watery night.

A man high on lust.

A Master getting off on doing unspeakable things.

I waited for an answering scream.

The tears of his prey.

Only silence.

A heavy, oppressive silence that felt…different.

Silence that wasn't just silence.

Silence that tugged me, taunted me, and cloaked me with far more energy than it should.

Energy that seemed…*familiar*.

My heart wrenched.

My feet stopped.

Breathing hard, I glowered at the satanic ceremony up ahead. Curtains of rain blurred the world, flicking it between reality and dreams.

That sensation of *elseness*.

That awareness of *someone*.

I'd felt that pull once before.

I'd sensed Ily's eyes on me before I'd ever spotted her in the club.

Her energy was a tangible thing, threading with mine, binding me to her even as I fought so fucking hard to bind her to me.

You're making it up.

You're drunk on the hunt and—

I shivered as another buffet of sentience quaked through me.

I swiped at my eyes, trying to see, but…I knew.

I knew before my brain could make sense of pictograms and pixels.

Vision could come in many forms.

Knowing could strike even the lowliest of creatures.

And this…it bypassed my paltry eyes, and I saw.

I saw with my fucking heart.

And I *ran*.

With a roar, I charged toward them.

They had her.

They hurt her.

They'll die.

The storm was my friend as I threw myself into whatever entity existed within me.

The diabolical.

The despicable.

The immoral and unhinged.

The strange sensations of my youth returned, but I didn't shut them down this time or convince myself they weren't real.

Familiar black hunger poured through every vein.

My hearing sharpened until the splashing of every raindrop ricocheted in my ears.

My nose became acute, scenting the musk of sex in the gloom.

And my teeth ached as if they lengthened, ready to tear flesh from bone and lap at hot marrow.

I ran faster.

The two men standing with their pants off saw me first.

Their greedy grins fell as I hurtled toward them.

With a snarl, I threw the stupid gem and hit one of them squarely in the forehead.

He stumbled backward, rubbing the mark only for the one on the ground to wrap his hand around a girl's throat and shift his hips.

Time seemed to slow as I looked at the jewel beneath him.

Black hair.

Thunder-dark skin.

Unparalleled beauty that fucking obliterated me.

Sickness gushed.

Possession flared.

And when I noticed her slack and empty face…

I

snapped.

I wasn't human.

I was death.

Everything became a hologram as if I'd stepped through the fabric of time and space.

I became one with everything.

My hands snatched at bodies. My fists punched against bone.

The feral shouts of men were drowned out by thunder as I hit and hit and *hit.*

I punched over and over.

I kicked. I killed. I shed off the restrictions of gravity and physics and was free.

Screams sounded. Curses bellowed.

The snap of feeble bodies and the satisfying delivery of my punishment.

I snatched at the animal on the ground and threw him straight through the air. I caught him before he landed and slammed him with inhuman strength into the ground.

He grunted.

He was naked.

I grabbed his cock and *tore.*

He screamed.

Fingers snatched me as I choked him.

Eyes locked on mine as I killed him.

But I wasn't aware.

Not really.

I was there but elsewhere.

I was floating and furious, violent and vicious.

No pain as men struck me from behind.

No awareness as my fist closed around someone's windpipe and twisted.

He went limp.

I went rogue.

I kicked the bastards trying to hurt me.

I attacked with every atom.

I lost all sense of time as I became carnage itself.

A man sobbed as I broke him.

Another bellowed as I tore him apart.

I relished in midnight-black blood.

I fed on their pleas.

Dined on their agony.

I siphoned down and down into darkness until I didn't remember why I fought.

I didn't know why I lost myself so completely.

Or how I'd ever stop.

All I knew was they had to die.

Die.

All of them.

Every single one—

Garish sunshine suddenly blinded me.

I hissed and raised a hand as another sun snapped on and another, trapping me in a triangle of blazing light.

"Stop. *Immediately*!" A voice boomed through the slapping rain, ringing in my teeth.

The only bastard still alive instantly dropped to his knees. Blood smeared his bare chest, his hands trembling as he raised them. "T-This man attacked us. Shoot him! He killed Dax and Roger!"

"Stay still. All of you!"

I stepped toward my final nemesis.

I licked my lips at the thought of feasting—

"You move, and we shoot!" Another spotlight, another holler. "We gave you an order! Obey it!"

Words.

I spoke those once upon a time.

They wriggled through my desperation to destroy...bringing with them memories of why.

The darkness in my mind receded.

The creature within me paused.

My hands flexed, feeling the tug of torn skin and the hot throb of bruises.

I looked at the carnage by my feet.

Two men.

One with his neck at an unnatural angle and another with a massive contusion where his mangled cock hung.

Both unconscious.

W-Where is she?

"The Master Jeweler is on his way," crackled the loudhailer. "Do. Not. Move."

Shielding my eyes, I looked up at the fortress walls. Massive spotlights angled toward my little massacre, and vague silhouettes of guards aimed sniper weapons in my direction.

The urge to keep killing bubbled in my gut.

I wanted everyone in motherfucking pieces.

But…

Her.

Spinning in the slushy grass, I searched the ground for—

"Ilyana." Her full name fell from my lips as I darted to her side and fell to one knee. She sat up in the rain, her head down and blue-black hair sticking to shock-washed cheeks.

I wasn't prepared for the slap of emotion.

The fist of feeling.

The godawful punch of home.

My heart stopped, then restarted, syncing to hers, always to hers.

"Ily…"

She didn't react as I gently touched her shoulder.

I splayed my hand on her icy skin and grunted as two polarising, primordial forces collided within me.

The beast inside me raged with the primal urge to fuck her as my right as conqueror.

I *despised* that another had put his hands on her.

Put his scent and DNA and—

She cried out as I squeezed her shoulder too hard.

I ripped my hand away.

Fucking calm down, Ri.

Flexing my fingers, my nostrils flared as I did my best to tame myself.

To save her from the unleashed anarchy within me.

I didn't trust myself around her.

Didn't trust I could touch her kindly when every part of me was mean and nasty and noxious.

Never taking my eyes off her, I sucked in deep breaths.

I focused on her and only her.

She caused such chaos inside me.

Such awful things and precious things.

Shame filled me that I hadn't protected her.

Despair that I'd been too late.

She didn't look at me.

I really needed her to look at me.

I needed to know.

What did they do…?

Inhaling a shuddering gasp, she drew up her knees and hugged herself.

She looked so small, so fragile.

The killer inside me raged again.

My monster refused to back the fuck down.

I was feral and raw, and both man and beast wanted to gift her every gory trophy I could.

To present her with the cock that'd hurt her.

To give her the hands that'd dared touch her.

The tongue of those who dared taste her.

The motherfucking souls of any and all who dared possess her.

Including mine.

I shook as urges came too thick, too strong.

I looked over my shoulder at the third man. The man who Victor had ordered to fuck her in front of me when I'd done my best to convince him I wasn't a cop.

He's dead.

Shifting on my knee, I went to stand…

But two things happened.

One, the softest puff of air shot past my face and a tuft of earth leapt from the ground.

And two, Ily touched my hand.

I froze as our eyes met.

My ears rang as the guards on the wall yelled in their loudhailer, "That was a warning fire. The next bullet won't miss!"

I glanced at the pockmark by my knee. I waited for a kick of concern that a sniper could so easily end me.

But I didn't care.

All I cared about was my little nightmare.

She's still alive.

With every blink of her golden stare, her emptiness filled with everything.

Anger, sorrow, hate, and pain.

I felt her emotions as if they were my own.

I *felt* her.

Tangibly, invisibly.

I shuddered with goddamn relief.

The unfightable connection was still there.

Still humming.

Still haunting my every thought and heartbeat.

Words felt foreign on my tongue. "*Est-ce qu'ils t'ont violé?*" (Did they rape you?)

Tears welled in her eyes but didn't fall.

With courage that made me hers for fucking life, she shook her head. "He…Y-You stopped him before—" Her face tightened. "No, he didn't."

All my rage snuffed out.

I bowed with relief.

Not too late.

Not too late.

I wanted to snatch her into my arms.

I wanted to kiss her. Hug her. Never let her go.

But she shifted away from me and tore out my putrid heart.

The animal inside me howled.

It couldn't tolerate her disgust of me when I'd done everything I could to deserve her.

I cupped her chin and tipped her eyes to mine.

She looked at me with sunshine all while I drowned in shadow.

I wanted to apologise.

I wanted to scold.

In the end, I just whispered, "*Tu es en sécurité maintenant.*" (You're safe now.)

She winced and looked down.

Her lashes lowered, refusing to show me just how badly they'd damaged her.

I'd stopped him in time…yet he'd still hurt her.

Rage siphoned through me again. My vision hazed red on the edges. My humanness drowned beneath homicidal violence.

Others had put *their hands* on her.

Another had dared scar her soul.

The only one with that permission was me.

Me.

No one else.

Fuck!

My teeth clenched as I resisted the urge to know everything in explicit fucking detail. I needed to know what they'd done. Needed to make them pay. I'd rouse them from the dead and murder them all over again.

My fingers tightened, *tightened* around her jaw.

"Henri…" She flinched and grabbed my wrist. "Y-You're hurting me."

"*Merde.*" Dropping my hand, I let her bury herself into her knees. "*Je suis désolé.*" (I'm sorry.)

I couldn't seem to remember English. My first language thick on my tongue.

She shook her head, not saying another word.

In her silence, other things came to my red-coated vision.

The way she quaked with a thousand shivers.

The way she moaned as if she couldn't breathe without mournful sound escaping.

But she didn't cry.

Her eyes were dry even as raindrops poured over her strained, stunning face.

She rattled with aftershocks; goosebumps puckered her grass-stained skin.

Without a word, I undid my shirt buttons, yanked the hem out of my trousers, and tore the soaking thing off my body. As tenderly as I could, I draped it over her trembling form. Bundling her into the wet fabric, she gave the softest whimper as I pulled her arms through the sleeves and buttoned her from throat to core.

Only once her nakedness was covered in sodden black cotton did I stand and bend over her.

"We said don't move!" ordered a guard on the wall.

"*Va te faire foutre*!" (Fuck you!) I shouted back.

I ducked.

She winced as I threaded one arm around her back and one beneath her legs. "W-What are you doing?"

I cursed her flinch.

I loathed her fear.

English returned along with human intelligence. "I won't hurt you. You're safe with me."

She sucked in a breath and shook her head.

I didn't know if she argued she was safe with me or didn't want me to pick her up.

Either way, both were happening.

"*Je jure*," (I swear), I breathed. "I'll take care of you."

She gave me nothing.

But I didn't need her to speak to hear her judgement.

I'd whittled away her trust ever since I told her I wasn't going to save her.

I would never get that back, and…in that storm with blood on my hands, it fucking hurt worse than anything.

Footsteps pounded behind me as I took her weight, plucked her from the ground, then hefted her into my arms. The cuts on my knuckles and radiating pain in my back didn't bother me.

Her silence and broken softness did.

It did horrible, horrible things to me.

It confused and bewildered me because the beast inside still very much wanted to hurt her. To stamp his brutal ownership on her and replace whatever mark that cunt had left behind, but…beneath that longing lurked another one just as strong…perhaps even stronger.

It wanted to hurt her, yes, but it wanted to hurt everyone else a *thousand times fucking worse.*

"Henri. What the *hell* is the meaning of this?" Victor yelled as he marched into our battleground. Four guards trailed him while a fifth held a black umbrella over Victor's head. The guard fought a war, trying to keep the wind from snatching it.

Words replaced the roars in my head.

I settled back into being nothing more than a man.

Swallowing back the taste of metallic blood—my blood—I cradled

Ily close and shrugged. "They touched what was mine."

Victor looked past us. "Who the fuck tied Peter to a tree? In a goddamn lightning storm?"

The skinny, pot-bellied man who I hadn't managed to murder staggered to his feet. "I-I did, Vic, but it was only—"

"Are you *trying* to turn him into a barbecue?" Victor snarled. "Because one bolt of lightning and poof." He snapped his fingers. "He's Sunday's roast."

"Sorry, Victor." The man dropped his eyes.

"Go release him and take him back to the stables." Victor glanced at one of the guards.

"Yes, Sir." The guard nodded and splashed through the grass to do what he'd been commanded.

"And *you*." Victor pointed at me. "Explain."

"I told you." I shrugged, my biceps bunching with Ily's weight. "She makes me irrational."

"*Mon Dieu*, you test me. *Je deviens trop vieux pour ces conneries*." (I'm getting too old for this fucking shit.) His eyes narrowed on the two men who hadn't moved. "Whatever you've done seem beyond the capabilities of Dr Belford." Pulling out a walkie-talkie from his blazer, he cupped it to avoid the rain. "Call Captain Roderigo. Two need to be airlifted to the hospital."

A crackle and a response. "Yes, Sir."

Shoving the walkie-talkie back into his pocket, he pinched the bridge of his nose as if I'd once again tried his infamous patience. Finally, he sighed, dropped his arm, and glowered. "If they're dead, you and I are having yet *another* fucking conversation."

I nodded. "I understand."

"Just…" He flung up his hands, hitting the brolly edges. "Just go to bloody bed, Henri. Before I shoot you."

I bowed my head. "As you wish." My eyes caught the discarded gem that I'd found and hurled at some Master's head. Clutching Ily tight to my chest, I grabbed it, placed it awkwardly on her stomach, then stalked through the thunderstorm. "Goodnight."

I didn't stop until I'd dripped all over Victor's stone pavers in the foyer, left a path of rain up the stairs, and sloshed my way down the storm-drafty corridor.

My hand slipped on my doorknob as I shifted Ily's weight in my arms.

She tried to get down, but I just shook my head, opened the door, kicked it closed, and carried her into the bathroom.

Placing her gently on her feet in the shower, I turned the water as hot as she liked it—boiling brimstone—and unbuttoned the same shirt I'd only buttoned up a few moments ago.

She didn't say a word as I stripped her.

Didn't move as I tossed the soaking material out of the shower, then tore off my own clothing. Only once I was bare as her did I reach for the sweet-smelling body wash and fill my palm.

Her eyes squeezed closed as I gently rubbed suds into her grass-stained skin. My teeth gritted as I fought prehistoric urges and focused on cleansing her from that other bastard.

I didn't look at her face. Didn't dare study her eyes. The only thing I could focus on was ensuring her bones weren't broken and her body wasn't destroyed. Her soul would come next…only once I was sure she was physically in one piece.

Keeping my attention on where I washed, I glowered at her shoulders, arms, wrists, and hands. My soapy fingers covered her in fragrant bubbles.

The cuts I'd given her a few days ago had healed nicely, slowly fading my autograph.

Was it wrong to hope those little slices would scar?

A permanent reminder that she belonged to me?

"Henri…I'm fine. You don't need—"

"I have to," I growled. "Just…let me, okay?"

Sighing, she nodded.

Her permission waked around me as I bathed her, scrutinised her, and kept my touch as detached as possible.

Her right arm was intact.

Good.

I turned to her left and repeated the inspection. Rinsing away green smudges, I glared at a couple of small scratches. A faint bruise on her elbow. A wince as I massaged her hand.

"That hurt?" I asked.

Her back tensed. "I hit Larry. I-I think something cracked."

"You *hit* him?"

Not looking up, she just huffed. "Fat lot of good it did."

My awe of her tumbled over. "You're far too brave, little nightmare."

"Not nearly brave enough," she whispered back.

Silence fell.

Letting her hand go, I slid my fingers to her shoulders and down her front. She flinched as I rubbed my thumbs over her nipples and caressed her full breasts.

Her eyes snapped closed. She stayed stiff and unyielding.

My heart thudded as I dropped my touch lower.

With gritted teeth, I washed between her legs.

"How close did he get?" I grunted at how soft she was, so delicate.

Her eyes flew wide. Her cheeks flushed, but she held my stare. "He…he breached a little but didn't get any further."

He was inside her…

Even a fraction.

Fuck!

Black-hot fury tore through me all over again.

How fucking *dare* he.

How fucking dare he touch her…*hurt* her.

I lost myself as I inserted a finger, desperate to eradicate him from her mind and memory. I struggled to stay human. "D-Did he hurt you…past the obvious?"

Temper flashed in her sunshine eyes; anger I wasn't prepared for. "No more than you."

I winced. Couldn't help it. The scorn and condemnation in her gaze arrowed directly into my heart. "I'm sorry."

"No, you're not," she said coldly. "If you were, you'd realise what you do to me. How you make me feel. How cruel you are even when you think you're being kind."

"*Cruel?*" I choked. I kept stroking, trying to remove as much of that bastard's imprint as possible. "I-I saved you."

I didn't think about the sexual implications. Didn't demand anything of her. This was clinical. Medical. Unemotional.

Unemotional?

Fuck.

I burned *alive* with emotion.

She jolted as I continued touching her, then looked away. "Yes, you did save me. And for that, I owe you a thank-you."

It felt as if my blood caught fire.

The creature within me wanted to do a thousand things to deserve another thank-you. To give her a million reasons to be grateful. To be worthy of her praise.

He almost stole her from me.

My finger hooked against my control.

Rip-roaring fury blazed as the mental image of that bastard on top of her exploded in my mind. Slaughterous contempt made my hand plunge deeper, driven by a mania I couldn't stop.

Twisted jealousy.

Rancid loathing.

Tangled self-disgust.

I wanted to beg for her forgiveness and roar at her for putting herself in danger.

I couldn't handle the unravelling of my sanity.

One finger became two.

She swayed on the spot, her stomach flexing. "Henri…stop. What are you—"

"I need him out of you. I need you to be okay."

"I'm fine." She sniffed, pushing at my trembling form. "You stopped him. He didn't—"

"He had you on your back."

"And you threw him off me before—"

"He should *never* have gotten that close to you."

Yanking at my wrist, she withdrew my fingers and glared. "Yes, well, that part is your fault."

"*My* fault?"

She shook her head with age-worn weariness. "You stole me, remember? You brought me here. You're the reason I've been molested by two men when—"

"Hang on." I frowned. "Two?"

She shrugged. "Do you honestly think I would've slept with you if you hadn't tricked me into playing along with you? Are you so corrupted by this place to believe I sleep with you by *choice*?" Her beautiful face turned nasty. "It was my choice to submit to that bastard Daxton tonight—not because I wanted him but because I wanted to stay *alive*. They were going to kill us. Me and Peter. And I made the choice. An unbearable choice. But I made it because I didn't have any other! And you know what? I'll probably have to make a similar choice in the future because you can't be everywhere at once, and one day, you won't be in time. One day, one of those bastards will hurt me, and I fucking *refuse* to let them break me."

She scoffed and laughed caustically. "And besides, you and I both know that eventually, Victor will ask for his turn, and then what will you do? Rip off his cock like you did Daxton?"

"Yes."

"You do, and he'll kill you."

"I don't, and I'll die anyway."

She rubbed her face and gave a tattered little scream. "Stop it. Just *stop it*!"

I frowned. "Stop what exactly? Caring for you? Cursing you?" I crowded her against the tiles. "You are *mine*, little nightmare, and I will defend you as such."

"You don't care about me. You only care that I'm your little chew toy and got jealous because someone else played with me!"

"Of course I fucking care!" I roared. "Have you not been listening? Jesus Christ, Ilyana, I almost lost myself seeing that cunt on top of you. I committed murder for you. I almost ripped off his cock for you. Why would I do that if I didn't care?"

Not letting her reply, I snarled, "And I'm fully aware you are not my toy. You are not my possession. But you *are* mine. You are my fucking *wife,* and if any other Master wants to test my commitment to you, then—"

"I'm not your wife, Henri," she cried with a strange, frustrated scream. "You're fooling yourself! Believing in things that aren't real. I will never be any more than what you turned me into. I'm a collared possession, nothing more!"

I staggered back, needles of firewater falling over me.

I'd expected her to snap into sobs, not bristle with barbaric rage.

The fall from earning her gratitude to being reminded of her hate fucking eviscerated me.

Wiping my mouth with a shaking hand, I struggled.

Fucking struggled with existing.

In that single second, every emotion I'd ever been denied suffocated me like toxic oil.

I shouldn't be surprised.

It shouldn't even hurt.

After a lifetime of being denied love, I'd grown rather used to it.

But now?

Fuck, *now*?

I didn't know what to feel.

Only that I felt *everything*

Every emotion.

All of them.

Craving and confusion, admiration and anger, disgust and despair. Horror, relief, grief—too many. Far, *far* too many.

Swooping into her, I grabbed her by the hips. "If I have to drag you before a priest and force you to say some binding words to make you believe my pledge to you, then so be it."

She squeaked as my fingers kept squeezing.

The bones in my wrists ached.

My knuckles turned white.

I couldn't unbury myself from the avalanche of feeling after feeling after *feeling.*

I'd never had someone to care about before. Never had a reason to hate if my loved one was threatened. Never suffered jealousy. Never learned how *violently* my heart would revolt at the thought of losing what was mine.

My fingernails dug into her.

Fury spilled like poison.

She's mine.

And they tried to take her from me.

That made me feel…

God, how does that make me feel?

Furious. Possessive. But…beneath all those self-serving, selfish rages, another one lurked. One that came with excruciating pain and screeched with absolute warning.

Sour sickness crawled up my throat.

Sickness I never wanted to suffer again.

Fuck!

"Henri…" Her fragile fingers landed on my shower-wet chest. "Y-You're hurting me."

"*Merde.*" Ripping my hands off her, I backed up.

She'd said the same thing when I'd grabbed her after I'd fought those bastards.

Such a condemning sentence delivered by the softest whisper.

"I didn't mean to…I—" I sighed heavily. "I'm sorry."

She hates me.

Her haunted eyes locked on mine as I stood ramrod straight.

I tripped into her stare, counting the swirling shadows and sorrow that hadn't been there before.

My stomach knotted.

I swayed back another step.

Instinct blared that the emotion currently welling in my every vein—the emotion coated in sickness—wasn't just possession but…

Fear.

It's fear.

…you're motherfucking terrified that you've lost her.

My hand lashed out.

I grabbed her chin and stepped forward.

She gasped as I crowded her.

Her fingers locked around my wrist, hot water sending curls of steam around her head as if she wore a halo. Her shoulders tried to brace, but they rolled instead, attempting to cocoon herself in protection. "Henri…stop it."

My arms longed to wrap her in a hug, but a lifetime with no intimacy meant I was an uneducated beast. A childhood of no embraces equalled an adulthood of lonely pain.

I didn't have the first fucking clue how to touch this girl.

I wanted her to see me as someone different.

I needed her to feel my regret instead of my darkness.

We stood there awkwardly, the shower pummelling us in scalding heat.

When I didn't speak, her tension dribbled down the drain, and she sighed. "Look…it's over, okay? I'm fine, thanks to you. He didn't hurt me…thanks to *you*. I'm grateful, Henri. Extremely grateful, but…you can't get angry with me for pointing out the truth."

"The truth?" I spoke around sharp gravel. "The truth that I'm no better than they are?" A red, horrible haze dripped over my eyes. "The truth that each time you sleep with me, it's because you don't have a choice? That you don't…enjoy it?"

Her lip curled as if to throw filth in my face. To deny her wetness or her orgasms.

I braced for it.

But then she slouched and said quietly, "I do enjoy it. Despite how I feel about you, our bodies are, unfortunately, perfect together."

A tragic laugh fell from my lips. "So our sex is perfect, but the rest—the stuff that knots souls together—is shit?"

Pinching the bridge of my nose, I backed up.

I couldn't find the shore in this tempest of emotions she drowned me in.

"I don't know what you want me to say." Her voice was too quiet, too soft.

"Say that you feel the same way as I do. Say that you'll give me a chance."

Her tears welled but didn't fall.

She never let them fall anymore.

"Seeing as you're so fond of the truth…fine." She balled her hands. "Allow me to tell you my honest-to-God feelings." Sucking in a breath, she murmured, "I like you. As awful as it is and as much as I don't want to…I like you. I like the man I see right here, standing before me. The man who rescued me, who looks at me as if I'm infinitely precious—the man who knows right from wrong."

My chest swelled with heat, only for her to puncture it.

"The moment I saw you in Paris, I felt something. Something strong and nonsensical. Something right in here." She pressed her fingertips over her heart. "You took my breath away, Henri. You made butterflies swarm in my stomach. When you offered money to sleep with me, I was flattered and aroused, and I thought…maybe."

"Maybe?" I whispered.

"Maybe it was destiny. Maybe it was fate. Maybe we knew each other in a different life, and that's why you felt so familiar." Her eyes hardened into amber chips. "But then you gave me to Victor, and all those maybes died. Maybe we might have been happy. Maybe we might've dated and fallen in love. Maybe we might've gotten married. Maybe we would've lived happily ever after. *Maybe*."

I cursed my stupid, stupid heart for its desperate eagerness. "We can still have those maybes, Ily. Just because our relationship isn't conventional doesn't mean—"

"The moment you turned your back on us—the second you refused to save the jewels—you made an unforgivable choice. A choice to become one of them and forsake all of us. You choose to abuse me all while calling it monogamy and marriage."

Stepping into me, her temper returned with wicked hellfire. "You brought me here. You condemned me to this. And you don't get to be angry with me for choosing to survive. You don't get to look at me as if I was stupid to fight back. You don't get to judge me, or scold me, or expect me to fall into your arms with sobs of gratitude. *Thank you* for saving me. *Thank you* for stopping him. For the first time since you chose to stay here, I see a shimmer of goodness still inside you. I wish that goodness would win. I wish you'd remember why you came here, but I know that most wishes don't come true, so…I will accept who you are, not the man I wish you would become."

"I'm—"

"I'm not finished." Her nose rose with aristocratic poise. "I will say it one last time so you know how genuine my feelings are. I will never forget what you did, and a part of me will always be grateful to you for protecting me despite everything else you do. But…I need you to see that what you did tonight was for your benefit, not mine."

"*My* benefit?"

"You saved me for yourself. You saved me because you think I belong to you, not because you care."

I swallowed hard, drowning beneath thick, rising nausea. "Don't assume you know how I feel, Ily. And you're wrong. You do. You *do* belong to me."

"No. I don't." Her eyes softened as if whatever she'd say next had the power to slaughter me. "You're lost, *Master* H. You're all alone. You were born alone. You will die alone. And while you keep me against my will, you will stay alone."

I staggered back.

Just like I'd never enjoyed love, I'd never learned that ordinary words in the mouth of someone you cared about could cut as deep as daggers.

They sliced me.

Wounded me.

My teeth bared to teach her a lesson.

My hand came up to grab her, but then…I took another tripping step backward instead.

She watched me warily.

I wanted her.

My hunger and thirst for her were fucking unbearable.

But that goddamn fear twisted everything.

I'd saved her because if anything happened to her—

Christ.

I twisted to face the wall and shoved a fist in my belly.

I swallowed hard as hot bile crawled up my throat. My nostrils flared as I did my best to lock down the old parts of me and embrace the ruthless comfort of finding a place where I belonged.

I reached for it.

Begged for it.

But then Ily shocked me stupid by slipping between me and the wall and dropping to her knees. She caught my eyes before grabbing my throbbing erection and sucking it into her wet, hot mouth.

That primitive creature inside me roared.

She dropped all my guards and arrowed into my heart.

Fuck.

I could come in a second.

Explode in a heartbeat.

I groaned and thrust forward, knocking her head against the wall.

She moaned in discomfort but didn't stop blowing me. She looked up the length of my body, and my hands landed on her temples, my fingers brushing through her soaking blue-black hair.

So soft.

So perfect.

So *mine.*

My soul burst open.

My blood shook off its ice and embraced sunshine instead.

In one submissive move, she fucking enslaved me.

"Ily…" I wanted to kiss her. I wanted to revoke that final rule about keeping intimacy out of our roleplay. I wanted her to fall in love with me. I *needed* her to care.

But then my hazy eyes met hers, and I froze.

She didn't watch me like I watched her. Didn't sink into feelings of awe and attraction.

Fuck no.

She watched me like an enemy sizing up their opponent. A talented little terrorist intent on using my weaknesses against me.

And I stupidly confessed my greatest weakness is her…

Yanking my cock out of her mouth, I swatted away her fist. "What the hell are you doing?"

Prim and far too composed, she dropped her hands onto her lap. "I'm adapting."

"Adapting?"

"To what's expected of me."

"What's that supposed to mean?"

"It means you didn't come at dinner. Victor's pissed at me for what I did, and you've been tasked with punishing me for it. I assumed that would be your next command. Especially now you've rescued me and cleansed me and fixed what went wrong. I'm yours again, aren't I? You want to make sure of it, am I right? You want to replace him with yourself. To ensure every piece still belongs to you." She laughed, shocking the hell out of me. "So…I made another choice. To be the slave you think I am. To serve you the way you think I should. To ensure neither of us forgets exactly what we are."

I hated that she could read me. That she'd seen all that and reduced our connection to nothing more than Master and slave when I wanted so, so much more.

"You're mistaken," I seethed. "I've told you time and again that I want more than just your body."

"Well, my body is all you'll get, *Master.*" Climbing to her feet, she splayed her hands. "Release me. If you don't want to fuck me, then let me return to the jewel quarters and—"

"You're not going anywhere. And don't use that address when we're alone, especially not in that tone. Call me Henri or nothing at all."

Her face etched with annoyance. "Make up your damn mind."

"Excuse me?"

"You told me to call you Master H at dinner."

"When we're in company only."

"Fine." She smiled full of poisonous sugar. "If you're not going to use me, *Henri,* then…what's the point?"

"What's the *point*?" My mouth hung wide. Words deserted me. The punching agony in my chest made it hard to catch a breath. "The point, you beautiful, psychotic little nightmare, is I *like* you. I like your company. I like arguing with you, talking with you, and yes…I like fucking you. You left my side for all of two minutes tonight, and another man had you on your back, so forgive me if I never let you out of my motherfucking sight again!"

She didn't so much as flinch.

Not a single reaction to my confession that I liked her back.

More than liked her.

I…

"Well…" She slowly turned around and turned the shower off. Silence rained between us; the tendrils of steam no longer just wisped around her but fogged the entire bathroom. "If you're not going to have sex with me, what *do* you want?"

I pinched the bridge of my nose again.

Christ, didn't she know?

It was fucking obvious!

I opened my mouth.

I scrambled for words.

And…nothing.

I couldn't stay here.

I'd do something bad.

Stalking from the shower, I shot out of the bathroom and dripped water all over the bedroom carpet. Wrenching open the mini-fridge by the throne chair, I grabbed an icy beer.

Fucking woman.

Fucking jewel.

Fucking pathetic human heart.

I'd hunted for her because she belonged to me.

I'd killed for her because the thought of her dead or broken ripped out my guts and hung me from the gargoyle-infested parapets.

What was the point in talking to her when she flatly refused to see what I wanted? Why should I run the risk of allowing the heartsick idiot inside me to resurrect when she didn't want a single scrap of my affection?

Fuck it.

I'd gone to war tonight.

I'd murdered in her name.

And somehow, with that stupid act of goodness, she stripped me of my newfound happiness.

Broke my blissful sanctuary.

And ensured the acerbity of nausea tainted every swallow of my beer.

I'd been free of that curse.

Free of feeling.

I wasn't equipped to go back there.

Wasn't strong enough to survive craving again. Longing again. Not after a lifetime of begging someone, *anyone*, to see me, want me, love me.

Was that so much to ask?

Was I that unlovable that even the girl I'd killed for wanted nothing to fucking do with me?

Fuck!

My hand curled around the beer bottle.

My insides turned glacial.

No more.

I'd tried. I really had.

I'd hoped. Against all odds.

And now I had to face the facts…

She would always hate me.

I would never be able to change her mind.

If I had to turn my back on wanting her heart and soul to protect my sanity, then so be it.

I'd settle for her body and her fear.

Screw affection.

Fuck connection.

She wanted to be my slave?

Well then…

She just got her wish.

Chapter Fifteen

Ily

I TREMBLED BENEATH HOT WATER.

I needed a moment.

A million moments.

After Henri stalked out of the bathroom, I didn't have the strength to follow him. Didn't have the courage to survive another fight, so…I chickened out.

I turned the shower back on and raised my face to the rinsing heat, begging it to wash out my mind as well as my body.

Flashbacks of Daxton.

Echoes of Peter telling me to run.

I shuddered.

I wanted to go back to the jewel quarters. To make sure Peter was okay and the others had survived the treasure hunt.

Go out there and ask nicely.

He's just as angry as you are…it makes sense to have some space from each other rather than stew all night in bed.

Nodding with bravery I didn't feel, I turned off the water and grabbed a towel.

I'll go out there and thank him again. I won't remind him that he's responsible. I'll act as if he's my hero in every way, and then…he'll let me go, and I can have a night in peace.

Drying my hair, then wrapping the towel tightly around me, I sucked in a deep breath and crept out of my steamy sanctuary.

My eyes shot to the throne chair in the corner.

Empty.

I glanced at the bed.

Also empty.

My heart rabbited with hope that he'd left and then stopped dead as Henri cleared his throat from behind me.

Spinning on the spot, I clutched my towel as he leaned against the wall by the bathroom door. Naked and still slightly damp, draped in shadow where the side lights didn't reach. He watched me with eyelashes at half-mast, casting his grey stare in absolute darkness.

His tongue ran along his bottom lip as he looked me up and down. "Seeing as you're fine enough to argue with me. Seeing as you still have that intoxicating fire and fight in you and insist you're of sound mind to make choices to sleep with men you hate just to prolong your life. I'm going to ask you one simple question."

I backed up, heading toward the bed. "Henri…I think you're still infected with whatever energy the storm churned up." My eyes flashed to the curtain-blocked window. "It's gone now. The rain is slowing, and the thunder is gone. How about you calm down and—"

"Calm down?" He chuckled under his breath. "Calm down?" Pushing away from the wall, he stalked toward me. "I *am* calm, little nightmare. In fact, I'm the calmest I've been in days." Stopping close enough to touch but keeping his hands to himself, he canted his head and gave me a terrifying, totally arousing smile. "You see, I finally understand that no matter what I try to give you, you're unwilling to accept any of me. I am nothing to you. I will *remain* nothing to you. How did you so eloquently put it? I was born alone and will die alone?"

"I-I didn't mean it exactly like that."

"Oh?" He shrugged. "How did you mean it?"

"I just…" I pursed my lips. How could I tell him that watching him fight on my behalf did unconscionable things to me? That his violence turned me on. That his vengeance didn't just invoke gratitude but lust.

Sweet, savage lust that had no place in here.

No place with us.

No place *ever.*

Cursing my betraying body and the way he hunted me across the bedroom, I tipped up my chin and tried to hide everything. "I'm sorry if I hurt your feelings."

"The fact that you acknowledge I even have feelings is an improvement, I suppose."

I frowned. "Of course you have feelings. I never said you didn't. I just…they're not entirely normal, Henri."

He nodded. "I see."

Goosebumps shivered down my back. "You see what exactly?"

"You think I'm one of them."

I scowled. "I've told you that. You are. As long as you turn your back on the jewels and are complicit in what the other Masters do, you *are* one of them."

"Fine." He shrugged. "In that case, it won't matter what I do then, will it?"

I gulped. "W-What are you going to do?"

"Get rid of the towel."

"What? No—"

"I wasn't asking. Drop it, little nightmare. *Now.*"

My eyes flashed to the door.

"Run and see how that ends for you." He shuddered and wrapped a hand around his hard length. "Actually, I'll *tell* you how that ends for you." Backing me closer to the bed, he whispered, "If you run, Ilyana, I will chase you. I will catch you, and I'll slam you against a wall and fuck you until you scream." He closed his eyes and sucked in a breath, his fantasy playing out between us as if he'd projected it on a big screen. "I wouldn't be able to stop myself. I'm barely holding onto my sanity as it is. So please, if you want me to live up to the expectations you have of me—the expectations that I will hurt you, bruise you, and use you—then go right ahead."

My breath caught.

I couldn't stop the clench inside me. The sinful little flush. The awful, awful acknowledgement that the girl I'd been before…the nice girl…the kind, *normal* girl who didn't punch rapists in the nose and didn't trade her body for a friend's life hadn't died back there in the storm.

Whoever stood in her place, I didn't know her.

But I did know she wasn't nice.

She was dangerous and dirty and…

Stop it.

You're still you.

Just…changed.

He smiled tightly. "By the way, while we're on the topic of being used…" With speed too fast to stop, his hand lashed out and grabbed at the knot in my towel. With a fierce yank, he tore it off me, leaving me naked and shivering. "You used me at dinner. You're right about that. You used me as if I were some vibrator stored away in your nightstand."

His chin tipped down, darkening his eyes even more. "I was prepared to treat you like my wife tonight. The thought of another hurting you? Watching someone else put their hands on you? *Fuck.*" His fists balled, and his entire body flinched as if he suffered honest-to-God pain. "I can't get the pictures out of my head. Him on top of you. You blank-eyed." He shivered. "I thought you'd broken. I feared you'd snapped and left me. But…I should've known you were so fucking strong. So unbelievably, *deliciously* strong, and so…I'm going to treat you exactly as you expect to be treated. I will do it because I know you'll curse me and hate me, and if those are the only two emotions I can earn from you, then…fine. I'll take them because fuck knows you won't give me anything else."

"What are you saying?" I cupped my breasts, my entire nervous system on high alert.

Scalding heat simmered in my belly, catching fire to all my other cells.

Ever since we met.

Every second since we noticed each other, I'd been at the mercy of this…this unwanted affliction. He was a virus overtaking my system. An insidious illness turning my very wants and needs against me.

If I didn't find a cure soon, I would die—storm or no storm, island or no island.

"I'm saying that if you want to be my slave so badly…" He exhaled heavily. "If you want to keep that line drawn in the sand between us? So be it." Striding to the wardrobe, he yanked it open and grabbed the tie he'd been wearing at the nightclub.

The faint whiff of his woodsy, citrusy cologne from that night drugged me instantly.

Memories of the way our eyes had locked.

The way the stars had sung.

And fate had laughed.

I'd meant what I said in the shower.

He'd given me butterflies and every other winged stupid thing.

My eyes locked on his hands as he snapped the tie tight and gave me a dark, devilish look. "Stand by the four-poster. Hands up."

Another gush of need flowed through me.

I tried to stop it.

I *hated* that I couldn't.

His voice. His words. His body. His threats.

It made me a sick, sick person that everything about him terrified me and turned me the hell on. A trickle of moisture. A betrayal of everything I believed in.

I shifted my hips.

I tried to hide.

Too late.

His gaze dropped between my legs, his nostrils flaring. "Shit, y-you're wet."

"No, I—"

"Lie to me about that again, and I'll throw you onto the carpet, here and now."

Oh God.

The image.

The *need.*

His entire body trembled as he slowly lowered the tie and cocked his head. "Jesus Christ, how did I not see it?"

"See what?" My nose wrinkled, common sense pouring icy water on the flames in my blood. I looked down at my body, cursing the traitorous shimmer coating the inside of my thighs.

The spark between us threatened to explode.

This was different to when he'd drawn my blood in Victor's trophy slaughterhouse. Different to when he'd spanked me by the pond and different to all the other moments where we'd done things to survive—both of us knowing full well there'd always been *something* lurking beneath our acting.

I couldn't get wet if I wasn't drawn to him, and he couldn't get hard unless he wanted me.

That was the truth right there.

The *only* truth.

The one thing that condemned us because as much as I didn't want to play this twisted game, I couldn't deny I was complicit in it.

Marching into me, he grabbed a handful of my hair and held me tight. His eyes lit up with blinding silver. He was starving…starving for the very thing he kept asking for that I couldn't deliver.

"It's true. Fuck…I…" His fingers scalded; his body heat seared.

I swallowed hard as electricity crackled between us. His eyes fell to my lips.

For a moment, I feared he'd kiss me.

The one thing he never did.

I had a horrible suspicion of why that was.

Why we both stopped at that line.

A kiss was intense and intimate.

Taste and truth.

Both those things had the potential to decimate the cardboard fortress that kept wilting around my heart.

"If I told you that I have dreams of rutting into you on the lawn. Of making you sob as you come and screaming my name as I bruise you…how does that make you feel?"

I convulsed.

The sickness tore through me, hijacking all my control.

His eyes turned black; his voice thick. "If I told you I wanted to string you up and gag you. If I admitted I wanted to eat you out, then cut the inside of your thigh with my sharp little knife…what parts of you respond?"

What parts?

God, *all* of them.

I grew damp and hot and wet.

Horribly, *disturbingly* wet.

I couldn't help it.

I'd never been able to help it.

Why can't I help it?

I hated this man.

I feared this man.

He was the reason my life was ruined, yet…right here, right now, I'd never felt so alive. So cherished as he'd pummelled those who hurt me. So precious as he killed for me—

God, Ily…stop—

"If I told you I wanted to drag you into the dungeons. If I admitted I wanted to whip that hate right out of you and force you to feel every part of me…would you fight me or bow for me?"

Fire.

Everything was on fire.

He was flames and fury, burning me alive with his wrath.

I didn't believe in fairy-tales.

I didn't really believe in destiny.

So why did Henri and I burn so badly together?

No, not just burned…*blazed.*

There was a name for that.

A label for that.

My eyes flew wide.

Horror filled me.

A Vedic astrologer told me once.

He warned me—

No.

It can't be.

It can't—

Henri spun me around, then marched me back until my spine slammed against the wall. Tugging my head aside with his fist in my hair, he pressed his lips to my throat. "If I told you that my teeth literally ache to bite you. That my tongue stings with the need to taste you. That my body is moments away from taking yours—with or without your permission—what would you say?" His teeth threatened to puncture. "Answer me. Or I'll answer for you, and if I do…there'll be no going back."

I gasped as he licked me.

My heart thundered as he bit above my collar.

Gently at first.

Then harder, *harder.*

His arms bunched as if trying to restrain himself, caging me against the wall.

I tried to speak. I tried to push him away but every sense, every awareness locked on his hot, hot mouth pressed against my highly sensitive skin.

He trembled as his self-control snapped.

With a guttural groan torn from the depths of his monstrosity, he tossed away the tie and sank his incisors into me.

I fought him.

Instinct made me struggle to get away.

But at the same time, a heaviness fell over me—a haven full of dizzy desperation.

I submitted.

Just like a deer in a lion's mouth.

Just like a fox in a trap.

I went loose and full of longing, all while I did my best to get free.

I tangled with two very different, very potent things.

He groaned as he broke my skin.

I flinched and cried out in pain.

Pain that morphed into mind-scrambling pleasure.

He snarled as he tasted my blood for the second time.

I was burning, *burning.*

I'd never been so hot, so tight, so needy.

The word for what we could be together shot into my head again.

A word full of could haves and maybes.

A word full of destiny and star-crossed fate.

He could've been my everything.

He could've been my only.

But not here.

Never here.

He lapped me, inhaled me.

I couldn't stop him.

Kicking my ankle aside, he wedged himself between my thighs and hoisted me up the wall. My legs automatically wrapped around his hips. His throbbing hardness pressed against my core.

I couldn't keep fighting anymore.

I felt faint and woozy and upside down.

W-What's happening to me?

My hips rocked forward on their own accord, needing, needing, *needing.*

Cupping my cheek, his fingers shook as he pulled away from the wound he'd caused and licked at a ruby streak on his bottom lip. "Goddammit, little nightmare…"

My chin came up.

His tipped down.

He came so, *so* close to kissing me.

My heart burst wide open.

He hurt me worse than anyone.

He was driven by demons I could never exorcise.

Yet as he stood there, crazy-eyed and dripping in need, I saw him.

The *real* him.

The lonely boy. The tortured man. The feral monster.

And in that single moment of time, I forgave him, wanted him, *begged* him.

Pressing his forehead to mine, he reached down and angled his cock to find me.

I didn't judge my complicity. Didn't care the bite on my neck drove me deeper into delicious hell. We were a match made in perfect fucked-up heaven, and I clawed at his back to finish what he started.

I needed to be claimed, bruised…awakened into this new misery where I'd fallen.

Henri stroked his thumbs on my hipbones—that maddening, mocking swirl. "It's driving you insane, isn't it?" His entire face resembled that of the beast inside him—cut with shadows and hollow with wanting. "Now you know how I feel every second I'm around you."

Every emotion overflowed.

Every heartache and fear.

With a cruel smile, he reached for my breast and twisted my nipple.

Hard.

"*Ahhh.*" I squirmed in his punishment, only to scream as he thrust violently inside me. "Oh God—"

Stabbed against the wall with his cock, I couldn't stop the convulsing clenches that sucked him deeper.

"Jesus Christ." He fisted my breast again, squeezing me so damn hard.

My eyes watered with agony.

My body reached another level of crazed.

"*Qu'est ce que tu es en train de me faire?*" (What are you doing to me?) His eyes tangled with mine, swarming with ghosts and monsters. "What the fuck is happening to me?"

The same question I'd thought.

And still no answers.

"I have no idea how to survive you." He twisted my breast again, his thumb digging into my nipple.

My vision was full colour.

My body a riot of anguish.

Any other man and I'd be in full combat mode.

Any other abuse and I'd be in tears.

But with this man and this abuse?

Fuck, I almost came.

He bent his head and lapped at the bite mark on my neck.

A full-body shudder had me falling into yet another level of desire.

I'd never felt this way. This unbound. This honest. This *free.*

Feeding a whisper directly into my wound, he rutted deeper, deeper into me. "You think I'm like them. You call me a rapist like the other Masters. But…you're wrong. I'm not a man who can hurt another and get off. I thought I was. I feared I was, but you…you showed me that I need someone to fight me. To be brave enough to survive me. I need *you.*" He groaned as he bit me again, tonguing my blood. "Christ, I need you. *Only* you. You make me so goddamn hard. You're messing with my mind, Ily. But…if I'm brave enough to face what I am, then you better be too."

Pulling away, he glowered at me as if he truly hated me, all while falling into war with me. "I'm a sadist, little nightmare. There, I said it. I confess I want to string you up, whip you, bleed you, and do a thousand bad things to you—"

"Oh my God." My head fell back.

I wanted to tell him to stop. To shut up. To keep his perversions to himself.

Yet my ears rang for more.

My core fisted his penetrating length.

I throbbed.

I *ached*—

"Fucking hell." His forehead landed on mine, our sweat mingling, our essence binding. "You're perfect. So damn perfect." Nuzzling my cheek, he whispered, "If I'm a sadist—if I'm finally ready to admit that word—then, I hate to tell you, little nightmare, but you—with all your morals and sweetness, beneath all your goodness and bravery—you are nothing more than my angry, dirty masochist."

My eyes flew wide. "What—?"

"I'm not done." He couldn't look away from my mouth, his face tight with hunger. "And the best part is…you don't even know it."

Masochist.

The word echoed.

It grew teeth and chewed into me.

It became a dagger and slaughtered me.

Because I suddenly *did* know.

It answered my question.

T-That's what's wrong with me.

That's why—

"The label fits, doesn't it?" He swayed closer to my lips, hypnotized against his will. "I might not have seen who you truly are beneath your prickly ferocity, but I did wonder the moment I realised what I am. You grow so wet for me despite your hatred. You fuck me like you love me, all while despising my touch. You were desperate at dinner because I spanked you and didn't finish you off, yet you covered it up with a nasty powerplay of taking from me."

Lowering his voice, he came so close to my mouth. "Tell me, Ily…didn't that feel wrong to you? Taking from me instead of letting me give you what you deserve?"

"What I *deserve*?" I glowered, doing my best to see straight when every molecule vibrated out of control. I swallowed a groan as he continued to rock into me. "You think I deserve all this pain?"

"Yes." His gaze darkened to a flat sterling. "I do. Because you cause me pain just by existing."

His mouth came closer, closer. His lips agonisingly near, too near, tinglingly near.

My heart kicked.

I swayed forward despite myself, summoned as if he was a necromancer bringing a black, black part of me to life.

That creature in the storm—the girl who was ready to murder and turn her back on everything—stalked bolder through my veins. My claws kept growing. My needs kept changing. Metamorphosing and rewiring the last of my pieces until I had no idea what I'd become.

His chest heaved, scattering the last remaining droplets on his skin.

I was afraid of him.

Wet for him.

Exhausted by him.

But I really, *really* needed him to kiss me.

A shocking, soul-wrenching connection weaved between us.

The way he'd defended me tonight.

The way he begged me to accept his black-riddled heart.

I had no immunity anymore.

No defence against him when he had an uncanny knack of making me see the tortured boy within, all while layering me in bruises.

Swallowing hard, he grunted, "This is me, Ily. *All of me.* You can't change me. I. Can't. Change. God knows I've tried. I hate being this way. I hate that I can't let you go. I hate that I can't stop. I hate that you hate me, but when you look at me the way you are—without all that loathing I deserve—you make me wonder if I could have your heart…after all."

I couldn't look away.

The hollowness of his cheeks and intensity of his smoky eyes…

It was a terrible, *terrible* thing to be in lust with your enemy.

A tragic, tragic thing to completely forget why you should hate him when every part of your heart said ***mine.***

God, this needs to stop…before it's too late.

His hips drove into mine, fucking me slowly, thoroughly.

Ahhh, don't stop…I take it back.

Don't.

Stop.

My clit hummed.

My lower belly tightened.

My vision grew hazy as he grabbed my throat and added punishment to my pleasure. Squeezing me above my collar, he hovered over my mouth again. His pace increasing. His cock plunging and withdrawing.

"*Fuck*, you feel so good."

His curse almost made me come.

I moaned as he rutted shallower, crueller—

"You're mine, Ilyana," he growled. "Every piece. You're mine to use. My slave to fuck." His voice turned guttural. "Mine to defend. Mine to kill for. *Mine*, do you hear me? All mine, always mine…whether you hate me or not."

I couldn't speak anymore.

Deny anymore.
He blinded me, deafened me—
"Kiss me," he suddenly whispered, his plea hot on my lips.
My eyes shot wide, fogged with clouds of passion.
Our stare locked.
His breath caught.
And then…
…his mouth *slammed* over mine.
I froze.
I died.
I waited for him to realise his mistake and stop…
Only this time—
He didn't.
Plastering me to the wall, he fucked me.
And while his body violently claimed mine, his tongue speared into my mouth.
Trapped against his powerful bulk I had nowhere to go, nowhere to flee.
He kissed me.
Kissed me.
Damn, did he kiss me.
His tongue hunted mine. His dark taste full of rain and lightning.
His primal growl detonated every piece of cellotape holding my cardboard fortress together.
Not just a kiss.
A reckoning.
A plundering.
A takeover.
His hands pawed at my body, setting fire to every cell. His touch brutal and unkind. His fingers decorating me with pain and ownership.
Every thrust, he grunted.
Every plunge, he shuddered.
He kissed me as if I was his only reason for existing.
And I had no choice.
None whatsoever.
He stole a kiss, but he gave me his soul.
And an exchange happened right there against the wall.
A forlorn heart for a lonely heart.
A forsaken life for a forbidden life.
And I broke.
I slung my arms around his shoulders.

I opened my legs wider.

I kissed him back.

The moment I licked him, his restraint—*what restraint?*—exploded.

Our kiss turned demonic. Violent. Hedonistic.

We went to war with each other; we *devoured* each other.

Our teeth clacked, our breaths threaded, our lips bruised and worshipped.

And that was where it happened.

A meditative quality cascaded over my mind, silencing all thoughts, worries, and fears. My spirit expanded through my body, billowing from my chest into every organ, bone, and limb.

I tingled in my extremities.

My sensitivity became excruciating.

My awareness arrowed on him.

Just him.

Always him.

His hot hands on my breasts.

His hot tongue in my mouth.

His burning, burning body as he rode me and smothered me, trying to crawl all the way inside me.

Our hearts synchronized.

Our souls forged.

I became aware of *everything,* all while knowing nothing at all.

Energy spiralled between us.

A vortex, a helix…

Synergy.

Salvation.

An orgasm tingled.

A full-body, heart-bonded release—

"Ily—" He bit my throat, making me bleed again.

Knowing he took my lifeforce.

Knowing he needed such primitive connection.

My climax hovered on a painful crest.

And for a moment, I touched pure, pure happiness.

Yes.

Yes…

"Fuck—" His black voice entered my subspace. "I need you to come. Come for me, little dream. Come because you want me…just as much as I want you."

My eyes flew wide.

Dream.

He sucked in a breath, noticing his slip.

His rhythm faltered just for a second.

Just enough for the rapture within me to crack.

Heinous truth flooded back.

This is wrong.

He's *wrong.*

What on earth are you doing?

What mad delusion had I drunk to believe, even for a second, that I wanted this man after what he'd done to me.

"Stop," I whimpered.

"*Merde*, you taste divine. I've been wanting to kiss you for so damn long." He kissed my cheeks, my eyes, my nose. "Every damn day."

He kissed my lips.

Drinking me down.

Drugging me.

"Stop," I whispered into his mouth. "You have to—"

"Come," he groaned. "Come with me—"

"*Stop*," I snapped. "Henri, please."

He didn't hear me.

Too far gone.

Too deep.

Too dark.

I was shattering, splintering—

"*Let me go*!" I scratched his shoulders, all while my body tensed to release in rip-roaring agony.

He thrust.

Hard.

Viciously, brutally hard.

Short, sharp, savage pumps.

An assault on my body and mind.

Breathe.

Just breathe.

That meditative fog only grew thicker, making me heavy and lost.

My blood sang.

My core clenched.

My climax didn't belong to me anymore.

It belonged to him.

"Stop…" I begged even as my hips gyrated and back arched.

My mind said no more, but my body said give me everything.

I split in two.

Battling right and wrong.

The more I struggled to get away, the more my body burned.

"Don't." I felt as if I'd break apart—shatter into the cosmos and become stardust. "Henri, stop!"

The refusal, the fight—it twisted and tangled, tempting the madness inside me and his lonely monster.

"Christ, yes." His snarl as he jack-knifed into me made my hair stand on end. "God, I love feeling you struggle."

I fought harder.

Grew wetter.

Climbed up that high, high mountain of bliss.

This was no longer about physical survival.

It's spiritual.

"Henri…"

"Ily." He kissed me again, gagging me and destroying me in one brilliant move.

He licked me.

Oh God—

Everything turned into a supernova.

A nebula of light.

A blackhole of endings.

I lost.

I came.

I came *excruciatingly* hard.

I screamed.

I became a different person.

Nothing more than flesh and feeling as I impaled myself on him and gave him everything.

He grunted as if I'd ripped out his heart and crushed it in my bare hands.

He thickened inside me.

His rampaging hips almost shunted me through the wall.

"God*dammit*," he roared.

The crown of his cock pounded against my G-spot.

I didn't stand a chance.

My second orgasm didn't just detonate in my core but in my very spirit.

"Stop. Oh God. Oh God. Stop. *Please* stop."

He was killing me.

Suffocating me by pleasure.

On and on.

My body fisted him.

Rippling.

Milking.

"*Fuck*!" The jerks as he came.

The shudders as he spilled inside.

Spurting deep, deep within—coating me, marking me, making me his.

A full body quake as he fed me his final drop.

Panting hard, he slammed his forehead against the wall by my ear as he struggled to breathe.

And that was where horror found me.

What we'd done.

How I'd felt.

What he'd called me.

And the awful truth about everything.

I felt as if I'd leap out of my skin.

My heart was a traitor.

My body my biggest enemy.

I need to run…

"Henri..." My voice caught on tears. Tears I would never shed in his company. Tears that threatened to river. "Let me go. Please…*please* let me go."

Slowly, he reared back.

His lust-glazed eyes met mine.

He went to kiss me with awe and affection, but…whatever he saw made him trip backward, disengage, and shove me far, far away from him.

Chapter Sixteen

Henri

JESUS CHRIST, WHAT DID I JUST DO?

What the fuck did I do?

She stood there.

Wide-eyed, white-shocked, my cum oozing down her inner thigh.

She told me to stop.

Merde, how long had she been begging me to stop?

How had I not heard her?

How had I lost myself so completely?

I tripped back another step.

Echoes of my orgasm butchered me. Memories of her body fisting my cock mocked me.

I-I kissed her.

Fucking hell, ***why*** *did I kiss her?*

I'd ruined everything.

Every goddamn thing I'd turned my back on.

Every monstrous thing I'd become.

My past and present tangled and tore, leaving me in a wasteland of feelings and guilt.

Such motherfucking *guilt.*

My lips stung from her taste. My tongue burned from her blood.

The moment I'd taken her mouth, I'd broken.

I'd forgotten all her promises to hate me.

I'd shredded all the despair between us.

I'd seen a fresh start.

Hope.

Whatever intelligence inside me that spoke words and walked on two feet died beneath the prehistoric awakening where only two emotions existed.

Love and longing.

I'd fallen into the pit of both.

I'd shattered my legs on impact; cracked open my soul upon

descent.

I'd felt more from a single kiss than I had in my entire godforsaken life, and instead of feeling the same tidal wave of connection, Ily looked at me as if I'd destroyed her.

Not her choice.

I forced her.

"*Are you so corrupted by this place to believe I sleep with you by choice?*" Her cutting question in the shower slapped me around the head. *"I'm not your wife, Henri. I will never be any more than what you turned me into."*

I couldn't breathe.

"The moment I saw you in Paris, I felt something. But then you gave me to Victor, and all those maybes died."

I crippled beneath loss.

And fear.

Such motherfucking fear.

I wanted to turn back the clock and never steal her.

I wanted to wind it back until I was never born.

"You were born alone. You will die alone. And while you keep me against my will, you will stay alone."

Fuck.

I bordered hyperventilation.

The fear became too much.

The fear of losing her to another. Of losing her to Victor and death and this place.

But really…I couldn't lose something I'd never had.

I couldn't miss something she'd never given me.

Couldn't hoard something I'd never earned.

Sucking on air, I did my best to claw my pieces back into place.

I needed that darkness. Craved to return to that black abyss.

I couldn't cope like this.

Feeling like this.

So what if I'd drowned in ravenous devotion while she'd begged me to stop?

So what if I didn't stop?

So what if I used her?

I'd told her I would.

She was my *slave.*

She said it herself that was all she'd ever be.

I did nothing wrong!

So why did everything feel so fucked up?

That kiss.

That goddamn kiss ruined *everything.*

Ah, Christ…

Raking both hands through my hair, I choked with a gush of nausea.

Daxton almost raped her tonight.

He'd tried and failed.

But me?

I'd succeeded.

I didn't stop.

I stumbled again, punched and kicked by the truth.

I didn't stop.

I hadn't stopped when I took her against her will in Victor's dead zoo either.

This is what I am.

This is what I wanted.

So why did I choke on shame? Why did I break beneath grief and guilt and grotesque self-hatred?

Because of that motherfucking kiss!

The moment her tongue touched mine, I'd hoped.

The second she opened wide, I swore her heart reached out to mine. There'd been something. Something transcendental. Something ethereal and sacred and—

Christ, you're a fool.

Completely screwed in the head.

She didn't kiss me back.

She fought me off!

Look!

Look at what you did.

Look at what you've become.

Blood trickled beneath her collar.

Shadowy bruises marked her breasts.

Teeth marks punctured her throat.

She looked as if she'd been attacked.

Not by the man I'd killed to keep her safe but by a man who'd let evil turn him into something un-fucking-forgivable.

And instead of kneeling for her forgiveness. Instead of flaying myself alive for ever laying a finger on her…I felt pride for marking her as mine.

Balling a hand in my gut, I turned away from her.

This was by far the worst thing I'd ever done.

Not because I'd done exactly what I promised and treated her like my jewel but because…I'd thought she *wanted* it.

Damn, even the monsters inside this castle didn't slip that far into insanity.

They knew their boundaries.

They accepted they would never have the love of a jewel and contented themselves with their pain instead.

But me?

Me?

Ha!

I'd deluded myself into thinking she could forgive me.

Believed in a fucking fairy-tale that she'd suddenly switch from hate to love and choose me.

Choose me?!

No one would *ever* choose me.

Because I didn't deserve to be chosen.

Sighing heavily, I slowly turned back to face her.

Gritting my teeth against her tear-brimming eyes, I swallowed the razors in my throat. "Go to bed, little nightmare."

And then I barged past her and imprisoned myself in the bathroom.

I needed bars.

And locks.

And chains.

I needed to get a fucking grip before I killed her, all because she'd just killed me.

Chapter Seventeen

Ily

"WHERE THE HELL DID YOU learn to fight like that?"

I looked up from where I kneeled beside Henri. The wooden deck beneath my bare legs was comfortingly warm, the new sunshine extra bright as if shining in apology for the storm's wrath three nights ago.

God…has it really been three nights?

Time had never passed so slowly or so awkwardly.

The energy in Victor's citadel was electric with animosity.

All the Masters kept a careful, hateful eye on Henri, avoiding him as if he might suddenly kill another of their ranks. No guest dared come near me. No one even looked in my direction.

It was as if we'd been in a snow globe of untouchability for the past three days—thanks to Henri's ruthlessness during the treasure hunt and Victor's ominous disappearance.

Seventy-two hours he'd been missing, and now…*here he is.*

Lucky me.

I schooled my face to remain impassive as I glanced up at the lord of this despicable estate. He looked as cool and collected as usual, with orange-tinted sunglasses perched on his sharp nose.

Henri shifted in his chair, finishing his swallow of coffee as he looked up at Victor. "Excuse me?"

Victor helped himself to an unoccupied chair and sat down. Dressed in a beige polo and linen shorts, he was the epitome of a rich asshole on holiday.

An inconspicuous waitstaff appeared, placing a plate of cut fruits, mini pastries, and a freshly brewed cup of coffee before Victor.

Grabbing a piece of pineapple, Victor plopped it onto his tongue and said midst-chew, "What you did to my two unfortunate guests the other night. Where did you learn to do that?"

I shot Henri a look.

His white t-shirt almost blinded, and blue jeans made him far more handsome than any man had the right to be. Even now, after everything,

I still couldn't look at him without a kick of unbearable attraction. It didn't help that his knuckles were still raw, and a few bruises hinted he'd been in a brawl and won.

A small smile crossed his face, sinfully hot and devilishly gorgeous.

Ever since what happened between us.

Ever since my body proved exactly what it needed and embraced the awful word Henri called me, I hummed with vicious arousal.

His every move, his smell, his presence.

Watching him read was pure torture.

Having him refuse to talk to me was ridiculous foreplay.

Masochist.

I'm a masochist.

I wished it wasn't true.

I waited for my heart to refute it, but…he'd weaved a curse around me.

As soon as he'd mentioned that damn word, I was his.

Unbearably, unwillingly his—and he'd avoided me ever since.

"So?" Victor scowled, yanking me out of my thoughts. "You gonna tell me how you did what you did, or is it some sort of secret?"

Henri dabbed his mouth with a napkin, wincing a little as the cuts on his knuckles refused to heal. "Secret? Why would it be a secret?"

"Oh, I don't know." Victor rolled his eyes behind his tangerine lenses. "The fact that secrets seem to be a trend with you? First, you sneak into my home under false pretences, then you announce you're a Mercer, and now you murder as easily as if you're a hired assassin." Leaning closer, he smirked dangerously. "What other skeletons are in your closet, *mon ami*?"

Henri flicked me a look, his eyes black and stony.

God, my golden collar and cuffs seemed extra heavy today.

The bite mark on my neck ultra bright.

For three days, he'd shut down.

Buried himself in books and closed out the world.

The longing I'd grown used to—the unshielded yearning within him that made my heart flutter despite myself…all gone.

Or at least…hidden.

He'd been monosyllabic ever since he'd left me dripping against the wall, and I probably deserved it.

He saved me.

Avenged me.

That one act of kindness had somehow negated all his badness…at least in my newly twisted mind. I curled my fingers into fists on my knees, ignoring the small twinge in my hand from punching Larry.

When Henri had exploded out of the darkness like some murderous werewolf—when he'd given a lupine howl on the storm's wind and morphed from a man into a tornado of violence…that'd been the moment things had changed for me.

Not in the shower.

Not in our bedroom.

That moment.

And…no matter how hard I tried, I couldn't undo that moment or change how my heart now felt.

He'd saved my mind from ruination.

Protected me from a lifetime of emotional scars.

He's still good…deep, deep inside.

I know it.

Running his fingers over my bare shoulder, Henri didn't seem aware he'd reached for me as he tipped his chin at Victor. "No more skeletons, Vic. I swear."

The way he reached for me…even now. The bond between us…despite everything.

I'd been wrong to think he was heartless.

If anything, he was heartful.

Too full.

Overflowing.

Drowning.

"Fine…tell me, then. How did you fight so well?" Victor asked.

"Would you believe me if I said I have no idea?"

"No idea?" Victor's eyebrows rose. "You're saying it was all instinct?"

Henri continued caressing me.

I wished he wouldn't.

Wished I didn't have to shift to hide what he did to me.

"I'm saying they made me irrational," he said. "*She* makes me irrational."

"Ah, yes." Victor scowled. "You became…how did you put it? Murderous?" He dropped his navy stare to where Henri stroked me. "Tell me, have all your crushes created this sort of violence in you, or is it just lucky Ilyana?"

My nipples pebbled beneath the scant silver bikini a maid had delivered after Henri had called for clothes for me. Something suitable for swimming. Something that allowed him to see me but hid forbidden parts from others.

Not that I was complaining.

The stretchy Lycra was the most decency I'd had since arriving here.

"Just her, I'm afraid," Henri muttered. "And as much as I wish I could undo her hold on me, I can't. Besides, I did warn everyone not to touch her." He threw a scowl at the guests having their breakfast, deliberately ignoring our table. "Least they're aware now."

My skin broke out in goosebumps as my heart quickened.

The longer Henri touched me, the harder it was to ignore the rapidly building fire between us. A fire that only seemed to grow stronger every time we were near.

Flames incinerated my insides the longer this awful silence between us stretched.

Say the word…

Admit what he might be…

You were warned by that astrologer. He said one day you'd find your—

Enough!

Just like I knew Peter wasn't my soulmate, I refused to entertain the idea that Henri might be my…

I shut that thought down.

God…if only he'd kept fighting that night.

If only he'd grabbed me and run the opposite way—toward the drawbridge and onto the plane—like a true gallant knight should. Everyone knew the saviour *saved* the damsel, not carted her back to the tower to ravage her.

And wow, did he ravage me.

"I need information, Henri," Victor clipped. "Tell me how you did it."

"I have nothing to tell. I just…let myself go." Henri shrugged, his fingers still sending pinwheels of heat through my blood. "I wasn't thinking about anything apart from making them pay."

"And you've never trained in Muay Thai or mixed marital arts?"

I looked between the two men.

Was Henri a master in warfare like Victor suspected?

The way he'd attacked those creeps. The typhoon of fists and hurricane of violence.

I could see why Victor was interested.

He'd seemed…inhuman.

"Never." Henri shrugged. "However, now that you mention it, I used to watch quite a few matches on YouTube when I wasn't working at the bar. MMA has always interested me. Brutal sport. Maybe I picked up a few tricks that way?"

"Perhaps," Victor muttered, all while looking highly doubtful. "From the accounts of my battlement guards, it sounds as if you turned into a death machine."

"I'll take that as a compliment."

"I wouldn't, if I were you." Victor smiled thinly. "It's got me thinking…"

Henri finally stopped touching me and placed his hands on his lap. "Thinking about what exactly?"

Victor just tapped his nose.

"Am I in trouble, then?" Henri raised an eyebrow. "Is that why you've been MIA for three days?"

"Trouble?" Victor blinked away his thoughts. "Frankly, you're always in trouble, Mercer. And no, I had other urgent business come up." He sighed. "To be honest, if your last name wasn't Mercer and I didn't get such a kick out of befriending my enemy's brother, I think I would've tossed you in the sea by now."

Henri chuckled.

Chuckled!

As if Victor—one of the most unpredictable, menacing men I'd ever met—just made a joke.

"Ah, come now, Vic." He smirked, the bruise on his freshly shaved jaw from someone's punch slightly green in the sun. "You'd miss me far too much."

Victor's mouth twitched. "And there is the crux of my little problem."

"Your problem being that you like me?"

Victor huffed. "Strong word."

"So…did I kill them?" Henri asked warily. "You said if I killed them, we'd be having another conversation. Is this another conversation?"

Biting into a strawberry puff pastry, Victor pouted as if he honestly didn't know if he enjoyed Henri's company or wanted to choke him with his danish. "A friend of mine at the local hospital called yesterday. Daxton passed away, but Roger is stable. However, he'll never walk again, seeing as you snapped his neck."

Henri leaned back with a scowl. "Isn't a broken neck usually a death sentence?"

"Not if the spinal cord isn't damaged. You were close." His face darkened. "Lucky for you, you didn't succeed."

"But Daxton—the one who hurt Ily…he's dead. That's a bonus."

Victor shot me a black look. "Pronounced deceased at five a.m. that morning." He pinned Henri with a judgy glower. "Died of a ruptured penis, if you must know. Apparently, whatever trauma you delivered created a hematoma that burst. He bled out before they could operate."

"Serves him right." Henri toasted Victor with his coffee. "He shouldn't have touched her."

The sun slithered behind a cloud, drenching all of us in shadow.

My skin prickled with goosebumps at the callous way Henri spoke of killing someone. He didn't exactly rejoice, but he didn't show any remorse for stealing a life, either.

Did that make him crazy or sane?

Safe or dangerous?

His eyes flickered to mine as if he sensed me questioning so many things.

My heart stopped.

He jerked.

All those guarded feelings in him crowded behind the walls he'd tried to erect.

He looked as if I truly undid him, only this time…he'd begun to despise it.

"You know, *mon ami*, if you enjoy dispatching my guests so much, perhaps I will put you to work, hmm?" Victor sipped his coffee, watching Henri over the rim.

Henri tore his gaze from mine. "What's that supposed to mean?"

Victor shrugged. "I should be reprimanding you. All my guests are aware I don't tolerate brawls or in-house violence. To fight one another equals immediate chastisement or a revocation of their invitation. I even sent Larry home yesterday as I'm not in the mood to listen to his whining. But…"

"But?" Henri stiffened.

"Lucky for you, you actually did me a tiny favour."

"How so?" His forehead furrowed.

Victor carelessly tossed me a blueberry and custard tart and lowered his voice. "A little birdie told me that Daxton wasn't keeping secrets as well as he should. He informed someone about the location of my Elysium. I obviously don't need to tell you what a big fucking no-no that is. Especially with your brother hunting. He was one of the scant few who I let boat here. The rest I fly in—windows blindfolded and no address given. I thought he was trustworthy after a decade of his company. I was wrong."

"Do you think Q was behind it?" Henri asked. "Bribed him to talk?"

"Who can say?" Victor leaned back. "All I know is…Daxton Hall was a walking dead man. And it pleased me to think of him enjoying himself, one last time, all while knowing he wouldn't be leaving here on Sunday when he was due to go back home to his wife and three little girls."

I froze with the sticky, sweet tart at my lips.

My stomach growled.

My appetite roared.

But the thought that the man who'd almost raped me had three daughters? That he had no empathy to be able to put his own flesh and blood into my shoes. Or imagine how he'd feel if another man did to them what he did to me…

My mouth gushed with sick saliva.

I threw the tart onto the grass. A cloud of cheeky sparrows descended in glee.

Henri's gaze cut to me.

I looked up.

Our eyes caught all over again, and he did yet another of his heart-scrambling tricks. Bending a little, he tucked a few straight strands behind my ear and continued talking to Victor as if he hadn't just blown my aching chest apart.

"How many of your guests know your exact location?"

Victor smirked. "Why? Do you want it?"

"I won't deny that I'm curious." Henri glanced around the glittering castle, gardens, and wealth. "It's my new home, after all. Even if I have made a reputation to be avoided in here. I'd like to know my address."

Victor kept a careful eye on Henri before he smiled. "If you're still curious in a decade, I will tell you." He waggled a finger. "As long as you behave and stop giving me reasons to murder you, of course. And don't worry, they'll come around. They're only waiting on my verdict."

"Your verdict?"

"To kill you, banish you, or forgive you."

"Gotcha." Henri tossed back the dregs of his coffee. "Well, I hate to tell you, Vic, but if you haven't killed me by now, I think I'm safe."

"Yes, you definitely act like it."

Henri laughed.

Victor didn't.

"Right, if that's everything you wanted to discuss?" Henri stood and tapped me on the shoulder. "Come, little nightmare. I fancy a fuck by the pool. If you'll excuse us, Vic—"

"Not so fast, Mercer." Victor stood too, his gaze snagging on his preferred jewel, Rachel, as she appeared from the citadel's wide-open doors.

I didn't know if Henri meant what he said about taking me by the pool—considering he hadn't touched me in days—but all my wondering paused as my eyes locked on Rachel.

On the stiff way she walked.

How she cradled her middle as if her innards would come tumbling out.

How her body shimmered with black and blue bruises beneath her see-through teal dressing gown.

What the hell happened to her?

Or a better question…*who* the hell happened to her?

Victor ran his tongue over his bottom lip, keeping a careful eye on her as she hobbled toward our small group. "Thanks to you, there's far too much pent-up testosterone in here, Henri. I will take partial blame by making the mistake of introducing Ily to my esteemed guests and then forbidding them from touching her. But you made it worse by breaking my laws and flouting your possessiveness." He smiled tightly. "Things are not balanced, and if monsters are to play nice, there must always be balance."

Henri stiffened. "What are you saying?"

"I'm saying I need a few new jewels…to soothe over the current upsy-daisy."

"Ah." Henri didn't dare look at me. "You're going hunting. Where?"

Victor gave a thin, smarmy grin. "Normally, I would go myself. I'd actually planned such a trip a few days ago. I was going to leave the morning after the treasure hunt, but…your latest fuckup ensured I had to stay, and then I received some news that I'm still…processing."

"News?"

"We'll get to that." Victor shrugged. "So you see, *mon ami*, not only did you prevent me from going on a little foraging expedition—where I happen to like sampling new *bijoux* before bringing them back to my friends—but you've also ensured I need to rebalance the energy in my home."

Flicking me a look, he added, "In an ideal world, I'd toss your jewel to another Master and take you with me for some 'bonding'. Your handsome face could help me fish all kinds of beauties. But alas…" He sighed dramatically. "I can't fly you off my island because of the risk of fratricide by your sibling, and I need to oversee a few things here. Therefore, I've arranged a few business associates to gather at least three new gems. They have my requirements and will be delivered momentarily."

I almost vomited on the deck.

More girls and boys.

More like me.

Targeted, taken…never to be seen again.

I wanted to *kill* him.

To stop him from stealing the lives of poor, unsuspecting—

"Fascinating," Henri drawled. "I'm glad you know how to remedy the situation." He glanced at me with guilty eyes. "You're very proficient, Vic. But now…if you don't mind, I really am itching for a fuck, so—"

"So impatient." Victor smirked and beckoned Rachel to walk faster. "As it so happens, I have the exact same affliction, but we both must wait. What have I told you before about patience being a virtue?"

Rachel's lips thinned in pain as she came to a stop. With trembling hands, she lowered her arms from her bruised middle and gave Victor a tight smile. Lowering her head, she presented herself docile and serene, but her curvaceous figure trembled, sending her gown shivering around her legs.

My heart convulsed.

I wanted to hug her.

To tell her that her agony would stop…one day.

Somehow.

For all my complicated desire for Henri, I hadn't forgotten my promise.

Or my determination to get the fuck out of here.

"I have a proposition for you." Victor smiled as he tucked raven locks behind Rachel's ear. She gasped and went to kneel, but he clucked his tongue. "No, no, stay standing, sweetling." With a doting caress on her cheek, he reached into his pocket and withdrew a leather leash. Clipping it onto her collar, he looked at Henri. "I would so hate to have to punish you, Henri…after everything we've gone through together."

Henri stiffened. "*Punish* me?"

"You did me a favour by ending Daxton and his snitching. And I forgive you for Roger. I never really liked him. With your violent skills, I feel comfortable that Joyero will be safe if and when I do leave on business—as long as you're fighting on the right side."

"Of course," Henri muttered. "I apologise for my behaviour, and you know I'm on your side. I've proven that—"

"You have, and I appreciate it. I also appreciate this new skillset of yours. You see…I catalogue all my guest's strengths and weaknesses, and you've turned out to be a gift that keeps on giving. If a time comes when I need your ruthless abilities, you better be prepared to aid me."

"Aid you how?" His face filled with shadowy wariness.

"Kill." Victor laughed. "What else? Did you think your money would ensure you didn't have to work to stay here?" He clucked his tongue. "Silly boy."

Henri didn't say anything for a moment. "Who…who do you expect me to kill?"

"Well…" His eyes flickered to Rachel. "It's not who but how many, but to start with…you could aid me in dispatching this one. I don't really care how you do it. Just that it's done."

"Wait, *what*?" Henri staggered back. "You want me to kill your jewel? Have you lost your fucking mind? I thought she was your favourite."

"She was. And I wish it didn't have to come down to this, but she disappointed me and needs to be punished."

Henri choked. "Punishment isn't usually fucking murder, Vic."

"The retaliation must match the level of rebellion."

"What rebellion?"

Victor ran a hand through his hair. "She's pregnant."

My heart stopped.

A gush of sickness twisted my stomach.

Oh God.

No…

"What do you mean…she's pregnant?" Henri went fatally still. His grey eyes landed on bruised, shaking Rachel. "H-How?"

"The usual way, I suspect." Victor sniffed as if she was dirt on his shoe. "She did it deliberately, the little witch." His face turned black. "Probably thought she could use me to elevate her position. Dr Belford assures me her contraception was up to date, so—"

"It's not one hundred percent foolproof, you prick," I hissed, unable to stop myself. "Are you that fucking diabolical that you'd kill your own child?"

Victor glowered at me. "It's not mine."

"You told me yourself that you don't loan her out to just anyone anymore." Henri wiped his mouth with his hand. "How long has it been since she was with anyone but you?"

Victor paused and actually did some math. Eventually, he said with a trace of annoyance, "Months."

"And how far along is she?" Henri dropped his stare to Rachel's sensuously curved belly. She didn't look pregnant, but that didn't mean—

"Six weeks or so."

"So, it's yours." Henri crossed his arms. "She's carrying your child."

"And I don't want it," Victor snapped, tossing Rachel toward him. "So…do something about it."

Henri caught Rachel and gently pushed her into the chair he'd vacated. Breathing hard, he scrambled for something to say. "Back in your office. The day you made me talk to my brother. Do you remember what you said?"

"Is this your way of trying to get out of your duties, Mercer?"

"Just answer the fucking question," Henri snarled. "What did you say to me?"

I shot a look between them, remembering the way Victor had softened and looked at Henri with almost wistful eyes. I'd struggled to breathe. Winded from Victor's backhand and cradled in Henri's arms…but I remembered.

It'd given me chills.

Filled me with horror.

The thought of a child being raised in this place…*good God.*

But if it saved Rachel's life…

"You said you were in need of an heir," I whispered. "You said that you created this island because you don't fit in anywhere else. Henri reminded you that sometimes…you still feel that loneliness."

Henri threw me a look then nodded. "Ily's right." Pointing at Rachel, who sat slouched and crying, he snarled, "There's your goddamn heir, Vic. *Your* blood. *Your* kin."

Victor crossed his arms.

His face remained unreadable as he studied the jewel he'd so callously asked Henri to dispatch.

It took forever.

His decision came with so many terrible consequences: accept his offspring and innocence would be born into hell. Don't accept his offspring, and Rachel would die, and Henri would be the one to do it.

Tears stung my eyes as I reached for Rachel's shaking hands.

I squeezed her.

She squeezed me back.

Finally, Victor nodded. "Fine. If she doesn't miscarry from the beating I gave her, and survives today's game, then I'm open to discussion."

My mind raced.

He'd beaten her hard enough to warrant a miscarriage?

What game?

Maybe it's kinder to end her.

To just free every jewel in this place and be done with it…including me.

A horribly morbid thought filled my head.

Henri could be our executioner.

A black-hooded, axe-wielding executioner, beheading all of us in one long line.

Henri glanced at me. He flinched at whatever he saw in my eyes.

Tearing his stare away, he shoved his hands into his jeans pockets. "What game?"

"Oh…didn't I tell you?" Victor grinned, bright and slightly unhinged. "I told you the atmosphere in here is unbalanced. Well, I mean to rebalance it. The new jewels will take time to arrive, but I need to eradicate this tension today, so…" He grinned and tapped his nose. "First, I have a few little housekeeping things to cover, and then Rachel—seeing as her lifespan has just been extended—can take Ily to join the others in preparation."

Before Henri could speak, he added, "Also, before I forget, I did as you requested. I ordered you a laptop for your writing venture and a small wardrobe for your jewel in appreciation of your fealty. They have already arrived and are in your chambers as we speak." He bowed his head regally. "I trust that you will be satisfied?"

"*Merci beaucoup*." Henri tilted his chin, his wariness growing by the heartbeat. "You're very generous."

"Generosity has nothing to do with it. I'm a businessman. And right now, our alliance is beneficial. Let's keep it that way, shall we?"

"Of course."

"Which leads me to my next point." He tugged on the leash, forcing Rachel to stagger out of the chair and trip into him. Wrapping his arm around her waist, he purred, "I know you have urges, my young friend, and frankly…so do I. But before we get to the dick-wetting part, you must indulge me in playing something I like to call Emerald Bruises."

Henri stepped a little closer to me, nudging his knee against my shoulder. "And what are the rules of Emerald Bruises?"

"Don't fret about that right now. I'll fill you in once our jewels have departed, but I have been remiss in helping you break your Ilyana. I'm hoping today will help bring her into line."

Prickles coated my skin.

My pulse picked up.

"You know what?" Henri tapped my shoulder, signalling me to stand. "I actually have my own plans for—"

"Plans that can wait." Victor's face blackened. "You both displeased me the night of the treasure hunt. I also didn't particularly like what I saw on camera in your room afterward." His gaze dropped to the bite mark on my neck. "You might have used her, but there was far too much talking for my taste. And besides, you have apologised. But her? She has not."

Apologise?

Never.

No way.

Not for anything.

Rachel gave me a worried look as I swooped to my feet. My bikini sparkled silver in the sun; I couldn't help my hate spilling free. "You're a bastard."

"Yes, I am." He grinned. "And you should remember that." Ignoring me, he narrowed his eyes on Henri. "Your jewel is pissing me off, Mercer. She is unruly, stupid, and flouting the rules. Her influence infected Peter with the foolhardy belief that she could offer him a different life. She's undermined his discipline and turned one of my best jewels against me."

Glowering at me, he hissed, "I might not have been able to hear over the rain that night, but I could read your body language. I saw you two talking *very* intently. I saw Peter refuse you. I saw you push him. And I also saw him finally agree." His hand shook with barely concealed temper as he ran it over his perfect greying hair. "He attacked a Master on your behalf. You made him do something completely out of character, and then you attacked another of my esteemed guests because you're idiotic and reckless. Needless to say, you both sentenced yourselves to severe punishment."

"Fucking hell." Henri sucked in a breath, grabbing my shoulder with pinching fingers. "What did you do, Ily?"

My heart absolutely shattered, full of panic for my friend.

Three days where I'd been encased in Henri's room and forbidden from leaving his company all while Peter suffered for my mistakes.

Three days was an *eternity*.

Shrugging off Henri's touch, I only had eyes for Victor. Deplorable vile, *vile* Victor. "What did you do to him?" I wanted to rake my fingernails over his soulless face. "Where the hell is he?"

Victor sighed with utter boredom. "Peter has been reminded of his place. And if Henri does not do the same to you, under my strict tutelage I might add, you will join him. If it were up to me, I would give you a week in the snuffbox before I trusted that you finally saw the error of your ways—stubborn little thing that you are."

My stomach dropped.

My fault.

Peter had told me not to fight, and what had I done?

I'd been stubborn and stupid and non-thinking, and…*someone else has paid my price.*

The awful knowledge that I was the cause of Peter's pain stopped me dead.

Letting Rachel go, Victor stepped into me and grabbed a fistful of my hair. "The things I would do to you. The breaking you require." He pressed a smacking kiss right over my lips. "Fuck, it would be my absolute pleasure to shatter you."

Henri snapped a leash to my collar and reeled me back into him with a steady pull. I choked and stumbled to his side. Hugging me with an arm that offered comfort as well as damnation, he said, "She's mine to teach, Vic. I thought we'd agreed on that."

"*Oui, oui.*" Victor exhaled. "You are in charge of her education, but you haven't been teaching her, and I'm sick of her fucking attitude. I've had it with her disruption. You will get her in line, Mercer. Today."

"I will." Henri nodded. "You have my word."

"Oh, I don't need your word." Victor smirked. "I'll see for myself. Now, Rachel darling, please take Ily to get prepared. You're both running behind."

"Yes, Sir V." She bowed with a wince.

Victor unclipped the leash from her collar and stepped back. "By the way, what do you say to Master H?"

Turning to Henri, Rachel bowed even deeper. "Thank you for showing my Master that I wasn't trying to trick him into anything. I-It just happened. And…and I'm incredibly grateful to be carrying my Master's child. If that…if that's what he wants." She swallowed hard. "It's an honour to be the mother of his heir."

"Yes, yes, away with you now." Victor rolled his eyes. "We shall see if you're still pregnant by the end of the day. Then I suppose we'll have yet another chat. All I seem to be doing lately is conversing with people.

I'm getting rather bored."

"Yes, Sir V."

"Henri, unhook your jewel. She's leaving."

With flared nostrils, Henri obeyed and reluctantly untethered me.

The horrible sensation of no longer being connected to him, even if it was by a stupid piece of leather, cast me adrift.

My stomach churned.

My heart flurried.

And I held his haunted stare as Rachel took my hand and led me away.

Chapter Eighteen

Henri

NEITHER VICTOR NOR I SPOKE UNTIL Ily and Rachel vanished into the castle.

The moment I couldn't see her anymore, the icy gale in my chest increased until I swore a blizzard lived inside me.

I'd been bad the past few days.

Positively OCD with my need to keep her close and safe.

I hadn't been able to touch her.

Talk to her.

I'd reverted to my childhood self that checked out of life and found salvation in the pages of someone else's troubles.

Books.

Fuck, what would I do without books?

"Right." Victor clapped his hands and gave me a wink. "Now they're gone, let's tell the others what's on today's agenda, shall we? They're going to be oh so pleased."

Blinking away my yearning hollowness, I smiled. "Sure."

"You know what? You can do it." Victor gave my shoulder a kind squeeze. "I've noticed how out of sorts you've been, my friend. You came to us alone, and I'm sure it hurts to remain alone, even amongst your own kind."

A group of Masters, crowded at a nearby table, chose that moment to laugh obnoxiously. Proving that for all my willingness to become one of them, the chances of that happening were probably fucking zero.

For one, I needed a jewel who wasn't broken.

And two, I didn't like many people.

"I'm not alone, though." I braced myself, shaking off his touch. "I have Ily."

"Yes, your nightmare."

My lips quirked. "She's certainly living up to that nickname."

"Unfortunately." Victor pouted. "But…I wonder if she's the right choice for you. Haven't you begun to suspect she might not be worth the trouble?" He pointed at a few jewels currently serving. A couple kneeled by their Master's feet. Others on the laps of those who'd finished their breakfast and felt like a different sort of snack. "There are so many other gems to sample. Much better-behaved girls and boys who would be honoured to accept your attention."

"Yes, well, you know my answer to that." My eyes swept back to the sliding doors where Ily had disappeared. "I'm still rather attached."

And, if I'm honest, I would give anything to be free.

I didn't want to feel this way anymore.

I'd done my best to sink back into my monster's darkness, but each time she looked at me, that flare of fear and longing kept me awfully fucking...*human.*

Instead of being free to be who I truly was, it felt as if she'd wrapped a net around me. A net that kept tightening and tightening—a noose that kept strangling, strangling—tying me up in knots and confusing the goddamn shit out of me.

If only the treasure hunt hadn't happened.

If only I'd found her first and fucked her on the lawn.

If only I didn't bloody kiss her!

I could've remained a beast—as deplorable and as depraved as that was.

Perhaps he's right.

Maybe I do need to discipline her.

To re-establish our roles in this new life and find my way back to that exquisite sensation of being home.

Sucking in a deep breath, I prepared to step back into the shoes I'd purchased. I might have made my bed by calling my brother and telling him I was staying, but I hadn't fully dressed in the clothes of my new self.

Today...that changes.

Today, I would be free again, and that jackass part of myself that howled for love would be well and truly slaughtered.

Good fucking riddance.

Grinning, I asked, "What do you want me to tell them? I'm ready to play. I think it will be good...for all of us."

"That's the spirit." Victor slugged me on the arm. "Tell them that I've improved Emerald Bruises and increased the stakes. They'll know what you mean." He glanced at his diamond-encrusted Rolex—a stark difference to my chipped old Casio. "Announce that the game will begin at the drawbridge, and I have gifts for everyone."

At the drawbridge?

What on earth did this game entail?

Almost on cue, a procession of guards suddenly marched over the daisy-splashed lawn, spilling from one of the many side entrances of the gothic stronghold. Two pairs of black-suited men carried a heavy crate between them.

"Ah, perfect timing." Victor nodded at me and strode to the edge of the deck. He waited until the guards placed the heavy crates down and unwound their fingers from the coarse rope handles.

Smiling with gratitude, Victor waited until the men had retreated to their posts and then turned to his guests. "Friends, gentlemen. Can I have your attention, please?"

Beckoning me to his side, he grinned. "Henri has something he'd like to say. But please allow me to say something first." Waiting until the fourteen or so guests ceased what they were doing and looked our way, he nodded at the scant jewels. "Sweetlings, please scurry along to the grounds behind the kitchens. You're the last to prepare. Hurry now."

Without a word of protest, the four slaves tucked their chins and vanished into the castle.

Once they were gone, Victor sighed happily. "My friends. I appreciate your loyalty, but you can welcome Henri back into the fold. Yes, he's forgiven. Yes, he's staying. And no, he's not a cop. Let's put the past in the past, shall we?" He shrugged. "Daxton was a snitch and got what was coming. As long as no one else betrays me, then we're all one big happy family!"

The change in atmosphere visibly lightened.

A few men toasted me with their coffee cups. "Understood."

Charles winked. "Welcome back, old chap."

"All yours," Victor murmured, stepping away and giving me centre stage. The clip of his shoes on the deck steps echoed as he strode toward the first crate and popped the two catches on the lid.

One by one, men left their tables, all coming to see what new toys Victor had brought. Turning to face the stunning gardens, gazing at the drawbridge in the distance, I froze as the heavy metal barrier cracked open. With cranks of chains and toil, the entrance—the one and only doorway into this place—descended, forming a bridge over the wide moat glittering beyond.

Sunlight spilled inside.

Sea spray twinkled in the sky as waves crashed against the cliffs.

It felt odd to see the outside world.

Frankly terrifying to be reminded of a place I'd forsaken. It suited me better to pretend the outside world had been decimated by some disaster—leaving us as the only survivors.

At least then the rules of old didn't matter. The laws of society were eradicated which meant my decisions didn't have consequences.

But it's still there…

The world I never fit into.

Laws still exist, lives still go on…

***He** still lives on.*

A chill scattered down my spine that my brother might appear at any moment and butcher me.

"Henri, if you don't mind." Victor interrupted my thoughts.

"Sorry." Swallowing hard, I tore my eyes off the open gap in the wall and said, "Emerald Bruises is about to be played. It's new and improved with even greater stakes than before."

Men shifted on the spot and elbowed each other as Victor lifted an assault rifle.

My mouth went as dry as fucking cotton.

Jesus Christ, what the hell is this game?

Stalking down the steps, I snatched a gun from the closest crate.

Heavy, well-made, oiled mechanisms and…not real.

Not real?

Frowning, I looked up. "What the hell are we about to play, Vic?"

He smirked and began passing out weapons. "Paintball."

"Paintball?"

"With a twist." He laughed.

"Hell yeah." Patrick, one of the guests I recognised, grabbed a gun and squeezed the empty trigger a few times. "New and improved, you say? Shit, this is gonna be good."

"How's it improved, Vic?" Ferdinand—the guy who had sick, sick fetishes—grabbed his own gun.

"Well, you're all aware that usually the winner is decided by the number of bruises they leave on a particular jewel. We've used all manner of tools in the past. Paddles, rolling pins, canes—"

"Billiard balls are my favourite." Charles interrupted. "Laying a jewel on the pool table, then scoring a shot with them lying in the middle. Dane had a nice array of round-shaped bruises all along his sides for weeks."

"Lawn bowls was great for me." Roland chuckled. "Using Molly as the jack and trying to get as many to whack into her as possible was addictive. And a good work-out." He jiggled his large belly. "Definitely worked up an appetite."

My hands clenched tighter around my gun.

"Yes, well. This time, I upped the ante." Victor tossed the final few assault weapons to his guests. They sailed through the air looking exactly like AK-47s. "Usually, the winner gets to enjoy a night of their choice in the snuffbox or dungeon, painting their jewel with a few more bruises if they feel so inclined. They're still bound by my guidelines, and I don't tolerate unnecessary violence, but…it's always been good fun."

"What do the winners get today, then?" Patrick asked, swiping his hand beneath his nose, looking cracked out with eagerness to begin.

Grinning like a puppeteer pulling everyone's nasty strings, Victor announced, "I'm aware some of you might be feeling a tad, shall we say…*stifled* under my many rules. And so…my gift to you is…no rules."

Men looked at one another in confusion.

But then...that confusion slowly switched to understanding and finally to fucking glee.

"You mean it, Vic?" Charles asked. "You truly mean we can do whatever the fuck we want?"

Nodding, Victor slammed a crate closed and leapt onto it like a goddamn spider monkey. Spreading his arms, he glowed beneath the sunshine. "Each gun will be loaded with a particular colour. That colour will determine the winner. The one who manages to shoot and paint a jewel the most—layering him or her with bruises at the same time—will win the right to do whatever their blackened heart desires."

"Even mutilation?" Ferdinand asked quietly.

"Yep." Victor nodded. "With my blessing."

"Asphyxiation?" Charles asked.

"Of course."

"Hook play?"

What the fuck is hook play?

"Mm-hmm." Victor smiled.

"Death?" Roland smiled like a psychopath. "What about that?"

Victor didn't reply for a moment, dragging out the suspense and my damn heartrate. Finally, he clasped his hands and pinned all of us with a blank, deadly serious stare.

His temper rose without warning—his frustration and intolerance, and every sick emotion he harboured that was usually so well covered with careful veneer—crawled to the surface and rained over us like acid.

"You hunt to eat, don't you? You shoot to kill, yes? Well, my beloved friends…today is that hunt. Today is that kill. So yes. Whoever wins this game has my unequivocal permission to do whatever he fucking wants. My gems have been protected by my rules for long enough and deserve a refresher for just how good they have it."

He swiped away a fake tear. "Am I not good to them? Do I not provide them comfy beds, healthy food, and good healthcare?"

"You do, Vic. You're a fabulous father."

"And so why must they keep chipping away at my magnanimity? Why must I stoop to their level to remind them that they are fucking *nothing to me*? They are *mine. My* flock. *My* sheep. My little herd to do whatever I fucking well please with. They're spoiled and ungrateful, and after today…they *will* remember their place." Breathing hard, he raked both hands through his hair and smiled. "After today, you'll see…we will have peace again, and all this nasty tension will be behind us."

Leaping down from the crate, he grabbed his own gun. "Now, arm up, gentlemen, the hunt is about to begin."

Chapter Nineteen

Ily

I STUMBLED OVER THE KITCHEN's threshold, unable to believe my eyes.

I'd thought Rachel was taking us to the jewel quarters.

A part of me longed to return to all those rows of neat beds where everyone supported one another. Where no one judged and all shared a safe space to air their fears, worries, and pain.

I wanted to share so many things.

I wanted to apologise to Peter and make sure he was okay.

I wanted to talk to each jewel and prepare them for an uprising.

But Rachel guided me away from that wing and toward the back of the citadel instead.

She kept her fingers locked tight around mine, tugging me farther and farther from Henri. Down long, drafty corridors and around ominous bends. Tapestries gave way to stone blocks, and fancy sconces became bare lightbulbs by the time we popped into the working heart of this trafficker's palace.

I felt as if I'd fallen through time as I blinked at the controlled chaos.

At least ten people bustled about in a huge kitchen. The ceilings were curved and low, soot-stained and weathered like similar manors I'd explored in England. Huge ovens and stovetops, massive chopping blocks with knife marks and rusty spots of blood. Big windows spilled sunlight onto racks of gleaming knives while the coppery glow of polished pots and pans hung from large hooks.

Unlike in the ancient eras, where whole hogs were spit-roasted in open fireplaces and pheasants were plucked in buckets by the back door, Victor's kitchen blended modern with old.

Stainless steel tables cut the kitchen in half, some covered in flour while staff kneaded dough and layered huge trays full of intricate fruit pastries ready to go into the oven.

Someone stirred a giant cauldron, giving off steamy tendrils laced with tarragon and garlic. Another poured melted butter over a roasting pan full of chicken breasts.

A grey-headed man with a hair-net on and crow's feet pinching weary brown eyes waved us away with a wooden spoon dripping with red sauce. "They're all out back. Hurry now. Oh, and take these with you. You're gonna need it." Snapping his fingers at a stout elderly woman beside him, she nodded and grabbed a basket covered in a blue-and-white chequered tea-towel.

Darting around the mayhem in the kitchen and bringing with her a whiff of delicious chocolate, she passed me the basket. "Ensure every jewel has one. It will give you energy for the long day ahead." Cupping Rachel's chin, she sighed sadly. "Did that tonic help ease any of your pains, my dear?"

Rachel patted her hand and nodded. "It did. Thanks, May. Who knew dandelion roots and nettle could ease such things."

"My grandmama taught me." May gave her another unhappy look, her mousy hair lank from the kitchen's humidity. "I can try to make you a concoction to help you lose the child…" She shrugged. "I can't promise it will work, but…"

Rachel winced and cupped her belly. "Pretty sure I'll lose it after how many times that bastard kicked my stomach this morning." She flicked me a look. "If I survive today, then yes, I'll take you up on the offer. Dr Belford also said she'll help induce my losing it—as long as Victor doesn't insist he wants it now. Fuck." She shuddered. "The thought of having a baby in here, to *him*?" Fierce tears filmed her vibrant blue eyes. "I can't. I literally *can't*."

"But if you raised them right…they might inherit it all and let us go."

Rachel laughed under her breath. "You're basing your freedom on a fantasy that wouldn't come true for at least twenty years…if at all." She shot me another look and dove her hand beneath the tea-towel of the basket I held.

Pulling out a thick muesli slice full of oats, fruits, treacle, and nuts, she nibbled on the end. "Besides, this is his kid we're talking about. It'll be raised to be even worse than its father. So no." She swallowed hard. "Victor will destroy it. He'll turn it into a creature not fit for this earth." Her shoulders braced. "I'd rather die with innocence in my belly than give birth to evil."

May rolled her shoulders and nodded. "Well, we're here if you need anything." Arching her chin at the open doorway leading outside, she added, "Keep an eye on Peter, will you, dear? He's not doing too well."

"Crap, is he still high?" Rachel lowered her voice, glancing at the cameras blinking red in the corner of the curved ceiling.

I stiffened. "C-Can they hear us?"

May gave me half a smile. "They say they can, but after years of working down here, I can tell you they don't hear shit of what we talk about. I think the extraction fans, constant boiling, and other ambient noise acts like a shield."

Interesting…

"And yes, he is." May answered Rachel. "I know Dr Belford trusts you guys not to overindulge, and usually he's so careful not to incapacitate himself, knowing the consequences of not obeying, but…" She dabbed at a sudden tear in the corner of her eye. "I'm scared he doesn't really care anymore."

Rachel glanced at me, her dark hair making her skin milky with horror. "Of all the days for him to snap." Grabbing my wrist above my cuff, she squeezed me. "We stick together, okay? No matter what happens out there, we don't let each other out of our sights."

I cupped her elbow and nodded, sharing in her quaking. "I promise. I won't leave your side."

She gave me a small smile. "I have no idea what Victor is planning, but…he's in a bad mood, new girl. And when he gets in a bad mood…well, our numbers always seem to go down."

May drew a cross over her ample bosom and lifted her eyes heavenward. "Please, Jesus, keep these dear ones safe. They've suffered enough. Let freedom come soon. Amen."

Rachel sniffed. "Prayers don't work, May. But I appreciate it."

"Prayers do work…if enough people do them at once," May said. "It's all about faith."

"Faith that if we repent and are punished enough, we'll be allowed out of hell?" Rachel asked with a snide tone.

"You know I mean well—"

"Yes, I know." Rachel shook her head. "I'm sorry. I'm just—"

"May," the chef by the huge pot barked. "Get back to work. Let them get on now. If they're not finished by the time the gong goes, there'll be even worse hell to pay."

"Yes, yes, you're quite right." May pressed a dry kiss on Rachel's cheek and then on mine. "Get one of those muesli bars into your tummies. And look after each other. We'll be here when you need us."

Unwinding her fingers from my wrist, Rachel went to move, but she stumbled.

Moaning, she cupped her middle as she snapped in half. "*Ahhh.*"

"What is it?" I hugged her close, trying to take some of her weight. "Cramps?"

Biting her bottom lip, she nodded. "Fucking bastard…*owww…*"

Sweat broke out over her forehead.

True terror filled me.

I had no idea what this game entailed, but she could barely stand up, let alone do anything else. Glancing at the camera, I whisper-hissed, "May…"

The older woman looked at us from her position stirring the big pot. "Yeah?"

"Is there a cellar down here? Could you hide Peter and Rachel? Just until tonight?"

She wrinkled her nose with sorrow. "Victor will do a head count. He always does. There's no getting out of it. Just…eat up. And…good luck."

"Come on." Rachel wiped at the sweat on her temples and stood upright. "I'm okay. It's passed." With her chin tipped like a queen, she guided me through the bustle and out the back door.

Just like a typical working castle, this forgery fortress was no different.

Cobblestones led left and right toward outbuildings, no doubt housing potatoes, mushrooms, and other produce requiring dark, cool places. A red brick larder with a huge slab of beef hung in the shadows, and bushels of leafy greens waited by the wall to be washed and prepared for dinner.

"Come on." Rachel guided me down the little laneways until we popped out into a small field where a hen house sat with its blue shingled roof and a busy flock of hens going about their morning.

Around another bend and my feet slammed to a stop.

A few sheds dotted about. Handyman sheds complete with tools, ladders leaning against dusty bricks, and a wheelbarrow full of gardening implements.

Amongst the litter of life—the everyday drudgery by those unseen who kept the flowers pruned and gutters clean—hovered every jewel in this godforsaken place.

They seemed out of place.

Terribly vulnerable.

I didn't know what I was expecting but…this?

I blinked at the long row of identically painted slaves.

What on earth—

Rachel blanched. "Well…this isn't good."

Swallowing hard, I went to agree, but Peter looked up from where he slouched against the wall of a muddy handyman shed. Wearing a pair of tanned boxer-briefs and nothing else, he threw up his arms and limp-ran toward us. "Rachie! Ily! Where have you two been? I've missed you so, so much!"

Rachel and I both stumbled as he crashed into us.

His skin felt damp and feverish, his pulse pounding visibly in his neck.

For a second, I couldn't see much wrong with him.

For a heartbeat, I hoped whatever Victor had done for three days wasn't that bad after all.

But then, I noticed.

And almost threw up on the grass.

"Oh God…Peter. No…"

He giggled and held up his palms.

His burned and awfully charred palms.

No bandages, no creams, nothing to protect his raw, red-black, oozing flesh. "Oh, these? Nah, it's fine, *jaanu*. Don't feel it. In fact, the smell reminds me of barbecue. See? Smell it. Makes me hungry." He shoved his hand under my nose, smearing my upper lip with whatever fluid his body produced, doing its best to heal.

"Peter, you need to snap out of it. Okay?" Rachel yanked his hand away and marched him back to the others. "Where are your slippers? Citra gave you a pair of her handmade slippers this morning, remember? You need to wear them."

"Nah." Peter shook his head, stumbling drunkenly as he waved at all the other jewels. "Not allowed." Every single one wore underwear matching their skin colour, making it seem like they wore nothing at all.

The fact that they actually wore underwear ought to be the most shocking part, if it wasn't for the giant bullseye painted right on their chests.

No…not just their chests.

Peter spun in place and tipped his head back to the sun, revealing his back.

Beneath the lashings from the night of the treasure hunt, a bright red dot marked the centre of his spine with ever-expanding circles in black and white.

Sick.

Twisted.

Evil.

I struggled to breathe as Rachel grabbed the basket from my slack hand and shoved a muesli bar into Peter's burned one. "Here. Eat this. Maybe it will sober you up a bit."

"Oh, yum! Thanks, Rach." He tore into it. "Better than eating myself, I suppose, seeing as I smell so fucking tasty!" Kicking up his left leg, he showed me his sole. "Tempted to gnaw on this if I'm honest."

My knees gave out.

I staggered to the side before I caught myself. "Fuck, Peter."

I couldn't tell if I wanted to burst into manic, morbid giggles or die of a broken, battered heart.

If I thought his hands were bad, his feet were atrocious. His heels were cracked with blackened flesh. His toes raw with burns. His arches even had a strip of skin hanging off, looking like overdone bacon.

I-I'm going to throw up.

"Ah, it's okay. Don't worry." He swooped into me and cupped my cheeks with his treacle and blood-sticky hands. "I'm fine. More than fine. I don't feel a thing. Couldn't walk before, but wow, those are some potent pills Rose gave me. And besides…" His eyes dropped to my mouth. "It was worth it. Should've done it years ago."

I hadn't cried since I'd vowed I would never shed another tear the night Henri drew my blood. Not a single tear. Not for Henri. Not for myself. Not for any other jewel.

But for him?

Right there with my friend in pieces and high as a fucking kite?

My friend who I'd hurt in ways I'd never hurt anyone else?

I couldn't stop.

Hot, stinging tears swelled and fell.

Crystal trails gushed down my cheeks as I struggled not to sob. "Paavak, I'm so, *so* sorry."

He pressed his forehead to mine. "Don't be. He might've burned my feet to remind me there's no running, and he might've burned my hands for touching what wasn't mine to touch, but…fuck 'im. I don't give a shit anymore. We're leaving." He grinned ever so bright, his brown hair flopping over one eye. "We're gonna get out of here. Together. And when we do, I'm gonna ask you out on a proper date. We're gonna fly to India and go to my cousin's restaurant. We're gonna hold hands and kiss under the moon and—"

"Let her go." Rachel tugged Peter off me and beckoned Kirk to join us. "Can you get some shoes for him? He's gonna die from infection if we don't do something."

"He's probably gonna die from shock before that happens." Kirk sniffed sadly. "Look at him. When I was ten, my little sister accidentally spilled hot oil on me when she climbed onto the kitchen counter while the fryer was on. I could barely move for months. It's still the most pain I've ever felt. So…how?" He waved his hand at Peter. "How is he even standing?"

"'Cause I'm responsible for all of you and I'm gonna get you out." Peter slung a fever-sweaty arm around my shoulders. Me and Ily. We're gonna—"

"Hush up." Kirk drew a finger over his throat. "That's fighting talk, Pete."

"Damn right it is." Peter nodded. "No pain, no gain. I've got plenty of pain, so we'll make lots of gain. We're gonna fight to make it right." He giggled. "Hey, I rhymed. I should become a poet when I get out of here."

"Fuck, he's lost it." Kirk winced at Rachel. "He's not gonna make it through the day."

"Says who?" Peter barked, letting me go and wagging his finger like a drunken headmaster. "Now give me Citra's slippers and—"

"You know you can't have them." Kirk looked on the verge of tears. "Strict orders, remember?" He cupped Peter's cheek, his face drawn and aged by a decade. "We're only allowed what we're wearing, man. Just…stay high. That's the only protection you have from the agony."

"Will do." Peter swayed forward and placed a smacking kiss on Kirk's cheek. "You look like such a grump but you're such a softie. Gonna hook you up with my second cousin when we get home. You deserve someone who can return all your softiness." He frowned. "Softiness. Is that a word? Sounds funny—"

"Someone grab me a shovel," Rachel muttered under her breath. "Maybe if we knock him out, we can say he fainted from the burns and can't serve. He might survive that way."

Peter crossed his arms, his blackened hands oozing in the sunlight. "Anyone tries that and I'll swing back."

"Yeah, yeah." Rachel sighed heavily, her own pain flushing her cheeks. Ignoring Peter she asked Kirk, "Do you know what's gonna happen?"

Kirk squeezed the back of his neck. "Nah. The guards who painted us didn't tell us jack. But we're painted with a fucking bullseye, so I'm guessing we're about to get shot."

"Like the dart boards!" Peter chuckled as Rachel braced through another cramp before brushing away her own stray tears. "Remember, Kirk? They threw darts at us after dinner one night? Got a few lodged in our thigh."

"Yep." Kirk pinched the bridge of his nose. "I remember, Pete."

"Bet Molly remembers too. One cunt got her in the tit."

"Yep." Kirk dropped his hand. "How about you just eat your muesli bar and get ready, huh? Save your energy, okay?"

"Wise man." Peter saluted him with his sticky bar. "I have a feeling we're all gonna have to run like mad, so…we all look after the slowest of us, yeah?" Limping on charred, tattered feet, Peter headed toward the throng of silent, bullseye-painted slaves. "No one is left behind. We all run as one, got it? Stay as a crowd, and they can't thin us out. And if we get a chance to retaliate, we *shoot them—*"

"Whoa, whoa, whoa." Dane dashed forward and clamped a hand over Peter's mouth. "That's enough, mate. You trying to give Vile Vic a reason to burn your tongue now, too?"

Peter struggled but then slouched. Tapping Dane's arm, he licked his lips as Dane let him go. "You're right. Gotta keep the uprising a secret."

"Uprising?" Dane blanched and backed up. "Bloody hell, someone put a gag on him. He's gonna get us all murdered."

My fault.

Fuck, this is all my fault.

Bolting to Peter, I guided him away a little, limping and stumbling, before whispering in his ear. "I don't think now is the right time to talk about that, do you?"

He shivered dramatically. "Having you this close does things to me." He giggled. "He'll probably burn my cock off next, seeing as I can't seem to help myself around you." Looking down his front, he shrugged as his cock remained flaccid in his briefs. "Huh. Stupid thing. Wake up—"

"No, no, it's fine. I think…I think your body is dealing with a lot of trauma, and you need to rest."

"Can't." He bopped me on the nose with a burned finger. "Going hunting. Well." He grinned. "*We're* the hunted but still…don't have time to rest." Swaying into me, he whispered, "So…when are we gonna finish what we started? I tried telling the others that we're gonna get them out of here, but they think I'm high. I mean…" He laughed. "They're not wrong, but I'm not talking shit. I'm done, Ily. I'm *so* fucking done. This ends. Now."

God, I've broken him.

Me and my stupid big mouth have destroyed this wonderful soul.

Giving him a soft smile, I nodded. "I believe you, but we have to stay quiet, okay? It's a secret, remember?"

"Right. Secret." He zipped up his lips. "Can't let them know."

"Exactly."

"Right, you two. Come 'ere." A guard snapped his fingers at Rachel and me. Tossing us two pairs of knickers and bras in a slightly lighter skin tone than my natural shade, he ordered, "Put those on and go see Smith. He'll paint you up." Checking his wristwatch, he added, "You have five minutes."

Rachel pushed Peter out of the way. "Sit down for five minutes, Pete. Give your poor feet a rest." Grabbing my hand, she guided me toward the hen house. A chicken darted between my legs, clucking with annoyance.

Once we were apart from the others—all whispering worriedly and looking at each other's painted skin—she slipped out of her teal see-through gown and sniffed. "Is this your fault? Is Peter talking about escape because you think it's possible?"

Unknotting my bikini top, I tossed it to the ground before securing the bra and shoving my arms through the straps. "Yes." I couldn't meet her eyes as I shimmied from bikini bottoms into cotton knickers. "I was such an idiot. I-I think I broke him."

She winced as she slipped her own pair of knickers into place, her bruises stark against her pale flesh. I expected her to tear into me. She came across prickly and reserved, but she shocked me stupid by breathing, "I'm in." Her eyes narrowed pointedly. "If you and Peter are planning something. I'm in. We all are."

The urge to hug her exploded through my arms.

Ideas flowed.

Plans of using the noisy kitchen as our undercover meeting spot.

Fantasies of chopping up Masters like meat on a butcher's block—

But then commonsense slapped me around the head.

Victor was all seeing, all hearing, all knowing.

To even think we had a chance against him was idiotic. Worse than idiotic, *it's suicidal.*

Somehow, all my grand ideas of fleeing were replaced with behaving the best I could so no one else got hurt.

I sighed heavily.

Peter used to be the careful leader, protecting his flock.

I used to be the wild card, instigating an insurrection.

Somehow, our roles had reversed.

And the thought of being the cause of any more pain filled me with absolute horror.

"Let's talk about it another day—"

"Gotta talk about that bite on your neck and the way you looked at your Master too," Rachel muttered. "Don't you remember anything Peter told you? Guard yourself. Don't let them into your heart, new girl. That's just asking for trouble. Pregnant trouble."

I cupped the small scabs left by Henri's teeth.

I had no idea how to explain what'd come over me that night or why I couldn't seem to stop this…this *addiction.*

Looking at a chicken pecking in the grass, I sighed. "I'm doing my best—"

"Get over here." A guard waiting by a table with three pots of paint waved a paint-brush in our direction. "Time to mark you."

With a sharp nod, Rachel whispered, "I'll help you with whatever you're feeling. I've been Victor's fave for three years, and I wouldn't be honest if I didn't say at least once in that time I've had feelings for him. But…whatever you think you're feeling is just survival. Your heart is trying to make this easier on you. Your body is doing the only thing it can to endure."

Squeezing my hand, she stepped closer. "If I survive today and don't miscarry, I flatly refuse to have this kid in here. You're getting us out before then." Her eyes narrowed. "We'll do whatever you think will work. But…we're doing it. We're at least gonna try. Our countdown has officially started because we can't stay here. None of us can."

My heart thundered as she guided me toward the guards and their paint. We held eye contact as red dots were painted right on our sternum and spine, then rings of white and black feathered outward.

On the last circle, a twanging noise rang out across the gardens.

A gong.

Every jewel froze.

The guards smiled.

Peter glittered in sweat, his body beyond abuse and most likely going into shock.

What if he dies today?

What if he died because his heart went into cardiac arrest from running on burned feet?

More tears glossed.

Agony pierced my chest.

I choked on terror as the guards rounded us up at gunpoint then marched us in a neat line away from the service area of the castle and toward the open drawbridge in the far, far distance.

Chapter Twenty

Henri

I COULDN'T FUCKING MOVE AS thirty jewels appeared in the distance around the back of the castle. Some hobbled, some shuffled, some cried, some glowered, but all of them were marked with a target.

White and black circles with red marking the spot.

The gun in my hand weighed a million tonnes.

The top canister screwed into place was full of tiny balls containing paint.

I had no idea what colour had been assigned to me.

Didn't want to know.

For all my urges and all my inhuman tendencies, I wasn't down with this.

This wasn't sexy or fun.

This was fucking…*barbaric.*

Other Masters chuckled and chatted amongst themselves.

Charles tried to strike up a conversation with me, but I turned my back and walked away.

I couldn't.

Fuck, I could barely stop myself from shooting all these motherfuckers. Let alone indulge in blood sport convo before the big hunt.

Staff in frilly pinafores handed out flasks of liquor. Trays of dainty snacks and cakes were offered.

If the Masters wore tweed and hounds circled our feet, it truly would be a medieval hunt.

Instead of muskets and swords, the Masters mingled in modern dress and patrolled with paintball guns. Everything about it was a farce, a mockery but still so fucking…*wrong.*

"Ah!" Victor stepped onto the open drawbridge. The sun gilded him in sunshine like a demented god. "Here are my sweetlings now, and don't they look so fine."

"They'll look better covered in my paint!" A Master cackled.

"Do you mean paint or cum?" Another winked.

"Both!"

Laughter broke out.

Sweat rolled down my spine.

My eyes raked down the line of slaves, searching, searching…

Ily.

I froze as our gazes locked.

She stood next to Peter with Rachel on the other side of him. Dressed in hideous underwear that didn't match her gorgeous rich honey skin, the target lines painted on her chest made me see fucking red.

The treasure hunt had almost gotten her raped and me murdered.

That'd been tame compared to this.

A quick little game of hide-and-seek in thunder and lightning, compared to a full day of 'shoot the mostly-naked slave'.

Peter limped strangely, his eyes overly wide, his chest dripping with sweat. Part of his target mark had run, streaking down his lean belly.

I waited for the sickening rush of jealousy.

The unquenchable desire to grab Ily and lock her by my side.

But whatever emotions existed within me were mysteriously absent. Buried beneath rapidly growing terror that no matter what happened here today…nothing would be the same afterward.

Counting silently, Victor darted his finger in the air, doing a head count of his jewels. When he reached thirty, he clasped his hands and grinned. "It seems we are all assembled! Who wants to hear what's in store?"

Every Master apart from me shoved up their hand like a teacher's pet.

Victor chuckled. "So eager." Shooting me a questioning look, he said, "The rules are simple. You will have an hour before sundown to hunt. When you hear the gong, you must return." He swept his stare over everyone, jewels included. "*Everyone*, do I make myself clear?"

His gems all nodded obediently.

"Good." Slipping his hand into the pocket of his linen shorts, he held up a familiar black device.

Every jewel tensed. Some even dropped to their knees, anticipating a shock.

"No, no, it's okay." Victor soothed in a sinister sing-song voice. "Today, you have no need to fear electricity, my pets. See?" Stabbing his thumb into a second button on the remote, he pointed it at each jewel for a few seconds, slowly working his way down the line.

No one convulsed.

No one fried.

Only once he'd finished did he slip the remote back into his pocket and clasp his hands again. "Your collars have been deactivated."

Instantly, the jewels looked at one another, sensing a trap.

Victor chuckled. "I'm not lying. For today only, your collars are completely useless in making you compliant. You can run, fight, go wherever you please. The invisible fence is shut off and you have my absolute word as a gentleman that you will not get shocked if you get too close to it. In fact." He side-stepped on the drawbridge, drawing everyone's attention to the lush landing strip outside. The tail of his private plane could just be seen peeking from the left. "I've decided to give you all a sporting chance."

Jewels shrank back, bumping into one another as Masters bristled with eagerness.

"Here's what's going to happen, my sweetlings." Victor marched toward the edge of the drawbridge and dropped every poise and mask. "You have all disappointed me, upset me, and shown me that I have been far too lenient with you. You are spoiled, lazy, and frankly…I would not be distraught if a few of you decided *not* to return tonight, after all." He shrugged. "The cliffs are right there if you wish to use them. Jump for all I care. End your life. The life I so painstakingly nurture and tend. If you don't appreciate everything I fucking do for you, then fine. You're free."

A jewel dared step forward, her strawberry-blonde hair looking almost pink in the sun. "A-And if we don't. If we come back like you request…will we be forgiven whatever transgressions we've committed?"

Ily sucked in a breath.

Peter chuckled.

Rachel seemed to sway.

Victor took his time answering. "You know how precious you are to me. Some of you have been here close to a decade and some of you are new. You know how kind I can be; you also know how strict I can be when that kindness is abused." He smiled and placed a hand over his heart. "You have my word that after today, I will judge your transgressions paid, and we can go on with fresh purpose. How about that?"

"Yes, Sir V. Thank you, Sir V." The girl backed up and returned to her spot in the line.

Another girl squeezed her hand; they shared a look I couldn't decipher.

Merde, how many of them would be missing by roll-call tonight? How many would take the leap? And why did that fucking wrench at my heart?

I felt responsible.

Like I'd failed even though their lives were not my responsibility.

Ily's life was the only one I was in control of.

No one else's.

"Q would disagree," that angel on my shoulder muttered obnoxiously.

Q can bite my ass.

"Right, someone hand me a gun. Actually, Henri. Come up here and join me." Victor beckoned, his greying blond hair twinkling like tinsel. "Don't be shy."

Jesus Christ.

He had to pick me.

Giving him a tight smile, I stepped around a few of the other Masters and joined Victor on the drawbridge. "What's up?"

"Shoot one."

I raised an eyebrow. "Excuse me?"

"Shoot one. Let's see how the paintballs work, and then I'll explain the rest. Hurry now. Snap, snap."

God's sake.

Who?

I wasn't personally acquainted with the pain of being shot with a paintball, but I'd watched enough movies where people were shot to know it didn't look pleasant. Especially without any shields or thick clothing.

Swinging my gun, I angled the muzzle at Peter.

He flung his arms out, puffing up his chest. "Shoot me, oh Master C!" He snickered. "Oh, sorry. Not C. Not cunt—"

"Hush." Both Rachel and Ily dove for him, dragging his arms down and tripping with him as he swayed.

Bile filled my mouth as I noticed his hands.

His bleeding, burned hands.

My eyes shot to Victor's. "You burned him?"

He shrugged. "The lightning storm gave me inspiration. Just a teeny reminder to behave, that's all." Throwing a bemused smile at Peter, he laughed. "I think someone is a little high, Peter sweetling. I'll give you that one slip-up as it was rather amusing, but test me again, and your tongue will be next."

Peter didn't blanch or bow or back down.

He merely saluted Victor like a drunken sailor. "Aye, aye, captain."

Victor just snickered. "That boy. Honestly. I will miss him when he's reached his use-by date."

My stomach churned as Ily gave Peter a heartbroken look.

She pushed his thick brown hair aside, brushing it away from his sweaty forehead.

I froze.

I waited for rage. For possessiveness. For jealousy.

But…I finally saw what she'd been telling me all along.

He definitely had feelings for her.

I sensed it in every molecule of my body. But her…? The way she touched him and sniffed back tears at his abuse? The way she watched him, desperately wishing she could protect him, looked exactly like one would protect a…brother.

Shit.

My mind suddenly filled with a very different scene.

Children all tucked up in bed, some crying in the dark, others huddling together under blankets. Outside the barred window, the haunting hoots of owls terrified us along with the screams of our mothers.

The door slammed open.

A man marched in.

Drunk and slurring, French and rotten.

He tossed a woman into the middle of our bedroom and spat on the floor. "You have an hour with your spawn."

The kid closest to me—a little girl who I did my best to keep smiling—flung herself into the woman's arms and—

The vision ended.

I shook my head.

The rush of nausea crashed over me, remembering, realising…

I have siblings.

Not just the one I'd begged to accept me, but…

More.

Others.

Brothers and sisters all bred by the same monster who'd sired me.

I'd lived with them at the same estate where I'd gone to visit my eldest brother.

I'd once looked at them the way Ily looked at Peter.

That same despairing, harrowing look of wishing you were stronger, bigger, better—not to get yourself out of hell but to save all those in there with you.

"Henri…I'm waiting." Victor tapped his watch.

I made a split-second decision.

The only choice I could as the monster inside me grew longer fangs and sharper claws. I shuddered on the drawbridge as my clothing felt too tight, and my feet ached to run.

Whatever creature lived within me woke up again.

Only this time…it didn't want to dine on tears.

It wanted to dine on death.

Raising my gun, I pressed the trigger.

Ily cried out and staggered back, taking Peter and Rachel with her. Pressing her forefinger to the splodge of bright orange on her upper thigh, she looked at me as if I'd just shattered her already broken heart.

"There." I lowered my arm. "I shot her. My colour is on her skin. No one else is to fire at what is already mine."

Victor pursed his lips, watching Ily wince as she prodded the bruise I'd given her. "Unfortunately, Henri…today the rules are slightly different." Looking at his guests, he raised his voice. "My island is large and can be quite dangerous if you don't know the terrain. There are loose rocks by the cliffs and blowholes by the ocean. The caves burrow through the island like worms through soil, and some footing is unstable. The forest is wild, and if I believe my land keepers' remarks, there's also quicksand in the marsh. The tides come in fast, and if you're caught in a part of the cave system that gets cut off at high tide, then you might very well drown. But!" He grinned. "The stakes are worth it, gentlemen, because…my own personal favourite, Rachel, is available to anyone who can fire the most shots at her. And Henri's—the forbidden jewel that started a war—is also free game."

"What?" I choked. "No, she's—"

"The winner is whoever covers the jewel of his choice in as many paint bullets as possible. Empty your clip at them, my friends. Cover them in bruises. Your choice of what to do with the jewel you win is entirely up to you."

Pulling a pistol from his waistband, he aimed it at my heart. "Any objections, *mon ami*?"

I shot Ily a look.

She gave me an unreadable stare back.

Her hate for me cloaked the entire drawbridge, but I didn't care.

I would fight for her…like I fought for a sister I didn't remember.

I would protect her…like the wife she would never be.

I gave her a nod; she looked away.

My heart twinged with despair.

Swallowing hard, I grunted, "No, Vic. No objections."

I had none because no one would get within firing distance of her.

I'll make fucking sure of it.

"Great!" Passing me the gun, he inconspicuously looked at the guards with their sniper rifles on the battlement. Snipers all aimed at me. "In that case, how about you do the honours?"

"Fine." I took the Glock.

The temptation to shoot him in the head made my palm sweat.

Pasting on a smile, I raised the gun to the sky. "Ready whenever you are."

Victor grinned. "How nice." Looking at his jewels, he stepped off the drawbridge, beckoning me to follow him. The avenue leading through the wall and toward the outside world hummed with ocean song and freedom.

The jewels all naturally swayed toward it, summoned by the allure of hope.

"You have a fifteen-minute head start, my pets," Victor said gleefully. "Fifteen minutes to scurry your way across my island before we come after you. And that countdown begins…"

I closed my eyes.

Begged the fucking universe to give me luck.

I fired at the clouds.

BANG.

Gunpowder.

Ears ringing.

Hand vibrating.

I almost swallowed my own tongue. "Emerald Bruises begins *now.*"

I looked at Ily and imprinted her to memory.

I memorised her golden eyes, inky hair, and the soul that'd ensnared mine the moment I'd seen her in Paris.

If we survived this, things were changing.

I didn't know how.

I didn't know what I'd become.

But I did know I couldn't stand this level of emotion anymore.

This agony of wanting and not deserving.

This despair and desire and decimating thirst for things I'd never had and things I would never earn.

I would win this game.

I would become the worst fucking monster to triumph over all other beasts.

I would cut away the strings of feelings and sink deep, deep into the black-fanged creature within me.

Who knew if I'd ever be human again.

Who knew what I would do out there.

All I knew was…*I'm done.*

She needs to go.

The metallic rust of blood coated my tongue.

The urge to chase and pillage, savage and ruin made me shudder.

She needs to go ***now.***

Smiling like a murderer, I lowered my arm and said softly, "What are you all doing standing there? *Run.*"

It took a moment for my command to ripple from ears to muscles.

A heartbeat for everyone to break ranks and go.

With sharp inhales and panicked looks, they bolted as one.

Up the drawbridge and across the heavy wooden bridge.

The thunder of thirty pairs of feet sounded like a stampede of wild horses.

Shadows swallowed them as they cut through the thick wall, then sunshine drenched them again as they reached the other side.

Water dapples from the moat painted their galloping legs.

Target marks bounced as they ran.

And like a flock of hungry birds, they all vanished to the left.

Thirty priceless jewels disappeared in a puff of diamond dust.

The Masters began to pace.

And I morphed into something obscene.

Black and seething.

Dreadful and diabolical.

Victor gave me a smile.

I sank into bloodshed.

And

the

clock

started

ticking

…

Henri and Ily's tale continues in

Sapphire Scars...

Henri is a hunter, Ily is his prey…what will happen when he catches her?

www.pepperwinters.com

If you haven't met Q and Tess yet, their New York Times Bestselling Dark Romance is available and complete now! Start with Tears of Tess

Sapphire Scars

"I thought I was strong enough to survive this awful nightmare. I did my best to take back my power and refused to let my heart fall. Only problem is…my heart is an idiot."

It only took one droplet of blood to forever change me.
Her blood.
The taste of it. The heat of it.
I swallowed her down and devoured her.
For a while, it was enough.
My monster was content. I believed I'd found where I belonged.
But now…that droplet is no longer enough.
I want rivers of it. Oceans of it.
I want the world dripping in red and I honestly don't know who I'm hunting anymore.
Her?
Me?
Them?
One thing's for certain, someone is going to die today.
I just hope it won't be me.

Playlist

Just died in your arms tonight – Cutting Crew
Sail / Baby, I'm a different breed – Awolnation
Novocaine – The Unlikely Candidates
Training Season – Dua Lipa
Vampire - Olivia Rodrigo
Bury a friend – Billie Eilish
Slave - Brittany Spears
Killing me softly – Fugees
Starving – Hailee Steinfeld
Beautiful things – Benson Boone
Something in the way - Nirvana
What do you want from me - Adam Lambert
High above me – Tal Bachman
Golden - Harry Styles
Before you leave – Six60
Love from the other side – Fall out boy

Acknowledgements

This will be short and sweet, like most of my acknowledgements.
Thank you to my amazing beta readers—you guys go above and beyond.
Thank you to my amazing cover designer—Cleo, your work is insane.
Thank you to my narrators—Luke and Lucy, you guys are fabulous.
Thank you to my editor—Jenny, what would I do without you?
Thank you to my proofreader—Christina, you're a rock star.
Thank you to my sensitivity reader and Hindi translator—Shabnam, I love learning your language. It's so beautiful.
Thank you to my French translator—Aurelie, you're amazing.
Thank you to my wonderful assistant—Danielle, you have my back and I'm ever so grateful.
Thank you to my hubby—who lets me spend time with all these other men 😊
And last, but definitely not least, thank you to you, dear reader, for reading this dirty, dark tale.
I hope you join me on the next one…
Pepper
xxx

For 2024/2025 titles please visit *www.pepperwinters.com*

<u>RELEASE DAY ALERTS, SNEAK PEEKS, & NEWSLETTER</u>

To be the first to know about upcoming releases, please join Pepper's Newsletter (she promises never to spam or annoy you.)

Pepper's Newsletter

<u>SOCIAL MEDIA & WEBSITE</u>

Facebook: Peppers Books
Instagram: @pepperwinters
Facebook Group: Peppers Playgound
Website: www.pepperwinters.com
Tiktok: @pepperwintersbooks

Made in the USA
Columbia, SC
17 June 2025

59504726R00154